SANTA MAYBE

Also by Mary Jayne Baker

The 24-Hour Dating Agency
Love at First Fight
The Never Have I Ever Club
A Question of Us
The Perfect Fit
A Bicycle Made For Two
The Runaway Bride
Meet Me at the Lighthouse

SANTA MAYBE

Mary Jayne Baker

An Aria Book

First published in the UK in 2022 by Head of Zeus Ltd,
part of Bloomsbury Publishing Plc

Copyright © Mary Jayne Baker, 2022

The moral right of Mary Jayne Baker to be identified as the author of this work has been asserted in accordance with the Copyright, Designs and Patents Act of 1988.

All rights reserved. No part of this publication may be reproduced, stored in a retrieval system, or transmitted, in any form or by any means, electronic, mechanical, photocopying, recording, or otherwise, without the prior permission of both the copyright owner and the above publisher of this book.

This is a work of fiction. All characters, organizations, and events portrayed in this novel are either products of the author's imagination or are used fictitiously.

9 7 5 3 1 2 4 6 8

A catalogue record for this book is available from the British Library.

ISBN (PB): 9781800246317
ISBN (E): 9781800241657

Cover design: Carla Orozco

Typeset by Siliconchips Services Ltd UK

Printed and bound in Great Britain by
CPI Group (UK) Ltd, Croydon CR0 4YY

Head of Zeus Ltd
First Floor East
5–8 Hardwick Street
London EC1R 4RG

WWW.HEADOFZEUS.COM

To my agent Laura Longrigg, for her many years of support, encouragement and hard work.

1

'Excuse me. Do you have any Splattertrons?'

Elodie Martin was creating a display of Marvel action figures to entice customers into the Martin's Toy Kingdom superhero section. She finished positioning Hulk in a suitably smashy pose and turned to face the woman who'd addressed her. A small, sticky-looking child was watching Elodie suspiciously, clinging to its mother's hand.

Did they have any what now? Splattertrons? What the flip were Splattertrons? Every week it felt like there was some new must-have toy making large portions of Elodie's stock obsolete.

She took a mad stab in the dark. 'A Pokémon?'

'I understand it's a sort of water gun.' The woman looked down at her child. 'Is that right, dumpling?'

The sticky child known as 'dumpling' rolled its eyes.

'Noooo,' it said, with disdain so solid you could lick it. 'It's like a robot that turns into another robot, and if you touch the wrong bit it squirts you out of its nose but not always, and then you turn it back and it squirts you again but from its bum.'

The child's mother laughed. 'As clear as mud, Jasper, thank you.' She looked at Elodie. 'Do you have them? The buzz among the playground mums is that they're going to be the big seller for Christmas. Of course that's a way off yet, but it's Jasper's birthday next month and I was hoping I could get my hands on one before the rush.'

Elodie tried to stop her panic showing. The big seller! But all the trade mags had said that merch from the latest Pixar film was what the kids were going to be nuts for this Christmas. She'd never even heard of Splattoes or whatever they were called.

And now any stock was bound to be going for silly money. As if this Christmas wasn't going to be challenging enough for Martin's, with their regular Santa Claus… well, with things being different.

Christmas. Oh God, how Elodie hated Christmas. She never had as many migraines as she did during the so-called Most Wonderful Time of the Year (TM).

'Er, no,' she told the woman. 'But we're expecting a big shipment of, um… of those things very soon, so if you'd like to come back in a few weeks…'

'I'm afraid we're in rather a hurry. People will be starting their Christmas shopping soon and I'd like to get my hands on one before things get manic. Already they're completely sold out online. If you don't have any, I suppose I'll try my luck at that department store in town.'

She tugged the child's hand and they started to go.

'We've got other robots,' Elodie called after them, slightly desperately. 'And Star Wars, Disney, Horrible Histories—'

Jasper shook his head. 'Want Splattertrons.'

His mum shrugged apologetically. 'Thank you anyway. We'll be back to see you at Christmas, of course. Jasper never misses your grotto.' She smiled at her son. 'This is where you find the Real McCoy, right, dumpling?'

Jasper nodded. 'The other Santas are so fake news. You can pull their beards off. I pulled your Santa's beard and he just said "ow".'

'Tugging Santa's beard, eh? Lump of coal for Jasper,' Elodie muttered as the bell above the door jangled to signal the pair's exit.

Elodie abandoned her Marvel display and headed upstairs. In the back room, her grandad – looking as avuncular and Father-Christmas-like as ever with his ruddy cheeks and bushy white beard, despite his recent health problems – was seated beside her seventeen-year-old cousin Summer as they rehearsed for the grotto.

'So thank you for your… letter,' Pops was saying in his toneless, stilted new voice. It made Elodie's heart hurt to hear it, although she'd rather poke hot bananas in her eyes than ever let him know that.

Saturday girl Summer was clearly relishing the role of 'tot meeting Santa'. Her eyes widened behind her round glasses and she clasped her hands to her mouth.

'Golly gosh and gee whiz!' she said, hamming for all she was worth. 'Did you really, truly read my letter, Father Christmas?'

'Of… course. I read all… the letters.'

'And will you bring what I asked for?'

This was the moment when Pops would usually make eye contact with the child's parent, who'd signal whether or not their offspring could expect to find what they'd asked for under the tree on Christmas morning, and then improvise some Santa banter accordingly. But instead he pulled his Santa hat off and threw it down on his lap.

'It's... no good,' he said to Elodie. 'I'm finished, Ellie. We can't afford... to take...' He took a deep breath as he struggled to queue up the words. 'To take a chance on me. It's time to hang up the suit.'

Elodie went to rest a hand on his shoulder. 'You don't get to retire, Pops, you're Santa – or you are to every kid who makes the trip to Martin's to see you. Without you, we might as well close down the grotto.'

'Then so be it,' Pops said despondently. 'Even Santas... reach the end of the road eventually. I've had a stroke, girls. How can you explain...' He trailed off, closing his eyes in frustration. 'How can you explain *this* to all those kiddies? I'll be letting them down. I'll be letting you down, Elodie. Martin's needs... its grotto.'

'I thought you were doing great, Pops,' Summer said with her usual earnest exuberance, tucking a strand of cherry-pink hair behind one ear. 'I hardly noticed the difference.'

Pops smiled in that lopsided way he'd developed since his stroke two months ago. 'Thanks, pet, but you're fooling no one.'

'Your speech therapist said you were coming on in leaps and bounds,' Elodie said soothingly. 'There's two months until the grotto opens. By then, you'll be chattering away as normal.'

Pops stared gloomily into the distance, apparently not hearing her. Elodie turned to her cousin.

'Summer, you know kids. Have you heard of some toy called a Splatto?'

'Splattertrons, you mean? Course,' Summer said. 'The

Cubs are all mad for them. I don't think there's a single kid who hasn't told me they've got one on their Christmas list.' Summer was a young leader with one of the Chessory Cub packs.

'But what are they?'

'They're sort of like... Transformers,' Pops said, zoning back into the conversation. 'Except bigger, and they squirt water if you...' deep breath '...if you can't change their shape fast enough.'

Elodie shook her head. 'How do you know about them when I don't?'

'Ashley Junior's got a display... in his big window.'

'Callum Ashley,' she muttered. 'Of course he has. I bet his bloody department store's cornered the market in Splattoes. He's probably got so many in stock he's using them as plant misters.' She looked at her cousin. 'You could've told me about them, Sum. This Christmas's most wanted toy, and Martin's has left it so late that you probably can't get stock in exchange for all major organs and your firstborn.'

Summer shrugged. 'I thought you'd be on top of it. You usually are.'

Elodie puffed away some frazzled sandy hair that had escaped from her messy bun. 'Well, this year I seem to have dropped a few juggling balls.'

The bell on the front door jangled to announce the arrival of a customer downstairs. The unfamiliar sound made Elodie jump. That in itself was pretty depressing.

'Summer, can you go serve them?' she asked. The teenager headed downstairs, a beaming smile fixed in place.

'It's... no good,' Pops said when they were alone. 'I'm sorry, Elodie. I just... can't do it. Not any more.'

She pressed his hand. 'Of course you can do it: you're *the* Santa. You've been everyone's favourite Santa for nearly forty years.'

'I had a good run. Now it's time… to say goodbye.'

'But you're only seventy-six,' Elodie protested. 'That's an infant in Santa years.'

'It's no good, kiddo. You can't… change my mind.' Pops spread his Santa hat across his knee, his hands moving reverently over the velvet. 'It was a privilege,' he said quietly. 'A joy and a privilege. All those little ones, seeing their faces light up with the magic of it all. But now… it's time, Ellie.'

Elodie bowed her head.

'You know, when I was a kid I really thought you were him,' she murmured. 'I remember how you used to tell me you were going to nip up to the North Pole and check on the elves. Where did you really go, Pops?'

He laughed. 'To the pub with your Great Uncle Geoff.'

'I boasted about it to everyone at school. "My grandad's Santa! The *real* Santa!"' Elodie smiled at the memory. 'Callum said there was no such person as Santa, but I knew he was wrong because I *knew* Santa. I knew him and he was my grandad. My God, I was proud of you.'

'I know.' He patted her shoulder. 'And I hope I'll always be… your Santa, Elodie. But for the next generation of Chessory children, it's time for someone new.'

Elodie scanned the supermarket for someone who looked like they might be in charge, her little card pinched tightly between her fingers.

'Excuse me,' she said to a passing staff member. 'I want to put an ad on your community noticeboard.'

'Nothing to do with me, hon. On my break.'

'Right. Then who can I—'

'On. My. Break,' the girl repeated, as if she thought Elodie must be a bit thick. She nodded to the single manned checkout then wandered off.

Was the girl saying Elodie should talk to the man on the checkout? With his boyish grin and the dark, curling hair flopping into his eyes, he looked too young to be in charge of community noticeboards – or of anything, for that matter. However, he was the only person around. Elodie hung awkwardly around the belt while she waited for him to finish scanning someone's shopping.

The lad seemed to take an age to put everything through. Meanwhile, the middle-aged woman whose shopping he was scanning was chattering away.

'...anyway, our Carol – you remember our Carol – she only caught Neil chasing the au pair around the kitchen in her frillies. The au pair was in her own frillies, I mean, not Neil in our Carol's.'

'She never did!' the checkout man said as he made leisurely work of weighing an aubergine. 'Not her own brother-in-law.'

'I know! I know!' the customer exclaimed gleefully. 'Well, then she had to decide whether to tell our Katie. I mean, they've three kiddies when all's said and done. No one wants to drop a bad news bomb like that.'

The man paused with a tin of condensed milk halfway to the scanner. 'Carol told her though, right?'

'What do you think?' The woman was evidently relishing having her audience eating out of the palm of her hand.

'She did. She told her so she could give that bar steward Neil his comeuppance. Sisters before misters forever.'

'Yes, she told her. So now I've got a houseful, haven't I? Katie and the kiddies are with us until she's decided what she wants to do about Neil. Lord knows where the au pair is. Back in Austria, I shouldn't wonder – hopefully with her clothes on.'

The man shook his head as he scanned her last item. 'Honestly, Janine, your life. You need to write a book. Write a book and get me a part in the film. I'd be a dab hand at chasing au pairs around in their frillies.'

Elodie, feeling this afternoon gossip session had gone on for quite long enough, cleared her throat. Janine looked at her.

'Sorry, I didn't realise I was holding anyone up,' she said, sounding resentful at having her social engagement cut short. 'Thanks, Nick. We'll catch up next week.'

Nick nodded as he took her payment. 'Always a pleasure, my darling. Oh, and I am *loving* the new hairdo, by the way.' He blew her a kiss as she left.

'Do you always take that long to scan someone's shopping?' Elodie asked. 'She only had a basketful.'

Nick shrugged. 'I'm here to provide a service you don't get from the self-checkout, aren't I? Not everything can be automated.'

'What service?'

'My dry wit and sparkling chat. Besides, serving Janine is the highlight of my week. *EastEnders* is like watching *The Waltons* after a dose of her family.'

Nick swivelled to face her. The beam on his face reminded her of Summer. Elodie could sense that there was no sarcasm, no insult, no grumpy retort that could dim its sunshine.

God save us from cheerful bastards…

'So did you want something?' Nick asked. 'I notice you're conspicuously grocery-less.'

Elodie pointed at the community noticeboard. 'Who's responsible for that? I've got a card I want to put up.'

'Ali, the manager. I'd find him for you, but I'm not supposed to wander off when I'm on the tills. What's the card?'

Elodie handed it over, and Nick read it enthusiastically. He looked like he did everything enthusiastically. Surely it was unnatural to be that happy without the aid of something with a street name.

'"Mature male character actor wanted",' he read. '"£25 per hour, beard and suit supplied. Open auditions Saturday 2nd October, 12noon–2pm, at the address below. Contact Elodie Martin for more details."' He frowned. 'I don't get it.'

'Well we had to be a bit sly, in case any kiddies read it.'

Realisation dawned.

'Santa?' Nick mouthed. Elodie nodded.

'Elodie Martin… hey, you're a Martin!' Nick fixed her in a starstruck gaze. 'You're one of *those* Martins, right? Of Martin's Toy Kingdom?'

Elodie laughed. 'You say it like we're the Kardashians.'

'Are you kidding? I *love* that place! When I was a kid, I used to go every year with my mum to see the big man. I genuinely believed your Santa was the real thing – I'm not sure I don't still. Is he retiring then?'

'That's right.' Elodie felt her throat constrict. 'He... thinks it's time for someone new to take over. Health problems.'

'Sorry to hear that.' Nick frowned at her expression. 'This is someone you're close to?'

'My grandad.' She held out her hand for the card. 'Anyway, thanks for your help. I'll go find the manager.'

'No need.' Nick tucked the card away. 'I can sort it for you.'

'I thought you said—'

'I'll be finishing my shift soon. I can arrange it with Ali when I'm done.'

'But isn't there a fee?'

'This is on me.' Nick smiled. 'Consider it payback for many happy Christmas visits to your grotto.'

'Oh,' Elodie said, blinking. 'Well, if you're sure. Thank you.'

2

Elodie drummed her fingers on the table in the upstairs storeroom. She nudged Pops.

'How long has it been now?'

'An hour.'

'It can't have been.'

She checked her watch. Pops was right. It was now 1pm, and not a single person had shown up to audition for the role of Father Christmas in this year's grotto. Surely there was someone who wanted the job? OK, Martin's rates weren't the best, but they weren't bad for a gig sitting on your backside.

Downstairs, the front door jangled. Elodie jumped.

'Relax,' Pops said soothingly. 'A watched... pot, remember. I'm sure they're all just... fashionably late.'

Elodie propped her chin on her fist. 'A fashionably late Father Christmas is the last thing we need.'

'Where did you advertise?'

'I put a card on the noticeboard in the big supermarket.'

'That's it?'

'Well, yes,' Elodie said. 'I thought word would get around. The old Chessory grapevine.'

'Did you send... an enquiry to that theatrical agency?'

She nodded glumly. 'It was like I thought. The pros are way out of our price range.'

Elodie sat up straight at the sound of footsteps. A second later, Summer's head peeped in.

'Please tell me you've got a ruddy, rotund old gent out there with his belly shaking like a bowlful of jelly,' Elodie said, clasping her hands.

'Um, well, there's someone here to audition.' Summer ushered in the man behind her. He was tall and skinny, dressed in a full-length tweed coat, black skinny tie and a shirt with the top button unfastened. He had dark, curly hair and a good-natured, youthful face that despite the absence of his supermarket uniform, Elodie recognised at once.

'You?'

Nick smiled bashfully. 'Me. Hi again.'

Elodie shook her head. 'Come on, you have got to be kidding me. What are you, twenty-five?'

'Way off, but thanks. I'm thirty-four.'

'Can I go?' asked Summer.

Pops nodded. 'Yes, go… back to the till. Thanks, pet.'

'You can't seriously be here to audition?' Elodie said to Nick.

'Why can't I? I was born for this role,' Nick said, his eyes sparkling. 'I knew it as soon as I read your card. "This is Fate, Nicky Boy." That's what I said to myself.'

'Born for it? Are you joking?'

'The card said "male character actor wanted". Well, that's me.'

'It said *mature* male character actor wanted. I mean, come on.' Elodie scanned the boyish frame under his bohemian-style coat. 'You're skinny, you're young, you're distinctly unruddy of cheek and nose, and I bet you couldn't grow a beard if you tried. Could you?'

Pops smiled wryly at Nick. 'She… gets her charm from me.'

'All right, so I'm lacking in a couple of areas,' Nick admitted. 'I've got the dimples though. Look.' He smiled broadly so they could see.

'Dimples alone aren't going to cut it,' Elodie told him shortly. 'Sorry, but you're basically the anti-Santa.'

Nick tossed his head. 'Isn't that why they call it acting, luvvie?'

'You can't be that good an actor. Come back in thirty years' and a lot of very lardy dinners' time.'

Pops nudged her. 'I don't think… we're allowed to say that kind of thing, are we?' he murmured. 'There's… all sorts of laws. Not allowed to discriminate based on appearance or age.'

'Yes, but within reason, surely,' she whispered back. 'He's auditioning to be Santa Claus!'

'Come on, give me a chance,' Nick said with a winning smile.

'Hmm.' Elodie looked at Pops. 'What do you think?'

Pops shrugged. 'He's not much younger… than I was when I started. It's all in the bearing.'

'Well… all right, I guess he can audition now he's here. No one else has turned up.' Elodie glared at Nick, who looked a bit smug for her liking. 'No one else has turned up *yet*, I mean. That doesn't mean the job's yours.' She gestured to a seat. 'Sit down then.'

Nick did as he was told, smiling widely. This annoyed Elodie. It looked a bit too much like he thought the job was in the bag.

'Age: thirty-four,' she said, making a note on her pad. 'Full name?'

'Nicholas Winter.'

She quirked an eyebrow. 'Seriously?'

'Is that a problem?'

'That's really your name? You've got the gall to march in here and tell me your name's Nicholas Winter and your dream job is Father bloody Christmas?'

'Um. Yes?'

'And that's your actual, genuine birth name?'

'No, my birth name was Jack Frost. I had it changed by deed poll.' He registered Elodie's unsmiling expression. 'Yes, Elodie. It's my actual, genuine birth name.'

'All right, if that's the story you're sticking to,' Elodie said, writing it down. 'What makes you think this is the job for you, so-called Nicholas Winter?'

Nick puffed himself up. 'Because I'm the king of Christmas, that's why. I love Christmas, me.'

'Really? Why?'

'What do you mean, why? Because it's Christmas! The most magical time of the whole year.' The disbelief in Nick's tone rang in the rafters above. 'Saying you hate Christmas is like saying you hate joy.'

Elodie shook her head. 'You are one weird guy.'

'Go on, ask me anything. I know everything there is to know about Christmas and the father thereof. *The Santa Clause, The Christmas Chronicles, Miracle on 34th Street* *both original and remake, Santa Claus: The Movie, Elf* – every Christmas film about Santa, I can pretty much recite it from memory.'

'I thought *Elf* was about an elf. There's a clue in the title.'

'Well yeah, but Santa's got a sizeable role.' Nick frowned. 'You're not seriously telling me you've never seen it?'

She shrugged. 'It's a kids' film. I'm neither a kid nor a parent of one.'

'Yeah, but it's *Elf*! Is it even really Christmas if you don't watch it?'

'Look, can we get on with this interview?' Elodie demanded.

'All right, ask me about Christmas then. Test me like I'm on *Mastermind*.'

Elodie shot a look at Pops, who gave her a resigned shrug.

'Reindeer?' he asked Nick.

'Dasher, Dancer, Prancer, Vixen, Comet, Cupid, Dunder, Blixem,' Nick reeled off promptly.

Elodie shook her head. 'Donner and Blitzen, not Dunder and whatever you said. As in, the German for thunder and lightning? Everyone knows that.'

'Wrong.' Nick looked pleased with himself. 'In the original text of "A Visit from St Nicholas" – better known as "'Twas the Night Before Christmas" – the names are in Dutch, not German. Dunder and Blixem. Look it up.'

'Hmm. And what about Rudolph?'

'Rudolph was created for a 1939 storybook as part of a marketing campaign by an American department store. He wasn't one of the original eight.'

Pops gave him an impressed nod. 'You know… your stuff, lad.'

'But dimples and reindeer trivia do not a Santa make,' Elodie said. 'Have you got any previous Santaing experience?'

Nick grimaced slightly. 'Well… kind of.'

'Kind of?'

'I haven't played Santa but I have played the Ghost of Christmas Present. Stage version of *A Christmas Carol*, St Peter's Hall, three Christmases ago.'

Elodie raised her eyebrows. 'St Peter's Hall?'

'That's right.'

Was that true? St Peter's wasn't some tinpot local theatre: it was big. Elodie had taken Summer and her brother Caleb to the star-studded panto there every year when they were little. She tried to keep her expression blank, however. She didn't want Nick to think he had the job all sewn up.

'Do you... act professionally then, Nick?' Pops asked.

'Often enough to keep me on the tills,' Nick said with a dry smile. 'I'm a trained thesp, if that's what you mean. Leeds Conservatoire, class of 2009. It's getting paid to do it that's the trick.'

'What's the Ghost of Christmas Present got to do with Santa?' Elodie asked.

'They're sort of connected. Santa wasn't really known in Britain when Dickens wrote the book. But Father Christmas was, and that's basically who the Ghost of Christmas Present is.'

Elodie frowned. 'Eh? He isn't Santa but he is Father Christmas?'

'The two were separate figures originally,' Nick said, his eyes shining as he dived back into his specialist subject. 'Santa Claus, or Sinterklaas – that's St Nicholas – was carried over to America by Dutch settlers. He went through something of an evolution, then he was exported to us in the 1850s and merged with the existing figure of Father Christmas. Unlike Santa, Father Christmas was just an anthropomorphism of the season who appeared on cards and—'

'All right, all right!' Elodie held up her hands. 'You know everything there is to know about Christmas; we get it. And don't think you're going to get the job just because you know the word "anthropomorphism" either. Are we going to see you in action then?'

'I thought you'd never ask.' Nick stood up and threw out his arms expansively. 'Come in, and know me better, man!'

Elodie blinked. 'Does Father Christmas say that?'

'Well, no. But the Ghost of Christmas Present does, and he's—'

'—basically the same thing. So you said. Is that it?'

'Haven't you got any banter?' Pops asked. 'You know, for... chatting with the kiddywinks?'

For the first time, Nick looked uncertain. 'Well, I have been practising a bit with my mum. Have you got a kid I can demonstrate it on?'

'You can demonstrate it on me. I used to help Pops rehearse.' Elodie pulled up a chair beside his. 'Right. I'll be a typical seven-year-old.'

'Hang on. I need to get into the part.'

Elodie rolled her eyes. 'Actors. All right, hurry up.'

Nick started muttering furiously.

'What's he saying?' Pops asked Elodie.

Elodie leaned in to listen. 'I think he's reciting the words to "Santa Claus is Coming to Town".'

Nick nodded. 'Just reminding myself of the guy's modus operandi. Knows when you've been naughty or nice, making a list, checking it twice, yada yada.' He took a deep breath. 'OK, let's go.'

Elodie stared at him, her eyes wide and unblinking.

'Well well well, who have we here?' Nick boomed in a deep Santa voice that Elodie was forced to admit was rather good. 'If it isn't young Elodie Martin. Funnily enough, I was just reading your letter before I left the North Pole. Now, remind me what you wanted.'

Elodie continued to stare, in as disconcerting a way as she could manage.

'Um, Elodie, it's your line,' Nick murmured.

'She's in character,' Pops said. 'About forty per cent of the kids I see are silent. Be prepared… to do most of the work.'

'Silent?' Nick said.

Elodie broke character and nodded. 'It's a scary business, meeting legendary magical figures with the fate of your Christmas presents in their hands. Some kids are shy, some are scared, and some just don't talk.'

'So what do I do if I get a non-speaker?'

'The parents usually speak for them,' Pops said. 'Just remember… to address yourself to the kid, even if they're non-verbal. Half the magic… is in the memory.'

'Right.' Nick slipped back into character. 'Well, Elodie, I know you've been good this year so I'm sure you'll get what you asked for. My elves are already hard at work making your present.'

Pops shook his head. 'Don't promise… what parents might not be able to deliver.'

'I might've written and asked for a pony,' Elodie said. 'Or a real-live velociraptor. Or an iPhone with an Oculus Quest headset when Mum and Dad have only got the budget for Lego. Not all families are rich enough to give their kids mega-expensive gifts.'

'I know that,' Nick said. 'So what's the right thing to say?'

'The parents… usually give a signal,' Pops said. 'Or just keep it vague. "I know there'll be something wonderful for you… under the tree." That sort of thing.'

'Right.' Nick sounded a little down.

'You're doing very well though,' Pops said kindly. 'A bit of practice… and you'll have it spot on. Ellie. Give him… the Violet Elizabeth.'

Elodie shook her head. 'No way he's ready for that.'

'I think he can take it.'

'Well, if you say so.' She turned to Nick again.

'That beard's not real,' she announced in an annoying know-it-all squeak.

Nick blinked. 'Eh?'

'And that's a pillow down your top. It's not proper fatness.'

Nick stared, then attempted to recover. 'Um… why do you say that?'

Pops shook his head. 'That'll only encourage her… to keep going. Get her off the subject, fast. Remind her what she's… here for.'

Nick looked lost for a moment.

'Presents?' he suggested.

'That's right. Exploit their greed.'

'My friend says Santa's not real,' Elodie went on in the same annoying voice. 'She says it's your mum and dad and you're just someone dressed up to get money.'

Nick looked panicked, but he quickly recovered. 'Then there's no point telling me what you want for Christmas, is there? Since I'm not really real. Of course, then I won't be able to bring it to you if it turns out I am real after all.'

Elodie pretended to think this over.

'I suppose I could tell you,' she said at last. 'Just in case.'

'But if you don't believe I'm real, I might not be able to get the magic to work. The elves and the reindeers need people to believe in them for there to be enough magic to fly and make toys.'

'So…'

'So I need you and all your friends to believe as hard as you can in me, then I can bring you all lovely things. Can you do that?'

Elodie hesitated, then nodded. 'I guess. If it'll help make the magic.'

'Thank you, Elodie.'

Pops beamed at him. 'Not bad. Not bad at all. Ellie, I think… we've seen enough.'

Elodie stopped being the Santa visitor from hell and went back to her place beside Pops.

'Do you get a lot of that?' Nick asked in his normal voice. 'The unbelievers?'

Pops nodded. 'Always a handful. Kids these days… think they know it all.'

'OK, we're done here,' Elodie said. 'Thanks for coming in, Nick.'

'Did I get the job?'

'If you leave your contact details with my cousin, we'll let you know in due course,' she said coolly, scribbling on her notepad. 'Bye then.'

'Elodie, can I have a word… in private?' Pops asked, laying a hand on her arm.

'What about?'

Pops turned to Nick. 'Can you wait outside a moment, lad? Don't go home… just yet.'

'Sure.' Nick went to wait outside the storeroom.

'Go on, get it out,' Elodie said to Pops when they were alone. 'You think I was too hard on him, don't you?'

'I think… we both were. Perhaps you were right. The Violet Elizabeth was too much.'

Elodie shrugged. 'He has to be prepared. The lad's so obsessed with Christmas he probably piddles sherry and farts cinnamon and cloves. He needs to know that despite what he's seen in his favourite films, being Santa isn't all candy canes and wide-eyed, adorable moppets.'

'He didn't do badly… for a first-timer. Impressed me.' Pops gave her a searching look. 'You don't like him.'

'I wouldn't say that. He's just a bit… odd.'

He laughed. 'This is coming from you?'

'I'm not odd. I'm prematurely old, bitter and cynical. That's completely different.'

'You didn't need to bite the boy's… head off, did you?'

She shrugged. 'Finding out if he can put up with me is half the audition.'

'And he did, didn't he? Give him a chance, Ellie. You and Nick Winter… could work well together.'

Elodie hesitated. 'I guess he's all right in a nauseatingly upbeat sort of way. He's obviously keen for the job. It's just that this is important, Pops. You know the grotto takings are all that keep us ticking along over Christmas. People might go to Ashley's for their shopping, but when it comes to seeing Santa, everyone knows it's Martin's where you'll find the real thing. We can't lose that reputation; it could ruin us.'

'We… won't.'

'Won't we? With a skinny, beardless boy Santa who crumples in the face of his first non-verbal?'

'There is no one else, Elodie,' Pops said quietly. 'It's 2pm. Nick Winter's… the only applicant.'

'I suppose he is.' Elodie lowered her head. 'Are you sure,

Pops?' she asked in a whisper. 'Are you really sure you have to give it up?'

'I'm sorry, kiddo.'

Elodie sighed. 'Let me tell him then. I hope he won't be too smug about it.' She leaned over to give her grandad a hug. 'Go home and have a lie-down, eh? You look tired.'

'I am a little.' Pops got stiffly to his feet. 'I'll send the young man back in... on my way out.'

When Nick entered, Elodie pointed to the chair he'd recently vacated.

'All right, sit down.'

'You know, for a toyshop owner you're one mean son of a bitch,' he observed affably. 'I thought you people were supposed to be all apple cheeks and merry, sparkling eyes.'

'Nope. I'm a hard-nosed businesswoman and proud son of a bitch, as you so astutely observe.'

'This is your place, is it? Or do you have some other, less grumpy Martins to help you? You seem young to be running the family business on your own.'

'It's just me. Pops is retired, so... that just leaves me.' She met his eyes. 'Why do you want this job, Nick? The truth, not all this "my mum was a plum pudding and my dad was Frosty the Snowman" bollocks.'

He shrugged. 'I need to eat. Pay bills. Like I said, I'm a trained actor, and I've had one job in four months. If this is the best I can do, so be it.'

'Don't do us any favours.'

'I didn't mean it like that.' He met her eye. 'I'll be good, Elodie. The best I can be.'

She stared him down. He beamed back like a human SpongeBob.

'Look, this might just be a job to you but it's bloody important to us,' she said. 'My grandad was the best in the business, for decades. You came here as a kid; you must know that.'

Nick looked awkward. 'His speech...'

'He had a stroke. Two months ago.' Elodie felt a lump rise in her throat and quickly moved on. 'Listen, Nick. Every year that eight-storey cement monstrosity of Callum Ashley's tries to outdo us with its Winter Wonderland grotto.'

'Callum Ashley – the guy who owns that department store in town, right?'

'Yeah,' Elodie muttered darkly. 'Smug bastard.'

'You know him then?'

'Sadly, yes. We were at school together. Last year his place was chocka with animatronic reindeers, a snow machine, a big-name celebrity to open the thing and God knows what else. But while Ashley's Department Store might be kicking our bottoms in every other respect, they've never been able to produce a Santa to rival ours. For five weeks every year, Callum's fancy Winter Wonderland grotto is virtually empty while we've got queues out of the door waiting to see Martin's Toy Kingdom's legendary Father Christmas. Are you hearing me?'

Nick blinked. 'Wow.'

'Wow is right. If you want this job, Nick Winter, you'll need to fill some bloody big snow boots.' Elodie held his gaze. 'Can you really be our Santa – *the* Santa?'

'You're right. Your grandad's a tough act to follow.' He didn't drop eye contact. 'But I'm still your best shot.'

3

Callum Ashley examined the toy soldiers that flanked this year's Winter Wonderland grotto. They stood ten feet tall, painted in bright, metallic colours and twinkling with multicoloured LEDs.

'Impressive, right?' said his store manager, Mike.

'Not bad,' Callum agreed. 'What do they do?'

'Hang on.'

Mike fiddled with the figures until the *Nutcracker Suite* chirruped out in the merry tones of a fairground organ. The soldiers swivelled on their bases and played their drums in time.

'Very nice,' Callum said absently. 'How's the budget looking for this year?'

'We're a bit over. You wanted separate scenes for the polar bears and the reindeer, remember. But it'll be worth it, I reckon.'

'Yes. We really want to give it all we've got this time.'

Callum cast his eye over the grotto door.

That door was impressive in itself. It could have been taken straight from a real gingerbread house – there were some serious Hansel and Gretel vibes. It was decorated with two candy canes, crossed like swords, with an arch of boiled sweets around it. The door alone was ten times more magical than anything Martin's would have in their makeshift cardboard-and-paper-chain affair, and more than ten times as expensive, he was sure.

Callum had spared no expense this year to infuse his grotto with as much magic as money could buy. The door and soldiers were at the end of an aisle of wonders that ran right through the toy department. At either side were scenes from the North Pole. Realistic moving elves, making toys in Santa's workshop. Mrs Claus, baking Christmas goodies. Polar bears and penguins, smiling as they skated. Christmas trees of all sizes; sacks filled with presents; giant gingerbread men and frolicking reindeer. Everything.

Callum, and his dad and grandad before him, had been throwing money at their grotto for decades, but until now it hadn't made a jot of difference. Because as long as Martin's had Jim Martin, all the frolicking reindeers in the world couldn't get the kids through their door. Not when everyone knew Martin's Toy Kingdom was the home of the actual, real Santa.

But not this year, Callum thought with a small smile. After Jim's stroke, Martin's grottopoly was surely over at last. This year, Ashley's finally had a chance to steal the holly crown.

'Something funny, boss?' Mike asked.

'Hmm? No.' Callum forced the smile down. It was unworthy of him. He'd known the Martins all his life and the annual grotto rivalry had never been anything personal. Certainly he wouldn't wish Jim any harm. He was a nice old chap.

Nevertheless, was it so wrong to feel that Martin's had

had their turn? Jim had been the reigning Santa around here for forty years. It was high time someone else had a chance – and why shouldn't that someone sit on the throne here, in the midst of the most magical, biggest-budget grotto experience in a twenty-mile radius?

No, he had nothing to reproach himself with. Callum had always dealt fairly with the Martins. Elodie knew that if she ever changed her mind about wanting to sell then he'd happily pay over the odds for that little shop, if only to have its inexplicably popular grotto out of his hair. He'd even offered her a job managing the toy department here at Ashley's. That offer was on the table whenever she chose to reconsider – and he was sure she would, one day. Martin's couldn't keep going forever.

It wasn't only about the shop. Elodie was a brilliant little businesswoman and she worked her backside off at that place. Of course it was still struggling to make money on everything except its grotto, like so many independent shops, but that was just the climate. Elodie's biggest fault, Callum knew, was her blind refusal to see that her family business's decline wasn't some temporary glitch. The age of the little shop was coming to an end, and if she wasn't such a stubborn little madam, she'd face up to that and come work for him. But let her live in her delusions. Callum Ashley had never begged for anything in his life. Martin's Toy Kingdom would die a death one of these days, and then she'd come running.

Still, he felt guilty for that cheap smile at Jim's expense. He was a kindly old soul who didn't deserve the bad luck he'd had. Callum hadn't seen him since his stroke either, although Jim and his own grandfather had been great friends on top of good-natured business rivals. That was remiss of him. He made a mental note to drop in at Martin's that afternoon with a get well card.

'Boss?'

Callum dragged himself back into the moment. 'What time are we meeting the new Santa, Mike?'

'Ten minutes.'

'OK. Let's go see if he's arrived.'

Ashley's had a fresh Santa every year. Every autumn Callum hired another St Nick, determined this time to find someone who could compete with Jim in the Martin's grotto, and each year they let him down. Callum could never work out what it was that made Jim such a hit and his Santa a flop. They had all the right ingredients. Bushy beards, suitably jolly ho-ho-hoing, fat tums and rosy cheeks. But somehow, while the ingredients were right for the perfect Santa, the finished product always fell down flat.

'Mike?' he said as they walked to the elevator that would take them to the top floor, where Callum's office was located.

'Yes, boss?'

'Did you go see Santa as a boy?'

'Course,' Mike said. 'Every kiddie sees Santa, don't they? Our mam took us second week in December, regular. Didn't you?'

'No, I was an early sceptic. I stopped believing in Father Christmas not long after I started school.'

Mike looked surprised. 'Really? How come?'

Callum shrugged. 'The magic soon wears off when you spend your childhood around this place. When I was five, I wandered into the grotto when our Santa was on his break. Caught him eating a Pot Noodle and flicking through the women's lingerie section of the Ashley's catalogue. That was it, after that. The lingerie was bad enough, but I couldn't bring myself to believe in a Santa who ate Pot Noodles.'

Mike looked hesitant, as if he couldn't decide whether this was a joke. Callum knew he had a reputation among his staff for being 'serious but fair'. A miserable sod with no sense of humour, in other words. He flashed Mike a small smile to let him know it was OK to laugh.

'Er, haha,' Mike said cautiously. 'So did that ruin it for you then? I used to think the jolly fat man was the best part of Christmas.'

'No,' Callum said as they entered the lift. 'Christmas for me was all about the presents; I didn't care much where they came from. Dad used to go all out for me – one benefit of being an only child. After the Santa myth died, I used to pick my presents out from our stock.'

'Oh.' Mike thought this over. 'Sort of not really the spirit of the thing though, would you say? Just picking something instead of getting it given.'

Callum shrugged. 'What did I care? I just wanted stuff. I wanted to see how jealous the other kids would be when school started and I showed them what I'd got. Watch them all falling over each other to make friends with me.'

Mike stared at him.

'What?' Callum said. 'I was a kid, wasn't I? The best of them are greedy, shallow little buggers. Santa Claus is just a way of dressing the greed up in a shiny velvet suit and calling it "magic". I didn't see the point in illusions, even at that age.'

'That's kind of sad, boss.'

'I never thought so. I had a very happy childhood.'

That was true. Callum had been happy, in his way.

His parents' marriage had been somewhat distant, with a significant age gap between Nate Ashley and Marie, his much younger wife, but in spite of that the pair had made sure their only child never wanted for anything. Still… there'd never been much laughter.

The lift stopped, and Callum stepped out with Mike.

The new Santa, Kenny, was seated outside his office. Callum examined him as they approached.

He'd used a different theatrical agency this time, and he had to admit Kenny looked the part. He was going to need very little in the way of padding or makeup. His cheeks had a natural rosy glow, and he filled what was no doubt his best suit – somewhat worn and ill-fitting – with a comforting plumpness. He even had the beard and a pair of half-moon spectacles.

Kenny beamed as they joined him.

'Ah, now one of you must be the chap I'm here to see.' His deep, cheerful voice was infused with a reassuring Scottish lilt.

'That would be me,' Callum said as he ushered Kenny inside his office. 'Callum Ashley. This is my store manager, Mike Steele. Thanks for coming today.'

Kenny shook Callum's hand vigorously, then Mike's, before taking a seat. 'Kenny Ross. It's a pleasure, lads.'

Callum was impressed. Their previous Santas had always been… adequate. Jolly and plump and so forth; everything Santas were supposed to be. But there'd always been something lacking. Callum had never understood what. He just knew, whenever he was looking at another year's abysmal grotto takings, that Jim Martin's Santa had something his own Santas never possessed.

But whatever that elusive quality was, this guy had it. Callum could sense it. This guy was the real deal – some proper *Miracle on 34th Street* shit. Kenny Ross was a gentle giant who filled the room with paternal warmth and personality, like… well, like Father Christmas.

'Right,' Callum said. 'There are a few issues of protocol to go over – timings, gifts, interacting with the kids – then we'll show you around the grotto. I think you'll be impressed.'

Kenny raised his eyebrows. 'Have I got the job then? The agency said you wanted an informal interview before you made a decision.'

'I did say that, yes.' Callum flashed him a rare smile. 'But now I've met you, Mr Ross, I don't think that will be necessary. I'm a man who always trusts his gut, and everything in mine is telling me that when it comes to Father Christmases, you're a natural.'

4

Nick arrived at Martin's Toy Kingdom for his fifth visit since his interview. There was only a month until the big grotto opening, and Elodie had requested that he was at the shop three times a week for training sessions with the old man, Jim. Nick didn't mind, as long as he was getting paid. With the state of his finances, he needed all the extra cash he could get.

Martin's was an old two-storey building in a smart wooded suburb. Nick's home of Chessory was a West Yorkshire town with pretentions to cosmopolitan chic, but in reality it was little more than a handful of shops, pubs and churches, with the odd theatre sprinkled in just to keep Nick's inbox adequately furnished with rejections. Above the town skyline loomed the ridge of the Pennines – wild moorland melting into harsh, jagged crags – just in case the little town nestled below started getting ideas above its station with its delusions of civility.

The street the toyshop was on, Whitsun Avenue, had once been home to quite a few shops. The other buildings were nearly all private residences now, but Nick could see evidence of the establishments they once were painted on to the stonework. One sign, worn and faded, announced that the long-gone shop had been licensed to sell tobacco. Another cottage had been a printer's and bookbinder's. But there were no shops on Whitsun Avenue now other than a small newsagent's and, of course, Martin's itself. Other businesses had closed or relocated as high street shops like Ashley's had pulled trade away from the outskirts of town. Somehow, though, the little toyshop was hanging on in there.

It was a pretty old building – Victorian, with two large windows each divided by wooden glazing bars into twenty rectangular panes. *Martin's Toy Kingdom* had been stencilled above the door in attractive gold lettering over claret-coloured paint. Nick could just imagine how it was going to look when the Christmas decorations went up, with seasonal toy displays in the glowing windows, a string of lights twined with holly over the window tops and a wreath on the front door. All it would need to complete the picture of Victorian Christmas charm was a cherry-cheeked tot eagerly pressing their nose against the glass. It certainly looked like the sort of place St Nick would pick for a holiday home.

Nick went in, hands thrust into the pockets of his big coat, and nodded a greeting to the pink-haired teen behind the counter. He guessed she only worked Saturdays. He hadn't seen her since she'd shown him upstairs the day he'd come to audition.

'Hi again,' the girl said. 'Are you here to see Elodie?'

'Yeah, she wanted to go over some things before my Santa lesson with her grandad.'

'She'll be down in a minute. She's just upstairs unpacking the grotto stuff from the storeroom.'

'Well, I've got nowhere better to be.' Nick leaned against the counter. 'So are you a Martin too?' He hadn't caught the teenager's name when they'd met briefly.

'No, a Rowan.' The girl paused. 'I mean, I guess by blood I am, same as Elodie – she's my cousin on her dad's side. But my mum changed her name when she got married.'

'What's your other name then, Miss Rowan?'

'Summer. What's yours?'

Nick laughed. 'Winter. Greetings, fellow season.'

'That's not your first name though?'

'No, my last name. You can call me Nick during the week or Nicholas on Sundays.'

'Like St Nicholas?' she said, laughing.

'Yep. The role I was born to play, dear girl.'

Nick glanced around the cluttered shop, looking just as he remembered it when he'd visited as a child. There were two floors, with toys on sale downstairs and children's books on a sort of mezzanine level, plus the storeroom-slash-office where he'd been interviewed. The ground floor was large and crammed with colour, as toyshops ought to be. Shelves of toys divided the room into aisles, and there was a carpeted corner with beanbag chairs, colouring books and a toybox full of old stock. A couple of small kids were playing with a Scalextric set while their parents browsed the shelves. Other than that, there were no customers in.

'What's it like working here at Christmas?' Nick asked Summer.

'Oh, I love it,' she breathed. 'I can't wait until the decorations go up, Elodie lets me put the Christmas playlist on and the littlies start coming to see Santa. I've got friends working in retail who say they have homicidal thoughts about Mariah Carey, but I legit can't hear "All I Want for Christmas is You" too many times.'

'What about your cousin? She doesn't exactly seem brimming with the merry.'

'Nah, Elodie hates Christmas.'

Nick shook his head. 'That's so weird.'

'Isn't it? She always says she can't wait to get it over with. I don't get how anyone can't love that time of year though.'

'Me either. Especially when they own a toyshop.'

'It's probably a bit sad for El, not having her parents around. I guess being an orphan hits you more at Christmas, especially when you're an only child.'

Nick frowned. 'She lost her parents?'

Summer nodded soberly. 'When she was little. Car accident. Pops and Nana brought her up after that. Our nana died three years ago though.'

It's just me. That's what Elodie had said the day of his audition, when Nick had asked if she ran the shop with other members of the Martin family. *It's just me...*

'That's a lot of loss for such a short life,' Nick said feelingly. 'How old is she? Not much more than thirty, I'd guess.'

'She's thirty-one.'

'I suppose that would affect your view of Christmas. All the focus on families.' Nick took another look around the shop. 'Quiet in here for a Saturday, isn't it?'

'It always is,' Summer said, lowering her voice. 'Until the grotto opens.'

'How come?'

'Dunno. I'd think maybe people didn't know we were here, except they come to see Santa so they must do. Maybe it seems like too big an effort to make the trip out here just for us.' Summer looked at the smattering of customers. 'I'm sure Elodie only took me on because I'm family. Martin's doesn't need a Saturday girl.'

'She said she managed the place on her own. Does that mean she's the sole owner?'

'She is now. She was made manager when Pops and Nana owned the place. Then when Nana died, Pops decided to retire and offered to sign what would've been El's dad's share in the business over to her. My mum was offered a share too but she didn't want it, so Elodie got it all.'

'How come your mum didn't want her share?'

'She reckons Martin's is a lame duck, with Amazon and the toyshops in town offering discounts we can't afford to match. She thinks it's only a matter of time until—'

They were interrupted by Elodie coming downstairs. Summer fell silent.

'Oh good, you're here,' Elodie said to Nick in her usual brusque manner. 'Come up to the second floor. I want to show you something.'

'I'm fine, thanks. How are you?'

'We don't have time for all that "more tea, Vicar?" crap. Come on.'

Nick followed her upstairs, trying not to smile. Something about the spiky little toyshop owner was kind of adorable, although he suspected she'd swing for him if he ever said so out loud.

There was a strange sort of charm about Elodie Martin, he'd discovered, which was ironic given she did her damnedest to push people away. Nick couldn't quite put his finger on why. Was it the way her nose twitched when he made a joke, as if she was trying not to laugh? Or the tender quality in her voice when she fussed around her grandad? It couldn't be her looks, surely. Not that Elodie wasn't pretty – she had a fresh, sweet look that was completely at odds with the sort of fierce, hard-as-hobnails image she seemed determined to project. But the thick blonde hair pushed up into a frazzled bun, coupled with the bare minimum of makeup and clothes that looked like they'd been dragged out of a pile of laundry, sometimes gave her the rumpled look of a female Columbo.

'Elodie. Such a sweet, musical name,' Nick said as they climbed the stairs. 'Was it supposed to be ironic?'

'Funny.' They reached the second floor and she turned to look at him. 'At least I don't dress like I'm on my way to a *Doctor Who* convention. What's with your dress sense? Is it a hipster thing?'

Nick glanced down at his favourite long tweed coat. 'Hipster thing? How dare you.'

'Come on. You look like you're one step away from a cravat.'

'Maybe a waistcoat. I draw the line at cravats.' Nick smoothed his hands over his coat. 'I was going for "eccentric, pale and interesting". The sort of vibe that makes directors stop in the street and say: "Who is that fascinating young man? He's got just the look I had in mind for my Jamie Tyrone!"'

'Jamie Tyrone can wait. You need to be channelling Father Christmas from now until the grotto closes on the 24th,' Elodie said firmly. 'Your DBS check came back yesterday, which means we're all paperworked up for the opening. I thought me and you could talk through how the grotto works before your lesson.'

'Hit me.'

Elodie gestured around the shelves of books that filled the second floor. 'We set it up here. You'll be in the storeroom, which'll be suitably Christmassy. Then there's a rope cordon down the middle of the books for people to queue.'

'You put the grotto up here?' Nick asked.

'That's right, so the downstairs stays uncluttered for people to browse.'

'But if you had people queueing in the same place as your main stock, you'd get more impulse sales, surely.'

'We get long queues for the grotto. We couldn't have that many people standing about, getting in the way of the Christmas shoppers.'

'Then bring some of your stock up here,' Nick said. 'Create a few displays of the most popular Christmas toys so bored mums and dads can grab them for their baskets.'

'Except they won't. They'll snap a photo on their phones, then they'll buy them online or from Callum Ashley's place because he can afford to sell his stock with heavy discounts and we can't.'

'Still. It feels like a wasted opportunity.'

Elodie glared at him. 'Look, are you here to learn how to be Santa or are you here to tell me how to do my job?'

He shrugged. 'I can do both. So what do you do grotto-wise?'

'How do you mean?'

'What decorations do you have?'

'Well, there's Santa's throne – it's just an old chair painted gold with a red velvet cushion, but it looks pretty good,' Elodie said. 'Then we have an arch of plastic holly for the door, plus the Christmas tree.'

'That's it?'

'Yeah, apart from Santa and his elf.'

'Don't you think you could make it a bit more of an experience? You know, give it a real North Pole vibe?'

Elodie shook her head. 'We can't afford all that fancy stuff Callum pays through the nose for: CGI reindeer that really fly or whatever. No one expects that here. We're a small family business, not a town centre department store.'

'You don't need to spend big bucks. I just think you could—'

'Look, thanks for the advice, Nick, but Pops taught me a great phrase when I was a kid that goes "if it ain't broke, don't fix it",' Elodie said firmly. 'Our grotto is the most popular in the area and it has been for decades. We don't need special effects and gaudy plastic tat to make it an experience. Our Santa Claus *is* the experience.'

She wasn't wrong. Nick had come here as a boy and he knew that at Martin's, Santa always had been the experience – when Santa had been Jim Martin. How would they fare now that Santa was just out-of-work actor and checkout legend Nick Winter? He ran one finger under his tweed collar.

'Sorry,' he said. 'Just trying to make myself useful.'

'Then listen to your grotto instructions,' Elodie said, tapping her temple to indicate she wanted him to engage his brain. 'It's no more than five minutes per kid so try to keep on schedule, OK? The entry fee is a fiver each, so if they're in too long it eats into our profits. By your throne you'll have three sacks of presents with gift-wrapped toys from old stock. We used to do Boys, Girls and Neutral, but we've modernised a bit so it's Superheroes, Princesses or Puzzle.

They'll be colour-coded – green for Superheroes, purple for Princesses and yellow for Puzzle. You'll get a five-minute wee-wee break every two hours and an hour for your dinner. Grotto opens at 10am and closes when the shop does at six, apart from late-night shopping every Thursday, when we close at nine. All clear?'

Nick stared blankly at her. 'Sorry, can you run all that by me again?'

She took a piece of paper from her pocket. 'Here, I wrote it down. Be sure to memorise it.'

'Thanks. Do I need to eat it afterwards?'

She shrugged. 'Help yourself, if it gives you joy.'

The bell on the front door jangled.

'That'll be my grandad here for your Santa lesson,' Elodie said.

She headed downstairs, Nick following. But it wasn't Jim. The person who'd just come in was a tall, earnest young man in an expensive-looking charcoal suit, clutching an impressive bunch of flowers. Elodie's brow knit. Whoever the man was, she was obviously far from thrilled to see him.

5

Who was this flower-clutching new arrival, Nick wondered? A boyfriend come to make up after a row? He was very good-looking, in a corporate, Christian Grey sort of way: designer suit, gelled black hair. He was also vaguely familiar, as if Nick had seen him somewhere before.

'Hello,' Elodie said, nodding coldly to the man. 'To what do we owe this pleasure?'

'I just thought that since I was passing, um...' The man looked a bit lost. 'Is your grandfather here?'

'No. Why, did you want to see him?'

'Yes. I brought him these.' He waggled his bouquet. 'To wish him a speedy recovery.'

Elodie took the flowers with icy politeness. 'Thank you, that's very kind. He'll be thrilled to know you've been thinking about him since he came out of hospital three months ago.'

The man winced at the unsubtle reproach.

'Yes, well, you know how it is. Christmas season coming up and everything. Time just... runs away from you.' He seemed to recover his equilibrium a bit and glanced at Nick. 'Who's this?'

Elodie grimaced. 'No one. He's... helping with the grotto.'

'Or something like that,' Nick said.

Elodie turned her glare on him, and Nick decided it would be a wise move to stop talking. He sidled over to Summer.

'Is it me or did it just get very chilly in here?' he whispered.

'Arctic,' she whispered back, shivering theatrically.

'Who's the hottie? Ex-boyfriend?'

Summer shook her head. 'Don't you recognise him? He has his photo in the paper all the time. It's Callum Ashley.'

'Oh yeah, the department store guy.' Nick examined the man with interest. 'I thought he looked familiar. How does Elodie know him again?'

'They were in the same class at school. El hates him.'

'Why?'

Summer shrugged. 'Because he makes tons of money and we don't. Oh, and she says he's a smug prick who was born with a silver spoon up his bum and has never had to do a hard day's work in his life.'

Nick laughed. 'She doesn't mince her words, does she?'

'Never.'

Nick turned back to the little scene. Callum had his hands thrust awkwardly into the pockets of his suit trousers, his body language suggesting he was longing to be anywhere but here. Elodie, too, looked like she was wishing him somewhere else. But for some reason, Callum seemed determined to keep their painful conversation going.

'How are the grotto plans developing?' he asked her. 'I suppose things are going to be tough for you this year.'

Elodie smiled sweetly. 'Very considerate of you to ask, Callum. Actually I think we might be looking at our best year yet.'

Callum blinked. 'You mean your grandad's still—'

'Oh no, Pops is retiring, naturally. He has to put his

health first. But we've got a brilliant new Santa lined up to take the throne, don't you worry.'

'I'm thrilled to hear it. We've got rather a good prospect ourselves this year.' Callum paused, looking embarrassed. 'Look, Elodie. I was thinking about you this morning – I mean, about this place – and I just wanted to say that my old offer still stands. If you ever want me to take the shop off your hands, just let me know. I'll always have a job for you at Ashley's.'

'How very, very, very kind. What would we little people do without millionaire philanthropists like yourself looking out for our interests?'

'Come on, El, there's no need to be like that. I'm trying to help.'

'The hell you are.' Any pretence of civility on Elodie's part had evaporated completely now. 'What have you got lined up this year then? Real elves imported through a rip in the space-time continuum? Rides on a jet-engine-propelled sleigh? I'm sure you've thrown a small fortune at your tacky Winter Wonderland again to try to steal the one thing we have that actually makes us money.'

'Good thing all the customers left,' Nick whispered to Summer. 'It's looking like fireworks.'

'Well, I'm a businessman, aren't I?' Callum said to Elodie. 'Of course I want my grotto to be successful. It's not a crime to try to make a profit, Elodie.'

'You just can't stand that this is our thing, can you?' Elodie snapped. 'You've got everything, Callum. A huge fortune, your own department store, a monopoly on pretty much everything that gets bought or sold around here, and all Martin's has got – all it's ever had – is a single five-week period when our grotto is the best and busiest in the area. And for years, you've been trying to take that too. Not because you need it, not even because you want it, but because you can't bear for there to be anything around here that you don't own.' She thrust the bouquet back into his arms. 'You don't care about Pops. You came here to gloat, didn't you? Because you think that now he's ill, Ashley's Winter Wonderland will finally come out on top.'

A flicker of guilt ran over Callum's face.

'God, I'm right, aren't I?' she said in a low voice, her lip curling.

Callum pulled himself up. 'I came because your grandad and mine were old friends and it seemed like the right thing to do.'

'Yeah? Then where were you three months ago?'

'Well, I... like I said, it's been busy.' Callum put the flowers down on the counter. 'I ought to go. I'm sorry if I upset you. It wasn't my intention.'

He turned to leave. Nick could hear Elodie muttering under her breath. He couldn't quite make out what she was saying, although the words 'smug oily stuffed-shirt wanker' seemed to feature heavily.

'Callum!' she called as he pushed open the door.

He turned. 'Yes?'

'Uh-oh,' Summer whispered to Nick.

'What?' he whispered back.

'I know that look. When El wrinkles her nose like that, it never leads anywhere good.'

'Care to put your money where your mouth is?' Elodie demanded of Callum.

He blinked. 'What?'

'How about a little bet? If you're not too scared.'

'A bet? What sort of a bet?'

'I'll bet you that our grotto's takings knock yours right out of the water again.'

He laughed. 'You're joking.'

'Come on, how about it? You know you can't resist trying to get one over on us. Might as well make it official.'

'OK,' Callum said slowly. 'Say I agree. What are we betting for, exactly?'

'Well…' Elodie paused. 'Half our grotto profit if you win. And if we win, half of what you take – just the profits from what the kids pay to see Santa, not including toy sales. I mean, it's hardly even a bet for you, is it? You wouldn't miss the money.'

'Yeah, but you would. You can't need cash so badly you'd take a gamble that big.'

'Oh, this has nothing to do with the money, sunshine,' Elodie said in a low voice. 'This is about teaching you a lesson. About you finally learning that there are some things even money can't buy.'

Nick approached Elodie and put a hand on her arm.

'Elodie, what the hell are you playing at?' he whispered. She ignored him.

'Well?' she said to Callum. 'Is it a bet?'

Callum looked like a battle was going on inside him. Nick wasn't sure whether it was the angel or the demon on his shoulder that ultimately won, but after a moment Callum nodded and grasped the hand Elodie had stretched out.

'All right,' he said. 'May the best Santa win.'

***

Ashley's was buzzing when Callum got back to work. The Christmas shopping season had started in earnest, and he could barely squeeze through the crowds to reach the private staff lift.

When he got to his office, he found his PA, Sam, sifting through some of the correspondence on his desk.

'Sorry, Callum. I'll be out of your hair in a tick,' she said. 'I can take this lot through to my office to deal with. I've left you the letters from charities. We still need to pick a beneficiary as our official grotto charity.'

The grotto charity – shit! Ashley's always chose a local children's charity to receive ten per cent of their profits. Callum hadn't even considered that when he'd agreed to Elodie's ridiculous bet. He'd just gone along with it, acting like he had a right to dispose of the company profits any way he wanted. Which he did to an extent: since his father's death, he was the sole shareholder and he had no one to answer to except himself and the taxman. Still, it had been stupid – immature and stupid.

Why had he done it? He knew exactly why. It had been that look in Elodie's eye, the one that had flashed so much fire and contempt. All Callum's life he'd been surrounded by sycophants and yes-men, even in the school playground. Elodie Martin had been the one person who, from their childhood onwards, had made no secret of the fact she neither liked nor respected him. When she'd thrown down her challenge, the competitive spirit that led Callum to strive year on year to create the best grotto experience in the area had been stirred up past resistance.

But… there was something else. He wanted to… to *impress* her. He wanted Elodie Martin to see him succeed at something that hadn't been handed to him by privilege and birth. Something he, Callum Ashley, had achieved with his own insight and graft.

The thought almost made him laugh. When had he cared enough about a woman, or about anyone, to go to an effort to impress them? He'd never needed to. He knew with all due modesty that he was rich, cultured and well-dressed, and good-looking too. That tended to be enough – for everyone except Elodie Martin.

What had she said to him? That she wanted to teach him there were some things money couldn't buy? In the depths of his soul, Callum was forced to confess that the one thing his wealth had never been able to buy him that he badly, badly wanted was… Elodie herself.

'Callum?' Sam said.

He was staring into space again. He really needed to stop doing that.

'Sorry.' He took a seat at his desk. 'Yes, that's fine. I'll make a decision on the official charity by the end of the day.'

'Cheers.' Sam tucked the letters under her arm as she prepared to leave. 'Hey. A few of us are going for a drink at the George after work. Fancy joining us?'

'Hmm?' Callum looked up. 'Oh. No, I won't, thanks anyway. No one wants the boss hanging around when they're trying to relax.'

'You sure? We'd love to have you.'

'No, you go have fun.' He hesitated. 'Sam?'

'Yes?'

'Do you think I'm selfish?'

She blinked. 'Well that's a hell of a question.'

'Do you though? Don't give me the boss's answer.'

'No, Callum, I don't think you're selfish.' She nodded to the letters on his desk. 'You're about to donate some of your hard-earned profits to charity. No one makes you do that, do they?'

'That's nothing,' Callum said, flicking a hand dismissively. 'PR, that's all. If I really cared, I'd do it anonymously. Not make a big song and dance with the obligatory giant cheque photo op.'

Sam searched his face. 'So you don't care.'

Did he? Callum looked inside himself, trying to work out how he felt. There wasn't much in there to go on.

'I suppose I care in a general sort of way,' he said at last. 'I firmly believe human beings should have the right to all they need in life. I hate the idea of anyone suffering, especially kids or animals. But I don't *feel* it. When I try to imagine someone experiencing that sort of suffering, I just feel sort of… numb.' He met her eye. 'Is that bad? Does it make me a sociopath or something?'

'To be honest, Callum, I'm a bit out of my depth with this conversation. I'm your PA, not your shrink.' Sam took a seat at the other side of his desk. 'What's brought this attack of the deep and meaningfuls on?'

'Just something someone said to me. About valuing money more than I value anything else.'

'Why let that get to you? People who say stuff like that are mostly just jealous.'

'Not this person. Anyway, she's right, isn't she? I've spent my life chasing the next buck, to the exclusion of everything else. I've got no partner, no kids… no friends really, apart from business contacts. Other people get invited to parties, I get invited to networking events.'

'Of course you've got friends.' Sam reached out to awkwardly pat his hand. 'We think very highly of you. Your staff, I mean. Why not come out for that drink?'

He smiled. 'Thanks, Sam. No, I won't join you – you can probably tell I'm not in a mood to be very jolly company. But I appreciate being asked.'

'Well, if you change your mind you know where we'll be. Think happy thoughts, eh?' She departed for her own office.

Callum was left to reflect on what she'd said. *The staff think very highly of you.* So that was what he had in place of friendships – employees who didn't hate him. When he thought about it, Sam was probably the closest thing he had to a friend. She'd worked for him for eight years, and she was the only person he ever felt comfortable opening up to. She made semi-regular attempts to get him out to the pub; invitations he always found an excuse to refuse. And yet Sam wasn't really a friend, was she? She was an employee. All the people he felt he was closest to, the ones he interacted with most regularly, were on his payroll.

God, that was a depressing thought.

And that was why Elodie despised him. In her mind, he was an overprivileged rich boy who valued money over people. And for some reason, she was the only person whose poor opinion of him really bothered Callum. Everyone else could think what they liked, but when it was Elodie Martin…

What to do about it though? If he won the bet, he'd be taking half her grotto profits. That was a sizeable portion of the little toyshop's annual turnover – perhaps even a ruinous amount for them to lose. Maybe the chivalrous thing to do would be to let her win by somehow sabotaging his own grotto.

Could Callum bring himself to do that? It would hurt, after all the effort he'd put into making his Winter Wonderland the best. The competitive spirit of the Ashleys – that overwhelming need to be a winner and not a loser, in his dad's words – recoiled in revulsion from the idea. But that didn't mean it wasn't the right thing to do.

Then again, if he lost he'd just be confirming to Elodie that he was exactly the snivelling worm she thought he was, wouldn't he? That without Daddy's money, he was nobody. He could achieve nothing.

And if you win, you might get exactly what you've always wanted, a treacherous little voice whispered. *Martin's out of business. Your grotto on top. And your very own Elodie Martin. She'll have to come and work for you when she's got no other options.*

Callum tried to ignore it. He steepled his fingers as he pondered what was best to be done – what was right to be done. Then he made a decision.

He would win, and he'd win right. He'd show Elodie Martin that there was more to him than his inheritance by doing this the hard way – through Christmas spirit alone, whatever that meant. And after he'd won, he'd wave a magnanimous hand and tell her to keep her precious profits. And then maybe, just maybe, she might look at him with something approaching respect.

Callum picked up the phone and dialled an internal number.

'Mike?' he said when the store manager answered. 'Can you come up a mo? I've had a major rethink on this year's grotto.'

6

'All right, Elodie, what the hell?' Nick demanded. She was still glaring at the door.

'Can you believe that bastard?' she growled. 'Coming here to gloat over a sick man. Always profit before people – that must be the Ashley family motto.'

'But you didn't have to bet him half of *our* profits, did you?' Summer said.

'Well, why not? He needs teaching a lesson.'

'You say that like we're going to win, El.'

'Course we're going to win. His grotto's never beaten ours yet.'

'Yes, but…' Summer cast a guilty glance at Nick. 'Well, um, we had Pops then, didn't we?'

'Yes, of course we—' Elodie's eyes widened. 'Oh *shit*!'

Nick shook his head. 'You forgot, didn't you? You forgot you'd only have me this year.'

'Well, I… I was in the moment. I didn't think…'

Elodie had started swaying slightly as the full reality of what she'd committed to sank in. Nick grabbed the swivel chair from behind the counter and wheeled it round for her.

'Oh God.' Elodie pushed her fingers into her hair. 'Oh *God*! What the hell did I do?'

'Why did you let that Callum guy rile you up?' Nick asked.

'I don't know,' Elodie muttered. 'He just... he always has that effect on me. Spoilt little rich boy. I bet this was his plan all along, coming here to sneer at the poor folk.'

'Don't try to put this on him. It wasn't Callum Ashley who suggested this ridiculous bet, was it?'

'Can't you call him and tell him you take it back?' Summer asked.

Elodie snorted. 'What, beg him to spare me? Admit we've got no hope of taking him on? I'd never give him the satisfaction.'

'But you would give him half your badly needed profits.' Nick shook his head. 'You bloody idiot, Elodie.'

Elodie recovered enough to glare at him. 'Listen, new boy, don't push it. Remember whose shop this is.'

'It'll be nobody's soon, if you're going to continue making business decisions based entirely on hormones and hate.' He put a hand to his forehead. 'Oh God. And now it's all down to me. Be the best Santa since someone first set fire to a Christmas pud or watch Martin's Toy Kingdom go up in metaphorical flames. Thank you, Elodie Martin, thank you so very, very much.'

'You what? I thought this was the role you were born to play.'

'Yeah, well you'd better hope for your sake that I'm right.'

'Mum?' Nick called when he arrived back at their small flat following a supermarket shift.

No answer. He dumped his bag of groceries and poked his head into the living room. His mum was watching

TV with headphones on, deaf to everything except the machinations of whoever the current villain of the piece was in *Coronation Street*. Nick went to wave a hand in front of her face.

She smiled, taking off her headphones. 'You're home then.'

'I appear to be.' He planted a kiss on her greying hair. 'I wish you'd turn those things down so you could hear the door.'

'It's the only way I could shut out the sound of Karen and Peter having another blazing row next door. The sordid details of her latest affair were fun at first but the novelty's worn off now. I prefer the soaps for drama.'

As much as his mum made a joke of it, the flat's paper-thin walls weren't much fun. As well as the lack of privacy, it was a real struggle keeping the heat in.

'I worry when I call for you and there's no answer,' Nick said.

'Oh, you and your worrying.' She struggled to her feet and grabbed the stick leaning against the wall. 'I'm not such a helpless invalid as all that, Nick. Did you pick up something for tea?'

'It's a bit of a hodgepodge. Some jars of sauce past their date I saved from the bins, plus some frozen veg and a bag of spuds. I think we ought to be able to cobble together a curry.'

'The economy drive continues, eh?'

He sighed. 'And will for some time, at the rate I'm getting acting work. Sorry, Mum. I know I said I'd just give it one more year, but…'

'…but you can't quite bring yourself to give up on it,' she finished for him. 'And why should you, with all that talent? I know it's only looking after me that's stopped you conquering the West End.'

He laughed. 'Er, yeah. That must be it.'

'Well, sit down and we'll have a cuppa before I put the food on.' She hobbled to the door to put the kettle on.

Nick tried not to let his worry show as she disappeared. His mum was trying to hide it, but there was no doubt that the pain was getting worse. He could see her wince whenever she put weight on her right side, where MS had left her with partial paralysis, and he was sure she was looking frailer. There wasn't a spare ounce on her these days.

'I'll cook tea,' he called to her. 'You chill out with your soaps.'

'Don't be daft,' she called back. 'You've been working hard while I've been sitting on my bottom getting fat. The least I can do is look after you when you get home.'

'Honestly, it relaxes me. Cooking's my yoga.'

She came back in with a cup of tea for him, then went back for her own. Nick didn't offer to help. His mum could be fierce if she thought people were trying to 'baby' her, as she put it.

'Anyway, I need the practice,' he said when they were both sitting down, picking up the thread of their conversation. 'It's only a matter of time until I meet the future Mr or Mrs Winter. I need to be working on my Happily Married Man skills.'

His mum smiled. 'I'm glad you haven't given up looking. I was starting to wonder. You haven't been out on a date in months, Nick. Or seen your friends or been out for a run, or done anything but work and sit around this place watching TV with your mum.'

He sighed. 'I know, I should make more of an effort. Between shifts at the shop and this new job, it's hard to find the energy for extra-curricular activities.'

'Hmm. You're not getting any younger, you know. Not that I'm trying to get rid of you, but you can't hang around here all your life looking after someone who really doesn't need looking after.'

He leaned over to give her a squeeze. 'Maybe she doesn't, but I like looking after her.'

His mum put down her cup, uncurling her fingers from the handle with an effort. 'I wasn't joking before. I can't help feeling that it's me who's holding you back. In love, in your career…'

'You've never held me back from anything. It was only thanks to you geeing me up that I had the confidence to aim for drama school. I had enough folk telling me that boys from my background didn't go in for that sort of thing, but you always believed in me.'

'For all the good it did you.' She sighed. 'How was Santa practice today?'

He grimaced. 'Scary. I hope I haven't bitten off more than I can chew. The woman who runs the place is a real dragon.'

'What, not old Jim Martin's granddaughter? That sweet little thing who was always skipping around the shop when she was a kiddie?'

'Yeah, Elodie. Losing her parents seems to have made her kind of hard. Although I'm convinced it's a bit of a front, personally.'

'What makes you say that?'

'Just an instinct, I suppose.'

His mum examined him. 'You like her then?'

Nick laughed. 'Not like that. God, I wouldn't dare. I just think there's more to her than this badass bitch persona she likes to project. Plus I can't believe any true Martin of

Martin's Toy Kingdom could really hate Christmas the way Elodie pretends to.'

'I remember taking you there when you were a little boy,' his mum said with a faraway smile. 'You were such a little crawler, Nick. Always sucking up to Father Christmas in the hope of better presents.'

'Why thank you, Mother. You spoil me with all these compliments.'

'You were always taking him things: pictures you'd drawn and those free toys that came in cereal packets. When you were six you even took him a Mars Bar you bought with your pocket money.'

Nick laughed. 'I'd forgotten about that. I must remind Jim next time he's training me that he owes me a Mars Bar.'

His mum was still in the past.

'I never could give you the presents you asked for in your letter to him, however hard I saved,' she said dreamily. 'But you never complained. You were a good little boy.'

'I was an ungrateful swine,' Nick said. 'I couldn't help resenting the fact that Santa always brought better presents to the well-off kids. Still, I loved it. Christmas.'

'Why?'

Nick stared into his cup. The truth was that in a childhood marred by a poverty that had seen him often cold and sometimes hungry, Christmas had been one day of solid joy and magic. At Christmas, everything was colourful. Everything glowed, everything sparkled. It smelled good and it tasted good, and on that day, at least, there was enough. His mum didn't have to work and they could spend the whole day together, playing board games and laughing at Christmas cracker jokes in their silly paper crowns.

Yes, the richer kids had better presents. Nick never got what he asked Santa for no matter how good he tried to be, for reasons he couldn't fathom at the time. But that didn't matter. For a small boy who had little of wonder in his everyday existence, Christmas had given Nick Winter something to dream about. Christmas was hope.

But he couldn't say that to his mum. He'd never want to remind her that she hadn't been able to give him everything he needed when he was growing up. None of their deprivations had been her fault; she'd worked bloody hard, even after her health had started to deteriorate.

'I suppose I got carried away by all that season of goodwill stuff,' he said, shrugging. 'I never did grow out of it.'

'I know.' His mum looked guilty. 'I'm sorry, Nicky, but I told your Aunty Alice I'd help with the pensioners' Christmas dinner again this year. You don't mind, do you? I hate leaving you on your own on Christmas Day, but I don't want to let the old folk down.'

'Of course not. I'll help too if you like.'

'No, we've got enough hands now. Besides, you'll have been working double shifts all week. You stay at home and relax.' She raised an eyebrow. 'Perhaps you might even find some Christmas romance while your mum's out of the way. Why don't you ask that girl from the toyshop over for a festive drink?'

He laughed. 'I told you, Elodie Martin loathes Christmas nearly as much as I love it. Besides, I'm pretty sure her affections are otherwise engaged.'

Nick couldn't help feeling that no one could hate someone as much as Elodie claimed to hate Callum Ashley unless they were overcompensating for something.

7

Elodie glanced at her watch. The shop was closing soon, and Nick was ten minutes late for this evening's Santa lesson. She hoped that wasn't going to become a habit. So far he'd managed to at least be punctual, whatever his other shortcomings in the Father Christmas department might be.

Martin's was practically empty as usual. The only people in were a red-headed girl of about seven, accompanied by a teenager who Elodie guessed was her big sister. They approached the counter, the little girl hugging a plastic egg.

'Ask the lady,' the bigger girl prompted.

The child held out the egg to Elodie. 'Can I please buy this please, Miss?'

The girl looked so afraid she might say no that Elodie couldn't help smiling. 'I can't see any reason why not.'

Her sister nudged her. 'You need to ask how much it is first, Soph.'

'I brung my birthday money,' Sophie told Elodie eagerly. 'My aunty gave me ten pounds, and Mummy said I could spend it how I wanted and I said I wanted the Hatchimals Playdate egg.'

'Oh sweetie, I'm sorry,' Elodie said, smiling apologetically.

'Those playsets are £14.99 each. You're a little bit short, I'm afraid.'

Sophie looked crestfallen. She gave her sister a helpless look.

'Aww, Soph, never mind,' the bigger girl said. 'Let's go see if there's something else you can get. Maybe Santa will bring your egg thing if you write to him.'

Sophie nodded with an air of mute tragedy and took her sister's hand.

'Oh for God's sake,' Elodie muttered as they walked off. She closed her eyes for a moment before calling to the girls. 'Er, hey. Wait up a sec.'

They turned back to look at her.

'Sorry, is that the Playdate Pack you've got there?' Elodie asked. Sophie nodded.

'I've just remembered, we've got a special offer on that. It's been reduced to £9.99 – just for today.'

Sophie's face brightened and she drew her sleeve across damp eyes. '£9.99 is less than ten pounds.' She turned gleefully to her sister. 'I've got ten pounds!'

Her sister smiled. 'Yeah.'

'All right, come on, before I change my mind,' Elodie said, smiling too. 'We're closing in a minute.'

Sophie fished out her birthday money to pay then skipped out clutching her new toy. Elodie was aware that Nick had turned up at some point and was lurking by the till grinning at her.

'OK, it's gone six,' she said, turning to him. 'Flip the sign, can you?'

He was still grinning.

'What?' Elodie said, flicking a wisp of hair out of her eye.

'Special one-day sale, eh?'

'Yeah, it's a new initiative. Random flash sales. Just one of my many bright ideas.'

'Cute kid, that,' Nick observed nonchalantly.

Elodie shrugged. 'I hadn't noticed.'

He nudged her. 'I knew all along you weren't really mean.'

'How dare you. I'm mean as hell. I kick hamsters for fun and... eat little old ladies for breakfast.'

'You're a big softie, Elodie Martin. All it takes is a kid blinking their big eyes at you and you melt into a puddle.'

'I'm a businesswoman, that's all,' Elodie informed him loftily. 'If the kid's got ten quid to spend then I'd rather sell at that price than nothing. We're so overstocked on those Hatchimal things, I'll never shift them at full price. I was planning to reduce them tomorrow.'

'Course you were.'

She glared at him. 'Look, are you going to flip the sign so we can get on with this lesson? I've got a life to lead that doesn't begin and end with Nick Winter, you might be surprised to learn.'

'All right.' Nick went to turn the sign. 'What sort of life do you lead, Elodie?'

'I'm sorry?'

'You know, the life that doesn't begin and end with me? I mean, what do you do for fun when you're not behind a toyshop counter? I'm assuming you've got hobbies. Friends.'

'Why would you assume that?'

'Well, because everyone does.'

She shrugged as she locked the till. 'I've got hobbies. I mean, I've got Netflix. Friends... friends are overrated.'

'You can't mean that.'

She turned to look at him. 'Why can't I? Not everyone craves company. I've always been happiest on my own.'

'Why though?'

'Because that's me. It's who I am.' She reached up to rub the worried furrow that always appeared between her eyes when she was tired. 'I guess someone like you would find that hard to get your head around. You enjoy being with people. I'm just someone who's happiest by themselves.'

'Yeah, but everyone needs people, even if they do enjoy their own company,' Nick said, pig-headedly refusing to take her at her word. 'You know, for emotional support, affection, conversation; all that stuff. It's like John Lennon said – no one is an island, sufficient in themselves.'

'John Donne said that. John Lennon said he was the walrus, coo coo ca choo.'

'Well whoever it was, he was very wise. No one is an island, Elodie, not even you.'

'That just shows how little you know me. Come on, let's get to work.'

She strode towards the stairs, Nick trotting after her.

'Your grandad's not here yet,' he pointed out.

'No, I gave him the week off. He's been better lately but he still needs to make sure he's getting enough rest.' Elodie glanced back over her shoulder. 'I'm going to give you a lesson.'

'You?'

'Yeah.' She flashed him a tight smile. 'Santaing runs in my family, don't forget.'

He followed her to the storeroom, which was gradually looking more grotto-like as paper chains and other decorations started to appear. 'What are we going to learn then, Miss?'

There was a tablet on the table. Elodie propped it up on a stand and pulled a couple of chairs in front of it.

'Do you have any young family members?' she asked Nick. 'Nieces or nephews?' She paused. 'Kids of your own?'

'Er, no. No nephews or nieces. None of my own either.' Nick looked awkward. 'I always hoped... I guess the clock's ticking, but if I met the right someone, um... well, you know how it is.'

Elodie wondered why her tummy felt suddenly... strange. Why should she care about Nick's home life? This was the first time she'd really considered him as a person who existed outside of his appearances at the shop.

'I didn't ask for a relationship history,' she said, trying to keep up her usual brisk tone. 'I just wondered how well you understood modern kids.'

'I'm an only child, same as you, but I see my cousin's kids relatively often,' Nick said. 'They're eight and twelve.'

'Twelve's outside the usual believer age. What does the eight-year-old like?'

'Charlie?' He shrugged. 'Scrounging sweets and being annoying. Why?'

'I thought it'd help for you to do some revision,' Elodie said, turning on the tablet. 'A good Santa knows what kids in the believer range are into. He understands what toys they like, what they watch on TV, what games they play, and he can make easy conversation with them about their interests. Something that I'm guessing you can't. Can you?'

'I suppose I am a bit out of touch on cartoons and that sort of thing,' Nick admitted.

'That's why tonight's lesson is going to be a marathon *Bluey* session,' Elodie said as she queued up a few videos.

'I've got a list of stuff I want you to research in your own time as well. Your homework is to play at least two hours of *Minecraft*.'

'OK. *Minecraft* I'm aware of. What's *Bluey*?'

'Cartoon about a little Australian puppy. Very big with the fives to sevens,' Elodie told him. 'You'll like it. It's cute and funny.'

'Like me, right?'

She ignored that comment and started the first video.

Elodie was gratified to see that Nick agreed with her review. He was soon laughing at Bluey and Bingo's antics. It was a compelling sound: warm, merry and unrestrained, crinkling his eyes at the corners. Elodie felt rather envious of that laugh. There was something about it that seemed... sort of freeing, in a way she wasn't sure she'd ever experienced.

During their sixth episode, Nick glanced at her. 'It's fine for you to laugh too, Elodie. I promise not to spread it around that you can.'

'I'm laughing on the inside.'

'Well, how about giving it a go on the outside too?'

She shrugged. 'I'm not really a laughing-out-loud kind of person.'

'Yeah, right. Your nose is twitching like a rabbit with hay fever. I know you do that when you're trying not to giggle.' Nick paused the episode and twisted in his chair to face her. 'Why hold it in? If you want to laugh, laugh. You'll enjoy it.'

'I'm not holding it in.'

'Fibber.' He smiled. 'Tell you what, I'll make a bet with you. You like making bets, right?'

Elodie narrowed one eye at him. 'Maybe. What sort of bet?'

'I bet you I can tell you a joke that'll make you properly, full-on belly laugh.'

Elodie's mouth twitched. 'Not a chance.'

'We'll see.'

'What would we be betting for?'

'A drink at the pub after this,' Nick said. 'If you lose, you get the beers in. If I lose, you can go home to your Netflix and I'll never try to nag you out of your miserable solitude again.' He held out a hand. 'So, are we on?'

Elodie couldn't help smiling at his earnest expression. 'You promise that when – that's when, not if – you lose this bet, you'll give up trying to convince me I need some sort of social life?'

'Scout's honour.'

She shook his hand. 'All right, bet accepted. Give it your best shot.'

'OK. No one can resist a really top-notch groanworthy dad joke. Try this one on for size.' Nick rolled up his sleeves and adopted a sober expression. 'Hey, guess what. I've just been diagnosed colour-blind.'

Elodie blinked. 'I don't get it.'

'That's the feed line. Now you say "gosh, how terrible!" or something like that.'

'All right. Gosh, how terrible.'

'I know, right? It was a real bolt out of the orange.'

She groaned. 'Seriously?'

Nick lifted his deadpan joke-delivering expression into a grin. 'Aha!'

'Aha what?'

'Your nose twitched. That's Elodie code for a laugh.'

'No it isn't. It's Elodie code for an itchy nose.'

'All right, best of three. I've got a million of them,' Nick said cheerfully. 'Last night, me and my mum watched TV back to back.'

He paused, which Elodie sensed was the cue for her to respond.

'Er, did you?' she said.

'Yep. Luckily I was the one facing the TV.'

She groaned, but she couldn't help letting out a little snort. Nick beamed.

'I win,' he said, folding his arms triumphantly.

'I wasn't laughing at the joke. I was laughing at… how bad it was.'

'One more then, and any snorting counts as a win to me. I say I say I say! What do you call bears with no ears?'

'I don't know, what do you call bears with no ears?' Elodie said, feeling like she was getting the hang of things now.

'B.'

This time, she couldn't help a proper giggle.

'Yes! I knew I could do it.' Nick smiled at her. 'Be honest. It feels good to lighten up a bit, doesn't it? You're too young to be digging in with the frown lines.'

Elodie let herself smile too. 'I suppose it has its merits.'

'You know, Elodie, I can't work you out,' Nick said. 'Sometimes I think you really don't like me. Other times I think the problem is that you don't know how to show me you do. Which is it?'

'I don't like you.'

'I refuse to believe that. Everyone likes me. I'm a very likeable man.'

'I know, it's sickening.' She closed her eyes. 'Nick, look,

I… this is new territory for me, OK? I've been on my own so long, pushing people away has kind of become an instinct. It's nothing personal. I mean, I do like you. I'm just… not really sure what to do with that.'

Nick blinked. 'Wow. I've never heard you say so many words together that didn't include an insult.'

She sighed. 'Sorry. Like I said, I don't really know how to do this – I mean the making friends thing. I wish I did, but I'm not like you. I've always felt… even when I was a kid, it just felt safer to be alone, you know?'

'Sounds a lonely way to live,' Nick said quietly.

Elodie shrugged. 'People only let you down. They leave, or they die, and then all you've got left is yourself. Better to embrace being alone on your own terms than have it thrust upon you.'

Nick was silent, examining her face. Then he stood up.

'Come on,' he said, holding out a hand to help her to her feet.

She blinked. 'Where are we going?'

'I won a bet, didn't I? We're going to the pub.'

'Oh. OK.'

Elodie got up to follow him with the distinct feeling this marked the beginning of something new in her life. She couldn't help wondering what exactly that was going to be.

8

'Again.'

'Ho ho ho,' Nick responded obediently.

'And again.'

'Ho ho ho.'

'Deeper. Softer. Pull it up… from the depths of your belly.' Jim guided his shoulders back so he was in a more appropriate stance for ho-ho-hoing. 'And imagine that belly… is twenty stone heavier.'

Nick tried again. 'Ho! Ho! Ho!'

Jim shook his head. 'Too deep that time. You don't want to scare the kids. Make it… warmer. Smile while you ho.'

Nick plastered on a grin. 'Like this?'

Jim grimaced. 'No teeth… for God's sake. Just smile enough to give you cherry cheeks and… a twinkle in your eye. Think of the Coca-Cola poster.'

'You show me.'

'All right.' Jim hooked his thumbs into his waistband, smiled warmly with the parts of his face he still had full command over and gave a deep, throaty chuckle that echoed around the rafters.

Nick smiled. 'Still got it, eh, Santa?'

'Some of it. Go on, your turn.'

Nick tried to emulate Jim's stance, sticking out his tummy, shoulders back, thumbs hooked in his jeans and smiling just enough to give his face the required amount of merriment. Then he let rip with a good, deep 'ho ho ho'.

Jim nodded approvingly. 'By George, I think he's got it. Just… keep practising, lad.'

'We open next week, Jim.'

'Exactly. Your homework is half an hour's ho-ho-hoing every day until then.'

Nick rubbed the stubble that was all he'd managed to grow so far of his Father Christmas beard. He was aiming for close-cropped modern Santa, since he knew anything truly bushy was going to be beyond him. Nature had not designed him to be hirsute. What he really coveted beard-wise was the Kurt Russell silver fox number from *The Christmas Chronicles* – and quite possibly also Kurt himself, circa 1987 – but he knew both were sadly well out of his reach.

'Jim, I'm worried,' he said in a low voice.

'About the grotto opening?'

'Yeah. What if I can't do it? No one's coming to see me – they're coming to see you.'

'Don't worry about that.' The old man slapped him on the back. 'You're a natural, son. Trust me, I know… a fellow Santa when I see one.'

Nick smiled. 'That means a lot coming from you. Still, there's a lot riding on me getting it right.'

'Don't you let my granddaughter and this daft bloody war of hers with… Callum Ashley get to you. Just do the best you can and… you've done all you can.'

'Thanks, Jim. I'll try not to let you down.'

Jim shook his head. 'They need their heads banging together. There's always been rivalry… over the grotto, since back when I bought this place and my old mate Terry Ashley had just taken over the big shop from his dad, but… it was all in fun. After Christmas we'd buy each other a pint and compare notes. I liked to have my gloat over the grotto and Terry liked to have his gloat about… well, everything else, but there was no malice in it. Not sure why this generation've made it personal.'

'Personality clash, I reckon,' Nick said. 'Sounds like the warring goes back to schooldays.'

Jim smiled. 'At least she's got you, eh?'

Nick blinked. 'Me?'

'I noticed… she's been finding ways to spend time with you. This field trip today, for example.'

'You think that's what she's doing?'

'Trust me. I raised that little girl… for most of her life. I'm tuned in to these things.'

Was that true? Elodie was certainly always around when Nick came into the shop, even if she didn't need to be. These days she often sat and observed his Santa training sessions with Jim, a small smile on her face as she watched the two men working. He'd even managed to lure her to the pub a few times.

'I guess she's lonely,' he said. 'I know Elodie doesn't have many people she's close to.'

'She never wanted them… until you came along. I can't remember when she last made a friend, Nicky. It's warmed my old heart, I must admit.'

'That's, um… well, I'm glad.' Nick squinted at him. 'Your speech seems a lot better lately.'

'Glad you think so. My speech therapist says if I keep up with the...' Jim paused a moment '...with the exercises, I could be almost back to where I was before the stroke within a year.' He sighed. 'Daft, isn't it? All this effort... just to learn to talk. It seemed so easy the first time round.'

'So I guess next year I'll be out of a job, will I?'

Jim shook his head. 'No, lad, I've had my time. You're our Father Christmas now. I know... you'll do me proud.'

'Cheers, Santa,' Nick said, smiling. 'You still owe me that Mars Bar though.'

They were interrupted by Elodie barging in.

'Well, Nick, are we going?' she said. 'I take it you managed to arrange our undercover agent.'

Nick nodded. 'She's meeting us outside the caf across the road from Ashley's.'

'I'd better drive, since we need to make this quick.' She gave her grandad a kiss. 'Thanks for minding the shop, Pops. Don't work too hard.'

'Take care of Santa's apprentice!' Jim called as they left. 'I didn't spend all this time on his training... for you to lose him at the shops.'

As they drove towards the town centre, Nick noticed Elodie kept glancing over at him.

'Why do you keep looking at me? Is there something on my face?'

'You could say that.' She nodded to his jaw. 'What's with the designer stubble?'

'It's my Santa beard, isn't it? Well, it will be.'

'You don't need to do that, Nick. We can get you a false one.'

Nick shook his head. 'If I'm doing this, I'm doing it properly. I've got some white dye ready as well.'

'It is quite sexy on you actually,' Elodie said, smiling.

Nick raised an eyebrow. 'Did you just pay me a compliment?'

'Yeah. Don't let it go to your head.'

'Well, thanks.' He rubbed his stubble. 'I wouldn't expect much from me beard-wise though, Elodie. I've always struggled to overcome my natural twinkiness, as much as I dream of something in the Kurt Russell mould.'

'I still can't believe him in those films. Who knew Santa could be hot?'

'Yeah well, you haven't seen me yet, have you? You'll be swooning on the shop floor once I get that suit on.' Nick glanced at his sparse stubble in the rear-view mirror, contrasting it enviously with the curly, flowing Santa beard of his imagination. 'I'm with you there though. I have to say, Kurt as Santa made for some very odd erotic dreams.'

'Right?'

Nick grinned at her. 'Hey. First you paid me a compliment, now we've got something in common. I guess we really are friends.'

Elodie indicated to take the road into Chessory town centre. 'No, we're love rivals. And I bagsied Kurt when I saw him in *Backdraft* in 1991, so I've got the prior claim.'

Nick flicked a dismissive hand. 'Sweetie, please. *Overboard*, 1987.'

'Doesn't count. You were a baby in 1987. That means you saw a telly repeat, which means my claim trumps yours.'

'And how old were you in 1991? Smells rotten to me.'

Elodie laughed. 'I don't know who we think we're kidding anyway. Who can compete with Goldie?'

'No one, obviously. Goldie's a goddess. Still, we can dream.' Nick swivelled to look at her. 'Is it me, or are you in a – I think they call it a "good mood"?'

Elodie shrugged. 'Even I have one every once in a while.'

'Your grandad seems to be coming on in leaps and bounds, doesn't he?'

She smiled. 'Well guessed. Yeah, that is what's behind the good mood.'

They were approaching Ashley's Department Store now. Nick spotted his mum outside the café opposite as Elodie turned into the car park.

When Elodie had parked, she followed Nick across the road to the café where they'd arranged to meet his mum. She assumed that was her outside: the haggard, middle-aged woman leaning on a walking stick, looking at them keenly with Nick's deep brown eyes. The woman's face was good-natured, like her son's, but nevertheless she had a fierce, determined look, as if daring the world to underestimate her. A little blonde girl stood at her elbow, stuffing huge handfuls of popcorn into her mouth.

'That's our spy?' Elodie asked Nick.

Nick nodded. 'My Aunty Alice's granddaughter, Charlie. I've arranged for us to borrow her for an hour.'

'Will she be any good?'

'She should be. She's inherited the drama-loving gene of the Winters,' Nick said. 'Don't let the innocent face deceive you either. She might look like an adorable little poppet of eight, but she's got the bitter, cynical soul of a thrice-divorced forty-five-year-old. The kid'll do anything for cold, hard cash.'

Elodie nodded as they reached Nick's mum and young cousin. 'Mrs Winter?'

'Actually it's Miss, but Sheila will do fine.' Sheila Winter smiled at her. 'Now then. I remember you, don't I?'

'Do you?'

'Of course. You were always around Martin's as a tiny thing, bouncing around the shop with your dress tucked into your knickers.'

Elodie laughed. 'Well, that was a long time ago. It must be at least three years since I flashed my pants at a customer.' She looked down at Charlie. 'And this is our spy. I'm Elodie.'

The child stared, unblinking, for a moment.

'Aunty Sheila said you'd give me ten pounds,' she said.

Nick raised an eyebrow. 'Ten? I thought we agreed five.'

Sheila grimaced. 'She talked me up, Nick, sorry.'

'I think we can stretch to a tenner,' Elodie said.

Charlie examined the department store with a calculating gaze.

'And some sweets,' she said. 'They look like they sell good sweets.'

Nick shook his head. 'Sweets as well? You've just woofed down a jumbo bag of popcorn.'

Charlie shrugged. 'So?'

'All right, and some sweets,' Elodie said. 'Can we go, Charlie? I need to get back to work.'

'OK.'

'I'll wait in the café,' Sheila said. 'Good luck.'

Nick rested a hand on Charlie's shoulder to guide her across the road.

'So have you rehearsed your part?' he asked.

Charlie nodded. 'I have to call you Dad and her Mum, and be annoying and ask the questions Aunty Sheila told me. And then you'll give me ten pounds and some sweets.'

'If you do a good job, yes.'

'I will,' Charlie said, with the unshakeable confidence of an Eton-educated cabinet minister on *Newsnight*.

Elodie glanced at Nick. 'I see what you mean. She's hard as nails.'

'Scary, isn't it?'

They stopped when they reached the department store, gazing up at the concrete monstrosity.

It was an eyesore: a Sixties-era building with too many edges, made up of discoloured beige slabs and grimy windows. It had been plonked between a couple of stately Victorian shops, as if to cock a snook at the high street's grand past. Elodie couldn't understand how Callum's great-grandad had got permission to build such a blot.

Not that the ugliness of the place seemed to affect business. Shoppers hurried out with branded Ashley's bags as they neared mid-November and the Christmas shopping season stepped up a gear. A sign outside announced 'Winter Wonderland grotto opens today! Meet the genuine, one-and-only Santa Claus at Ashley's!'

'Huh,' she muttered. 'We'll see about that.'

'We're not likely to run into your friend Mr Ashley, are we?' Nick asked.

'I doubt it. He'll be up in his office. Still, just in case he's lurking around I brought these.' She handed Nick a spectacles case, then produced a baseball cap and jammed it on her head, threading her long hair through the hole in the back.

Nick peered around as if he'd lost something. 'Hey, where did Elodie go? She just disappeared right before my eyes!' His young cousin giggled.

'Very funny,' Elodie said, rolling her eyes.

'Well. You're not exactly a mistress of disguise in your little hat, are you?'

'I'm sorry that I don't keep a wardrobe of costume changes for when I need to go undercover at department stores. Now put your glasses on.'

Nick put on the heavy specs and blinked. 'Elodie, I can't see a thing. Whose are these?'

'They're my grandad's spare reading glasses.' She grabbed his arm as he very nearly walked headlong into a lamppost.

'I'm going to do myself an injury,' he said.

She sighed. 'Fine, take them off until we get up there. Hopefully the stubble will be enough of a disguise, since Callum's only seen you once.'

The little group went inside and headed for the escalator that would take them to the toy department.

'Hold my hand,' Nick said to Charlie.

She shot it a look of disgust. 'Ew. No. Someone from school might see.'

'Come on, I'm your fake dad for the next half an hour. Can't you pretend you like me a bit more than the average stinky grown-up cousin?'

'All right, if I have to.' Charlie grudgingly took his hand, grasped Elodie's on her other side, and they stepped on to the escalator.

9

Elodie frowned when they got to the toy department. There was the rope cordon that led to the grotto, but…

'This isn't right,' she murmured.

Nick looked around. 'It's a bit bare. I thought you said Ashley went all out.'

'He does. Whenever I've been in before it's looked like a movie set in here.' She shook her head. 'What the hell is going on?'

'What the *heck* is going on?' Nick said. 'You're a mum now. Mind the mouth.'

'Sorry,' Elodie said to Charlie. The little girl shrugged.

They went to join the sparse queue, Elodie looking around in bemusement.

It wasn't entirely bare. There were a couple of small Christmas trees flanking the entrance to the grotto, and some plastic candy canes on the door. Snowflakes hung from the ceiling, and there were a few mail sacks around filled, presumably, with letters to Father Christmas. But it was verging on false advertising to call the place a Winter Wonderland.

Was this about their bet? Elodie's brow knit as an idea formed.

'It's a taunt,' she muttered to Nick. 'He's done this on purpose to mock me.'

'Eh? How do you work that out?'

'Because he thinks he's going to win! He thinks that without Pops, he can beat me on quality of Santa alone,' Elodie said. 'That's why he's got rid of all the usual fancy stuff – so that when he wins, he can gloat that he's beaten me fair and square. Really revel in humiliating me.'

Charlie, bored of this grown-up conversation, had taken her phone out and was engrossed in a game.

'You really think that's what's behind it?' Nick asked Elodie.

'What else could it be?'

Nick shrugged. 'Maybe Callum regretted making the bet and decided to let you win.'

Elodie laughed. 'An Ashley lose a bet on purpose? You really don't know that guy.'

'No, but I like to give people the benefit of the doubt.'

'I wouldn't bother. Not for Callum.' She shook her head. 'God, he gets on my wick.'

'Yeah, I can see why. Handsome, charming millionaires are hard men to like, aren't they?'

'They are when they're malodorous gits intent on ruining your livelihood.'

Nick squinted at her. 'What's with you two? Why always at each other's throats? Your grandad said it never used to be that way in his day.'

'Callum just winds me up,' Elodie muttered. 'He was such a spoilt brat at school, always flaunting the fact he had more than the rest of us.'

'Did he really offer you a job?'

'Yeah,' Elodie said darkly. 'He offered to buy the shop at some daft price a few years back. Protect us from losing everything when we inevitably went out of business, he said. And the sweetener was supposed to be a job managing his toy department, with Pops installed as the Santa here.'

'And you told him to shove it, did you?'

'Damn right.'

'So why do you think he renewed the offer?' Nick asked. 'Your grandad's retired, so if it was him Callum was after then there's not much point pursuing it.'

She laughed bitterly. 'Oh, he loves playing the magnanimous little prince. I'm sure it silenced his conscience, if he's got one: knowing he offered to buy the shop at well over its market value. But with Callum it's never about doing the right thing; it's only ever about winning. His dad was exactly the same. There's something around here Callum can't own and it gnaws at him constantly.'

'You mean your shop?'

'No, I mean us. The Martins. Maybe he can't get Pops but he'd love me to be his paid lackey: legendary Santa Jim Martin's granddaughter. If he owns me, he can finally say he owns Christmas.' Elodie turned to look at him. 'We need to win this bet, Nick. If all I'm getting for Christmas is a flop grotto, a potentially business-destroying bill and a gloating Callum, I may just give up on the season altogether.'

Nick jabbed a finger at her. 'Aha! So you haven't completely given up on it. I knew you hadn't.'

She smiled. 'All right, maybe not entirely. Don't push it though.'

'Too late. I swear I'll have you donning a Christmas jumper and singing "Jingle Bells" by the big day.'

'Now you're being delusional.' She met his eyes. 'Nick, can I ask you something?'

'If you like.'

'Is your mum... I mean, sorry, I know it's none of my business. But I didn't realise when you said you lived with her that you had additional responsibilities at home.'

Nick turned to avoid her eye, his smile disappearing. 'It's fine. We're OK.'

'But if you're working two jobs and caring for her as well—'

'I said it's fine. She's got MS, yes, but she's not an invalid. She can still drive and care for herself, except on the really bad days.'

'I just didn't realise you had so much on your plate. Does she work?'

He was silent.

'It's OK, Nick,' Elodie said, resting a hand on his arm. 'I've got a sick loved one of my own to give me sleepless nights. There's no need to shut down on me.'

'No.' He sighed. 'She's not working. Technically she could – at least, the authorities think so, which means she's not entitled to much in the way of benefits. But there's not a lot suitable for a fifty-six-year-old with mobility issues and little in the way of skills or education.'

'So you're supporting the both of you?'

'Trying to. We've mostly been surviving on out-of-date stock from the supermarket.' Nick shrugged. 'But we're used to making do. In a single-parent family, you learn that skill early on.'

'What will you do after Christmas? I guess you're only getting minimum wage at the supermarket.'

'Look for acting jobs – the usual routine. And if I can't find anything… well, I guess it's time to think about pursuing a career that's a bit more suited to paying the bills.'

'It'd be a shame if you had to give up acting. You're very good.'

He smiled. 'Two compliments in one day. Elodie Martin, are you flirting with me?'

'I just wanted you to know that if I can help…'

'In what way?' Nick said, laughing. 'I don't think Martin's is in a position to offer me a permanent job, is it? Unless you're planning on keeping your grotto open all year round.'

They were at the front of the queue now. The door opened, and a young woman dressed as an elf appeared.

'Santa Claus can see you now,' she told them cheerily. 'What's the name of the child?'

'Charlie.' Elodie handed over the five-pound entry fee and they followed the elf inside.

'OK, this is it,' Nick murmured, putting on the too-thick glasses. 'Charlie, set brat level to max. It's time to give the performance of a lifetime.'

Charlie looked determined as she put her phone away and once again grasped both their hands.

As the elf led them to Santa, Elodie took a look around the inner sanctum of the grotto.

Stripped to the bare essentials, Ashley's grotto didn't look vastly different from their own. Yes, there was the big gold throne that would have towered over their spray-painted dining chair, but other than that and a Christmas tree there wasn't much in the way of frippery.

But the old man in the chair gave her a jolt. Elodie almost

stopped in her tracks, he reminded her so much of Pops. Not that they looked alike, aside from the white beard and red suit that she always associated with her grandad. There was just… something. Something indefinable. Something magical. Something… Christmas.

Surely Callum hadn't finally found a real Santa of his own?

The Santa smiled warmly as they approached.

'Now then, who do we have here?' he said to Charlie, a soft Scottish burr infusing his deep voice.

Nick nudged her. 'Tell him, pumpkin.'

Charlie flashed him a disgusted look that conveyed only too well what she thought of the endearment 'pumpkin' before turning to Santa.

'Don't you know who I am?' she demanded, folding her arms. 'I thought you knew all the children.'

Santa didn't miss a beat. 'Of course, but you've grown so much since last year that I hardly recognised you.' His elf bent to whisper something. 'Ah, yes, now I know you. It's wee Charlie, isn't it?'

Charlie glanced suspiciously at his elf. 'She told you.'

'Nonsense. I knew as soon as I got a closer look at your face. My eyes aren't what they used to be, I'm afraid. Come and sit by me, Charlie.'

Charlie looked up at her pretend parents before going to sit on the small chair.

'I got your letter,' Santa said to her. 'I was so pleased to get a proper, old-fashioned letter. So many children prefer to email now, but as Mrs Claus will tell you, I'm an old duffer about technology. The elves are always teasing me about it.'

Oh, he was good. How did he know Charlie had written

by hand, Elodie wondered? He must be playing the odds. That had to be a lie about children choosing to email. The annual letter to Santa was surely one thing nearly everyone still did the old-fashioned way.

Some of the cynicism was starting to sap from Charlie's face now. She stared at the Santa with fascination.

'What did my letter say?' she demanded. 'I bet you don't know what I want for Christmas.'

Santa looked at Elodie and Nick. Elodie kept her face fixed, refusing to give him any clues.

'Well, a Splattertron, of course,' Santa said.

Charlie's eyes popped. A little 'wow!' escaped from her lips.

Oh yes, he knew all the tricks. If in doubt, try plumping for that Christmas's most popular toy and you'd be bound to be on to a winner.

Anyway, Charlie seemed convinced. She shuffled in her chair to get closer to Father Christmas.

'I've been good,' she told him. 'Really good, honest.'

Nick snorted, then hastily turned it into a cough.

'I know you have,' Santa said with a warm smile. 'I checked my list before I flew over and there was your name, right on top. I hope to see it there again next year.'

'Will you bring it? I mean, please will you?'

'We'll have to see, won't we? There are still a lot of days until Christmas. Let's just see if we can keep that name on the Nice List.' He rummaged in his sack and handed Charlie a gift. 'Here's a little treat until I bring your proper presents. I'll see you soon, Charlie.'

As soon as they were outside the grotto, Charlie tore open her gift. It was a packet of hot chocolate bombs: milk chocolate balls containing mini marshmallows that melted in a mug of hot milk.

'Cool! I love these.' Charlie turned to her cousin accusingly. 'You said he wasn't the real one, Nick.'

Nick seemed distracted. He took off Pops's thick glasses, staring off at nothing. 'Hmm?'

'The real Santa. You said that wasn't him and it totally was. He knew everything about me!'

'He didn't really. He just—' Elodie looked at the little girl's face, glowing with the thrill of belief, and stopped herself. 'Never mind.'

'He was real though, wasn't he?'

'Yeah. Sorry, Charlie, we didn't know it was really going to be him.'

'That's OK.' Charlie was happily examining her hot chocolate bombs. 'You don't need to give me money if you don't want. I don't mind coming to see the real Santa. Anyway, it might not be good to ask for money to do things. I don't want to be on the bad list.'

'That's all right, you've earned it. Let's go get your sweets.'

Charlie was suitably paid with a ten-pound note and a jar of chocolate reindeers, then they delivered her back to her Aunty Sheila and Elodie offered Nick a lift to the supermarket, where he had an afternoon shift. He remained silent throughout the car journey.

'Something up?' Elodie asked when she pulled up outside the big shop. 'You're uncharacteristically quiet.'

'Yeah,' he said vaguely. 'That Santa… he was good, right?'

Elodie shrugged. 'Better than their usual ones. Anyway, I feel better now we've scoped it out.'

Nick laughed. 'You what? Why?'

'Because now I know what we're up against, don't I?'

'Well I don't feel better. I feel awful.' He turned to face her. 'That guy wasn't just good, Elodie, he was bloody amazing. He even convinced Charlie he could read her mind, and you have to get up very early in the morning to get one over on that kid. How am I supposed to compete with that?'

'Come on.' Elodie tried to sound soothing. 'What happened to "I'm the king of Christmas"? What happened to it being fated – the role you were born to play?'

'Who did I think was kidding? I'm not Santa.' Nick rubbed at his stubble as if it suddenly irritated him. 'Your grandad was Santa, and now that bloke at Ashley's is Santa. What I am is a thirty-four-year-old checkout boy who's spent his whole adult life kidding himself he's an actor.'

'You are an actor. You're a great actor.'

'It's no good, Elodie. You can lie to me but I can't lie to myself.' He rubbed his stubble again. 'You don't need me. You need someone who can win your bet for you.'

'But that is you. You're right, Nick, it was fate. The fact it was you who took my card in the supermarket, that you were the only applicant...'

Nick laughed bitterly. 'Oh my God. No, Elodie. No it wasn't.'

'What?'

'I was the only applicant because... because I was the only one who knew about it. I never gave the card to my manager.'

She frowned. 'What?'

'I fixed it so I'd get the job. Fate had nothing to do with it.'

'But... why would you do that?'

'Because I was desperate for an acting job, you were offering an hourly rate more than double what I was getting for checkout work, and despite being about thirty years too young and fifteen stone too light for the part, I still thought I could do a half-decent job. I wanted to make sure I didn't miss out on the opportunity – on the money. Then you started making bets, turning up the pressure…' Nick trailed off. 'It's all my fault,' he said quietly. 'Callum's going to win the bet because… because I lied to you. I'm not good enough; I never was. I'm sorry, I should've told you before.'

'Nick…'

He opened the door and got out. 'It's not too late, Elodie. You can still hire someone who can win this thing for you.'

'What're you saying?'

'I'm saying I resign. Tell your grandad I'm sorry. I'm really, really sorry.' Nick trudged off towards the supermarket.

10

When Elodie got back to the shop, Pops told her he was happy to man the counter while she did some work on the grotto. She was grateful for that. Her head was in a whirl, and she badly needed some time to process what had happened with Nick.

So he'd tricked them into giving him the Santa job. Hid her card so they'd be forced to hire him by default. Then she'd made that stupid bet, not realising that Callum had managed to hire the best grotto Santa since… well, since Jim Martin. It didn't matter that Callum had stripped his grotto down to bare essentials. With his new Santa, he didn't need anything else to get the kids through the door once word got around – and it would, with a week's head start on them. The department store always opened their grotto first. Now the Ashley's Santa *was* the experience, just as Santa had been here during Pops's reign.

And yet Elodie was finding it hard to be angry. She wasn't sure why. Elodie sometimes felt that her default state was a sort of ambient rage at the world in general. But when she pictured Sheila Winter, looking almost as fierce as she was frail, and remembered what Nick had said about how they lived – surviving on meals of out-of-date supermarket stock – Elodie couldn't feel really pissed off with him.

That didn't mean she wasn't hurt though. He'd lied to her, all these weeks they'd been getting to know one another. Elodie wasn't someone who found it easy to form bonds with other human beings. Since the death of her parents she'd been more or less a loner, with no one she was close to outside her immediate family. Relationships had fizzled out quickly, and friendships were even harder. At least dating had a rulebook. Making friends had hardly seemed worth the effort, even when loneliness started to gnaw. Elodie had actually managed to convince herself she liked life that way, empty of people and the stress that went with them, until… well, until Nick Winter.

Nick was the first person who'd managed to battle his way through all Elodie's attempts to keep him at arm's length. Something about his cheerfulness felt infectious, even to a world-weary soul like herself. Elodie had discovered with surprise that she'd come to really look forward to the days Nick was due at the shop. That they'd become friends.

These past five weeks, Nick's visits to Martin's had been the one bright spot in her life. Once she'd allowed herself to lower her guard, Elodie had enjoyed their fun, silly chats about everything and nothing; chats that didn't have to be about serious, anxiety-generating things like her struggling business or her grandad's ill health, but could be for the sheer, simple joy of human interaction. Nick had made her laugh even when she'd tried not to, until she stopped trying not to and just enjoyed the freedom of letting go. That made it hurt all the more now she discovered he'd been concealing the truth from her.

She caught her thumb on the craft knife she was using to cut out snowflake shapes and swore as she lifted it to her mouth.

Sentimentality. It never did any good. Let yourself get close and you let yourself get hurt. What Elodie needed to focus on was saving the Martin's grotto, and winning her bet against Callum.

Well, she was free of Nick Winter now. He was almost certainly right: how could Nick triumph over the Ashley's Santa, with his fresh face and skinny frame? OK, it was hard to beat the boy for jolliness, and he was a damn good actor. Obviously his love for Christmas was the real deal, and his sense of humour was spot on. But physically Nick was so far off what he ought to be that there was no way they could hope to fool the kids into thinking he was the real thing.

Elodie made up her mind. Tomorrow she'd go to the theatrical agency she'd written off as too expensive and see if they had any Santas on their books who weren't engaged. Cost be damned. This was too important to take chances.

There was a knock and Pops came in.

'All shut up… downstairs,' he told her.

'You get off home,' Elodie said. 'I'm going to put in another hour. Not long now.'

'How was the field trip?'

'Come on, Pops, are you retired or aren't you? You've been nose to the grindstone all afternoon. Go home and rest.'

'It's not fair to leave me dangling,' Pops said. 'Come on, did you find out… anything?'

Elodie smiled as brightly as she could. 'Only that we've got nothing to worry about. Their man's not a patch on you.'

'But it's not me you need to be thinking about, is it? What did… young Nicky think?'

Elodie couldn't hold back her flinch.

Pops frowned. 'Ellie, what is it?'

'Nick's… resigned, Pops. I'm going to hire us someone from an agency tomorrow. He said to tell you he was sorry.'

'But why on earth… would he go and do… that?'

His speech had been a hundred times better recently, but under stress, Pops always found it harder to get at the words he needed.

'It's not a problem,' Elodie told him, trying to sound nonchalant about it. 'He had personal reasons; nothing to do with us. To be honest I'm relieved. He was far too young to be convincing.'

'If you're relieved then… you're a bigger bloody fool than I took you for.' Pops searched her face. 'Tell me the truth.'

'I told you, he—'

He held up a hand. 'Elodie Martin, I've raised you since you… were eight… years old. Don't think I don't know when you're lying.'

She sighed. 'Sit down.'

Pops took a seat on the Santa throne with Elodie cross-legged on the floor leaning against the side of it, as if she were a child still and he was sitting on the sofa with her nana. She picked up one of her paper snowflakes and dropped it so she could watch it flutter to the floor.

'Well, what happened?' Pops asked.

'He lied to us, Pops. The day he auditioned, the reason he was the only one was because he hid my card so no one else knew to turn up.'

'Why… would he do that?'

'He needed money. His mum's ill and can't work so he supports them both. The salary was too good to ignore.'

Elodie realised she sounded defensive on Nick's behalf, and wondered who she thought she was arguing with. Herself, probably.

Pops was silent.

'I really like that boy,' he said at last.

She shrugged noncommittally.

'Now don't... give me that,' Pops said sternly. 'Elodie, you haven't made a new friend since 1998.'

'OK, so I liked him too,' she admitted. 'He still lied to us.'

'Well, wouldn't you in his... circumstances?'

'Perhaps. What do you want me to do about it though? He saw the Ashley's Santa, freaked out and threw the towel in. Nothing to do with me.'

'I want you to talk him out of it, don't I?'

'Why?'

'Because the boy's a born Father Christmas, that's why. And because...' Pops took a deep breath. 'Because he puts a smile on your face. That's reason enough... for me to want to keep him around.'

She summoned a smile. 'You're not matchmaking for me, are you? Because I hate to disappoint you but I'm not Nick's type. His heart belongs to Kurt Russell.'

'When he's here... you're happy. That's all I know.'

She sighed. 'He is fun to have around. But he's so... well, skinny. And young. And... and everything Santas aren't. What are we going to tell people, that we're the first grotto to use age-blind casting?'

'His age won't matter. Not if... he's good enough.'

'Don't you think we'd be better going to a theatrical agency? Getting a proper pro?'

'I do not,' Pops said firmly. 'Ellie, would you say that… your old Pops might know a thing or two about Santaing?'

She smiled. 'Maybe.'

'Then take his advice… and go get us back the best successor I could have hoped for.'

'You really think he's that good?'

'I think he will be.'

'But how do I get him back?' Elodie asked. 'The Ashley's Santa totally shook his confidence. I don't know what I can do about that, if it turns out he's really determined to quit. He might not even let me talk to him.'

'You know a bit about him by now. Use your… brains. What's the best way to get around him?'

'You're glum tonight,' Nick's mum observed as they sat on the sofa, watching some celebrity show where they had to dance or ice-skate or something. He wasn't really paying attention. 'You normally laugh your head off when they fall over.'

'Hmm?' Nick forced himself to focus. 'Sorry, Mum, I was miles away.'

'I know. You have been all night.' She examined his face closely. 'Charlie was full of today's trip to Santa. She genuinely seemed to think he was the real deal.'

'I guess she would.'

Sheila turned off the TV. 'What's wrong, Nicky?' she asked gently.

'Just… thinking, that's all.' He couldn't bring himself to

tell her he'd resigned from the Santa job yet; not when they'd been counting on the money to get through Christmas.

'You know you can talk to me, don't you?'

'I know.' He forced a smile. 'Thanks, Mum.'

They were interrupted by the rattle of the letterbox.

'Who's putting stuff in at this time?' Sheila said, tutting. 'It'll be another of those damn takeaway leaflets – no wonder we're losing the rainforests at the rate we are. Ninety per cent of them are now Balti menus. Grab it for me, can you, Nicky?'

Nick went to pick up the letter and carried it back in.

'Is it the Chinese?' his mum asked. 'They seem to change their prices every week.'

'No.' It was a small envelope with just his first name, *Nick*, scrawled on the front. 'It's... for me.'

She frowned. 'They're not bringing post at this time, are they?'

'It's not been sent in the post. Someone dropped it in.'

'Must be a Christmas card. Well, open it.'

Nick tore open the flap and took out a little strip of paper.

'What does it say?' his mum asked.

'It says "How does King Wenceslas like his pizzas? Deep pan, crisp and even".'

'Eh?'

'It's a Christmas cracker joke.'

'Why on earth is someone sending you a Christmas cracker joke?'

'I've got no idea.'

'Does it say anything else?'

'No.' Nick turned it over. 'Oh. Yes. It says, "I'm outside".'

'Who's outside?'

'I guess I'll have to go see.'

Nick went to open the door. Elodie Martin was out there. She was wearing a Santa hat and an eye-watering Christmas jumper bearing a picture of a psychedelic snowman.

'Ta-da,' she said, doing jazz hands.

Nick couldn't help laughing. 'Can this really be Ebenezer Martin on my doorstep, bearing novelty hats, Christmas jumpers and cheesy pizza jokes?'

'You can't beat a top-notch groanworthy dad joke, I always say.'

'You always say that, do you?' Nick said, smiling. 'What's with all the Christmas, Elodie?'

'Pops said if I wanted to be sure you'd talk to me then I had to figure out the best way to get round you. *What's Nick Winter a sucker for?* I asked myself.'

He laughed. 'Am I that predictable?'

'I'm afraid so,' Elodie said, smiling. 'Can I come in, or are you going to make me sing "Jingle Bells" first?'

'You can come in.'

'Mum!' Nick called as Elodie followed him inside. 'I'm just going to talk to Elodie in my room, OK?'

'OK,' his mum called back. He grimaced at the smirk in her tone. 'Would you like me to make myself scarce?'

'No, we won't be long.' Hastily he waved Elodie towards his bedroom.

'Sorry,' he said when he'd closed the door. 'It's pretty normal for me to feel like I'm thirty-four going on fourteen. I forget how weird it must be for people who drop round.'

'She knows she's got nothing to worry about from me, doesn't she?'

'Are you kidding? Her desperation to see me married

off to literally anyone reached epic proportions long ago. She'll have the vicar waiting for us when we come out.' He gestured to his bed. 'Er, take a seat.'

Elodie sat down, glancing at the monitor on his desk. He'd installed a *Bluey* screensaver and the little puppy and her sister were currently chasing each other across the screen.

'So you're a fan now, are you?' Elodie asked, raising an eyebrow.

'Kind of, yeah. It's moreish, isn't it?'

'I know what you mean.'

Nick planted himself awkwardly beside Elodie, feeling self-conscious about his room. It was the same one he'd had all his life: small and poky, with its single bed making it look a little like a bedroom in a homeless hostel. Or a prison. He'd done his best to give it a more grown-up vibe when he'd moved home after graduating, but somehow no matter how he decorated, it always felt like the room of a teenager. One good thing about being thirty-four was that dates, at least, usually had their own places to invite him back to. Or so he remembered. It'd been a while.

He got the impression Elodie was looking around his room while trying not to look like she was looking around his room. Judging it.

Well, and why wouldn't she? Nick was well aware that the bleak little room was beyond pathetic. He thought he'd made his peace with that, but now Elodie Martin was sitting all pretty and colourful in the middle of it, the contrast made it sting afresh.

'So, um, what did you want to talk to me about?' he asked.

'Nick, look. About the thing with the card—'

He winced. 'I'm so sorry, Elodie. I didn't realise when I decided to hide it that the shop was relying on the grotto for its future. I just thought… well, I knew it was a bad thing to do, but I was desperate and I convinced myself the universe would forgive me for one little fib. Can you understand that?'

'It was bad, but I get why you did it. What hurt is that you didn't tell me until today.' She looked down at his threadbare carpet. 'I thought… we were friends. I know I'm a prickly cow and I haven't made myself easy for you to like, but… well, I thought you might have started to all the same. You know having friends is a bit of a novelty for me.'

'We were friends – we are. I might've come clean sooner if it hadn't been for the bet. After that…' He sighed. 'I didn't want to let you down. Then today, seeing Ashley's guy… it shattered my confidence, if you really want to know. You're better off without me.'

'That's up to me and Pops, isn't it? And he very much disagrees.'

He smiled. 'I don't know why he likes me so much.'

'Because as you once told me, you're a very likeable man. Even I like you, and I hate about ninety-nine per cent of people.'

'No you don't. Not really.'

Elodie smiled. 'Nick, you're the only person I've ever known who's been convinced I've got some secret better nature.' She reached for his hands. 'Come back, please. Pops firmly believes no one can save Christmas at Martin's Toy Kingdom except you, and in my soul I can't help agreeing with him.'

'Why?'

'God knows. You're the wrong age, the wrong shape, the wrong everything. But some sixth sense is telling me none of that matters. Because you're Santa.'

Nick looked down at his fingers pressed in hers. Skin on skin. There was a strange, unfamiliar sensation fluttering in him that made him feel sort of… warm. He filed it away to analyse later.

'But there's still Ashley's guy,' he said. 'That's a tough act to compete with. Charlie thinks he's the real Santa, and she's an actual kid.'

'She's wrong. You're the real Santa.' Elodie plucked the hat from her head and put it on his. 'Well?'

'I don't want to ruin this for you, Elodie.' He reached up to rub his stubble. 'I'll never forgive myself if I stuff it up.'

'And I'll never forgive you if you don't come back to work and give it all you've got.' She leaned over to peck his cheek. 'I believe in you, Nick.'

He felt the colour rise in his cheeks. 'Thanks. That… means a lot.'

'So? Will you come back and be our Santa? I'd rather not get down on my knees and beg, but I will if I have to.'

'All right, I'll come back. On one condition.'

'What is it?'

'If you're doing Christmas properly now, ex-Grinch Elodie Martin, you have to do it my way.'

She frowned. 'Eh?'

'Have you really not seen *Elf*?'

'No, why?'

He shook his head. 'That's an actual, real-life tragedy.

I mean, you've literally wasted your life up until this point. Have you seen any Christmas films?'

She hesitated. 'I've seen… *Die Hard*. That's a Christmas film, right?'

'Opinion on the subject is divided. Anything else?'

'No, I don't think so.'

'Right.' Nick put the Santa hat back on her head. 'In that case, Ebenezer, strap yourself in. Because this week, I'm taking you on a journey through Christmas Past.'

11

Elodie was putting the finishing touches to her makeup when there was a knock at the door of her cottage.

She wasn't sure why she was bothering to put any on. It was only a film night. She was in pyjamas, for God's sake – all right, new pyjamas that she'd bought especially for the occasion, but pyjamas nevertheless. Obviously she wasn't trying to impress Nick. Whatever thoughts she might have been entertaining about the potential for romance between them – and there'd been more than the odd thought in that direction, she couldn't deny it – had been knocked firmly on the head when he'd made his preferences clear to her in the car the other day.

It had been good of him to drop her a hint. He must've been worried she'd get the wrong idea about his overtures of friendship and wanted to spare her embarrassment. Elodie was grateful for that. She'd have hated to make a fool of herself with him.

She always had been terrible at this sort of thing – reading signals, recognising feelings, working out where the line was between friendship and romance. It felt like a game – all those subtle touches, the flirting that might not be flirting – and Elodie couldn't stand games where she didn't understand the rules. It felt like adults were always playing them, and she'd never got the knack of figuring them out.

She guessed that was why she quite liked chatting to the kids who came into the shop: the fact that there was no pretence about them. Their conversation was so much easier than adult small talk. Kids said what they thought, brutal as that could sometimes be, and they didn't hide what they really meant. They laughed when they were happy and cried when they were sad, and they didn't expect you to guess which was which. It was a shame grown-ups couldn't learn a thing or two from them. It'd make the world a much more Elodie-friendly place.

There'd been a twinge of disappointment when her new friend had taken pains to make it clear to her that he was gay, true. Elodie hadn't been able to help thinking about it – Nick, and her, and the possibility they could be more than just friends in future. Elodie knew she could be quite socially naive, but she was aware that when two people of compatible sexualities started to grow closer, that often came with some sort of subtext. But there'd been relief mingled with the disappointment: knowing she'd made a friend who could be just a friend, with no subtexts involved. She hated subtexts. Why did they have to be sub? Why couldn't they just be texts? It was just one of the many things about human interactions that Elodie couldn't get her head around. Anyway, friends had always been harder to find than lovers – at least for her. It was better this way.

Still, she'd felt the need for a bit of lipstick and foundation before Nick's arrival tonight. Not because this was in any way a date; just that it felt… sort of symbolic. Elodie didn't generally spend much time thinking about how she looked because she was too busy living in her own head, enjoying her own company. If she was going to start experimenting with spending time on the outside, she'd feel more confident knowing she was someone it didn't hurt people's eyes to look at.

She went to answer the door. Nick was outside in that big shabby coat he loved, holding a stack of DVDs. He was wearing jeans under his coat and carrying a rucksack over one shoulder.

'Well swit-swoo,' he said, glancing down at her candy-cane-print pyjamas.

She shook her head, beckoning him inside. 'I'm disappointed in you, Nick. I made it quite clear this was a pyjama party and you show up in jeans.'

'Au contraire.' He threw off the rucksack and removed his big coat, revealing a black sweatshirt with a colourful dinosaur print. When he'd unzipped his jeans and struggled out of them, Elodie could see he had matching bottoms on underneath.

She laughed. 'Sexy.'

'Right? Nothing's sexier than dinosaurs.'

She glanced at the DVDs he'd dumped on the coffee table. Just looking at the spines, she could see there was a worrying abundance of snowflakes on them.

'Which of these Christmas horrors are you going to force me to watch then?' she asked.

'Well, all of them.'

She laughed. 'You what? We'll be here till Monday.'

'Not in one go. But I fully intend to show you every one of these stone-cold classics before we open the grotto next week.' Nick glanced at the DVDs. 'I reckon we can get through… at least three tonight.'

'Come on!'

'It's Saturday night, Elodie. You can sleep it off tomorrow.' He opened his rucksack and took out a bottle of white wine, a jumbo pack of toffee popcorn and a folder. 'Naturally I brought supplies.'

Elodie smiled. 'You're the perfect date.'

'So I've been told.'

'Let me put your wine in the fridge. I've got a cold one we can have first.'

She went into the kitchen to put the wine away, then came back in with the chilled bottle in a cooler and two glasses. Nick had already made himself at home on the sofa, looking very cosy in his pyjamas with his feet tucked under his bum.

'What's in the folder?' she asked as she poured them each a wine.

'Bingo cards.'

She blinked. 'Bingo?'

'Yep,' Nick said, grinning. 'It's a game of my own devising: Christmas Film Bingo. That's copyright Nicholas Winter.'

Elodie opened the folder to take a look at one of the cards. It included the following:

Someone does some baking
A character wears red
Kissing in the snow
A Christmas miracle occurs
Someone who hates Christmas learns to love it
A doubter comes to believe in Santa

Workaholic parent
Matchmaking child
Snowball fight
Love triangle
Perfectly timed snowfall

'And if you're the first to get a line you win a prize,' Nick said. 'I won't give too much away but it involves chocolate.'

'You realise this reads like a list of reasons I've tried to avoid ever watching a Christmas film? They sound like pure schmaltz.'

'I know. Great, isn't it?'

She shook her head. 'I can't believe you're making me do this, Nick.'

'Someone who hates Christmas learns to love it,' Nick murmured, taking the card from her. 'I'll be ticking that one off this week.'

Elodie turned on the DVD player. 'Seriously. Why are you making me do this?'

'Because I know you're secretly desperate to be convinced. Hollywood and Charles Dickens have decreed that it's the fate of all grinches to become Christmas converts.' He raised an eyebrow. 'Anyway, less of the cynicism. You promised me you'd keep an open mind during Christmas movie marathon week.'

'Only because you threatened to leave us Santaless if I didn't.'

'Tough love. It's for your own good.' He handed her one of the DVDs. 'We'll start with this. I've never known anyone not to love this.'

She glanced at it. '*It's A Wonderful Life?* That title's a lie, for a start.'

'This is the grandaddy of Christmas classics. Trust me, you're in for a treat.'

Elodie put it on, turned down the lights and sat next to Nick with her wine. He opened the bag of popcorn and held it out to her.

'Now is this so bad?' he asked as she helped herself to a handful.

'I'll let you know in half an hour.'

'Not the film. This. Us. Spending your chill time with someone else instead of watching Netflix on your own.'

She smiled at him. 'It has its charms, I guess.'

At first, Elodie diligently checked off her Christmas bingo card as they watched the old black-and-white film. Not that she wanted to look too invested – she didn't want Nick crowing about having converted her too soon – but hey, chocolate was chocolate.

But as the film went on, Elodie became oblivious to the pen in her hand. She stopped noticing the bag of popcorn Nick kept waving under her nose, forgot about her half-drunk glass of wine; in fact she forgot about everything except what was happening on the screen. She gasped when the young George Bailey was given a ringing slap by his drunken boss at the drugstore, and when an adult George gave up his honeymoon money to bail out the depression-hit folk of Bedford Falls, she even found a tear in her eye.

'You've won.'

'Hmm?' Her attention was dragged back to the here and now as Nick tapped at her card with his pen.

'You've won. Look, you've got a line there. You've forgotten to check off two, that's all.'

Elodie looked at her card, which was swimming a bit. She paused the DVD so she wouldn't miss anything and turned away from Nick to wipe her eyes.

Nick nudged her. 'Told you, didn't I?'

'All right, so it's a great film. Don't be too smug about it.'

'I'm not smug. I'm happy.' He smiled at her. 'I knew I was right about you. You are a softie.'

To Elodie's surprise, Nick stretched an arm around her shoulders and gave her a squeeze. Elodie had never been on squeezing terms with anyone before; not even with her handful of short-lived boyfriends. At first she stiffened, her body's natural defence mechanism kicking in at the unfamiliar situation it found itself in… then she relaxed. Nick left his arm there, and she let herself snuggle closer.

'There's only ten minutes left,' she said. 'What are we watching after this, Nick?'

'And now she's hungry for more,' Nick observed to the universe at large. 'My work here is nearly complete.'

Elodie looked up to smile at him. 'You're not my guardian angel, are you?'

'That'd be telling.'

'You are, aren't you?'

'I'm someone who's on your side. It seemed to take a while for you to believe that, but we got there.'

'I guess we did.' She leaned her weight comfortably against him. 'I'm glad you came into my life, Nick. You're… weird.'

'Gee, thanks.'

'I mean a good weird. A different kind of weird to my

weird. It feels like yours sort of fits mine. I mean we fit, you know?'

'That must be the wine talking.' Nick reached for the bottle. 'Here, have some more. I like you like this.'

'Thanks.' Elodie's gaze fixed on the face of George Bailey frozen on screen, looking utterly distraught as he realised his wife no longer recognised him in the alternative reality of Pottersville. 'I like you too, Nick.'

12

Callum was at a cocktail party. Well, it was sort of a cocktail party. There were definitely cocktails – he'd hired a bevy of attractive people to serve his guests with a range of fruity alcoholic beverages, as well as some unpronounceable canapés. Everyone was wearing cocktail-drinking attire: smart, sexy dresses for the women; black tie for the men. The extent to which it was a party, though, could be debated. What it actually was was Ashley's Department Store's annual 'nice to have done business with you' Christmas bash for their suppliers and contacts, held in the meeting-slash-function room next door to Callum's office. He'd been beyond bored for the last hour, and his smile was starting to feel sprayed on.

But his evening was looking up. The woman who ran the theatrical agency he'd used to hire Kenny was making eye contact from across the room while she ate an olive on a stick – ate it pretty suggestively, Callum thought. Angela was a stunning older woman of around fifty, wearing a figure-hugging black dress that left very little to the imagination.

He grabbed a couple of drinks and approached her.

'Can I tempt you?' he asked, offering one to her.

'You can certainly do that,' she said, smiling as she took the champagne cocktail.

'I just wanted to thank you for sending us Kenny Ross. He's proved a real treasure.'

'We don't have to talk about work, do we, Mr Ashley?' Angela purred, resting long fingernails on his arm. 'I'm sure there's something more intimate we could discuss. Perhaps somewhere private?'

Callum blinked. He'd met plenty of women who didn't waste any time, but this one was setting a new record.

'Well, there's my office—' he began, before he was interrupted by a throat clearing. He turned to see who was trying to attract his attention.

'Mike. Is anything wrong?'

Mike didn't answer. His attention had been claimed by Angela's prominent cleavage, which he'd got an eyeful of when Callum had stood aside.

'Mike?' Callum said.

'Oh. Right.' Mike tore his gaze from Angela's horizon-dominating rack. 'Sorry for interrupting, boss. It's just that I was checking the recent security footage and there's something I think you ought to see.'

'That can wait. Why don't you grab yourself a drink?'

He turned back to Angela but Mike tapped his elbow. 'You'll want to see this. I guarantee it.'

Callum sighed. 'Sorry about this, Angela. Don't go anywhere.'

He followed Mike to the control room where their security guard usually sat, monitoring the screens connected to the store's CCTV cameras.

'OK, what's so important?' he asked.

'Sorry to drag you off when you were on a promi— I mean, when you were enjoying yourself,' Mike said. 'I knew you'd want to be told about this right away. I always have a scroll-through near the end of the month, and I spotted – well, you'll see for yourself.'

'Has one of the staff had their hand in the tills or something?'

'No. Here.' Mike pulled up a video. 'Watch this and tell me if that's who I think it is.'

Callum watched the footage in silence.

'Elodie Martin,' he said quietly. His mouth flickered. 'Only Elodie could convince herself that putting on a baseball cap would make her unrecognisable to someone who's known her all her life.'

'You think she was trying to pilfer our man?'

'She couldn't make him a better offer. Anyway, I don't think she'd stoop to that sort of thing.'

That was more Callum's line, wasn't it? Throw money at the thing, and if that didn't work, try to buy someone else's thing instead. He'd made enough offers to Elodie and Jim in his desperation to get them on board at Ashley's. Actual Santa-stealing hadn't been an option, with Jim part of the family business rather than a bribable hired hand, and it would be nice if Callum could say he wouldn't have lowered himself to that even so. It would be a lie though. Of course he would.

'What's with the crappy disguise, do you think?' Mike asked. 'She must be up to no good if she's trying to hide her face.'

'I suppose she's scoping us out. Seeing what we've got in our grotto.' Callum skipped back to watch the footage again. Elodie and that man from the shop were waiting in the grotto queue with a little girl.

'Do you recognise the bloke and the kid?' Mike asked.

'I've never seen the girl before but I know the man. He's a handyman or something. When I saw him at the shop, Elodie told me he was helping her install the grotto.'

'What's she brought him for?'

'He was the only age-appropriate fake spouse she could find to play happy families with, probably.' Callum's brow wrinkled. 'Unless…'

Callum had assumed, when Elodie had said the man was helping with the grotto, that he was a carpenter or electrician or something. But suppose he was helping out in a more… personal capacity?

The idea that Elodie might have a new boyfriend was more irritating than Callum would have expected. Not that he was jealous exactly. He admired Elodie, and yes, he was attracted to her on some level too. People who knew how he lived might be surprised by that. Elodie was careless of her appearance but nevertheless pretty in a girl-next-door sort of way. However, she was far from a beauty; nothing to compare with the women Callum dated. His female companions were beautiful, well-groomed, seductive, oozing sex appeal – women like Angela Weston, who was even now waiting in the function room impatient for an opportunity to tear his dinner suit off, Callum remembered vaguely.

Still, he didn't need to talk to a therapist to get to the bottom of his feelings for ordinary, averagely pretty Elodie Martin. Out of everyone he'd known, she was the one person who didn't constantly blow smoke up his backside – who made no secret of the fact that she thought Callum Ashley was far from being God's gift to the universe. Maybe it wasn't the sign of a healthy, well-adjusted libido, but he couldn't help finding her dislike of him… well, kind of a turn-on.

He didn't feel jealous though. Callum knew what jealousy felt like. So what exactly was gnawing at him?

Callum had always got what he wanted. All through childhood, he'd only had to point at something and his dad would buy it. In adult life, if he'd wanted something – possessions, women – they'd almost always been available to him if he made sure the price was right. But Elodie Martin had never been available to him. And the more she'd made that clear, the more he'd longed for her.

That was it. It wasn't about jealousy – it was about possession. Callum couldn't have Elodie, so he resented the idea anyone else could. It wasn't about them. It was about him.

It was always about him.

'You think he's a boyfriend?' Mike asked.

'It's possible.' Callum tried not to display any emotion. That, at least, was something he was good at. He paused the footage at a point when Elodie and her gentleman friend had unknowingly turned to face the security camera.

'Funny sort of date,' Mike observed. 'Not like there's much for them to see this year either, grotto-wise.'

Callum couldn't ignore the note of reproach in his store manager's voice.

'Look, Mike, I told you. I know what I'm doing.'

'At least tell me what this is all about, boss. We spend megabucks creating a grotto the likes of which this town has never seen, then all of a sudden you're demanding I have it all sent back. A string of fairy lights and a few scrappy bits of tinsel is hardly what I'd call a Winter Wonderland. Your old man would've blown a gasket if he'd seen this year's effort.' Mike squinted at Callum. 'Here. You're not having one of them nervous breakdowns, are you?'

Callum sometimes felt Mike relied too much on the fact he'd worked for his father to say things to him his other staff would never dare.

'No, Michael, I'm not having one of them nervous breakdowns.' He shrugged. 'I just want to make sure we're doing things fairly. We've already got a big lead over the other local grottoes with Kenny on our team. It doesn't seem right to push our advantage.'

'Since when do you care what's right? I thought this was about being the best.'

'Yes, well, I've been doing some thinking lately. Maybe things are finally changing. I'm changing.'

Mike shook his head. 'I've seen that look in people's eyes before. Please tell me you haven't found Jesus.'

Callum smiled. 'Nothing that drastic. I just want to make my life going forward a bit more worthwhile than my life up to now. Take more notice of what other people need instead of just… what I want.'

'Ah, right. I see.'

Mike looked at the screen, then back to his boss. Something like realisation seemed to be dawning on his solid, sensible face.

'I see,' he said again, slowly. 'Pretty little thing, old Martin's granddaughter.'

Callum shrugged. 'She's passable. Or she might be, if she put a bit of lipstick on occasionally.'

'You wouldn't, er… have any sort of history there, would you, boss? Not meaning to pry, but you've been acting bloody weird since you went to see her that day.'

'We were at school together. She hated me then and she hates me even more now,' Callum told him shortly. 'We haven't had sex, if that's what you're getting at.'

'Right. So you're not trying to impress her to get into her knickers or anything.'

'She's got nothing to do with it,' Callum lied. 'I told you. For once in my life, I'm trying to do the right thing.'

That was true, at least. Did Elodie realise that? Callum would love to know what she'd thought about the changes to the Ashley's grotto this year. It tore him up that he cared whether she thought well of him, but there it was. He did.

His gaze was drawn to that cute, determined face under the baseball cap. Elodie seemed to be deep in conversation with the young man, who looked different than he had when Callum had met him. Kind of… well, kind of hairier. Had Elodie persuaded him to grow a beard? He had no idea she had a taste for facial hair.

Slowly, his brain started to fight back against the two cocktails he'd drunk and whir into life.

He's helping with the grotto. That's what Elodie had said – and yes, she'd looked embarrassed too. And then the man had said 'or something like that'.

'Oh dear God,' Callum muttered.

'What?' Mike said.

'I think I might just have worked out why Elodie wanted

that guy to keep her company for her spot of espionage. And why she's got a sudden taste for men with beards.'

'Eh? Why?'

Callum laughed. 'I can't believe this. Surely she'd never be such a fool. Never take such a risk with her business. She loves that crumbling old place.'

And if she had, that opened up a whole new train of thought, didn't it? Callum didn't have to take her money, of course, when he won the bet. That had actually been his plan all along: to refuse his winnings, be magnanimous in victory, in the hope… well, he wasn't sure what he hoped except to win in one sense or another. But there was always the chance that Elodie would insist on giving him his dues – it'd be typical of her pride. And if Callum won the bet now, knowing this…

'What can't you believe?' Mike asked. 'Sorry, boss, but I'm not following you.'

'I mean, I knew she had a blind spot when it came to that doomed shop, but other than that I always respected her for her sound business sense,' Callum murmured, still talking half to himself. 'I can't believe she'd make such a ridiculous bet while knowing that all her grotto had to offer this year was… well, him.'

'Callum, do you mind telling me what on earth you're blathering about?'

'The skinny, baby-faced boyfriend.' Callum shook his head, laughing. 'He's Martin's new Santa.'

13

It was the evening before Martin's Toy Kingdom's grand grotto opening. Elodie was humming as she wrapped presents for the Santa sacks with Summer, who'd come round after college to lend a hand. Nick was upstairs, trying on his costume.

'You sound happy,' Summer observed. 'Normally the night before opening, you're under the counter rocking and sobbing.'

'Weird, isn't it?' Elodie used her scissors to curl the ribbon on the Captain America figure she'd just wrapped and dropped it into the superhero sack. 'I don't know if it's because I really think we can win or my brain's just accepted we're doomed, but I'm feeling oddly relaxed about this year's grotto.'

'What're you humming?' Summer frowned. 'Is that from *Muppet Christmas Carol*?'

Elodie flushed. 'Probably. Nick's had me on a diet of at least one Christmas film a day for the past week. He says it's an essential part of my education if I want to put my Grinchy ways behind me.'

'What, you guys have been hanging out?'

Elodie nodded. 'Quite a bit. We have a good laugh.'

'Aww. It's nice you made a new friend, El.'

Elodie laughed. 'Well that makes me feel pathetic.'

'No way, I totally get it. It can be tough if you're not, like, a really outgoing person.'

'You're wise beyond your years, Summer.'

Summer reached for the scissors to curl her ribbon. 'It's easier when someone's gay, I always think. I mean, if you're a girl and he's a boy. Otherwise you get that whole thing where you're like, "Is he into me? Am I giving the wrong signals? Was that flirting or joking?" It can spoil a friendship when you don't know what the other person wants.'

'It certainly makes things easier when you don't need to be constantly second-guessing one another.' Elodie spotted Nick coming down the stairs in his Santa suit. 'Speak of the devil.'

'Ta-da!' Nick said, twirling. 'Well, girls, how do I look? Sexy, right?'

'Like you're wearing next year's school uniform.' Elodie smiled. 'It's not bad though: you just need to fill it out. Have you got a big enough pillow?'

'Even better. My Aunty Alice is a nurse. She's arranged for me to borrow one of those fake pregnancy bellies.' Nick patted his non-existent tummy. 'That way, no wardrobe malfunctions from inadequately secured pillows.'

'Well, I hope it's twins. You need all the help you can get. When are you dying the beard?'

Nick reached up to rub his facial hair, still short but a passable length for a Father Christmas who had modern tastes in personal grooming. 'In the morning, I think: as close to opening as possible. Minimise any roots.'

'Surely it isn't growing that fast.'

'Maybe not, but I'm not taking any chances.'

They looked around as the bell on the door chimed.

'We're closed,' Elodie started to say, then stopped. Callum Ashley had walked in, done up like a dog's dinner and smirking all over his face.

'So it's true,' he said, looking at Nick in his Santa suit. 'Jesus Christ, Elodie. What the hell do you think you're doing?'

Elodie glared at him. 'What's it to you?'

'Callum.' Nick nodded to his dinner suit. 'Is it prom night?'

'Says you, Kris Kringle.' Callum looked highly amused as he examined Nick's costume.

'I saw you trying to infiltrate my grotto,' he informed them conversationally. 'He's good, isn't he? His name's Kenny Ross. I got him from an agency. I've already booked him for the next three years.'

'Look, we are actually closed,' Nick told him. 'It's not against the law to take my little cousin to see Santa, is it? Now if you don't mind, we've got a lot to do so…'

Callum beamed at him almost affably. Elodie had never seen him in such a relaxed mood.

'How old are you, kid?' he asked.

'Older than you. Kid.'

'I can't believe that. Go on, how old?'

'I'm thirty-four, not that it's any of your business,' Nick told him shortly. Elodie had never heard Nick being short with anyone before.

'Really?' Callum said. 'Heh, you are older than me. You don't look it.'

Elodie shook her head. 'Callum, can you please just sod

off? I hate to deprive you of your pre-Christmas gloat, but we are opening tomorrow. Like Nick said, we've got a lot to do.'

'Nick.' Callum nodded. 'Good name. It suits him.'

'Just go, can you? Or did you come for something other than taking the piss?'

'I came to tell you I'm calling off the bet, didn't I? I can't go on with it now. It'd be ridiculous.'

Elodie frowned. 'And what's that supposed to mean?'

'Well, come on, El. When I agreed to it, I assumed you knew what you were doing. But this… it'd be like shooting fish in a barrel. I couldn't do it to you.'

'Well of all the arrogant, up-themselves little…' Elodie glanced at Nick. 'Ignore him. He's just trying to break your confidence.'

Nick nodded. 'I can see exactly what he's trying to do.'

Callum held his hands up. 'Honestly, this is for real. This isn't a bet any more, it's… it's virtually a robbery. I thought when I stripped my grotto down that I was at least giving you a sporting chance, but now…'

'God, you're something.' Nick stepped towards him. 'Look, Mr Callum Ashley, you've already been asked to leave multiple times. Now are you going to get the hell out or do I have to make you?'

Callum laughed. 'What, are you going to ask me to step outside? I mean, I always feel Christmas isn't Christmas unless I've had a fist fight in the street with a man dressed as Santa Claus.'

'Do as he says, Callum,' Elodie said in a low voice. 'We know what you're trying to do and it won't work.'

'Look, sorry. You're right, I've done this all wrong.'

Callum turned away from Nick. 'I didn't mean to laugh, it's just funny. Him, I mean. But I am one hundred per cent serious when I say I came to call off the bet. It was always a stupid idea, and now I know…' He glanced back at Nick. 'Well, without insulting anyone here further, it's sufficient to say I don't feel right about it. Let's forget the whole thing, shall we?'

'Running scared, are you?'

'Elodie, you're being absurd. Don't let your pride get in the way of your business sense. You know I'm right about this.'

Elodie drew herself up. 'I don't know any such thing. I have complete confidence in Martin's Santa when it comes to bringing home the bacon, and I've got absolutely no intention of calling anything off.' She nodded to the door. 'Goodbye, Callum.'

He shook his head. 'I've known you a long time, Elodie. I knew you were stubborn, proud, headstrong and impulsive, but the one thing I've never believed you were was stupid. But if this is what you want… well, on your head be it.' With a last scathing look at Nick, Callum left the shop.

Elodie could feel herself shaking. 'Jesus. Nicky, can you believe that guy?'

'You think he meant it?' Nick asked. 'About wanting to cancel the bet?'

'No. He came to crow, that's all – and to knock your confidence because he knows we open tomorrow. We should be flattered he was worried enough to try intimidation tactics.'

'He gave you the perfect opportunity to get out of the bet though, El,' Summer said.

'Back down? Let him think he's beaten us?' Elodie folded her arms. 'Not a snowball's. He knew I wouldn't agree or he'd never have made the offer.'

'I see what you mean about that guy,' Nick said. 'He knows how to get you riled up, doesn't he?'

Elodie smiled at him. 'Were you really going to fight him for me?'

'Too right. I'll have you know I know kung fu.'

She raised an eyebrow. 'You don't, do you?'

'Well, I've seen *Kung Fu Panda* a few times. I must've picked up some moves.' Nick glared at the door. 'Ladies, we are so winning this bet. No way I'm letting that dinner-suited creep get one over on me.'

'How though?' Summer asked.

'Well for a start, we can get that grotto of ours looking like a contender. Roll up your sleeves, gang. We've got a lot of work to do.'

14

'Like this, Nick?' Summer asked, holding a chain of paper Christmas trees against one of the pillars that stood either side of the grotto door.

Nick, who'd got changed out of his Father Christmas gear, looked over from the table of Splattertrons he was arranging. 'No, diagonally. I want trees and snowmen alternating with rows of fairy lights.'

'Yes, Santa.' Summer started arranging them as instructed.

Elodie glanced up from the floor, where she was sitting cutting out the paper chains. 'Careful with those splatter thingies, Nick. I had to pay through the nose to get stock in at the last minute.'

'I'll treat them as tenderly as my own unborn children.'

'We're going to spend all our profits paying the electricity bill for these lights,' Elodie said, looking around at the strings of fairy lights. 'That'll keep them out of Callum's coffers if we lose, I suppose.'

The second floor had been transformed over the last couple of hours. It was sparkling with tinsel and lights, while displays of toys flanked the rope cordon to tempt Christmas shoppers. Winter greenery – holly and pine boughs Summer had collected – hung everywhere, adorned with cotton wool snow. It wasn't expensive – everything had been made with things they'd had lying around, or cobbled together from the woods and corner shop – but it was still magical. Nick felt a surge of pride as he looked around.

'We actually did it, didn't we?' he said. 'We *Elf*ed the place.'

Summer shook her head. 'It's no good talking about *Elf* in front of Elodie. She won't get it.'

'Yes I do,' Elodie said. 'Buddy works all night to decorate the Gimbels toy department ready for Santa.'

Summer blinked, then turned to Nick. 'Wow. I've been nagging her to watch that with me every year since I was about four. What did you do to her, Nick?'

'Hey. You're talking to the Ghost of Christmas Present, St Peter's Hall, Christmas 2018 here.' He smiled at Elodie. 'I knew you weren't a real Scrooge though, El.'

'Bah humbug.'

He wagged a finger at her. 'None of that. Not allowed after the way you soaked my shoulder when Muppet Tiny Tim died.'

'I'm ready to admit there's some quality Christmas programming I've missed out on,' she conceded. 'Still, it's a big fuss over one little solstice. Bloody Dickens.'

'Don't blame Charlie. Washington Irving has got at least as much to answer for when it comes to making Christmas the solstice celebration we all know and love.'

'Who?'

'He was the American writer who gave us Rip van Winkle and the headless horseman of Sleepy Hollow. And created the modern Santa, if you're interested.'

Elodie shook her head, smiling. 'You and your Christmas trivia.'

Nick smiled back. 'You love me for it though.'

'Maybe. It still seems like a lot of trouble for one day.'

'Now come on, I know you don't mean that. Not after all the work I put in festiving you up.' He finished his Splattertron display and stood back to admire it. 'What do you do at Christmas, Ellie?'

'Work too hard. Why do you think I've always disliked it?'

'Not the Christmas season; Christmas Day itself. How do you celebrate?'

She shrugged. 'I don't really. I mean, we used to do all the usual stuff. Me and my parents would get together with family for a big dinner, games, all that type of thing. Then when my mum and dad died, it all sort of… stopped.'

Nick turned to look at her. 'How come?'

'I think the rest of the family thought it might upset me, when the grief was still fresh. I lost my parents just before Christmas so big celebrations didn't seem appropriate afterwards. We got into the routine of having a smaller celebration on Christmas Day – just me, Nana and Pops, quietly remembering the people we'd lost. Then Nana died and it just left the two of us.'

'I didn't realise,' Nick said quietly. 'Sorry, El.'

'That's OK.'

'You know we'd always love to see you and Pops at ours for Christmas dinner, El,' Summer said. 'All the cousins and aunts and uncles from my dad's side of the family are coming. Mum's ordered a turkey big enough to feed a small country. Even between fifteen of us, we'll never manage to finish it.'

'Thanks, Sum, but you know we prefer to keep it low-key. Big family Christmases just depress me, and then I bring everyone down. We'll see you guys at New Year as usual.' She summoned a smile for Nick. 'How about you, Nick: what do you do? I'm sure the Christmas King has a pretty impressive itinerary.'

'Not so much these days. My mum and Aunty Alice have been volunteering to help with the pensioners' Christmas dinner at the town hall the last few years, so I'm usually left eating pigs in blankets on my own.'

Summer finished attaching fairy lights to the pillar. 'Elodie, I have to get off. I told my mum I'd be home before ten. I can come in early if you need me to.'

'Yes, you get home: you've already stayed longer than you should have,' Elodie said. 'Thanks, Summer.'

Summer said goodbye and left them to finish off.

'I don't think we've much left to do,' Nick said. 'What do you think: pub after? We've earned it.'

'All right, just for one,' Elodie said. 'You need to be on top form tomorrow. No one likes a hungover Santa.'

'I hope I didn't upset you before,' Nick said as he started decorating the other pillar. 'I didn't realise it was Christmastime when you lost your parents. If I had, I wouldn't have been such a big blunderbuss with all that "most wonderful time of the year" stuff.'

'It's OK. I don't really associate Christmas with them dying. I mean I always think of it, when the decorations go up and I know the anniversary's approaching, but that's not why I started disliking this time of year.' She paused.

'Or maybe it is, partly. Not because it reminded me of the accident, but because it felt like… like every year we were sitting down to Christmas dinner and there were fewer and fewer people to eat it with us. First my mum and dad, then Nana.' She laughed damply. 'When I was a kid I looked forward to what I might get given at Christmas, you know? As I got older, I couldn't help thinking about everything I'd lost. After Pops had his stroke, I really thought another seat at the table was going to be left empty. That I'd be the last one left.'

'Aww, El, you poor soul. I never thought of it like that.' Nick left off decorating to sit on the floor beside her, stretching an arm around her shoulders. 'How come you don't spend it with your Aunty Helen? Summer sounded keen to have you there.'

Elodie hesitated. 'I suppose… because Aunty Helen's the only one there who'd remember my mum and dad. She hadn't met her husband Dave when they died, and Summer and Caleb weren't born, obviously. She invites us every year, but she never really expects us to accept. She knows Pops and me prefer to spend Christmas Day quietly, so we can think about the people we've lost when we need to. We have a smaller family dinner with Helen, Dave and the kids on New Year's Day instead.'

'I've been an insensitive bastard, haven't I? I had no idea Christmas was such a bittersweet time for you when I kept going on about it. I am sorry.'

'You haven't at all. You've been great.' She looked up at him. 'What is it about you?'

'How do you mean?'

'Ask anyone who knows me well and they'll tell you I've

spent my life pushing people away. I could count the people in this world I really care about – the ones I actually love – on the fingers of one hand.' She smiled weakly. 'And then you come barging into my life with your big clumping Santa boots, Nick Winter, and somehow manage to make me care about you in spite of my best efforts not to.'

He smiled too. 'A sixth sense told me you weren't the hopeless case you pretended to be.'

'What's your Christmas tragedy, Nicky? Who's missing from your dinner table?'

'No one really. It's always just been me and Mum. Sometimes her sister invites us to have Christmas dinner with her family, but mostly it's just the two of us.'

'Your dad's never been part of your life?'

Nick shook his head. 'My parents were never what you'd call together. It was just a fling. I'm a fling baby.'

'But you've met him, surely?'

'No. He never showed any interest in me so I never had any in him.'

'Aren't you curious about what he's like?'

'I was curious to know if he had other kids. When I was in my teens I went to some effort to find out. He didn't, as it turned out: there was just me. My interest dried up after that.'

'That's sort of sad.'

He shrugged. 'Not really. I think never knowing my dad was easier in some ways than if he'd walked out on us when I was young. Being a single-parent family was far harder on my mum than me, having to bring me up alone on pittance wages. Especially after her health got worse.'

'You're a good lad to look after her.'

'That isn't what it's like. We look after each other.' He looked into her damp eyes. 'You OK, El?'

'Yeah.' She smiled through her tears. 'Sorry. Are you OK?'

Nick rubbed his nose. 'I'll be all right.' He looked down at the paper chains by her feet. 'I suppose we should stop being all Ghost of Christmas Past-y and get on with this.'

'Just… give me a minute. It feels good, having you there.' She rested her head on his shoulder.

Nick had never seen Elodie quite like this before: so vulnerable and open. Their bond had really grown since his impromptu resignation – watching films together, going to the pub – but he could sense Elodie never dropped her guard entirely. Tonight was different though. Tonight she was just Elodie Martin: no defences, no masks, just the woman herself. It made Nick feel sort of… protective. Following an instinct, he reached up to stroke her hair.

'That's nice, Nicky,' she murmured. 'Hey, do you think you'll keep the beard after Christmas?'

Nick laughed. 'I shouldn't think so. Not really me, is it?'

'I think it suits you. Very male model.'

She was looking up at him, as if waiting. Did she… she didn't want him to kiss her? He wanted to, but… well, she was upset. That wasn't really the time to angle for a snog. And if he timed it wrong then she might go all defensive again, just when he was making progress breaking through all the Elodie barriers she put up to stop the world getting in and hurting her. Nick turned away, feeling awkward.

'Thanks,' he said lightly, in response to the compliment. 'Maybe I will keep it then, if it's going to make me a hit with the ladies.'

Elodie frowned. 'You what?'

'Well I'm not getting any less single, am I? Any other tips would be appreciated.'

She'd lifted her head and was staring at him. 'Are you… I mean, so you're not…'

'Not what?'

'Well, um… gay.'

'Eh? No.' Nick blinked. 'Is that what you thought then?'

'Well, yeah.'

'What, just because I'm an actor? It's not compulsory, you know.'

'No. You said you fancied Kurt Russell.' She shook her head. 'You're really telling me you don't like boys?'

'No, I do. But also, girls. More than two sexualities are available, Elodie.' He stared at her. 'I thought you knew. That I was bi.'

'How would I know that?'

'I guess I thought I'd mentioned it.'

'You didn't.' She rubbed her forehead. 'Sorry, Nick. I mean, I'm not bothered, obviously, and there was no reason you should've felt obligated to tell me. And no reason for me to assume you were gay or straight or… well, anything. I feel a bit stupid now.'

'It's fine. It was probably my fault,' Nick said, answering on autopilot as thoughts zoomed around his brain.

God, and he'd come so close to kissing her! Nick was sure there'd been something building between them. He remembered how an energy had seemed to flow from her to him when she'd held his hands that night over a week ago as she'd pleaded with him not to resign. Then they'd been spending all this time together: almost like dating. The envy Nick had felt when he'd fleetingly suspected her of repressed romantic feelings for Callum Ashley had been swallowed up in the euphoria of a connection as real and wonderful as anything he'd ever experienced. He'd loved learning more about her, this complicated, simple, sweet, grumpy, intelligent, multi-faceted person who'd started to fascinate him; loved the little, teasing glimpses she gave him of the real Elodie every time she opened up just a little more, a little more, a little more…

Then tonight, when she'd rested her head on his shoulder and talked about how few people in her life she cared for, Nick had really thought she might feel something equally powerful for him. But it was an illusion, after all. Elodie had only ever seen him as a friend. Just a nice, safe, non-sexy friend that she could touch and confide in and compliment without any subliminal meaning being read into it. Nick watched as the castle in the air he'd been building came tumbling down, brick by brick by brick.

'We're OK, aren't we?' Elodie was asking. 'I'm so sorry, Nick. I had no right to make assumptions about you.'

'We're OK,' Nick said vaguely.

'Well, shall we go to the pub? We can always finish decorating in the morning.'

'Hmm?'

'Pub. Come on, I'll buy you a pint.'

'Oh.' Nick pulled himself together. 'No, I'd better give it a miss. You're right, it's a big day for Martin's tomorrow – and for me.'

'All right, another time then.' She gave him a peck on the cheek that felt so miserably platonic he could've burst into tears right then and there. 'Night, Nick. Good luck tomorrow.'

15

'What time is it?' Elodie asked Summer. The cousins were behind the counter in matching Christmas elf costumes, ready for the grotto's grand opening. Pops, who as Martin's Toy Kingdom's illustrious founder was to be their celebrity ribbon-cutter, was resting on a chair beside them.

'The same time as when you asked me thirty seconds ago, Elodie,' Summer said, rolling her eyes. 'You've got a watch, haven't you?'

'I think it's broken. I feel like I'm checking it every ten minutes only to discover mere seconds have passed.' Elodie looked up at the queue outside the grotto: the kids humming with excited chatter as they took in the hastily constructed but nevertheless impressive North Pole decor the staff had cobbled together the night before. 'Where the hell is Nick?'

'He'll be on his way,' Pops reassured her. 'The grotto doesn't open... for half an hour yet.'

'Half an hour isn't long to get ready. He's cutting it bloody fine.'

'He'll be here any minute, I'm sure,' Summer said. 'Calm down, El.'

Elodie lowered her voice. 'I'm worried, you two. There's a lot of buzz about the new Ashley's Santa.'

'They're here, aren't they?' Pops said. 'I bet... young Callum can't boast a queue like ours this morning.'

'They're here because Martin's has still got a reputation as the place to see Santa,' Elodie said. 'The only reason we've pulled in a crowd is because no one knows you've retired from grotto duties. One bad day and we're sunk.'

'Nick'll do a good job. I trained him, didn't I?' But even Pops was sounding a bit doubtful this morning. He got to his feet. 'I'd better dig out my... ribbon-cutting scissors from the kitchen. Not long to go.'

'What time did you leave the pub?' Summer asked Elodie when Pops had gone. 'I hope you didn't get our Santa drunk the night before his big debut.'

'We didn't go in the end. Nick decided he should grab an early night.' Elodie grimaced. 'It was a bit awkward, after you left.'

'Why, what happened?'

'We were getting on great, talking through some emotional stuff, then I mentioned something about him being gay and he was really surprised. Turns out he's bi – he thought I knew already. I felt a right div.'

'But he told you he was gay, didn't he?'

'Not in so many words. I just assumed when he said he fancied Kurt Russell... I mean I thought he'd dropped it into the conversation deliberately to give me a hint. You know, so I wouldn't get the wrong idea about him trying to make friends.' She sighed. 'Another classic Elodie balls-up.'

Summer shrugged. 'Not necessarily. If you'd known he liked girls too you might've been more cautious about getting closer. And now you're best mates, see?'

'I guess that's true.'

'Do you think he likes you? Like, *likes* you likes you?'

'Nick? No.'

'You sound very sure.'

'I did wonder about it, before the muddle,' Elodie admitted. 'He's so touchy-feely, it's hard to tell where the line is between flirting and friend stuff – especially when you're me and you've spent your life avoiding people. But he never picked up on the hints I dropped that I might be interested.'

'What hints did you drop?'

'Well, I...' She paused. 'I asked him to the pub a few times. And once I told him his beard was sexy.'

Summer laughed. 'That's all? I say stuff like that to guy friends all the time. To girl friends too – I mean, not about their beards, obviously, but I tell them when they look sexy.'

'Ugh. I'm so bad at this stuff,' Elodie said, groaning. 'What should I have said?'

'Guys are dim about flirting,' said Summer, sage veteran of three whole years at the dating coalface. 'You have to properly spell it out for them. Like "Hey, Nick, I personally find you really sexy with that beard".' Summer narrowed one eye. 'So you like him that way then?'

'Well no, not any more. I mean, we're friends.'

'What about before?'

Elodie thought about this. She had felt something building, starting from the night she'd introduced Nick to *Bluey* and he'd vowed to make her laugh. A crush, you'd probably call it. But she'd stamped on that pretty quickly when she'd discovered – or thought she'd discovered – that Nick's romantic preferences couldn't include her. And now... now she was just glad to know him. To have someone in her life whose company she felt completely comfortable in.

'Maybe,' she said to Summer. 'At least, I wondered if there could be the potential for something. But Nick seemed totally uninterested in me in any romantic way, then I thought he actually *couldn't* be interested in me like that, and now... now we're just really good friends. And actually, I'm happier that's how it worked out. Boyfriends are easier to find than friends, but they're a lot harder to keep.'

Summer nodded. 'Yeah, I get that. Sex can really mess things up for a friendship.'

'I felt a right idiot when he told me he was bi though, after jumping to conclusions like that.' Elodie cast another glance at the door. 'I hope I didn't offend him.'

Summer was staring at something over Elodie's shoulder.

'Um, Elodie...'

'Yeah?'

Summer nodded to the window. 'That's Nick out there, isn't it?'

Elodie turned to look. A furtive red and white figure, just visible through the Christmas window display, seemed to be trying to attract her attention.

'Why the hell's he scampering about outside?' she said, shaking her head. 'Mind the till a minute. I'll go see what's up.'

As soon as she was through the door, Nick pulled her down the little ginnel between the shop and the building next door where they couldn't be seen.

'Nick. Why on earth—' Elodie stopped when she got a good look at his face. 'Oh my God!'

'It's not my fault,' Nick said in a pained voice. 'The photo on the box was white, Elodie, I swear.'

Elodie shook her head slowly. 'Jesus, Nicky.'

'I know, I know.'

'We can't let the kiddywinks see you looking like that. I mean, whoever heard of a platinum blond Santa?' She let out an involuntary snort. 'Sorry. I know I shouldn't laugh. It's just, you look like you're in a Nineties boy band.'

He glared at her. 'It's not funny, El. I'm supposed to make my debut as Santa in twenty-five minutes. No one's going to buy me as the real deal looking like this.'

Elodie looked more closely at his beard. 'You know, it's actually got a purple tint to it.'

'Elodie!'

'All right, all right, I'm thinking.' She pondered for a moment. 'Come round the back way, into the kitchen,' she said at last. 'Pops is in there. Maybe he'll have a brainwave.'

'Right.'

He followed her behind the shop.

'Zac Efron!' Elodie said suddenly. 'That's who you remind me of; after he went blond.' She glanced down at Nick's now sizeable gut, courtesy of the loaned pregnancy belly. 'I mean, if he'd let himself go a bit.'

'I can't believe you're laughing. I thought you'd be wailing and cursing the gods when you saw me in this state.'

'I'm sorry, I can't help it. You just look so... cute.'

'Cute?'

'Yeah. With your little purple-blond beard and your look of earnest dismay.' She forced herself into businesslike mode. 'But you're right, we need to sort it. Let's see what Pops has got to suggest.'

In the kitchen, Pops had the Brasso out and was giving the ribbon-cutting scissors a polish. He looked up when they came in.

'What happened... to you?' he asked Nick.

'Dye malfunction,' Nick said, grimacing.

'What can we do, Pops?' Elodie asked. 'It's too late to sort out another dye job.'

Pops looked thoughtful. 'Take the hat off,' he said to Nick.

Nick did so, and Elodie tried not to burst into laughter again at the sight of his matching locks: bleached blond with the lilac tint. She didn't know what was wrong with her. She ought to be panicking, but instead she just felt oddly light-headed and giggly. Maybe it was the fumes from Nick's hair.

'What did you do when you started playing Santa?' Nick asked Pops. 'You were only in your thirties, weren't you?'

'Wig and false beard. Not ideal if you get a doubter who fancies giving it a tug, but… kids weren't so cynical in those days.'

'That'd do until I can get to a barber. Have you still got them?'

Pops shook his head. 'Been a while since I needed them,' he said, giving his bushy beard a proud stroke.

'What about rubbing in a bit of flour?' Elodie suggested. 'I could run to the corner shop for some.'

Pops thought it over.

'I've got a better idea,' he said. 'Ellie, go get… some of those hair chalks.'

'Oooh, yes, that's an idea,' Nick said, brightening. 'I forgot hair chalks were a thing. Hey, do you guys sell face paints too?'

Elodie nodded. 'I'll fetch you some.'

She ran out into the shop to grab the bits they needed.

'Here you go,' she said, dumping them on the worktop. 'We need to hurry though, Santas. There's only twenty minutes left.'

'Right.' Nick slid her the hair chalks. 'You do it. Hair first, then beard.'

He sat down on a chair and Elodie stood behind him. She selected a grey chalk and got to work.

Pops smiled. 'This reminds me of when… your nana and me got you that Girl's World for your birthday, with the hair you could style. You did all sorts of… weird and wonderful things to it, Ellie.'

Elodie laughed. 'And then not satisfied with using my skills on the doll, I got to work on you and Nana. I think you were the only Santa who went to work with braids in his beard.'

Nick groaned. 'Please don't braid me.'

'Don't worry. I've come a long way since then.'

When Elodie had finished rubbing chalk into Nick's hair and beard, she stood back to admire the effect.

'That's really not bad. I think the two-tone effect actually makes it look more natural.'

'Here.' Pops passed Nick the chrome kettle to take a look at himself.

'Heh. If Santa had highlights,' Nick said, smiling at his reflection. 'I still look a bit young though. How long now, El?'

She looked at her watch. 'Nine minutes.'

'Right. I'll have to make this quick.' He grabbed the face paints. 'I've got a mate who's a makeup artist. She creates online tutorials for stuff like ageing effects. I've just got time to skim through one and age myself up.'

With less than two minutes until the big opening, Nick was finally ready. He picked up the sack of presents Elodie had fetched for him and slung it over one shoulder.

'Well, how do I look?'

Pops nodded. 'Impressive.'

'Nice job with the crow's feet,' Elodie said. 'How do you feel?'

'A bit sick. I think the nerves just kicked in.'

'You'll be grand,' Pops said, slapping him on the back. 'Go on, give us… a ho ho ho.'

Nick rested his hands on the fake belly. 'Ho ho ho!' he roared, jiggling his belly in time.

Pops gave him a thumbs-up. 'Perfect.'

'I don't know, Jim. I can't help thinking about that Santa at the department store. When Callum came in last night he said—'

'Oh, sod Callum,' Elodie said, scowling. 'He only came to put you off your game. Don't let him get to you.'

'I know. You're right.' Nick paused, his eyes fixed on the door. 'I hope I can win for you though, guys.'

'If you can't, no one can,' Pops said firmly. 'Now it's time to graduate from apprentice… to fully fledged Santa. Get out there and knock 'em dead.'

Nick's heart thumped violently against his chest as he strode out into the shop. The plan was that he would 'arrive' as Santa direct from the North Pole, ho-ho-hoing and chucking sweets to the kids. Then he'd go into the grotto with Summer the elf, Jim would give a speech about the shop's glorious history, cut the ribbon and they'd officially open for business.

Nick looked behind him at Elodie, who smiled reassuringly.

He didn't know why he was so nervous. He'd played to packed theatres several times and rarely experienced full-on stage fright. He didn't even have any lines to remember, other than 'ho ho ho'. But in his head Nick could see the perfectly upholstered figure of Callum Ashley, handsome and successful and everything else Nick wasn't, laughing at him and pleading with Elodie to cancel a bet she had no hope of winning.

Somehow, Nick made it through the crowd without mishaps. The kids were thrilled to see him, cheering and waving as he threw sweets. His ho-ho-hos, while definitely not his best work, still earned an approving nod from Jim. Nevertheless, Nick could feel himself trembling. He was grateful when he was safe in his grotto and had a brief hiatus for Jim to give his speech before the kids started coming in.

'That was great,' Summer said. 'Well done.'

He sank on to his gold-painted Santa throne. 'God, I was shaking like a leaf. I hope the kids didn't notice.'

'All they noticed were free sweets. They loved you, Nick. You've got this.'

He glanced around the storeroom-slash-grotto, lit only by strings of fairy lights. 'At least the lighting's low. Hopefully they won't notice the face paint and hair chalk.'

The side door opened and Elodie appeared. 'All ready, Santa?'

'Dunno. Yes. No. Maybe.'

She examined his face, which Nick suspected was slightly ashen under the face paint rouging his cheeks.

'Summer, can you man the till?' she asked. 'I'll take elf duty for the first hour.'

'I don't mind. I love being the elf.'

'You can do the rest of the day. I just want to be here for the first few kids.'

'All right, if you like.' Summer left them alone.

'Coming to keep an eye on me, boss?' Nick asked Elodie.

'You just look like you could do with some moral support. From a friend, I mean.'

'A friend. Yeah.' He fell silent. 'You're right. Thanks, Elodie.'

She went to rest a hand on his shoulder. 'Relax and try to enjoy yourself. This is your dream role, remember?'

'But what if I can't do it? What if the guy at Ashley's—'

'Never mind the guy at Ashley's. At Martin's we do it our way.' She pressed his shoulder. 'Just be yourself, Nick.'

He blinked. 'Myself?'

'Yeah. Kind, warm, jolly, cuddly. Be exactly who you already are and every kid'll leave here today knowing they've met the real thing.'

Nick smiled. 'Didn't you once tell me I was like the anti-Santa?'

'That was when I thought a beard and a big belly were all you needed to make a Father Christmas. I know better now,' Elodie said. 'Physically you might need a bit of help, but when it comes to the true essence of Christmas, Nicky, there's no one more genuinely Santa Claus than you.'

He looked up at her. 'You know, El, that might be the nicest thing anyone's ever said to me.'

'Well, it's true.' There was a knock at the door – Jim, letting them know the opening ceremony was over and the first visitors were ready to be let in. 'Here we go. Believe in yourself, Nick Winter.'

'Believe in myself. Believe in Santa.' He took a deep breath. 'Bring it on then.'

16

Elodie ushered in their first visitors: a mum with a little girl of about five clinging to her. The child had a piece of paper gripped in her free hand.

Be yourself. OK. Nick summoned his warmest smile for the kid.

'Now then, who do we have here?' he said in the deep, slightly gravelly jolly-old-man voice he'd been working on, trying to stop it from trembling. The little girl stared, then looked mutely up at her mum.

Great. Trust him to get a non-verbal for his very first one.

'This is Annalise, Father Christmas,' the mum told him. She was a no-nonsense-looking individual who stared him straight in the eyes in a way Nick found quite disconcerting.

'Of course it is. I'm sorry, Annalise. You've grown so much since last Christmas, I hardly recognised you,' Nick said, borrowing a bit of spiel from the Ashley's Santa.

He waited for the child or her mum to say something, but they both remained silent.

'Um.' He looked helplessly at Elodie.

'Do you want to tell Santa Claus what you'd like for Christmas, sweetie?' Elodie asked the little girl.

'We don't say Santa Claus,' the scary mum told her with

a censorious look. 'Santa Claus is a vulgar Americanism. Father Christmas is the proper name.'

'Actually the two were originally separate—' Nick began, then stopped himself. This wasn't the time for trivia.

'Annalise would like the Belle dress from *Beauty and the Beast*,' Annalise's mum told him. 'Wouldn't you, my love?'

Annalise shook her head.

Her mum dropped to a crouching position. 'Annalise, we talked about this.'

'Don't want it,' Annalise whispered. 'Want a robot.'

'Little girls don't play with robots. Wouldn't you rather play princesses with your friends?'

'My friends don't play princesses.' Annalise turned helplessly to Nick. 'Want a robot. Please.'

Nick smiled. 'I'm sure I can get my elves to make you a robot. Do you want to come here and tell me what sort?'

Annalise hung back, torn between fear and her desire for the robot. Nick cast around for a way to help her feel at ease, trying to remember his training.

He scanned the girl's outfit for clues, and a familiar cartoon figure on her jacket caught his eye.

Aha! Yes. This was where the mind-reading act came in.

'Annalise...' he said slowly, as if trying to place the name. 'Ah, of course, now I remember: you're the Annalise who likes *Bluey*, aren't you?'

Annalise's face lit up. 'I love *Bluey*!'

'I love it too.'

'Really?'

'Really.'

Annalise looked excitedly up at her mum. 'Mummy! Father Christmas likes *Bluey* too!'

'Mmm,' said the mum, her lips pursed. 'You really ought to have grown out of that cartoon by now, Annalise. It's for pre-schoolers.'

'Oh, you're never too old for *Bluey*,' Nick said cheerfully. 'I'm 1,752 years old and it's my favourite cartoon. What's your best episode, Annalise?'

Annalise pondered. 'I think maybe... where Bluey and Bingo play hotels?'

'That's one of my favourites too,' Nick said, awash with relief he'd managed to get the little girl to speak to him directly so he didn't have to talk to the stern mum. 'I like it when Dad lies on Bingo and says, "Hey, this is a crazy pillow!"'

Annalise giggled. 'Oh yeah! I forgot crazy pillow.'

She hesitated a moment, then went to sit in the little chair beside Nick's throne. He beamed at her. Thank God for *Bluey*!

'Now do you want to tell me about this robot you want?'

'Want one that dances,' she said. 'Like my friend Jake got for his birthday. And if you play with it, it learns the game and it learns talking.'

'That sounds like a fun toy.'

She nodded enthusiastically. 'Yeh, and its eyes glow and it can do different dances and it's got its own app.'

Annalise's mum was glaring at him, a look that said he'd better tell Annalise she was getting the princess dress her mum seemed to think was a more appropriate present for her gender. Nick ignored her.

'Well, since I know you've been very good this year, I'm certain you'll find it under the tree.' Nick nodded to the piece of paper in Annalise's hand. 'What's that you're holding?'

Annalise held it out shyly.

'It's a present,' she said. 'I drew it for you.'

Nick unfolded it and smiled at the drawing in coloured pencil. A red ball with stick arms and legs – not a bad portrayal of his current physique with the heavy pregnancy belly on – was standing on top of a roof next to a chimney. Through a window, a stick figure with long hair – Annalise, presumably – was lying on a bed. Just to make sure he knew she was playing by the rules, the word 'ASLEP' had been scrawled next to her.

Nick was touched. Annalise really believed in him, didn't she? He felt a warm glow of pride at the thought.

'Well, that's… thank you,' Nick said softly. 'I don't think anyone's ever given me such a nice present before.'

'Will you keep it forever?'

'I certainly will. I'm going to put it on the wall in my workshop, where the elves can look at it while they make toys. I think they'd like that, don't you?'

Annalise nodded vigorously, her eyes sparkling.

'And will they look at it while they make my robot?'

'Of course.' His hand hovered over the three sacks before selecting a gift from the yellow one, which was for puzzle toys. Annalise the robot fan seemed like a child interested in how things worked. 'And this is to play with until I visit on Christmas Eve with your proper presents. Stay good, Annalise.'

'I will. And I'm going to bring you a drawing of Bluey next year, Father Christmas. Bingo too.'

Nick smiled. 'I'd like that very much.'

Annalise beamed as she skipped back to her mum.

'Mummy, look!' she said, holding up her gift. 'This is for now and the elves are going to make my robot for Christmas, Father Christmas says.'

Her mum forced a smile. 'That's very kind of him. Now go outside – Daddy's waiting by the door with Noah. I just want to have a little word with Father Christmas about your present.'

Annalise nodded happily and disappeared.

'You're new, aren't you?' Annalise's mum asked Nick, narrowing her eyes.

'It's my first time manning a grotto, yes.'

'Well it seems you've got a lot to learn. Why on earth did you tell my daughter she could have a robot?'

Nick shrugged. 'Because she's on the Nice List and it was what she asked me for. That's my job.'

The woman stared at him, then turned to Elodie. 'Is he all right? He sounds like he really thinks he's Father Christmas.'

'He's a stage actor. Big fan of the Stanislavski Method,' Elodie said. 'Look, I'm sorry. You're right, we shouldn't promise gifts parents might not be able to give. But your little girl did seem to have her heart set on the robot, and, well, why shouldn't she get it? I know the model she's talking about. We've got plenty in stock, and they're no more expensive than the dress you wanted for her.'

'It's not for you to decide what's an appropriate gift and what isn't,' the woman said stiffly. 'Besides, we've already bought her present.'

'eBay it,' Nick said. 'You'll probably get more than you paid for it, this close to Christmas. Everyone's a winner.'

Annalise's mum flashed him a look of dislike. 'Robots aren't presents for little girls.'

'Oh, rubbish. They're presents for people who like robots. I may be nearly two thousand years old, but even I'm not trapped that far in the past.'

'I'll be making a complaint to the owner about this.'

Elodie smiled tightly. 'That would be me. Complaint duly noted.'

Annalise's mum glared at her then stormed out.

'Sorry about that,' Nick said, grimacing.

Elodie shook her head. 'Not a great start, Nick.'

'The kid believed in me, didn't she?'

'Yeah, and the mum made a complaint about you that she's probably now sharing with some of the other parents, who may well decide to go to Ashley's instead. You can't do stuff like that just because the parents piss you off.'

'I know, I know,' Nick said, closing his eyes. 'I hate all that gendered toy rubbish, that's all. Why shouldn't the kid get what she asked for instead of something she's got no interest in? It's not like she wanted a pony.'

'I agree, but it's not our place to question what the parents have decided to get them.'

'Isn't it? I'm Santa. Deciding what to give kids for Christmas is my whole thing.'

'There are rules, Nick. You're not actually a magical being with a workshop full of elves.'

'The kids believe I am. That's good enough for me.' He smiled at Annalise's picture. 'Look, El. She made me a present. How sweet is that?'

Elodie broke into a reluctant smile. 'OK, that was adorable. I'll show the next ones in. Try not to generate any more complaints, can you?'

The next child, a boy of seven or eight, certainly wasn't a victim of shyness. He hopped into the seat beside Nick before his parent had even got through the door.

'Hiya!' he said chummily. 'Remember me, Santa? It's Oliver Miller, from last year.'

'Oh, sure thing,' Nick said, grinning back. 'I couldn't forget you, could I, Oliver Miller?'

'Tell Santa what you want for Christmas, Oli,' said the lad's mum, who thankfully looked quite friendly.

'I told him already,' Oliver said. 'In my letter. Didn't you get it, Santa?'

'Of course. I get a lot of letters though. Now, remind me what it was you asked for – was it a Splattertron?'

Oliver's eyes went wide. 'Hey, you remembered! And you're, like, really old! My great-grandad says it's hard to remember things when you get old.'

Nick smiled. 'That's true, but I find it helps when you're as ancient as me to have a little magic to help you along.'

'How many letters do you get?'

'Oh, millions. Billions. I get letters from children all over the world.'

'How many though?'

'Er... 12.8 billion,' Nick fabricated wildly.

'Whoa! Does the postman bring them all?'

'That's right. But not at the same time because they'd be really, really heavy.'

Oliver giggled. 'Is it the same postman who comes to my house?'

'No, there's a special service to get the letters to the North Pole. It's called the Santa Express.'

'Do you have to open them all by yourself?'

'No, Mrs Claus and the elves help me.'

'Do children send them from other planets? Like, alien children? Or do they have their own Santas?'

Nick felt a bit out of his depth with that one. He was grateful when Oliver's mum interrupted the cross-examination.

'That's enough questions for now, Oli.' She smiled warmly at Nick. 'I'm sorry for the barrage, Santa. He's a big fan of yours.'

Her eyes skimmed Nick's face, with its artificially silvered beard and face-painted wrinkles. He wondered if she was trying to work out his real age. It had to be a good sign that Oliver didn't realise there was anything different from when he'd visited Jim the year before.

'Well, thank you, Oliver,' Nick said. 'I've always been a big fan of yours too. And I do appreciate the treats you're kind enough to leave out for me and the reindeer.'

'I left them chocolate biscuits last year,' Oliver informed him. 'Mum said it should be carrots but I thought they probably got bored of having the same stuff.'

'They enjoyed them very much. They like carrots but chocolate biscuits are lovely as a treat.'

Nick was getting quite into the role now. It was ages since he'd had the opportunity for a bit of improv, and the kids were brilliant. He loved how real it was to them; that look of awe and wonder in their eyes. It brought back to him all the magic of believing when he'd been a boy himself.

He reached into the green sack for a superhero toy. That seemed a safe bet if Oliver was a fan of Splattertrons.

'Here you go, Oliver,' he said, handing it to him. 'Just a little something to keep you entertained until Christmas Day. I'm looking forward to bringing the girls to see you again.'

Oliver frowned. 'Girls? What girls are you bringing?'

'The reindeer, of course. Didn't you know they were all girls?'

'No.'

'Lots of people think they're boys because of their antlers, but they're thinking of ordinary deer, not reindeer.' Nick lowered his voice. 'I'll tell you a big secret, Oliver. The antlers are the clue, you see, because male reindeer lose their antlers in early December. But female reindeer, like my little gang, they keep them all year round. So now you know something not many people do.'

'Wow!' Oliver sounded like a piston spurting steam. He beamed at his mum, who beamed back.

'Don't you have something to ask Santa before we go?' she said.

Oliver nodded. 'Can I have your autograph please, Santa? My mum said you'd sign my book for me.'

His mum laughed. 'I did tell you he was a fan.'

'So I see,' Nick said. 'Certainly, Oliver, I'd be happy to.'

Oliver's mum handed over a picture book of "'Twas the Night Before Christmas" and a pen. Nick turned to the title page and scrawled in a flourishing hand *To Oliver. Stay good, and thanks for the chocolate biscuits! From Santa Claus and the reindeer x*.

When the boy and his mum had gone, he turned to Elodie. 'Bloody hell. I'm a celebrity.'

Elodie smiled. 'Don't let it go to your head. That was great though, Nick.'

'I can see why your grandad loved this job.' Nick shook his head. 'You know, I was so worried they'd spot me for a fraud straight off but… they really think I'm him. I'm half wondering if I am.'

'The makeup and hair chalk is pretty effective in this light.' Elodie looked at him with one eye narrowed. 'I don't think it'd matter even if you hadn't bothered though. Pops is right – it's all in the attitude.'

'Oliver didn't even spot there was anything different about Santa since he saw your grandad last year,' Nick said. 'I felt like I was really getting into my stride with that one.'

'And you managed to make good use of your limitless Christmas trivia.' Elodie smiled. 'That mum had taken a bit of a shine to you, you know. I could see her checking you out.'

Nick laughed. 'Come on. I'm wearing a pregnancy belly that's really stretching the definition of the term "dadbod", I'm covered in fake wrinkles and I'm dressed as Father Christmas. I wouldn't call this my peak sexiness.'

'You have got a certain silver fox thing going on though. Almost Kurtesque, I'd say.'

'Sweet-talker. All right, my little elvish minion, show the next one in.'

Nick waited fifteen minutes after the last child and parent left, then he decided it was probably safe to emerge. It was after six, which meant Elodie must have flipped the sign.

Elodie was leaning against the counter with Summer, their elf costumes rather rumpled after a busy day. She smiled when she saw him.

'Summer, put the Santa Triumphant music on,' she said. Her cousin used her phone to change the track on the shop's sound system.

Nick laughed as 'I Saw Mommy Kissing Santa Claus' blared from the wall-mounted speakers. 'This one?'

'What else? You've been a big hit with the Yummy Mummy brigade, Nick – and a few of the Delicious Daddies as well.'

'Well I hope you gave them my number.'

Elodie shook her head. 'I told them they'd have to write and tell you what they wanted like the other boys and girls. Better be prepared for some smut in your postbag.'

Nick took his Santa hat off and rubbed his hair. 'I don't think you should be allowed to tease me after a hard day's Santaing.'

'She's not teasing, it's true,' Summer told him. 'We've had parents whispering about Martin's hot new Santa all over the shop. They've nicknamed you Father Dimples.'

'Come on. Stop winding me up, you two.'

'I'm telling you, Nick, being old suits you,' Elodie said. 'That kid Oliver's mum told me I was a marketing genius for thinking up the idea. All these weeks I was worrying you weren't the right age and physique for a Santa when it turns out that was our USP the whole time.'

'Did any of the kids spot you were fake old?' Summer asked.

Nick shook his head. 'I got a couple of Santa sceptics, but none who seemed to notice I didn't look right for the part.' He sank tiredly into the swivel chair behind the counter. 'I think as long as the beard's the right colour, you've got the suit on and there's a visible tummy, they fill in the rest with imagination.'

'A bit like magic,' Summer said.

He smiled at her. 'Exactly like magic.'

Elodie patted her cousin on the back. 'You can go, Summer. We'll see you for your Thursday night shift.' The teen was working extra hours over the festive season to accommodate late-night shopping evenings.

'Who plays my elf when she's at college?' Nick asked when Summer had gone.

'We hire a temp. There's not much to the elf job really. It's just showing parents in and out.' Elodie rested a hand on his shoulder. 'How about that pint now? You've earned it.'

Nick rubbed his forehead. 'I can't, I've got a supermarket shift at seven. God knows what they'll make of the hair but I haven't got time to wash it. I'll barely have time to change and scrub out the wrinkles.'

Elodie eyed him with concern. 'How long a shift?'

'Till ten.'

'And you're back here for ten tomorrow morning. When will you find time to eat?'

He shrugged. 'I'll grab a sandwich in my break.'

'You need to look after yourself, Nick. You'll make yourself ill burning the candle at both ends.'

'I have to, don't I? I need to be earning.'

'You look tired though.' She squinted at him. 'Or is that the face paint?'

'Bit of both.' He stood up. 'I'd better go. See you tomorrow.'

'OK.'

Nick started to leave, then turned back. 'Elodie?'

'Yeah?'

'That speech you gave me this morning. About me being more Santa than Santa.'

'What about it?'

'You were never one hundred per cent sure of me, were you? You were just trying to gee me up.'

'I meant it. Every word.' She grimaced. 'But perhaps...

I did still need the tiniest bit of convincing. Not because I didn't believe in you,' she added hastily. 'But because… well, you seemed so nervous. And like you said, Pops is a tough act to follow.'

'Did I do it? Convince you?'

'You had me worried with the first one, I have to admit.' She smiled. 'But in the end you convinced me and then some. You were great, Nick. A worthy successor to my grandad.'

Nick smiled back. 'Thanks, El. Was I a bet-winning worthy successor though? I did my best, but that guy at Ashley's was bloody good.'

'There's no point worrying about that. You just try to enjoy yourself.' Elodie looked up from counting the day's takings. 'Did you enjoy yourself? Was your dream role everything you hoped it would be?'

Nick thought about the kids he'd seen that day; the delight in their faces as they'd experienced the thrill of true belief.

'Yes,' he said. 'It really was.'

17

Considering they spent most of the year preparing for it, the grotto season seemed to flash by with barely time to draw breath. Almost as soon as they'd opened, it seemed, Elodie blinked and it was the final day.

She'd been so focused on the grotto, in fact, that until Nick had reminded her she'd completely forgotten that today was Christmas Eve. Early closing was at two, and then… well, then they'd know. Callum would be straight on the phone, no doubt, desperate to rub Elodie's face in his success.

Not that she was assuming he'd won, but she knew he'd had a cracking season. His Santa, Kenny Ross, had proven a huge success. For once, parents and kids had flocked to the Ashley's grotto. Elodie liked to go to the café across the road occasionally and glare at them. Some might say it was pretty difficult to resent bright-eyed, smiling children at Christmas, but Elodie found she was able to manage it with surprisingly little effort.

And as for Martin's Santa… she glanced at the queue on the second floor.

It wasn't a bad little queue. Smaller, perhaps, than the Christmas Eve queues in Pops's day, but it was still pretty healthy. Apart from the odd wobble in his first few days, their new Santa had done great work for them. Whether it was enough to beat Callum Elodie couldn't be sure, but Nick had done his level best, which was all you could ask of the boy.

He'd loved it too – making the kids smile. The proud, happy expression on Nick's face when he'd finished work each day had been enough to warm the hardest of hearts. It had even managed to warm the flintish shard in Elodie's chest – something she would have said was impossible this time three months ago. She'd been surprised, when she'd examined the unfamiliar feeling swelling inside her, to find that she was proud of him.

It was a bit weird, wasn't it, to suddenly have a friend – a best friend, even – after spending a lifetime convincing yourself you didn't need anyone? But Nick Winter had plenty of weirdness for the both of them.

Although grotto takings were below what they'd usually expect, they'd gained in other ways. Nick's suggestion of placing merchandise displays around the rope cordon, where bored parents could grab items for their baskets, had worked like a charm. Not that the increased sales profits were any help when it came to beating Callum, since it was profit from grotto entry fees that formed the foundation of their bet, but it was a comfort.

'He's been a blessing, that boy, hasn't he?' Pops said beside her, as if reading her thoughts. He'd joined them for the last day, to bring the grotto luck.

'How did you know that's what I was thinking about?'

'I can read you… like a book, Elodie Martin.' He followed her gaze to the grotto. 'Now don't forget to ask him like we agreed.'

'You're sure it's OK with you? I know we like to keep it low-key, but…'

'Of course. It's a brilliant idea.'

Elodie looked at her watch. 'Half an hour to go. Cross everything, Pops.'

He shook his head. 'I do wish… you and Callum would call off this ridiculous bet. Martin's is better than this. You're better than this.'

'I'm not, you know. This is absolutely my level. If Callum wants to play with the big boys, he'd better be prepared to get burned.'

He gave her a stern look. 'Young lady, don't ever mix a metaphor like that in my shop again.'

She laughed. 'Whose shop?'

'I knew it was a mistake signing it over to you,' he said, shaking his head. 'And what happens… when we lose half our grotto profits?'

'With the increase in sales, we can just about bear the loss. Not that that'll happen,' Elodie added quickly, worried she might be tempting fate. She glanced at the queue again. 'I think I'll go do some elving when it gets to the last one. See it off, sort of thing.'

When Elodie saw Summer appear at the grotto door to show in the last visitors, she headed upstairs and snuck inside.

'…and a Splattertron and a Barbie and a unicorn bracelet kit and more unicorn stuff and a 3D paint puzzle,' the child in the chair was saying while her little sister lurked shyly at her side.

'Wow. All that, eh?' Nick said.

'I've been really good though.' The little girl looked at her parent for validation. 'Haven't I, Daddy?'

The father laughed. 'I'm not sure anyone's been good enough for that long list, Lil. But I'm sure Santa Claus will have some lovely presents for you, won't you, Santa?'

'Of course. I've got them all wrapped up ready.' Nick turned to the smaller child, who couldn't have been more than five. 'What about you, sweetie?' he asked gently. 'What can I bring you on Christmas Day?'

The little girl whispered something to her sister.

'Carly says she likes dinosaur stuff,' the older child, Lily, told him. 'I think unicorns are better though.'

'Well, that's part of the fun of being human, that we all like different things.' Nick smiled at the shy younger sister. 'I've always thought dinosaurs were pretty cool too. Here's some presents to play with until I bring your real ones tonight. Don't forget to leave a mince pie out for me.'

Lily pulled a face. 'Yuck. I hate mince pies.' She glanced at her sister. 'I suppose coz we're all different and like different stuff. But that's OK.'

Nick selected a princess toy for unicorn-loving Lily, and a puzzle for dinosaur-mad Carly. The children dutifully thanked him, although Carly's thanks came via a whisper to her sister.

'All right, girls, come on,' their dad said. 'It'll be time for Christmas Eve boxes and new PJs when Mummy's home from work.'

'Yay!' Lily hopped down from her chair. 'Bye, Santa. Don't forget to come tonight.'

Nick smiled. 'You're at the top of my list, Lily.'

Carly started following her sister, then hesitated. Suddenly she ran back to throw her arms around Nick.

'Bye Santa,' she whispered, before running off again.

'Wow.' Nick looked a bit windswept as he turned to Summer and Elodie. 'Hey, did you see that? She hugged me.'

Summer smiled. 'That was cute.'

'And you taught the older one a bit of philosophy with your "it's OK that we're all different" speech,' Elodie said.

'Is that it then?'

Elodie nodded. 'Yes, we're all done. You can officially come out and start enjoying your Christmas.'

They headed downstairs. Pops had just ushered out Lily and Carly and was flipping the shop sign.

'I think this job is making me broody,' Nick told Elodie as they descended. 'Kids are pretty amazing, aren't they?'

She shrugged. 'They have their moments. But don't forget you only see them when they're trying their best to convince you how good they are.'

'Come on, I know you like them. I was surprised at how sweet you are to them, given your professed dislike of humankind.'

'That only applies to adults. Kids don't count.'

'Do you want a family of your own?'

'Never really thought about it,' Elodie said vaguely. 'Maybe.'

When they reached the counter, Nick sank into the swivel chair.

'So now we've finished work it's really Christmas,' Summer said.

'You elves might've finished your work,' Nick said. 'Some of us have got to hitch up the sleigh and deliver all those presents by morning.'

Elodie shook her head. 'You're never breaking character again, are you?'

Nick took off his hat. 'I will if it means I can get some rest. It's exhausting, being Santa.'

Summer laughed. 'You're not seriously telling me you're too tired for Christmas, Nick?'

He smiled. 'You're right, I'll soon get my second wind. Enough to squeeze in a quick wassail after my shift, at least.'

'You're not working… at the supermarket today, surely?' Jim said.

'Too right I am. I get time and a half, not to mention as many slightly wilted sprouts as I can carry. Don't worry though, we shut at six.'

'What is a wassail anyway?' Summer asked.

Elodie shook her head. 'You had to ask. You're going to get a ten-minute lecture on the history of the Christmas wassail now.'

Nick smiled. 'I'll spare you the full TED talk. Wassailing is boozy carolling, basically. "Wassail" was a hot mulled cider offered to householders by carol singers.'

'Is there anything you don't know about Christmas?' Summer asked.

Nick looked smug. 'Nope.'

Pops came forward to shake his former apprentice's hand. 'I've been hanging around to say… well done, lad. Made me proud to see you in action this year.'

Elodie was sure Nick genuinely blushed under his painted cheeks.

'Thanks, Jim,' he said. 'That means a lot coming from you.'

Pops raised his eyebrows at Elodie, who took the hint.

'Um, Nick, I was wondering… if you fancied coming over tomorrow,' she said, feeling embarrassed.

He frowned. 'Elodie, tomorrow's Christmas. I know it's not top of your priorities, but you surely didn't forget that.'

'That's what I mean. Me and Pops wanted to invite you for Christmas dinner. You said your mum's got plans, and it seems a shame for you to be on your own when we'd love to have you spend the afternoon with us.'

Nick seemed rather touched.

'I thought you had a special family tradition. Remembering the people you've lost and everything.' He grew suddenly awkward, dropping eye contact. 'Sorry, I shouldn't have mentioned that. I just mean, I wouldn't want to intrude.'

'You wouldn't be intruding at all. Pops and me agreed we'd love you to be there.'

Pops nodded. 'You work for Martin's now, Nick. That makes you… one of the family.'

Nick looked moved. 'Does it?'

'If you'd like to be,' Elodie said, meeting his eye.

'That's, um… wow. I mean, I'd love to join you if you really mean it. Thank you.'

The phone on the counter rang, making them all jump.

'If that's not Callum Ashley ringing me to gloat, I'll run naked round the shop singing "Grandma Got Run Over by a Reindeer",' Elodie announced.

Nick nudged Summer. 'Do you ever think your cousin might have a gambling problem? Seems to me she's addicted to making ridiculous bets.'

'All right, quiet, you lot,' Elodie said. 'The sooner I get this over with, the sooner I can get this over with. God, I'll lose the will to live if he's won.' She answered the phone. 'Hi, Callum.'

'How did you know it was me?'

'I'm only surprised you waited this long. Come on then, what are the scores on the doors?'

'I actually rang to offer you a last chance to call the whole thing off,' Callum said. 'Honestly, Elodie, there'd be no hard feelings. It was a stupid, childish, heat-of-the-moment thing. We should both know better.'

She glanced at Pops, who was watching her with that same disapproving expression he'd had on his face earlier when he, too, had told her she ought to know better.

'Why would I do that?' she demanded stubbornly. 'We've had a great year.'

'I believe you. And I'm sorry I was rude to whatsisname—'

'His name is Nick, as you know perfectly well.'

'OK, Nick then,' Callum said, his voice infuriatingly gentle. 'It's not about how good a year either of us have had. It's about doing what's right.'

She snorted. 'Is this Callum Ashley, expecting me to believe he suddenly cares about what's right?'

'Elodie, come on. You know I'm talking sense.'

Elodie hesitated.

She had been feeling increasingly guilty about the bet. Callum was right about one thing: it had been childish, made when she'd been so pissed off about the way he'd seemed to rejoice in her grandad's poor health. God knew they couldn't really afford to lose the money if Callum's grotto was triumphant, even with the increased Christmas sales.

But Elodie knew Callum would never offer to get her out of a hole unless he wanted something in exchange. This was probably part of a longer-term plot to get Elodie working for him in his soulless toy department. At the very least, he'd never let her hear the end of it if she backed out now.

'Not a chance,' she told him flatly. 'When I make a decision, Callum, I stick to it.'

He sighed. 'I knew you were going to say that. You were always stubborn to the point of ignoring your own best interests.'

'Yes, it's one of my more endearing qualities,' she said, smiling tightly. 'Come on, how much did you make?'

'You first.'

'All right.' Elodie flicked to the figure in her accounts book, although she knew it by heart. 'After all deductions... £9762.28.'

'Nine grand?'

Elodie bristled at something in his tone that might've been pity. 'Ten, if we're rounding to the nearest thousand. OK, it's a bit less than usual, but we made up for it in other ways. You want me to email you evidence so you know that's the true figure?'

'That won't be necessary. I trust your word.'

'Well?'

'Well... you win,' Callum said quietly.

Elodie frowned. 'What?'

'Ashley's grotto took a little over eight grand. I don't even need to adjust for the fact we were open a week longer. You win, Elodie.'

Elodie let this sink in. After everything they'd gone through, it felt weirdly anti-climactic that Callum should accept his defeat so calmly.

'So... you didn't have a good year?' she said.

'We had an excellent year. But the agency fees for Kenny

took a chunk of the takings – I suppose your friend Nick is rather cheaper. Hang on, let me pull up the actual figures.' There was silence while Callum opened his accounts. '£8409.12. I'll deduct ten per cent from that for the charity we support and send a cheque for half of the remainder from my private funds. I don't suppose you object to the charity getting their share, do you?'

'Um, no,' Elodie mumbled, feeling light-headed. 'Thanks, I guess.'

'I'd like to say it was my pleasure, but that would feel a little disingenuous. So in the spirit of sportsmanship, I'll just say well done. I suppose the best man won in the end.'

Elodie glanced at Nick. 'I suppose he did.'

She wasn't sure why she felt bad – an uncharacteristic attack of Christmas spirit, perhaps. Callum could easily afford his gambling debt, and he didn't exactly sound devastated. Still, Elodie couldn't help feeling guilty for taking his money. The bet had never been about that. She'd wanted to teach him a lesson, that was all – that money couldn't buy him everything he wanted.

'No hard feelings then, Callum?' she found herself saying.

'None at all. Still, let's not make a habit of it. Have a happy Christmas, El.'

'Thanks. Um, you too.'

'Remember me to your grandfather.' He hung up.

Elodie replaced the receiver and stared, unseeing, at Nick in his red suit.

'Well?' he asked. 'What happened? Did we win?'

'Yeah,' she said quietly.

Summer blinked. 'No way! Seriously?'

'Yeah. Callum's sending us a cheque for four grand. His

grotto took over a thousand less than ours.' She finally broke into a smile as her brain caught up. 'Bloody hell. We won, you guys.'

'Arghhh!' Nick came forward to hug her. 'That's amazing!'

'And now, Elodie, I hope you'll leave it at that,' Pops said firmly. 'This store-wars nonsense with Callum… has gone far enough.'

Elodie laughed. 'You know, I actually felt sorry for him. Losing must be a new experience for the great Callum Ashley.'

'It's a Christmas miracle,' Nick said, smiling. 'Tell you what, let's go to the pub and celebrate properly. I've got time for a quick one before I need to be at my other job.'

Callum looked up as a knock sounded at his office door. Mike strolled in, not bothering to wait for an invitation.

'Everything's closed and the staff have gone to the pub,' he announced. 'Me and you are invited too if you fancy it. I'd have told you sooner but I could see you were on the phone.'

'Mmm. Just rang an old friend to wish them a happy Christmas.'

Mike glanced at the spreadsheet open on his boss's laptop.

'Can't stop looking at it, eh?' he said with a smile. 'You know, when you told me to strip down the grotto I thought you'd gone off your noodle, but I'm not too proud to admit you were right. I don't know how you did it but you did it. Well done, boss.'

'It's Kenny who should get the credit,' Callum said, half on autopilot as he stared at the columns of figures.

'Twelve grand profit though,' Mike said in a satisfied voice. 'Best year we've ever had. Your dad'd be proud.'

'I'm not so sure,' Callum muttered.

'Eh?'

'Nothing.' Callum flipped the laptop closed. 'Sorry, Mike. What did you want to ask me?'

'Just wondered if you wanted to join the staff for a Christmas drink. I'm heading over now.'

'No, I won't. It's been a tiring few weeks.'

Mike laughed. 'Callum, it's half past two in the afternoon. It's Christmas Eve. Come and have a pint, you boring bugger.'

Callum smiled. 'I remember begging to go to bed at this time on Christmas Eve when I was a kid. My logic was that the sooner I was asleep, the sooner Father Christmas could come. Before I stopped believing, I mean.'

'I did the same. Happy days.' Mike slapped him on the back. 'Come on, come out for a few jars. It's Christmas. A time for peace and goodwill and friends and beer, and all that other bollocks.'

'I guess it is,' Callum said. 'OK, for once I'll let you twist my arm. Let's go.'

18

'Another yorkie?' Jim offered Nick the plate of Yorkshire puddings.

'I won't, thanks. I'm stuffed.'

'Pig in blanket?' Elodie asked.

'Honestly, Elodie, I couldn't eat another thing.' Nick paused. 'Well… one more.'

She speared one with the serving fork and put it on his plate. 'There's always room for one more pig in a blanket.'

'Help yourself to more sherry,' Jim said.

'Ah, the drink of the true Santa,' Nick said, refilling his glass. 'You have to feel sorry for the chap when he gets to America, don't you? I mean, with nothing stronger than milk and cookies to sustain him.'

'Keep eating like that and you'll be able to skip the pregnancy belly next year,' Elodie said, giving his tummy a pat.

'What can I say? Five weeks on grotto duty really works up an appetite.'

It had been a lovely afternoon. Nick had been hesitant about spending Christmas with Jim and Elodie despite their touching invitation, knowing it was a bittersweet time of year for them. But when he'd thought about eating his Christmas dinner off a tray, alone in that dismal little flat, Elodie's cosy cottage suddenly seemed very inviting indeed.

It had been the right thing to do. Elodie and Jim had welcomed him with open arms. Elodie, glowing with something that might actually be Christmas spirit (or a little too much sherry), had been all smiles and touchy-feelyness with him. He loved it when she smiled. It changed her round, care-filled little face into something different; something warm and young and joyous.

The meal had started with a toast to absent friends. Elodie and Jim had solemnly bowed their heads as they thought about the loved ones no longer here to celebrate, and Nick had joined in. It was a sober note to open Christmas dinner, but after that the meal had been full of warmth, laughter and some seriously groanworthy cracker jokes – his favourite kind.

'Christmas pud with brandy butter?' Jim asked Nick.

Nick laughed. 'Jim, I'll pop if I eat anything else. At least give me an hour to digest the twelve-person feast I've just shovelled into myself.'

'Let's do presents, if we're holding off on pudding,' Elodie said. Nick had learnt that the custom in the Martin house was to wait until after food to exchange gifts.

They went into the living room, leaving the washing up out of sight and out of mind for the moment, and Elodie sat on the floor by the tree to hand the gifts round.

'We don't do big presents,' she told Nick. 'Just the sort of little luxuries we don't tend to buy for ourselves.' She handed a gift to Jim. 'Pops, this is for you.'

Her grandfather took the long, tubular package and held

it under his nose, inhaling deeply. 'Ahh. I can guess what this is.'

'Same thing it is every year,' Elodie said, smiling.

He unwrapped it. Inside was a large Cuban cigar in a tin.

'I didn't know you smoked cigars, Jim,' Nick said.

'It's my Christmas treat. My missus... always used to evict me after dinner and... I took it to enjoy on my walk.'

Elodie opened her present from Jim, a bottle of perfume, before handing a parcel to Nick. 'From me, Pops and Summer.'

He blinked at the oblong package. 'You didn't have to get me anything.'

'Don't be daft. You have to have a present if you're joining in our Christmas.'

Inside the wrapping was a book: a handsome hardback edition of *A Christmas Carol*.

Nick ran his hands over the gold foil lettering. 'This is... gorgeous. Thanks, you two.'

'Elodie picked it – I can't take any credit,' Jim said. 'I just... signed my name on the bookplate.'

Nick opened the book. Elodie, Jim and Summer had all signed it, with the date and a dedication that read: *To Nick, our very own Ghost of Christmas Present and the best Santa's apprentice we could have hoped for.*

He smiled, feeling strangely moved – almost tearful, in fact – at the simple token of his new friends' affection.

'Thank you,' he said quietly. 'I'll treasure it.'

'All right, lad, don't get soppy on us,' Jim said with a grin. He got to his feet. 'And now... I'm going to leave you young folk to enjoy yourselves while I go out for a stroll with my Christmas present.'

'A stroll to the pub, by any chance?' Elodie asked, raising an eyebrow.

'There may be a hostelry… in my near future. I certainly can't rule it out.' He patted Nick on the back and headed for the door.

'There's a gang of old reprobates who slink off to the local after every Christmas dinner,' Elodie told Nick. 'They've probably already got him a pint in.'

'Let me do the washing up. Least I can do after you cooked me dinner.'

Elodie shook her head. 'You're the guest. Anyway, it won't take long to get it in the dishwasher.'

Nick didn't reply. His attention had been caught by the movement of Elodie's fair hair as she shook her head, flowing from under the paper crown she was wearing slightly askew. It seemed to glow under the fairy lights that adorned her little Christmas tree, almost like the angel that sat on the very top branch. He watched the light shift over the surface, fascinated.

'What are you smiling at?' Elodie asked.

Nick pulled himself together. 'Was I smiling?'

'You were. You've got a distinctly sherry-fuelled daft grin on your face.'

'I suppose I was just feeling a bit smug. You know, that I was right all along.'

'Right about what?'

'You. I knew you loved Christmas just as much as I did in your secret, secret heart.'

She laughed. 'Nick, no one loves Christmas as much as you do.'

'You do. I know you do. Don't you?'

Elodie flicked at a bauble on the Christmas tree. 'Perhaps I don't hate it as much as I like people to think.'

'Why do you like people to think that?'

'Well, it's a bit… wet, isn't it? Liking Christmas when you're a grown-up. I mean, it's not when you do it because you're that sort of person, all jolly and bouncy and weird, but I've got a reputation to uphold as a grumpy cow.'

'Why uphold it when it's not the real you? It's much more fun being jolly and weird.'

She shrugged. 'Because it keeps people away. Best place for them, I always think.'

'You don't mean that.'

'I used to do. I used to mean it with all my heart, until you came along.' She gave the bauble another flick, watching it swing from side to side. 'It feels different this year, Nick,' she said in a dreamy voice. 'Christmas.'

'How come?'

'Well, you're here, aren't you? Infecting me with all that nauseating Christmas cheer.'

'You're welcome.'

She smiled. 'It has done me good. I was in serious danger of turning into the world's leading miserable bastard when you came along. Now I'm practically Buddy the sodding elf. I sicken myself daily, but it's good for me.'

'You just needed to see Christmas through my eyes.' Nick flushed as he reached into his pocket. 'I, um… I got you a little something too.'

Elodie blinked as he handed her the gift he'd bought her. 'You got me a present?'

'Well, yeah. It kind of goes with the season.'

She opened it and placed the little snow globe on her

palm. Inside was a jolly little family, sitting around the table eating their Christmas dinner: Mum, Dad and their three children. Elodie shook it, and watched as the snow cascaded over them.

'They'll catch their deaths,' she murmured.

'I thought, um... that it'd remind you what Christmas is all about.' Nick's eyes widened as he caught her expression and realised how the gift must look. 'God, no, not like that! I didn't mean I got it to remind you about your parents not being here.'

'What did you get it to remind me of?'

'Well, that Christmas is for being with loved ones – the family we choose as well as the one we're born with. Because...'

Nick swallowed. He'd actually practised this speech on the walk over, but it seemed to be getting away from him.

'...because, er, well, you said I was part of the family, and I wanted you to know that... that you don't need to worry about empty chairs at your Christmas table as long as you've got me. I'll always be here for you, Elodie, at Christmas and whenever you need a... a friend.'

Elodie smiled, her gaze fixing on the little family. 'Like the brother I never had, you mean?'

Nick winced. No, that wasn't what he'd meant at all! How had he managed to cock this up so badly?

'Yeah,' he said helplessly. 'If you like.'

'Thanks, Nick. I love it.' She stood up to give him a hug.

God, that hug. How could something be so wonderful, so warm, smell so good, and be so very, very far from what he wanted? It absolutely screamed 'just good friends'. He patted Elodie awkwardly on the back while she held him.

'You know, for a skinny lad you're incredibly cuddly,' Elodie murmured.

Cuddly, yuck. Well that just wrapped it up, didn't it? There was nothing less sexy than the friend you designated 'cuddly'.

Elodie released him and sat by the tree again. Nick watched as she shook her snow globe and the flakes cascaded over the little family, feeling a lump rise in his throat. It was absurd, really. He'd laugh at himself if it wasn't all so bloody depressing.

It had been the last thing on his mind when Nick had made the spur-of-the-moment decision to hide Elodie's recruitment card so he could claim the Santa job for himself: falling in love. And yet somehow, that was what had happened.

He was in love with Elodie Martin. And he knew – her hug had told him as clearly as if it was tattooed on her forehead – that this was one thing he could never, ever tell her.

In a big white house on the outskirts of town, Callum Ashley was spending Christmas Day alone.

He didn't have to spend his Christmas alone. His mum, who was wintering in Marbella with her latest toy boy, had been keen to see him as always. Numerous women of his acquaintance had offered to share their tables and beds with him. So the fact Callum was by himself in his huge, minimally furnished sitting room when he could be enjoying a home-cooked meal with some steamy sex for dessert was entirely his own fault.

He hadn't been in the mood for company after yesterday's staff drinks. Mike had assured him he'd be welcome at the pub, and he had been – to an extent. Sam had been pleased to see him, making room for him in a seat next to hers. There'd even been a toast, to him and to the store, with three cheers that had sounded hearty and sincere. But Callum noticed the way people edged out of his way, and the worried look in their eye if he tried to join their conversation. He made peoplc nervous. That was what happened when you were the boss. He'd come home wishing he hadn't bothered going.

Even people he didn't employ seemed nervous in his company. He noticed it in his dates, sometimes. He wasn't sure whether it was something about his wealth they found intimidating, or something about him personally. Most likely it was the former. Would Callum's life have been very different if he hadn't been born into privilege? Would he have had friends – family? A wife, perhaps, and a bevy of happy, cheeky children to give his life meaning?

Callum's great-grandfather had been a former mill worker who'd grown up in poverty. When he'd founded the family business, it was as a modest menswear shop with a tearoom in the back: Ashley's Gentlemen's Outfitters. For some reason, trousers and tea had proven a winning combination. Within ten years, Callum's great-grandparents were earning enough to move into larger premises, and eventually to build the current Ashley's building. The business had gone from strength to strength under the next generation, Callum's grandad Terry, so that when his son Nate had taken over he'd inherited both a booming business and a significant private fortune.

And that was Callum Ashley's big problem: he was neither one thing nor the other. His dad had been born into wealth, but he'd also been abnormally proud of his working-class heritage. He'd talked a lot about how the Ashleys were destined to be winners – destined by birth, by blood, and by an ambition forged through the memory of a time when they had nothing. Nate had spoilt his only son – any gift he wanted, money no object – but he'd also insisted he was educated at the local state schools, 'to keep his feet on the ground'. Perhaps if Callum had grown up among people in situations like his, he wouldn't have spent his life feeling like an alien. If he'd had a sibling even, or anyone in his life who understood. His dad had given him everything... while condemning him to live his life alone.

Callum laughed softly at himself. *Poor little rich boy*. Funny how the voice in his head sounded exactly like Elodie Martin.

He swallowed the rest of his expensive brandy and reached for the bottle. This would be his third large measure. A liquid Christmas dinner of £3000-a-bottle Cognac: how very apt. Wasn't that just his whole life in a single, miserable image?

'Well, cheers, Dad,' he said, toasting the photo of his parents on the bureau. 'Here's to making you proud, eh?' He gave a bitter laugh and swallowed half the liquid in one mouthful, burning his throat.

What was Elodie doing right now, he wondered? Was she with her grandad? Or with the Santa guy – Nick? The idea of it made him angry. Callum had seen the way Nick looked at her, all cow-eyed and smitten. And while Elodie didn't seem equally moony over Nick, there was no doubt she liked him – liked him a lot. If she liked Nick, and Nick more than liked her, surely it wouldn't be too long until deeper feelings developed.

She'd probably invite Callum to the wedding. And he'd have to go, because it looks bad if you don't go to the wedding of a business rival whose family has always had a close relationship with yours, and he wouldn't be allowed a single flicker of emotion when he watched Elodie promise herself to someone else.

Callum lifted the remainder of the Cognac, then paused with it halfway to his lips.

He remembered primary school: the loneliness of the place, the isolation. He remembered Elodie at school, this feisty little tomboy who even in Reception class had had a crowd of little worshippers. He remembered there was something… different. Special. Something that made Elodie Martin stand out like the only three-dimensional person in Callum's flat picture-book world. They'd been rivals from birth, but they were friends of a kind too, when they were too young to realise what a chasm there was between them. She'd laughed at him and teased him, then, and Callum had liked it. For a little while, they'd been friends.

Before her parents had died, Callum remembered Elodie as a tough, hardy child, always in some scrape, with rips in her clothes and dirt in her hair. Even in those days, though, Elodie had been softer than she'd wanted people to realise. One incident in particular Callum remembered, when they were six years old and a fledgling crow had been discovered in a corner of the playground. Elodie had guarded the little bird fiercely, protecting it from the noisy, clumsy children who wanted to prod and pet it.

Only the persuasion of their class teacher, who promised Elodie the baby bird's mother would come back for it once everyone had gone, could convince Elodie to leave her charge at the end of the school day. And Callum remembered how she'd sobbed uncontrollably when the poor thing had been discovered dead the next morning, cradling its little body in her hands. A boy had laughed at her tears. Callum had pushed him.

Above all, Callum remembered the day everything changed – the day Elodie came back to school after her parents were killed in that horrific road accident. Her round face, pale and stern. Her eyes red and puffy, and yet their owner determined, this time, not to let them leak in front of her peers. Everyone had stared and whispered, the little bastards that they were, and Elodie had held her head up proudly as if she didn't hear. Suddenly the child of eight had looked far more grown up than any of her classmates. It had seemed to stir something in him – made Callum long, for the first time, to make things better for someone other than himself. Then came the frustration and anger when he'd realised that all his dad's money couldn't fix this for her. That being rich couldn't prevent you from being thoroughly, utterly powerless.

Elodie had grown up to resent him. Callum had never taken it personally. She resented everyone. Grief could do that to you. But he'd wished… he didn't know. Something.

Callum's eyes drifted to the photo of his dad. 'The most important thing you can be in life, Cal, is a winner,' Callum could hear him saying.

Callum glanced around the sparsely furnished room, devoid of human touch. Devoid of people, apart from its one lonely inhabitant getting drunk on his overpriced Cognac. His bank account was bulging, his shop was booming, yet somehow, Callum had never felt less like a winner.

He'd always thought it was his need to win that had led him to investing more into the Winter Wonderland grotto every year. His dad, and his grandad before him, had striven to make it better and better in the face of Martin's continued dominance, but it was during Callum's reign that it had gone the full Hollywood. He'd told himself he was just living up to his dad's expectations – making his grotto, and himself, a winner. But as Callum drained the last of his third drink, his subconscious forced him to confront the fact that the yearly grotto wars had been little more than a pathetic attempt to claim Elodie Martin's attention for just a few short weeks every year.

On a sudden impulse, he flung his crystal brandy glass at the wall and watched it shatter.

Elodie *fucking* Martin! Who the hell did that woman think she was? She was no one. She was ordinary. She was barely even pretty, really, except when she smiled. And he was Callum Ashley, with millions of pounds at his disposal, who could have any woman he wanted apart from that one stubborn cow over at Martin's.

What had she done to him? She'd made him like this. She was the reason he was drinking alone on Christmas Day. She'd got under Callum's skin somehow, like the little witch she'd always been; even got him lying about losing the bet just to spare her pain. And now he'd faced up to the fact he cared, he couldn't shake it off. He was in love with her, wasn't he? Probably had been for years. Of all the beautiful, fascinating women he'd known in his life, he'd somehow managed to fall for ordinary Elodie Martin. It was all so palpably absurd.

The shock of finally letting himself admit his feelings made Callum laugh out loud for a moment: a brutal, harsh snort. Disorientated, he reached for the brandy bottle and looked around for his glass to fill it up. His blurry gaze fell on the shards by the wall, and he laughed again before taking a slug straight from the bottle.

Well, it was practically the new year. Not too early to make a resolution. If he was going to Elodie's wedding, it damn well wasn't going to be to watch her marry another man. He was an Ashley, and when he wanted something, he got it.

Callum stood and held up the Cognac bottle, wobbling slightly as he made his vow.

'All right, you little witch,' he muttered. 'I don't care what I have to do to make it happen, but, Elodie Martin, I swear that by this time next year you'll be as much in love with me as I am with you. Just you wait and see.'

19

Elodie let herself into Pops's bungalow with her spare key. 'Knock knock! I've brought your shopping, Pops.'

'I'm in the study,' he called out.

'All right. I'll just put this stuff away.'

Elodie went into the kitchen and unpacked her bags of groceries. The freezer was freshly stocked with labelled Tupperware tubs, which told her that her Aunty Helen, Summer's mum, must have been over recently.

The Martins were a small family these days. Nana was gone now, as were Great Uncle Geoff – Pops's older brother – and his wife. And her parents, of course. Left were Elodie and Pops, her dad's little sister Helen and her husband Dave, and their two grown-up children, Summer and twenty-year-old Caleb. Since Nana's death, Elodie and Aunty Helen shared care of Pops in a constant battle to get him to eat something that wasn't a sodium-packed microwave meal.

Elodie glanced at the labels on the frozen meals. Turkey curry, turkey stew, turkey goulash… it looked like Aunty Helen had made good use of her Christmas leftovers. Helen alternated hosting Christmas with her sister-in-law, and their ongoing battle for dinner table supremacy was even more epic than Elodie's grotto rivalry with Callum Ashley.

Her aunt always bought what she called a 'centrepiece turkey', about five times too big for the number of people she had to feed. Elodie had seen this Christmas's offering. It looked like its mother had mated with an emu.

When she'd put the shopping away, Elodie headed to the study to find out what Pops was up to. She discovered him frowning at his computer.

'Who're you writing to?' Elodie asked when she'd planted a kiss on his snowy hair.

'I'm not. I'm making notes… for my memoirs.'

'You're writing your memoirs?'

Pops nodded. 'I'm calling them *Miracle on Whitsun Avenue: Memories of a Toyshop Santa*. You know, sort of… a play on *Miracle on 34th Street*.'

'What's the miracle?'

'I haven't decided yet.'

'Have you got far?' Elodie asked, perching on the window ledge.

'No, I only started today. I've got the title and a few notes.'

'Will you publish them?'

He shook his head. 'These are for the family. I wanted you all to have something… to remind you of the old man when he's gone.'

'What's brought this on, Pops?'

Pops took off his glasses and rubbed his eyes. 'I've been feeling very old… Ellie, since this last Christmas. It felt like I needed something to fill the days.'

Elodie examined him with concern. His crinkled blue eyes, almost always either stern or sparkling with merriment, had a wistful look in them.

'Is everything OK?' she asked gently. 'You sound low.'

'Getting old will do that to you,' he said with a sigh. 'To be honest, it's... not the years or the ill health. It's not even remembering the people you've lost, although God knows... no man expects to bury his child in his lifetime. It's the feeling you've lost your purpose. That there's nothing left to do but tick along more and more slowly until... well, until you stop.'

'What was it? Your purpose?'

He shrugged. 'The grotto, I suppose... once I was done raising kiddies. I was dreading having to give it up, but then fate brought young Nicky to us. Training him gave me a new purpose – a reason to get up in the morning. Now it's over... I'm feeling a bit bereft.'

Elodie twirled a strand of hair around her finger. 'I know what you mean. I've never been one for the post-Christmas blues, but January seems so much greyer this year.'

Pops swivelled his chair to face her. 'You miss the boy.'

She nodded. 'I'd got used to seeing his face around the shop, bringing all that sickening positivity. Martin's isn't the same without Nick, is it?'

'Have you heard from him?'

'No. I tried to ring him to wish him a happy new year but there was no answer. I suppose he's working all hours at that bloody supermarket.' She sighed. 'I hope him and his mum are OK. It seems very unfair the way he struggles to get acting work.'

'He should get himself registered... with one of those agencies that rents out Santas,' Pops said. 'You know, like the one Callum uses.'

'He can't do that when he's booked with us for next Christmas. Anyway, that'd be no good to him until grotto season. It's the rest of the year he's got to worry about.'

'They don't just do Santas though. If he gets on their books... it'll put him in the way of other work.'

'I'm sure he's thought of that.'

'I suppose so,' Pops said. 'Well, happen it'll all come right in the end.' But Elodie could sense his heart wasn't in it.

'Let's cheer up,' she said, forcing a smile. 'Have you made any new year's resolutions? Aunty Helen's seems to be to offload a food mountain of turkey leftovers on to you, I noticed.'

'No. No resolutions.' Pops's gaze had fixed on the page of memoir notes. 'Just a new year's wish. I was waiting for you to come over so I could talk to you about it.'

'A wish? What is it?'

He turned to face her. 'I wish you'd make it up with Callum, Ellie. It's been gnawing at me... all Christmas, this business of bets and suchlike. His grandad was a good friend, and... I always kept on good terms with his dad Nate when he was alive. Seems a shame you two should have inherited all the rivalry of previous generations with none of the bonhomie.'

'Did you really enjoy it?' Elodie asked. 'The grotto wars with Terry?'

'Highlight of the year,' Pops said, smiling at the memory. 'Whoever's grotto had most visitors... had to buy the other a Christmas drink, and whoever's shop made the most in sales did the same. Well, it was always our grotto... that had most visitors and Terry's toy department that outsold us, so we were effectively buying our own pints. He was a good lad though, Terry Ashley. A lot of people are ruined by money... but not him. He'd give you the shirt off his back if he thought you needed it.'

'Shame his grandson didn't inherit the same generous nature.'

'You're too hard on him. For a boy who's been spoilt rotten since the day he was born, Callum's fetched up all right – or at any rate, he could've turned out worse. It can be lonely at the top, Ellie. What he really needs… is a friend who can see past his money.'

She laughed. 'What, and you think that should be me?'

Pops shrugged. 'I think… you could keep things on good terms, at least. You've known each other since you were in your prams; that has to count for something. And he's lost people too.'

'His dad,' Elodie murmured. 'He was back at work the next day, wasn't he? That was either very hard or very sad, I remember thinking.'

'I'd lean towards the latter.' Pops rested a hand on her arm. 'Well? Will you make the lad a peace offering, for the sake of an old man… who wants to see things settled for all his kith and kin before he has to go?'

'You're not going anywhere yet. Don't you dare.'

'None of us know what tomorrow will bring. So?'

Elodie sighed. 'It really means that much to you?'

'It does.'

'OK, then I suppose…' She grimaced. 'He'll be so smug about it though.'

'You won your ridiculous bet, didn't you? Just offer him a frank handshake… and let him know this year is a clean slate for Ashley's and Martin's. For me, Ellie.'

'Well… I suppose he was a good sport about losing the bet. I do feel a bit guilty about taking his money.'

'You'll do it then?'

She sighed. 'All right, for your sake. I'll give him a ring and wish him a happy new year. Make it clear there're no hard feelings.'

Pops shook his head. 'In person.'

'Ugh. Really?' Elodie said, pulling a face.

'It'll do you good. You need to work on your people skills.'

'OK, OK. I'll do it next week.'

'No time like the present, I always say.' Pops turned his chair back to the computer. 'Go on, off you go. I've got memories to set down, before I lose... what few marbles I've got left.'

Elodie walked through Chessory town centre, half-heartedly aiming for Ashley's Department Store. It was Sunday and she was nursing a secret hope it might be closed, but no such luck. Ashley's never seemed to close. The place was bustling, packed with January bargain-hunters.

She was heading for the escalator when she spotted a familiar face behind a huge white beard. It took her a minute to place him, then she realised – it was Kenny Ross, the superstar Santa who'd given her and Nick so many sleepless nights, doing some shopping in his civilian clothes. He was examining a shelf of perfume with a puzzled look on his ruddy face.

'Hi,' Elodie said. 'Mr Ross, isn't it? Sorry, you probably don't remember me. My friend and I brought his little cousin to see you—' She stopped, glancing about for any young believers. 'I mean, to see Santa, of course.'

Kenny laughed. 'Thankfully I'm not in uniform so I'm spared having to pretend I know your name and what you asked for, for Christmas. I hope your wee friend enjoyed her visit.'

'Yes, she was very impressed.' Elodie lowered her voice. 'Actually, I came over to apologise. I have to confess that it was partly a research trip. I own a toyshop on the outskirts of town and I was curious to see what we were up against. Sorry, I know that was a bit devious, but Charlie really did have fun.'

Kenny raised one bushy eyebrow. 'You're not from Martin's?'

'Yes, do you know us?'

'Know you? Jim Martin's a legend in this business. Every shop Santa knows his name.'

Elodie smiled proudly. 'Thank you. I'll tell him you said so.'

Kenny squinted at her through his glasses. 'And you must be his… daughter?'

'Granddaughter. Elodie Martin. Pops is retired now – health issues.'

'Well, tell him from me that he'll be sorely missed.'

'I will. Thanks.'

'I bet he misses it, does he?'

Elodie nodded. 'He enjoyed training our new Santa though. I think he's feeling a bit lost now the Christmas season's over. He's decided to write his memoirs.'

'I know how he feels,' Kenny said with a sympathetic nod. 'Now, young lady, perhaps you might like to make amends for visiting me under false pretences.' He gestured to the shelf of perfume. 'It's my wife's birthday next week and she tells me she wants something to make her smell like Jennifer Lopez. Well, how do I know how Jennifer Lopez smells? All women smell like flowers and fruit and things.'

Elodie laughed, relieved there were no hard feelings. 'Can't you use your Santa present-detecting powers?'

Kenny smiled. 'I'm afraid they only work at Christmas. Once January arrives, I'm on my own.'

Elodie picked out a bottle of Promise by Jennifer Lopez. 'This ought to do the trick.'

'Ahh. Excellent.' Kenny took the box and held it up to squint at it. 'Thank you, Miss Martin. You've been a great help.'

'My pleasure.' Elodie turned to go, then she thought about Nick. 'Mr Ross?'

'Kenny, please.'

'Kenny, I hope you don't mind me asking but what do you do for work the rest of the year? Do you get much from the theatrical agency?'

Kenny shrugged. 'I don't work much outside Christmas, to be honest. I've been rather typecast since I started working grottoes – the big man is the only role I was ever any good in. I'm semi-retired from acting now anyway, but I can't deny it would be nice to bring home some extra pocket money outside the winter months.'

Elodie wasn't sure what she'd been expecting. A solution, she supposed, to Nick's struggle to find stage work. But if anything, it sounded like playing Santa was a bit of a curse when it came to getting gigs outside the season.

'Yes,' she said vaguely. 'I imagine it's tough.'

'Ah well, that's show business, as they say. Only a mug goes into this game to get rich.' He nodded. 'Nice to run into you, dear.'

'You too. I hope your wife enjoys her birthday.'

Elodie made her way to the escalator, her brain whirring.

20

Callum was in his office, working through the correspondence Sam had left him to deal with. Or he was trying to work through it. The letters kept dancing in front of his eyes.

He'd woken up on Boxing Day next to a puddle of Cognac worth probably a few hundred quid where he'd knocked the bottle off the table, but despite his hangover, the resolution he'd made on Christmas Day had remained strong. Now he'd confronted the fact that his feelings for Elodie weren't a passing attraction, he was resolved to create the answering feeling in her – one way or another.

He needed to woo her. That's what he needed to do. Elodie had probably never been wooed in the whole of her sheltered existence.

The problem was that for someone with a reputation as a ladies' man, Callum hadn't done much wooing either. He'd been on plenty of dates and he'd had plenty of sex, but those things had happened almost by themselves. It would be pretty tacky to go up to a woman and say 'Hello, my name's Callum Ashley and I'm very, very rich. Would you like to go to bed with me?' But in truth, that's what Callum's wooing technique had amounted to even if he'd never had to speak those words. The women he met knew he was very rich and they invariably did want to go to bed with him.

But he didn't just want to bed Elodie Martin: he wanted to make her love him, and that was new ground entirely. Besides, flashing cash and status wouldn't work on her. She already thought he was a spoilt, overprivileged little rich boy who relied on his family's money to open doors for him. He'd no doubt find a few slammed in his face if he tried that trick with her.

No, Elodie needed wooing of the old-fashioned variety. She needed to be courted properly and thoroughly, and made to feel like the princess she ought to be. If he could just work out how to make a start! It seemed pretty inadvisable to turn up on a woman's doorstep, brimming over with premium woo, when the woman in question had made it clear she couldn't stand you.

Callum pushed the letters aside and took out his iPhone. He opened a note titled 'The EM Project'. In it, he'd jotted down his ideas for wooing techniques.

Flowers
Wine
Fine dining
Chocolates
Jewellery

That was it. It was a pretty pathetic list, he was forced to admit. Nothing exactly groundbreaking on there, and certainly nothing that would break new ground with Elodie Martin.

Callum had tried thinking back to the few romance stories he'd read in his quest for new ideas, but there were no clues there. They'd studied *Wuthering Heights* at school, but all he remembered from that was some brooding, violent bastard who knocked the women in his life around and tortured small animals. That didn't sound very romantic. The copy of *Fifty Shades of Grey* he'd sneakily borrowed from the charity book table in the Ashley's staffroom had been no help either. The man in that seemed to do his wooing by presenting the object of his affections with presents like expensive first-edition classics or anal beads, depending on his mood. If Callum tried that with Elodie, he suspected it'd be the books and not the beads she'd be attempting to wedge up his backside.

In his next attempt at research, he'd binged all the romcoms he could find on Netflix. Again, they were no help. The problem was, women in books and films weren't Elodie Martin. If you stood outside her window with a boombox, she'd probably chuck a bucket of water over you. She never wore jewellery, she didn't appreciate poetry and she wasn't impressed by big spending. She was just fundamentally unwooable.

There was a knock at his office door, and a moment later his dream woman herself appeared. She had her arms folded and looked like she resented having to be anywhere near him, which proved it was the real Elodie and not a vision conjured by his smitten imagination.

He blinked. 'Elodie? What're you… um, I didn't expect you.'

Hastily Callum turned off his phone, which typically Elodie noticed.

'Sorry if I'm interrupting your regular lunchtime Pornhub session.'

'Never mind, I've got Premium,' he said, matching her deadpan tone. 'What's up?'

'Pops told me I had to come and see you.'

'Did he? Why?'

Elodie grimaced. 'Look, Callum, I don't want you to read too much into this, but… I came to do this.'

She leaned over his desk and thrust out her hand. Callum recoiled.

'You came to give me a slap?' he hazarded.

'I'm making a peace offering, aren't I? Well go on, shake it.'

Callum stared at the outstretched hand before gingerly giving it a shake.

'So, um, what's going on exactly?' he asked, bewildered by this new turn of events.

'We're making friends,' Elodie informed him, taking a seat. 'Well, no, friends is too strong a word. We're making… non-enemies.'

'Are we?' Callum said, feeling dazed. 'That'll be nice for us.'

'Yes, well, as much as I hate admitting you might've been right about something—'

'I was right about something?'

'A bit. Maybe. All this stuff, store wars and bets: it is childish, isn't it? We can't keep playing these games for the rest of our lives.'

Callum stared. 'So… you're going to be nice to me?'

'I'm going to be… not un-nice to you.' Elodie winced, as if the next bit was particularly galling. 'And… I want to invite you out for a drink.'

'Bloody hell! Do you?'

'Yeah, like our grandads used to do. Just one, to say no hard feelings about the grotto.' She screwed her eyes closed. 'God, I can't believe I'm actually going to do this. Just don't think this is any kind of apology, OK?'

'I can't, can I? I haven't heard it yet.'

'All right, here it is.' She kept her eyes closed, as if she were wringing out the words with great difficulty. 'Callum, I wanted to say I appreciate you being so gracious about losing the bet, and I accept that… you're not entirely awful. And as the last representatives of two families that have always managed to keep their business rivalry sporting and friendly, I think it's beholden on us to make sure there's no bad blood between Martin's Toy Kingdom and Ashley's. We're not kids any more.'

Callum felt like he was in a dream. Was this happening? He was sure Elodie Martin was sitting in front of him, not only telling him she wanted to put their long-standing rivalry behind her but that she wanted to go out for a drink. An actual drink! That was basically a date, wasn't it?

He felt a surge of triumph. For the past fortnight, he'd been making himself dizzy trying to work out how to make a start on his Elodie-wooing plan. And now she was practically doing the work for him! He couldn't have hoped for a better way in with her.

He rested his hand one of the envelopes he'd just opened. Yes! That would be perfect. It had wooing written all over it.

OK, Cal. Play it cool…

'You're absolutely right,' he told Elodie, keeping his tone steady. 'We're civilised adults, and it's high time we called a halt to the Santa wars. There's no reason we can't both have success with our grottoes, as this Christmas proved. Anyway, it's big of you to make the first move, Elodie.'

She shrugged. 'It was Pops really. When he started talking about how he didn't want to leave the world knowing there was bad blood between people he cared about, even my stubbornness had to crumble. He was very attached to your grandad.'

'And I've always had the greatest admiration for yours.' Callum's fingers pressed against the envelope. 'So, um, are you seeing much of that chap Nick now Christmas is over?'

'Nick? No. I mean, I will be. What do you care?'

He shrugged. 'Just curious. I've always wondered what Santas got up to out of season.'

'Slob around the North Pole, I expect, working on their ho-ho-hos,' Elodie said. 'Although I know one of them is down in your perfume department, arranging for Mrs Claus to smell like Jennifer Lopez.'

Callum laughed. 'Kenny?'

'Yep. We had a nice chat.'

'So did you mention going for a drink to toast this new era of peace and camaraderie?'

'Oh. Yeah,' Elodie said absently. 'Apparently it was a tradition that our grandads would buy each other a drink after the Christmas season to show there were no hard feelings. If you want to do that. It suits me if you'd prefer to leave it at a handshake.'

'I'd love to.'

She looked disappointed, but quickly rallied.

'OK, send us a text when you're free and we'll meet at the George for a pint.' Elodie, evidently relieved to have done her granddaughterly duty, stood up. 'See you, Callum.'

'Yeah, see you.' Callum hesitated a beat, then placed two fingers on his temple. 'Oh, actually, here's an idea. Are you free two weeks on Thursday?'

'I should think so. Why, is that a good night for you?'

'It's just I've got a couple of complimentary tickets to this wine-tasting thing; they came in the post this morning. I was going to throw them away, but we could always make that our peacemaking trip if you want?'

Elodie looked unconvinced.

'Free drinks,' Callum said hopefully. 'Shame to buy our own when we can get them for nothing.'

'I suppose. OK, text me the address and I'll meet you there.'

'That's all right, I'll pick you up.'

'Right.' Elodie had a faraway look in her eyes. 'I wonder though. What *does* a Santa do out of season?'

'Slob about working on his ho-ho-hos, didn't you say?'

'Yeah. That's exactly what he'd do.' To his surprise, Elodie burst into laughter. 'Ha! Thanks, Callum, you've been a big help.'

'You're welcome,' Callum said, blinking. 'Um, what did I do?'

'Nothing. Nothing. I just had an incredible idea, that's all. I'll see you in a couple of weeks for the thing.'

She hurtled out of his office like a tiny thunderbolt, leaving Callum staring after her in entranced puzzlement.

21

Nick was between customers during what felt like a long shift. January shifts always felt long: even more so this year when he didn't have the prospect of going to a job he actually enjoyed afterwards. He was using the free time to surreptitiously scroll through acting jobs on the Equity website.

As usual, there was very little. Some unpaid stuff, but Nick couldn't afford to work for free. He had enough experience that meant he shouldn't have to give his skills away for nothing. There was a paid job his finger hovered briefly over – character actors wanted to advertise crisps – but the fee was barely worth the trip down to London for the audition. Then a casting call for a big theatre, but again, actors were expected to have a London base. A talent agency was looking to get more people on their books – ah, but actors must be under thirty. And live in London. Typical.

What was this one? Improv actors with comic talent wanted for stage revue show in Leeds... Nick perked up. That sounded like more his thing, and the pay was £150–250 a day plus expenses. But... oh. Must have TV experience. So many seemed to want that nowadays, and he knew from previous auditions that a minor part in a Sugar

Puffs ad wasn't going to cut it. Sighing, Nick closed the website.

His Equity membership was up for renewal soon and he needed to make a decision on his future before he invested in another year. His choices at this stage were either to move to London, where the work was – which of course was impossible for various financial and filial reasons – to struggle on for a little longer in the hope something would turn up, or... well, to give up. See if he could retrain, or resign himself to a career scanning people's shopping for minimum wage. He was nearly thirty-five, a bad age to be a character actor, and it was getting harder and harder to find work on the stage. Nick had promised himself that this was the year he'd force himself to abandon his delusions, but he was still hoping for a miracle that would mean he didn't need to give up on acting as a career.

It was a grim sort of new year's resolution: giving up on your dreams. Being Santa had made it worse, somehow. It had reminded Nick exactly what he loved about the work, just to make sure that abandoning his chosen career was the good, hard kick in the plums it deserved to be.

At least he was guaranteed work at Martin's come the winter – Jim and Elodie had made it clear that he was now their Santa-in-residence for as long as he wanted the job. That was something. Not enough to stoke the fire of his acting ambitions in the face of a rapidly emptying bank account, but it was something.

Elodie was another thing Nick was trying not to think about. It was fitting though, because why shouldn't he start the new year with his love life in just as miserable a state as his career? Misery was what Januaries were all about.

This year's Christmas comedown was proving to be a real belter. Nick hadn't realised just how much colour and hope Elodie Martin had brought to his life these last few months. It's like the girl had been Christmas in human form, which was ironic given her views on the season. Now the trees were down, the lights had gone… and he had no Elodie to brighten his days. There'd never been a bleaker, greyer January than the one Nick Winter now found himself in.

It had been over a fortnight since they'd last seen each other on Christmas Day. She'd been trying to call him but Nick had avoided answering, sending vague texts about work. He felt like he needed some time to process his emotions. To work out if he could continue with a friendship that was going to bring him daily pain, with seemingly no chance of his feelings being reciprocated. Except he couldn't give it up now, could he? He couldn't go back to the empty Elodielessness of his life before – not now he'd experienced how different things could be.

Nick's phone started buzzing and he glanced at the screen, momentarily hopeful it might be someone wanting to offer him an audition.

Ugh. Elodie. He ignored the call and stuffed it in his pocket.

'Hi, Nick. Happy new year.'

Nick smiled wanly at his customer. 'Oh. Hey, Janine. Did you have a good Christmas, my love?'

He started scanning the items in her basket.

'A busy one. Katie and Neil have decided on a trial separation so her and the kiddies were with us. She'll crack and go back to him in the end though. Shame really – cheaters never change, I always say – but there you go.' Janine squinted at him through her glasses. 'You OK, are you?'

'Not really.'

'Why, what's up?'

Nick sighed. 'I managed to fall in love with my boss over Christmas.'

'Blimey!'

'I know. It's not requited, as you can probably guess from my handsome yet miserable face.'

'Well, that is a turn-up. Usually it's me bringing you the gossip.' Janine glanced at Ali, the grizzled middle-aged store manager, as he strode self-importantly around the shop. 'I'd not have pegged him for your type. Still, takes all sorts to make a world.'

Nick smiled. 'Not that boss, you daft ha'p'orth. At my other job.'

'At the toyshop?'

He nodded. 'I thought we had something building, me and her, but it turns out she thought I was gay the whole time.'

'Are you not then?'

'No, I'm bi.' He shook his head. 'I wish people would stop assuming that. It's starting to seriously limit my romantic prospects.'

'Well. You're on the stage, aren't you?'

'I'm not, you know. Santa aside, I haven't had an acting job in seven months.'

'Ah, something'll turn up for you.' Janine finished packing and took out her purse. 'Can you not just tell her you aren't gay, this woman?'

'I did. It was too late to make any difference by then though. She'd already filed me away as that platonic male friend who's like a brother to you.' He pulled a face. 'She called me cuddly.'

'Oh,' Janine said, her voice laden with concern. 'Oh dear.'

'Right?' His eyes widened when he spotted Elodie herself. She'd just entered the shop and was looking around for him.

'Bugger, that's her!' he whispered to Janine. 'Keep schtum, OK?'

Janine locked her lips with an invisible key. 'Not a word.'

Elodie had spotted him now and was making her way over. She had an odd look on her face – elated, and a little feverish. Her eyes were sparkling like they had on Christmas Day when she'd overdone it on the sherry.

'Um, hey,' Nick said when she reached him. He'd been deliberately avoiding her for a fortnight, yet he'd missed her every day. He couldn't stop his heart from leaping now that he was seeing her again.

'I thought you might be here,' she said, beaming at him. 'Nicky, I just had the most amazing—' She glanced at Janine. 'Oh, sorry. You're serving someone.'

'No, I'm all done,' Janine said, taking her bags. She gave Elodie a significant glance. 'You know, young lady, you're very lucky to have a friend like Nicholas here.'

Elodie blinked. 'I know I am.'

'I just hope you do, that's all. Because you could do a lot worse.' With a conspiratorial nod to Nick, Janine left.

'What was that about?' Elodie asked when she'd gone.

Nick rubbed his neck. 'Who knows? I think she might be in cahoots with my mum to get me married off.'

Elodie laughed. 'I'm sure there are plenty of options for Father Dimples, the Martin's grotto heart-throb.'

'Mmm. Fighting them off with sticks, I am.' Nick twirled his chair to face her. 'So, um, you wanted to tell me something? I'm due a break if you want to grab a coffee.'

'That'd be great.'

Nick exchanged till duties with one of his colleagues and they went to the supermarket café.

'I see the beard's gone,' Elodie said when they were sitting behind a mug each of something hot.

'Oh. Yeah.' Nick rubbed his bare chin. 'Don't worry though, it'll be back for next year.'

'Well, I'll miss it. I wasn't lying when I said it suited you.' She met his eye. 'I've been trying to call you.'

'Sorry. Like I said in my texts, I've been working a lot of shifts.'

'I know, wasting your talents flirting with the old dears. No luck finding anything on the stage?'

Nick shook his head glumly. 'Not unless I suddenly come into a fortune and can afford to move me and my mum down to London. I was just thinking it's time I stopped kidding myself and jacked the whole thing in. I'm not exactly a bright young thing any more who can keep convincing himself his big break must be just around the corner.'

Elodie still had that strange look on her face: the little smile, the sparkling eyes. Nick's tales of woe didn't seem to be having any dulling effect on her good mood.

'Nicky, suppose I told you I know of a way you could put your acting skills to good use and earn a tidy sum while you're doing it?' she said.

He blinked. 'Do you know of a way?'

'I might do.'

'What, you've heard of an acting job?'

'Nooo, not exactly. It's just that I bumped into Kenny Ross earlier at Ashley's, and then Callum said... well, I might just have had the most amazing idea.'

'All right,' Nick said cautiously. 'Care to share this amazing idea with me?'

'Callum made this throwaway comment, about what Santas do the rest of the year, and it got me thinking—'

'Callum? Did you go to Ashley's to see him?'

'Oh. Yeah. Pops wanted me to bury the hatchet over the grotto wars,' Elodie said, flushing slightly. 'Well, I thought that since we kicked his arse so thoroughly at Christmas then I could afford to be magnanimous.'

'So you guys are mates now?'

'God, no.' Elodie paused. 'I was impressed with how well he took losing though. I'm willing to entertain the idea he might not be one hundred per cent awful after all. Maybe only ninety-nine per cent.'

'I thought you said he was a smug, oily prick and you hated his guts.'

'The old Elodie said that. I suppose this Christmas changed me – gave me a new perspective on things. Life's too short for hate.' She smiled at him. 'I've got you to thank for that, Nick. Restoring my faith in humanity a bit.'

Oh, great. So not only had Nick scuppered any chance he might have had with Elodie Martin – he'd managed to push her into the arms of another man as well. A sexy, wealthy, successful man with whom he could never hope to compete. *Top work, Nicky.*

He smiled weakly back. 'I'm glad I played a part in converting Chessory's leading misanthrope.'

'Anyway, we're getting off the point,' Elodie said. 'Callum made a comment about what Santas do the rest of the year, and it got the cogs whirring. What do all the professional Santas do when it's not Christmas?'

Nick shrugged. 'Same as me, probably. Try to make ends meet any way they can. What's that got to do with anything?'

'It just seems daft you should have to scrabble about for jobs when you've got such a top skill set. Same for Kenny Ross, and my grandad. You're all great Santas. Why shouldn't you get to be great Santas all year round?'

Nick felt dizzy now.

'El, you've lost me,' he said. 'Are you saying you want to keep the grotto open all year? You'd have to move to Lapland to make that a viable business model.'

'Not that. It just occurred to me... well, you're doing a job you hate and struggling to pay the bills. My toyshop's fighting to survive. My grandad's depressed that after training you, his life feels suddenly purposeless. And Kenny Ross was bewailing the fact he struggles to get work outside the Christmas season because he's been typecast as a Santa.' She beamed. 'But I may have thought of a way to solve all our problems in one fell swoop.'

'What is it, this amazing idea?'

'OK, tell me this. What do you think of when you hear the name Martin's? Apart from toys, what's it associated with as a brand?'

'I guess... the grotto. Martin's is the home of Santa Claus, isn't it? That's what everyone round here calls it.'

'Right, and that's my idea exactly,' Elodie told him triumphantly. 'To turn Martin's into more than just a toyshop. To also make it the one-stop shop for grotto Santas.'

Nick didn't feel this made things any clearer.

'Are you talking about starting a theatrical agency specifically for Santas?' he hazarded.

'Yes, but more than that. It wouldn't just be an agency:

there'd be a training programme too, for people who want to become Santas. You and my grandad would be amazing instructors, and I was hoping Kenny might make a third.'

Nick took a sip of his coffee, hoping it would help this sink in.

'So it'd be a sort of Santa Academy,' he said at last.

'Yep. Those who can do and those who can't teach, the old saying goes. Well, you guys can only *do* at Christmas. But you can *teach* all year round.'

'And you had this idea when?'

Elodie beamed. 'About half an hour ago.'

'Don't you think it needs a bit more thinking through?'

'I have thought it through.' She reached for his hands, her eyes shining with eagerness. 'Nick, it's perfect! You'd be an ideal instructor. You're a great actor, you're good with people – you could do it with your eyes closed. And my grandad's such a big name in the Santa world, the marketing would practically do itself. We could repurpose part of the toyshop's second floor as a year-round training grotto. And the publicity would be bound to have a knock-on effect for the toy-selling side of the business. There's no downside.'

'Losing your family business if it doesn't work out would be a pretty big downside,' Nick pointed out.

'That could happen any time in the next five years if trade continues as poor as it has been. At least if I try something new we've got a shot.'

'But…' Nick was feeling dazed. 'All right, I'll admit the Santa School thing is a unique idea. But who's going to fund it? Who will your students be? How will you promote it?'

Elodie waved a dismissive hand. 'Those are minor details.

Come on, you must think it's a good business move for us. For Martin's, I mean.'

'I'm not saying I don't think that. I just want to make sure you've got a plan as well as an idea. There must be significant start-up costs involved – that's not what I'd call a minor detail. Will you go to the bank for a loan?'

'No. I'll use the money I won from Callum,' Elodie said, looking pleased with herself. 'I was thinking about it on the walk over. That's cash I never banked on having. I can ring-fence it as my start-up money.'

'Four grand?' Nick shook his head. 'That won't be enough.'

'It should be, shouldn't it? There are no premises to hire, and it ought to easily cover publicity costs.'

'Yes, but you'll have salaries for your instructors to pay on top of that, plus there'll probably be some sort of registration fee to set up the agency, the cost of course materials, paying for DBS checks for the students… it'll mount up, El.'

'Fees from the students will cover salaries, I hope.'

'If you can get students. It'll take time to build up numbers. You'll still have to pay your staff in the meantime, even if you only have a handful of people enrolled.'

Elodie looked put out at what probably felt like a barrage of negativity. She let go of his hands.

'Aren't you excited, Nicky? I thought you'd be all for it.'

'I'm just trying to be practical, for your sake. You don't want to be sinking money into this unless you can be damn sure it'll work. Have you thought about who the students will be?'

'Well, people like you. People who like the idea of playing Santa and want to earn a bit extra around the Christmas season.'

'Will there be grottoes to employ them all though?'

'I'm sure there will. Loads of shops and garden centres have grottoes, and then there are schools, nurseries, churches, village halls. We just need to make sure our agency is the go-to place for Santas.'

'And how will we do that?'

'By making sure our Santas are the best in the business. With you and Pops on board, Martin's will soon have a reputation for producing the crème de la crème of shop Santas.'

'It'd be Christmas until we could prove ourselves. We need students right away. How are you going to lure them in?'

'Publicity. It shouldn't be hard to promote. Like you said, it's unique.' Elodie's brow furrowed in thought. 'You're right though, I do need to think stuff through before I launch the thing. Thanks, Nick. I was getting carried away, wasn't I?'

Nick smiled. 'It is kind of adorable seeing you all excited. I'm just trying to make sure you don't adorably bankrupt yourself by jumping in at the deep end before you've learnt to swim. I care about you, you know, El. And about Martin's too.'

'I know you do,' Elodie said, smiling back. 'OK, I'll make sure I do it properly. Draw up a plan. Cost it all out, and apply for a bank loan if I need to.'

'That's all I wanted to hear.' Nick finished his coffee. 'I'd better get back to work.'

'Wait.' She rested a hand on his arm. 'Before you go. Just tell me, if I do decide to go ahead with this, can I count on you?'

Nick hesitated. Then he nodded. 'If you need me, then yes. I'm in.'

22

Nick stood at the door of Elodie's cottage, in his best shirt and clutching a bottle of wine, trying to summon the nerve to knock.

It was actually weird how nervous he felt. They'd hung out loads over Christmas and he'd never felt awkward. They'd just been friends spending time together, and he'd had the perfect excuse when he'd insisted she needed a full education in the art of festive merrymaking in order to abandon the Grinchy Elodie of old. As long as they'd been watching Christmas films or chatting about the grotto in the pub, everything had felt straightforward. Then there'd been his big realisation on Christmas Day, that his feelings for her were more than just a crush. And now…

It didn't help that they were no longer working together. Going for a drink after work had felt natural then: not too date-like. Then January happened. The decorations had gone down; the red suit was put away for another year. Once the warm haze of Christmas had disappeared, Nick had found himself plunged back into the daily non-Santa reality of his life. He was forced to face up to the real facts of Nick Winter's existence: that he was a nearly thirty-five-year-old man who'd failed in his chosen career, was surviving on out-of-date supermarket stock, hadn't had a proper relationship in two years and lived in his mum's spare room. And on top of all that he was in love with his best friend, who'd made it abundantly clear that she considered him about as sexually desirable as a Care Bear. If ever a new year had grabbed him by the testicles and stamped the word 'LOSER' on his face in big red letters, it was this one.

But as his mum often told him, you never got anywhere feeling sorry for yourself. Nick had thought it over last night, and given himself a stern talking-to about his defeatist attitude.

He didn't want to lose Elodie. If she really couldn't see him as anything but a friend, then so be it – he'd rather have her in his life as that than nothing at all, even if it caused him pain. Then again, though, why was he letting himself give up on romance this early in the game? They'd only been friends four months, and for much of that she hadn't even realised he was capable of being attracted to women. And wasn't that encouraging in itself: that they were friends? From an inauspicious start, an easy friendship had sprung up between two people who might from the outside seem like complete opposites. Elodie had said she was close to very few people in her life, and that he, Nick, was one of those few people. She'd come to care about him despite the fact he was broke, his career was screwed and he still lived with his mum. If that stuff didn't matter to Elodie when it came to their friendship, maybe she wouldn't write him off as boyfriend material either.

At the very least, he needed to make it clear he was interested in a relationship. It was no good wallowing in self-pity when he hadn't even told the object of his desires what his feelings were. Not that he was planning to go bounding in, dropping love declarations on the poor girl, but he could subtly start preparing the ground. A nice shirt here, a bottle of wine there, and maybe she'd start to think of Nick a bit less like a mate and a bit more like a date. At least, that was the plan.

And it was a plan that started here, tonight. When Elodie had texted to ask if he could spare half an hour to chat about the Santa School, Nick had paused only for a quick 'woohoo', then he'd donned his best shirt, picked up a bottle of wine from the shop – a £7.99 sauvignon, none of your rubbish – and practically jogged over to Elodie's place.

He was holding up his fist to knock when the door opened.

'Hi, Nick,' Elodie said. 'I thought it was you I spotted lurking out here.'

'Er, yeah, sorry.' He laughed awkwardly. 'I was just… lost in thought.'

'Right.' She glanced at what he was wearing. 'You look nice.'

Nick took in Elodie's own outfit of smart bootcut jeans and strappy top. Her hair was free of its messy bun, brushed into a golden sheen, and there was the subtle smell of perfume: the Chanel stuff he remembered Jim giving her for Christmas. She had makeup on as well – eyeliner and everything. He'd never seen her so dolled up.

His heart leapt. Oh God, it was a date! Had that been her plan when she'd texted him to come over? He'd been sitting at home worrying about how to take their friendship to the next level, and… could Elodie have been here wondering the very same thing?

OK, Nicky, don't get carried away…

'So do you,' he said, gesturing to her clothes. 'Love those jeans on you.'

She smiled. 'You're sweet. Come on in.'

Nick followed her to the living room. The atmosphere in there seemed equally optimistic. Lighting was low and romantic, and soft music emanated from the speakers.

'Um, I brought this,' he said, holding up his bottle of wine. 'I thought it'd be nice to have a couple of glasses while we talk business. Like old times, eh?'

Funny how their regular non-dates over Christmas already felt like 'old times', although barely a month had gone by.

She grimaced apologetically. 'Sorry, Nicky, I'd better not. I'm going out in forty-five minutes.'

'Oh.' Nick hoped the sensation of his heart sinking into his toes wasn't too obvious. 'Never mind, another time. Have you got a date?'

Elodie laughed. 'A date? God, no. Here, sit down.'

Nick took a seat on the sofa and Elodie threw herself down next to him.

'So who're you going out with then?' Nick asked. 'I thought you told me socialising made your ears cringe.'

'This isn't socialising so much as duty.' She pulled a face. 'I'm going wine-tasting with Callum Ashley.'

Nick stared at her. 'With…'

'Oh, don't look at me like that. I don't know how it happened. I said I'd buy him a pint, show there was no bad blood now we're calling time on the grotto wars – it used to be a tradition under previous generations of owners. Then somehow I got roped into wine-tasting. I was only half listening when he invited me. I'd just thought of the Santa School idea so all my attention was on that.'

So that was why she was all dressed up. Not for him. It was for Callum. Of course it was.

'Yes, but Callum Ashley?' Nick said. 'Won't you end up throttling him?'

'I certainly can't rule it out.' She shrugged. 'I'll probably only stay for one drink. Once I've done my duty as a Martin, we can call it quits till he makes it his mission to get on my tits again next Christmas.'

'Why go at all if you won't enjoy it?' Nick nudged her. 'Text him and tell him you've been headbutted in the bum by a rampant rhinoceros. We can watch a film and drink that wine I brought. It's ages since we hung out.'

Elodie sighed, snuggling against him. 'That does sound a hundred times more fun than playing out with Callum the human suit. But I promised Pops I'd make an effort, for his sake.'

Nick glanced down at her outfit. 'You've certainly dressed up for him.'

'It's Callum, isn't it? You know how he overdresses: he'd wear a dinner suit to a church jumble sale. I don't want to look like a scruffbag next to him.'

'Sure you're not trying to impress him?'

Elodie laughed. 'Why would I want to do that?'

'Well, because he's Callum Ashley. You know, Chessory's most eligible bachelor? Hot? Rich? Backside you could bounce a penny off?'

'Exactly. It'd take more than my best Topshop jeans to impress Callum. At least a pair of fake double-Ds and significant amounts of Botox, judging by the women he usually dates.' She narrowed one eye at him. 'How do you know he's got a backside you could bounce a penny off?'

Nick shrugged. 'It's those tailored trousers he wears. I couldn't help having a sly look.'

'Do you want to go on this date?'

'No thanks. I've got better things to do with my night than bounce pennies off Callum Ashley's buttocks.' He shuffled to face her. 'Anyway, I thought it wasn't a date.'

'Slip of the tongue.' She reached for a folder on the coffee table. 'Let's talk about something more interesting than Callum's arse, shall we? I did what you told me. Costed everything up, made a plan.'

'And?'

'Take a look at this.' She handed him a sheet of paper. 'I've based it around the training you got from Pops. Three one-hour sessions a week for six weeks makes eighteen hours of teaching time. Right?'

He nodded. 'It did feel rushed though. Plus don't forget I already had a bit of experience. I doubt most of your students will have acting backgrounds.'

'I know that. I was actually thinking we'd offer a course spread over eighteen weeks. Two one-hour sessions a week, with three instructors. So that's twice as much learning over a longer period – thirty-six hours' teaching time.'

'OK,' Nick said slowly. 'So me, your grandad and Kenny would be the instructors.'

'If Kenny wants to be involved. Pops is already on board. He can't wait to get started.'

'And we'd teach… what?'

'The same things Pops taught you. Santa banter, effective ho-ho-hoing, dealing with non-verbal kids, convincing doubters, kids' TV and toys, Christmas lore – that'll be your specialism, obviously – and the sort of mind-reading tricks Kenny seems to be good at. On top of that, I thought you could run some general acting sessions. Improvisation techniques and the like. And then makeup, hair and costume tips to get people looking the part.'

'That does sound fun,' Nick said. 'Sorry to be mercenary, but what sort of fee would I be looking at?'

Elodie looked embarrassed. 'Well, that depends.'

'Oh God.' Nick shook his head. 'Elodie, I love you, but please don't ask me to do it for the exposure. I did plenty of CV-filler freebies when I was freshly graduated. Exposure's all well and good but you can't eat it.'

'I wouldn't dream of asking you to do that. Part of the reason I wanted to do this was because it felt like a travesty that someone as talented as you wasn't able to earn from his skills.'

'Really?' Nick said, pleased.

She nodded. 'I've been thinking about your situation ever since Christmas. Wondering if there was some way Martin's could help. Like Pops said, you're part of the place now.'

'Oh. Well, that's... really lovely of you. Thanks, Ellie.'

She didn't answer. Just smiled and gave his leg a squeeze. Nick tried not to flinch at her touch.

'So what did you have in mind as an instructor fee?' he asked.

'I calculated the pay based on general salaries for drama tutors. Three instructors each teaching two hours per week with some shared sessions, plus course development time, we'd be looking at around £1200 per instructor, per course.' She pulled a face. 'Sorry. I know that doesn't sound like much.'

'As an hourly rate it's pretty good.'

'And once we've built up demand, we could be running the course twice a year: you never know,' Elodie said. 'So that'd be a few grand extra a year for you, and it might help lead to other acting or teaching work.'

'Why did you say it depends though?'

'Well I did wonder if instead of the fee the other instructors are getting… I mean, it's a bit of a risk, but since I'm using Callum's bet money and since it was really you who won it for us, I wondered if you'd be interested in taking a smaller fee of £900 per course plus a twenty-five per cent share of the profits. No investment required.'

Nick blinked. 'Like… a partnership?'

'If you wanted,' Elodie said, smiling awkwardly. 'I can't guarantee there'd be big money in it, or any money, but we do make a great team. And if it did start earning for Martin's, I'd like you to have a share of that too. I'd never have thought of it if it hadn't been for you.'

'You mean it?'

'Course. I mean, you don't have to make a decision right now. Take some time to think about it.'

'Right.' He was silent for a moment. 'So what about the other costs involved?'

'You were right that it's more than I thought,' she admitted. 'Once I'd tallied up fees for instructors, cost of advertising, website, branding, registration fees for the agency, DBS checks, classroom materials and so on, it came to around eight grand.'

'Have you got eight grand?'

'I've got nearly four from Callum that I ring-fenced, haven't I? I'm hoping the bank will agree to a loan to fund the rest. We'll soon recoup it when we start getting students.'

'How much are we going to charge them?'

'I thought £350 for the course didn't sound unreasonable.' She stood up. 'Tell you what, I will have a glass of wine with you. You've made me feel guilty now for hanging out with Callum instead of you. Rest assured it's not through preference.'

Nick smiled. 'You must be the only woman in Chessory who'd rather hang out with the local checkout boy than the town's playboy millionaire.'

'Don't do yourself down, Nicky. That's checkout boy, heart-throb Santa and acting instructor from now on.'

'I'm not sure about the heart-throb bit,' Nick said, laughing.

'Tough because I'm not letting you talk me out of it. You had hearts throbbing all over the shop this Christmas, not to mention a few other bits. I bet I'm the envy of every parent in town.'

He smiled. 'If you think flirting with me is going to get me to agree to be your business partner, you're absolutely right. Do carry on.'

'Drinks first. Flirting after.'

Elodie went into the kitchen to get them each a glass of wine. While she was out of the room, Nick stood up to examine her bookcase.

There was an ornament on one of the shelves, in the gap between a couple of hardbacks. It wasn't until he got closer that Nick realised it was the snow globe he'd given Elodie for Christmas. He picked it up and shook it, watching the flurry engulf the little family and their dinner.

'You'll bring yourself bad luck, keeping this out after Christmas,' he said to Elodie when she came back in and put the glasses of wine down on the coffee table.

'That's a risk I'm willing to take.' She smiled at the globe as he put it back. 'I couldn't bear to put it away with the other decorations. It reminded me of that Christmas Day. Best Christmas I've spent since…'

'Since when?'

'I suppose, since my nana and parents were alive. It's never felt… complete since then.' She looked at him, and her eyes seemed liquid in the lamplight. 'It was you, Nick. You filled the gap in my life – the one that made me shun people and dread Christmas. You pulled me back out of the dark.'

It was the same look she'd given him the night they'd decorated the grotto, when Nick had come so very, very close to kissing her. And now here they were again. God, he'd never wanted to take her in his arms so badly. Should he? Did she want him to?

This was it. This was his sign. It was time to put his heart on the line and take a chance. He moved closer, and for a moment he really thought it was going to happen. Then they were interrupted by the buzz of Elodie's phone on the table. She broke eye contact to glance at the screen.

'Callum.' She picked it up to read his text. 'Ugh, he's early. Apparently he's waiting outside. Sorry, Nick, we'll have to put the wine on hold.'

Nick stepped back, trying not to flinch as he realised he'd

once again managed to completely misread the situation. 'Oh. OK.'

'Oh God, where's my bag?' Elodie started hunting around for it. 'Is there anything worse than early men? Why can't he turn up when he says he's going to turn up? He can't be that desperate for my company.'

Nick went to twitch the curtain aside and stared. 'Bloody hell, Ellie.'

'What?'

'There's a Rolls-Royce out here that looks like it's worth more than your house.'

23

Callum glanced at his watch. He was fifteen minutes early. The traffic had been quieter than expected, and the Rolls was surprisingly speedy for an old girl. He hoped that wouldn't look too keen, turning up this far ahead of time. Mind you, if you were picking a woman up in a chauffeur-driven Rolls-Royce, the fact you were a bit early was the least of your worries.

He prayed the Rolls hadn't been a mistake. His dad's taste for classic cars and his own taste for speed had left Callum with a garage full of expensive machines of varying size, pace and vintage, all of which were likely to make Elodie roll her eyes. He'd picked the Rolls over the Porsche or the Lambo because it was luxurious without being too boy racer, but now he was here, in this leafy village street with its modest Toyotas and Vauxhalls, he knew his beast of a car was sticking out like a sore thumb. There were curtains twitching all along the row as Elodie's neighbours peeped out. She wasn't going to like that much, being the subject of gossip. Why the hell hadn't he just got a taxi like ordinary people did?

'Shall I knock, Mr Ashley?' asked Brian, the chauffeur.

'No need. I sent her a text; she knows we're waiting.'

Yet still no sign of her. He hoped she hadn't climbed down the back drainpipe when she'd spotted the car...

The front door of Elodie's cottage opened and Callum breathed a sigh of relief. Then he frowned when instead of Elodie, a man emerged.

It was Nick. He was pretty dressed up too, at least by his standards. What had he been doing here?

A moment later, Elodie appeared. Callum tried to summon the charm and conversational skill that came so naturally with any woman who wasn't Elodie Martin. He climbed out of the car so he could open the door for her.

'What the hell is this, Callum?' she demanded, just as he'd known she would.

'It's a Rolls.'

'I can see it's a Rolls. What's it doing outside my house? It's bigger than the front garden.'

'I know. I brought it especially so you could make derogatory jokes about the size of my penis. I thought you'd enjoy that.'

'I would enjoy that,' Elodie grudgingly agreed. She peered through the window. 'A chauffeur? Seriously?'

'Well I can't drive us, can I? It's a wine-tasting evening.' He nodded to the back seat. 'Get in then.'

Elodie hesitated before clambering in and making herself comfortable on the white leather seats.

'Rubbish,' she said when he'd climbed in beside her. 'It doesn't even have cupholders.'

'What an old banger, right? It was my dad's. I prefer something a little niftier myself, but I thought you might appreciate the leg room.'

'Um, hi, Mr Chauffeur,' Elodie said, waving to the back of Brian's cap. 'Thanks for the lift.'

'Good evening, Miss,' Brian said genially. 'Will you want the screen up, Mr Ashley?'

'Please. Thanks, Brian.'

Brian turned a handle, and a tinted screen slid into place between the front and rear seating.

'Nice,' Elodie said.

'Worrying. Makes you wonder what my dad used to get up to when he was out in this thing.' Callum glanced down at what she was wearing. 'You look nice.'

Elodie shook her head. 'Don't say that.'

'Why?'

'Because it's weird. We're not on a date. You don't need to pay me compliments.' She glanced around the spacious car with its walnut and leather interior. 'I only suggested a swift pint at the George. Now I'm in a chauffeur-driven Rolls with a man in a dinner suit. Do you live in that thing or what?'

Callum straightened his bow tie. 'It doesn't hurt to make an impression.'

'Yeah, if the impression you're going for is "oh look, it's that guy who always wears a dinner suit". What is this thing we're going to?'

'It's a promotional event for the British champagne industry. No, sorry, the British sparkling wine industry. They're not allowed to call it champagne.'

Elodie snorted. 'There's a British sparkling wine industry?'

'Yeah, why?'

'I don't believe you. There is no British sparkling wine

industry. The British sparkling wine industry is a Soda Stream and a bottle of Blue Nun.'

Callum laughed. 'You can't be too pissed off with me if you're doing jokes.'

Elodie shuffled in her seat to glare at him. 'Look, Callum Ashley, let's get one thing straight. I don't know quite how this whole thing happened but this is not a date, all right?'

'I never thought it was,' Callum lied.

'Really? Because I invited you for a strictly business goodwill drink at the pub and you showed up at my house in a chauffeur-driven Rolls-Royce and a dinner suit ready to ply me with Britain's answer to champagne.'

'I turned up at your house in a Rolls-Royce because I own a Rolls-Royce. I'm wearing a dinner suit because as you rightly point out, I'm the guy who always wears dinner suits. And I'm taking you out for sparkling wine because I had a spare ticket to a sparkling-wine-tasting event,' Callum said in as firm a tone as he could summon. 'This is the world I occupy; it contains very few pubs and quite a lot of complimentary tickets to wine-tasting events. Believe me, Elodie, if I'd wanted a date I've got plenty of options – but I'm sure you know that.'

Callum suppressed a grimace. Shit, had that been too much? There was playing it cool and there was playing it cool. He didn't want to scare Elodie off by seeming too keen, but he also didn't want to sound like he thought he was out of her league.

Elodie was still regarding him suspiciously. 'Because if you still had your eye on my shop, Callum, then I can tell you now that shagging me out of it is not going to be a workable plan. Martin's isn't for sale, and neither am I.'

'You really think that's my plan? I just want to put any bad blood behind us, same as you do.'

'Well, good. Strictly business then. One drink then we've paid our debt to our families and we can go back to ignoring each other until next Christmas.'

'Right.' He paused. 'So… was that Nick I just saw coming out of your place?'

'That's right. I invited him over to—' Elodie stopped, as if she'd been about to let something slip and bitten her tongue just in time. 'We were hanging out. You know, the way friends do.'

'Are you… I mean, I don't want to pry, but I did wonder…'

'What did you wonder?'

Callum loosened his bow tie slightly. 'Well, if you two might be… more than just friends. Not that I care. Just making conversation.'

'Me and Nick? No, we're just mates.'

'So you've got no irons in the fire then. Dating-wise, I mean.'

But Elodie's attention had been claimed by something else. They were pulling up outside the venue now: a large hotel. Her eyes were wide as she watched the other guests queueing to go inside.

'For Christ's sake, Callum!' she hissed.

'What?'

'They're wearing *ballgowns*!' She looked down at her jeans and top. 'Why didn't you tell me it was a ballgowns type of thing? I'm going to look a right div.'

'I didn't think,' Callum said, grimacing. 'I never noticed the women's dress code. You look great though.'

'I look all right for the pub. I look like I should be serving the drinks at this place, and I'd be underdressed for that.'

'You want Brian to drive you home so you can change?'

'Into what? The ballgown I keep in the back of the cupboard?' Elodie shook her head. 'It really is another world you live in, isn't it?'

'Oh, forget about it,' Callum said, nudging her. 'Who cares what anyone else thinks? The drinks are free. That's the main thing.'

'Hmm.' Elodie looked doubtful. 'Well, since I'm not planning to stay long. But you have to stand in front of me if anyone looks.'

Elodie followed Callum to the door, trying to stay behind him out of sight. Once again, she wondered how the hell this had happened. A pint at the pub: that was all it was supposed to be. Even that, she felt, had been going above and beyond when it came to hatchet-burying. Now she was queueing outside Chessory's biggest and swankiest hotel with a bunch of people who looked like escaped Moss Bros mannequins, on something that despite Callum's assurances still felt disconcertingly like a date.

She wasn't sure why it felt like a date. Callum was absolutely right when he'd said – maybe not in so many words but she wasn't an idiot – that he could do a hell of a lot better than her. She'd seen the sort of women he went out with: busty, stunning debutante types who dripped jewels and class. It was also true that this was Callum Ashley's world. Black-tie wine-tasting events were probably as everyday and familiar to him as the pub was to her. Still, something about it felt wrong to Elodie.

She peeped around Callum. She was guessing there'd be

some snooty butler type on the door, waiting to curl his lip at her Topshop ensemble. Maybe he wouldn't even let her in. After all, a dress code was a dress code, and these people looked like they wouldn't want to sully themselves mixing with the sort of oiks who had to buy their clothes from the high street.

Elodie brightened. That's right, maybe he wouldn't let her in. That was a pleasing thought.

They'd reached the front of the queue now. The ticket-checker was actually more bouncer than butler: broad and burly, in a suit that struggled to contain him. As she'd predicted, he cast an unimpressed glance at Elodie's outfit.

'You know this is a black-tie event, don't you, love?' he asked in that patronising tone common to doormen the world over.

'No, actually. Nobody told me.' Elodie sighed. 'What a terrible faux pas. Oh well, I suppose you can't let me in.'

'It was my fault,' Callum told the doorman. 'I forgot to fill my date in on the dress code.' He flashed the man a winning smile. 'I'm sure you can make an exception for me, can't you, Graham?'

'Oh. Mr Ashley.' The man straightened his tie, his voice suddenly full of servile respect. 'I didn't realise the young lady was with you. Of course, in you go. Sorry, just doing my job.'

'Thanks, it's much appreciated.' Callum subtly slipped the man a handsome tip-slash-bribe before taking Elodie's arm to guide her inside.

Elodie shook her head. 'Did you just pull a "don't you know who I am"?'

'I had to get you in, didn't I?'

'What did you tell him it was a date for?'

'What else was I going to tell him? That you're an old business rival who's grudgingly agreed to tolerate my company for an hour or so?'

'I'm not sure I'll be able to tolerate it that long,' Elodie muttered as they entered the main event room.

24

God, it looked like the ballroom on the *Titanic*: all chandeliers and crystal glassware and people who thought they were better than you. Was that woman's necklace made of real diamonds? And was that one of the dancers from *Strictly*? Elodie was still staring as Callum claimed some drinks and pressed one into her hand.

This was all Nick's fault, she decided. If she hadn't been worrying about his financial situation, she'd never have thought up the Santa School. And if she hadn't been thinking about the Santa School, she'd have been focusing properly on the sort of thing Callum had been inviting her to. This was what came of having friends.

'They all look so beautiful,' she murmured, watching women in glamorous, expensive-looking dresses sail around the room.

'Fine feathers make fine birds, as my grandmother used to say.' Callum nodded to the drink in her hand. 'Try it then.'

She took a sip. 'Actually, it's not bad, is it?'

'Better than your fizzy Blue Nun. Shall we find a seat or would you prefer to mingle?'

Elodie glanced around the room. There were a lot of people looking at them, and not in a particularly friendly way either. Actually, no, the men weren't looking at them: it was nearly all women whose eyes had turned in their direction. Were they sneering at her outfit? Or was it because she was with Callum?

It was a new experience for Elodie, drinking champagne with a handsome millionaire while finding herself an object of jealousy for a room full of rich, beautiful women. That was probably something a lot of people aspired to, but she wasn't madly keen on it. It made her feel like meat… or like prey, all those eyes narrowed in her direction. She felt like she was in the midst of a terribly formal zombie apocalypse.

'Can we sit down please?' she whispered to Callum. 'I don't think I'm much of a mingler.'

'No, I don't care for it much.' He took her arm to lead her towards a seating area.

'How many of the women in this room have you slept with?' Elodie asked.

'What makes you think I've slept with any of them?'

Elodie glanced over her shoulder at the resentful gazes following her. 'Call it a hunch.'

'I'm going to decline to answer that,' Callum said with a smile. 'More than one and fewer than all of them. That's all you're getting.'

'Right, I'll rephrase the question. How many women are going to be in the queue to scratch my eyes out?'

'You coward. Come on, you could take them.'

'With those manicures? Are you kidding?'

A woman turned to observe them. God, she was amazing: like a *Pretty Woman*-era Julia Roberts, auburn-haired and stunning in a skintight emerald dress. You could've rolled marbles down her curves and her hair extensions alone probably cost more than Elodie earned in months. She peeled away from the group she was with to speak to them.

'Callum,' she said, air-kissing him on each cheek. 'I'm glad you could join us.'

'Melissa. Hi,' Callum said. 'Thanks for the invitation.'

She turned her smile on Elodie. 'Do introduce me to your charming date.'

'This is Elodie Martin. Our families go way back.'

Melissa regarded her with more interest. 'Martin? Of the restaurateur Martins?'

'Um, no. The Santas.' Elodie summoned a smile for what she assumed was their host. 'Sorry about my clothes. Callum forgot to mention there was a dress code.'

'Oh, I barely noticed,' Melissa said, oozing coolness and charm. 'Would you like to join us? Cal, there are some people I'd love you to meet.'

'Maybe later,' Callum said politely. 'I promised my date we could spend some time together.'

'I understand. Have a nice time, both of you.'

Melissa returned to her equally magnificent-looking friends while Callum guided Elodie to a table.

'You have slept with that one though, right?' Elodie whispered.

'How did you know?'

'It doesn't take a genius. Can you stop telling people we're on a date?'

He shrugged. 'If they think we're a couple then they'll leave us alone. You were the one who didn't want to mingle.'

They reached the table and he pulled out a chair for her.

'You don't need to do all that door-opening chair-pulling stuff for me,' Elodie told him as she plonked her bum down.

'I'm a perfectly functional human being. Well, some of the time.'

'Sorry. Force of habit.' He claimed the chair next to hers.

She took another sip of her non-champers. 'I'll go when I finish this.'

'Don't be silly. We can't make peace over a drink that size. Besides, my reputation might never recover if people see my date walking out on me after one drink. You haven't got plans, have you?'

'I've got plans to be in bed by nine with a book and a hot water bottle, where there won't be gangs of posh lasses glaring at me.' She narrowed one eye at him. 'Why are you so keen to keep me around? I'm sure you can find some friendlier female company. Melissa, for example.'

Callum paused before answering, as if weighing something up. When he did speak his voice sounded different. Warmer, Elodie supposed. More earnest, less teasing.

'To be honest, Elodie… I like being around you. I always have.'

Elodie laughed. 'You what? We've done nothing but bicker since Year Four.'

He smiled. 'And don't even dare pretend you didn't enjoy every minute of it.'

Elodie wasn't sure how to respond to that. She drained the rest of her fizz, feeling a little dazed by the onslaught of bubbles and lights and colour.

'Let's assume I believe you,' she said. 'Why do you like being around me? I've never exactly been nice to you.'

'Maybe that is why. I spend a lot of time around people who tell me nothing but what they think I want to hear. It's quite refreshing to get a dose of hostility.' Callum paused to take a sip of his wine. 'And I suppose… I've always felt we were sort of alike.'

Elodie blinked. 'What, you and me?'

'Yeah. Don't you think so?'

'Well you're a multi-zillionaire and I haven't got a pot to piss in, so no, not really.'

'In a lot of ways we are,' Callum said. 'All that weight of expectation on us, as the last representatives of two old family businesses. Both with no life outside work; both lonely and sort of isolated. Plus we live for Christmas every year while hating the crap out of the whole bloody season. Fair assessment?'

'Pretty fair,' Elodie said vaguely. 'I didn't realise you knew so much about me.'

'I'm good at noticing what others don't.'

Another drink had magically appeared in front of her, presumably placed there by one of the silent, shuffling waiters in white jackets who were gliding around the room with loaded silver trays. Elodie swallowed a mouthful, once again feeling like she was in the ballroom on the *Titanic* while an iceberg loomed just ahead. In her brain, a tiny violinist played the first few bars of 'Abide With Me'.

'What's your reason for hating Christmas?' she asked Callum. 'It's made you enough money.'

'It irritates me,' Callum said, scowling into his drink. 'When people start talking about the true meaning of Christmas – all that BS about peace and love and goodwill – it sticks right in my craw. All I see at Christmas is greed, dressed up with a few baubles and fairy lights to pretend to be something better than it is. When you've watched a couple of mums having a literal fist fight over the last must-have toy on the shelves, you can see Christmas for what it truly is. You can see people for what they are too.'

Elodie blinked. 'You've really seen that?'

'And worse. Yes, my business depends on a good Christmas season, but that doesn't mean I have to like it.' Callum beckoned a waiter over to top up their glasses. 'Why do you hate it?'

Elodie watched the bubbles rise through her drink and burst on the surface. It reminded her of her snow globe, with its little family eating their snowy turkey.

'I didn't always. Christmas never felt really whole after my—' She stopped.

'After your parents died,' Callum said quietly. 'I remember.'

'After that it all felt different. And then seeing the tots come into the shop with their mums and dads, all excited…' She sighed. 'It just reminded me of everything I'd lost. Eventually I got bitter about the whole season.'

'I'm not surprised.'

'This Christmas just gone made me realise I was in serious danger of being eaten up by the darkest parts of myself. That's why I wanted to make things up with you; it wasn't only Pops.'

'Well, I'm glad,' Callum said. 'I'd like to be friends. Or at least, be friendlier enemies.'

'No. I'm done with enemies.' She glanced up at him. 'What do you remember?'

'Sorry?'

'You said you remembered. What do you remember?'

'I remember when your parents died. How everyone stared, and how brave you were.'

'I wasn't brave,' Elodie murmured. 'I just wanted life to

be normal again, and yet I knew it never could be. I feel like I stopped being a child that day.'

'I remember I wanted to fix it for you. I grew up that day too.' He shook his head. 'I was a selfish little brute. Always bragging about what I had; too shallow to realise the so-called friends who followed me around didn't give a damn about me as anything other than a source of sweets or toys. But when it hit home that all my dad's money couldn't bring your parents back for you… It wasn't much of a lesson, but it changed something in me.'

'Really?'

'Yeah.'

'I never realised you noticed so much back then. About me, I mean.'

Callum smiled. 'I don't know how anyone could not notice you.'

Elodie looked into his face. She felt like she was seeing him for the first time, almost. Looking past the face of her business rival to find the boy he'd been. There was a curl of the lip he'd inherited from his father that could be interpreted as either faintly amused or arrogant – Elodie had always assumed the latter. But in his eyes there was something… a vulnerability, almost fear…

'Is that how you felt when you lost your dad?' she asked quietly.

'Huh. No.' Callum stared past her, his eyes glassy. 'I didn't feel anything. Not a single, solitary thing.'

'Why? Was he cruel to you?'

'Just the opposite. He was exacting – he'd let me know about it if he didn't think I was giving my all in various areas of my life. He wasn't one for showing physical affection, or telling me he loved me, but he was generous to a fault when it came to money and gifts. I grew up spoilt, yet I can't remember if my dad ever hugged me. Still, he wasn't a bad man. He was what his life had made him, same as we all are.' He was silent for a long moment. 'I loved him.'

'You went back to work the next day,' Elodie murmured, half to herself. 'That's what I always remember. You went back to work the next day.'

'Well, why not? I couldn't grieve for him. I felt numb. I feel like I've been numb nearly all of my adult life.' To Elodie's surprise, he let out a sudden, choked sob. 'If you can call it a life.'

'Oh. Hey. No.' Elodie hesitated, then patted his hand in a helpless sort of way. 'Don't cry.'

Callum gave a damp laugh, taking out his handkerchief. '"Don't cry", Jesus. You're worse at this than me, El. I told you we were alike.'

'Sorry. I just… I didn't realise. How things have really been for you. You poor thing.'

'God, please don't. I don't think I can take pity from you, of all people.'

'It's not pity, Callum, it's empathy. There is a difference.'

'Is there?'

'Take my word for it.' Elodie let herself smile. 'Tell you what. How about we steal a bottle of bubbly and go drink it somewhere less fancy? I'll show you the park bench where the rebel kids used to take their cheap cider when we were at secondary.'

Callum glanced down at himself. 'What, dressed like this?'

'Come on, live a little. I bet you never broke a rule in your life, did you?'

'I took a sweet out of the Ashley's pick 'n' mix without paying for it once.'

'It's your shop, Callum.'

'True,' he conceded. 'All right. You sneak a bottle into your handbag while I cover you.'

'We should've borrowed a couple of glasses,' Callum said as Elodie produced the stolen fizz from her bag.

'Nope, not allowed. If we're drinking on a park bench like teenagers, we're doing it properly. Straight from the bottle.' She handed it to him. 'Here, you open it, Champagne Charlie.'

Callum popped the cork expertly and passed the bottle to Elodie, who took a swig and passed it back.

'So did you used to drink here with the rebel kids?' he asked when he'd had a drink.

'I wasn't really cool enough, but I came here a few times in Year 11 when I was going out with Ryan Hewitt. Remember him?'

'The emo kid with the lip piercing? I don't remember you going out with him.' He passed her the bottle.

'It was only for a month. That was usually the point I started to find every little thing about a boyfriend annoying.' She drank some wine and handed it back. 'It'd be nice if I'd grown out of it.'

'Didn't you?'

'Not really. I've got very low people tolerance.'

'I know what you mean. It's hard to find people I can be myself with. Take off the mask, you know?'

She turned to look at him. 'Haven't you got anyone?'

'My PA Sam maybe. You.'

'Me?'

'Yeah. I know we've mostly bickered, but I never felt like I had to pretend with you.' Callum took a thoughtful swig of wine. 'The depressing thing was you still believed the worst of me, even when I was just being myself. Every time I did something to try and impress you or to do the right thing, you thought I had some evil ulterior motive.'

'Well you did try to steal my shop.'

'If by "steal" you mean "offered to buy at well over its value", then yes, I did. Hard as it might be for you to believe, that was genuinely an attempt to help you out.'

'And to get me working for you.'

'OK, that was something I wanted,' Callum admitted. 'You're a good businesswoman and I believed – I still believe – that little outlier shops like Martin's have a limited shelf life. I wanted to snap you up before someone else did. I never pressured you, did I?'

Elodie grimaced. 'I know, sorry. You were just so bloody annoying. With your money and your suits and your I-can-buy-anything smirk.'

He shuffled round to look at her. '"Were" past tense? As in, I'm now less annoying?'

'Don't push it,' she said, smiling. 'But… perhaps I was a bit hard on you. You couldn't help being a spoilt brat, could you? Like you said, none of us can help what life makes us.'

'Thanks,' Callum said, passing her the bottle. 'And I

suppose you couldn't help being a grumpy, stubborn little madam either.'

'You're sweet.'

'Anything else you'd like to admit you were wrong about, while we're playing this game?'

'I guess… I shouldn't have said you've never needed to do a hard day's work in your life,' Elodie said. 'I mean, you've never *needed* to. You've got more money than the queen. But I know you work bloody hard.'

'A very Elodie compliment.' He glanced at the goose pimples on her neck and took off his suit jacket. 'That coat you're wearing's paper. Put this on.'

'I'm fine.'

'No you're not.' He draped it over her shoulders. 'Anything else you were wrong about then?'

She handed him the wine bottle. 'I was wrong to say you only cared about money and winning, never about people. Sorry, Callum.'

'No, that was fair. Money and winning were the only things I was ever taught to value. It's only lately I've been thinking…'

'Thinking what?'

'I've been sleepwalking all my life, Elodie. For some reason, this last grotto season, it became very important to me that I start trying to live with my eyes open.' He looked at her. 'My turn then?'

'Why? What did you assume about me that's wrong?'

'I thought you were tough as boot leather but you're not, are you? You're a bit of a softie.'

'That's what Nick always says,' Elodie said, smiling. 'I've given up trying to deny it.'

Callum passed the bottle to her. 'So has Nick already hit your boyfriend annoyance threshold? Is that why you and him aren't a thing?'

'No, me and him aren't a thing because we don't see each other that way. I guess it doesn't happen much in your world, Callum, because every woman you meet is a libidinous supermodel desperate to shag you, but in the universe of ordinary slobs like me, people of compatible sexualities can sometimes just be friends.'

'I just wondered. He looked a bit dressed up when I saw him leaving your place.'

Elodie laughed. 'Says James Bond Junior over here.'

Callum unfastened his bow tie, letting it hang loose, and undid his top button. 'There. Happy?'

'Exquisitely.' She passed him the wine bottle. 'Actually, Nick came round to talk over some business plans. I've got a new venture in mind using the Martin's brand. I'm pretty excited about it.'

So this was what Elodie had stopped herself from telling him earlier. He'd been worried it was something about her relationship with Nick. Anyway, she seemed quite happy to chat about it now. That was a good sign, wasn't it? If she was sharing business information with someone who until tonight had been her main rival, that meant she trusted him – or at least she was starting to. And she'd opened up to him about her parents, and hadn't run away when he'd rather randomly started crying for his dad six years after his death. It was going well – really well. At the very least, it felt like they were becoming friends.

Callum shuffled a little closer as he handed over the wine bottle. For a moment he toyed with the idea of stretching an arm over the back of the bench, behind Elodie, then he mentally slapped himself. That was too much. He couldn't lose his advantage now, when it was going so well.

What were the things that made Elodie tick? What did she care about? Well, her grandad, of course: that was a given. And that crumbling old toyshop. If he kept her talking about that, he could hopefully keep this date going as long as possible.

'That sounds interesting,' he said. 'Can you tell me more?'

'I was planning on setting up an agency for Santas, with an attached training programme. Martin's Santa Academy or something like that, we'll call it.'

Callum frowned. 'Training Santas?'

'It's what we're known for, isn't it? Martin's, the home of Santa Claus. Since the toy-selling business is a constant struggle, I thought this would be another string to our bow.'

'But you'd be creating competition for your own grotto.'

She laughed. 'Competition for yours, you mean.'

'That too,' he conceded. 'Ashley's doesn't depend on its grotto like you do though. Are you sure it's a good idea?'

She shook her head. 'Why are there always men trying to talk me out of this? There'll always be grottoes, Callum, and there'll always be Santas. We can't stop competition, but we can make it work to our advantage.'

'But if every shop has a Martin's Santa, why would kids still come to you?'

Elodie pulled his jacket tighter around her, shivering. 'We won't need them to. If the Santa School's a success, we won't be relying on our grotto for most of our Christmas income.' Her eyes went hazy. 'Every shop with a Martin's Santa. Just imagine that. Come on, you know it's a good idea.'

'All right, maybe I'm just jealous I didn't think of it,' Callum said, smiling. 'And how are you paying for this Santa School?'

'With your money. So thanks for that.'

He frowned. 'My money?'

'The money I won from you. That and a small bank loan.' Elodie looked at the wine bottle, which was nearly empty. 'I don't think I can manage more without burping. You finish it.'

Callum did so, pondering his next move.

It seemed like their date that wasn't a date was about to come to an end. He was definitely marking it down as a big success. Elodie was smiling at him now – actually smiling at him! But he didn't want to make his move too soon. First came friendship, bonding, gaining her trust. Then came the groundwork for a relationship: the little touches, the flirty signals that he liked her as more than just a friend. And then, when he was sure she was prepared, he'd strike.

'I suppose I should call Brian to pick us up,' he said.

Elodie laughed. 'That's going to be fun to explain. He dropped you off at a champagne reception and he's picking you up from a park bench.'

'He won't ask. He worked for my dad; he knows how to be discreet.' Callum stood, slightly woozily, and offered her his arm to help her up. 'Thanks for leading me astray, El. I missed out on all this as a teen. It's been fun catching up on some long overdue juvenile delinquency.'

'Thanks for inviting me.' She used his arm to hoist herself up. 'I don't want this to go to your head, but I've had a really nice time.'

'Told you it wasn't a date, didn't I?'

She laughed. 'And I thought it was all a dastardly scheme

to coerce me into selling my toyshop using your sexual wiles. Sorry, Callum.'

'So we're friends?'

'I guess we are. Hey, that brings my total up to a whole two.'

This was the difficult bit. Callum unfastened a second button on his dress shirt. 'And, um… shall we do it again?'

'Sure.' Elodie had taken out her phone and was scrolling her notifications. 'We can make it a tradition, same as our grandads did.'

'I was thinking a bit sooner than next Christmas.'

She looked up. 'I don't know, Callum. We've both got businesses to run, and as alike as you're convinced we are – and I'm not arguing there's plenty we have in common – it's two very different worlds we occupy. I'm not sure how I could fit into yours. I mean, you take a chauffeur-driven Rolls to swig wine on a park bench.'

'It doesn't have to be like that. We could meet in a pub or something. No chauffeurs, no suits: just to chat.'

'Everyone knows you though. I don't like the idea of people gossiping. Taking photos of us for the papers maybe, like the ones I see of you with dates.'

'I wouldn't let anything happen that might embarrass you. We'd just be old friends catching up.'

She narrowed one eye. 'Why is it so important to you?'

'I told you, I like being around you. I don't have many people I can be myself with, Elodie.'

'It's lonely at the top,' Elodie murmured.

'Sorry?'

'Just thinking about something Pops said. I'll think about it, OK, Callum?'

25

'You're back early,' Nick's mum observed when he trudged back into the flat.

'Mmm. Elodie had a social engagement.'

His mum raised an eyebrow. 'You mean a date?'

'She says not. I remain unconvinced.' He rubbed a hand over his forehead. 'Sorry, Mum, but do you mind if I grab an early night? I'm knackered.'

His mum regarded him for a moment. Then she switched off the TV.

'Sit down first,' she said. 'I want to talk to you.'

He grimaced. 'If I do, do you swear you're not going to give me the third degree about my love life?'

'I swear. Now sit.'

Reluctantly, he took a seat in the armchair.

'Now are you going to tell me just what your feelings are for this girl?' she demanded.

'Oooh, you liar!'

'Never mind that. Answer the question.'

'Can't I have any privacy?' Nick demanded, crossing his arms.

'Not when you walk in from seeing a girl with a face like a slapped backside.' She got painfully to her feet.

'There's hot chocolate in the cupboard. I'll make you one.'

'I'm not five, you know,' Nick called as she headed to the kitchen.

'Shut up and let me do my mumming.'

While she was in the kitchen, Nick closed his eyes, feeling unutterably weary.

What would Elodie be doing now, out with Callum? He'd seen the man in his dinner suit in the back of that ridiculous chauffeur-driven Rolls. Perhaps they were at a fancy restaurant: the sort of place people with Callum's level of wealth went to, where the meals were minuscule works of art and there were no prices on the menu. What was the best Nick could offer her? A bag of chips, supply your own vinegar?

Or maybe... maybe they were already back at Callum's place. Nick was well aware of the man's reputation. Maybe they hadn't even made it that far, and Callum had sent his chauffeur off somewhere while he and Elodie tore each other's clothes off on the back seat. Nick grimaced at the image that rose unbidden in his mind, of the person he loved naked and writhing in someone else's embrace.

A few minutes later his mum came back in with a watery hot chocolate and pushed it into Nick's hands.

'So what is going on with you and Elodie Martin?' she asked, sitting back down.

He sighed. 'It's like... we're best friends. And that's it.'

'You want to be more?'

He nodded. 'Very much.'

'And does she know you feel that way?'

'No. As far as she's concerned, we're just good friends.'

'Has she shown any interest in you, romantically speaking?'

Nick pushed his hair back from his forehead. 'That's just it: I don't know. She pays me compliments sometimes. Tells me I'm sexy even, in a way that's kind of half jokey. Touches me. I mean on the arm or leg, or a hug; the sort of thing that could be taken either way. I've got no idea if she's flirting with me or if it's just the sort of thing you do with a friend you feel totally comfortable around. That's kind of worse: that she sees me as so completely asexual, she can flirt without it meaning anything.'

'But it might mean something.'

'There's always that small hope,' he said, without much enthusiasm.

'Well there's no point you sitting about with that mardy face on if she doesn't know how you feel, is there?' his mum said, folding her arms. 'Tell her. Then if she's not interested you can feel miserable afterwards. You're wasting your time doing it before.'

Nick rubbed at a dusty mark on his jeans. 'I was going to. Not right away, but I was going to start preparing the ground. Then she told me about this non-date tonight that's definitely really a date.'

'Who's it with?'

'The department store guy, Callum Ashley.'

'But she doesn't like him, does she? I thought they were always fighting.'

'Yeah. In fact, she doesn't like him so much it makes me suspicious she likes him a hell of a lot. She certainly talks about him enough.' Nick sighed. 'You should've seen the car he picked her up in, Mum. I bet you could buy this flat three times over with what it must've been worth. Have you ever seen him?'

'No. What does he look like?'

Nick googled a picture of Callum on his phone. There were plenty, taken at business functions and that kind of thing. The man must have a whole apartment just for storing his dinner suits.

'There,' he said, showing his mum.

Sheila squinted at it. 'I see. Handsome lad.'

'Handsome. Rich. Successful. Money, cars and property all over the place, and then he's got this brooding, slightly vulnerable *Twilight* thing going on that has people swooning all over town for him. How do I compete with that?'

'Oh, rubbish,' his mum said, waving a hand. 'You're a good-looking boy too. What's more you're a good man, and there aren't bags of them around. You don't need to feel threatened by Callum Ashley.'

He laughed. 'Mum, I'm a skinny failed actor who works on the tills and still lives at home. Callum Ashley's got a huge private fortune, cars worth enough combined to buy a small private island, he wears designer clothes and he lives in a sodding mansion. I know you're highly biased in my favour, but even you have to admit that when it comes to rivalling Callum for anyone's affections, I've got the losing hand here.'

'Money isn't everything, Nicky. Do you think any of that would impress Elodie?'

He stared into his hot chocolate. 'I don't know. I think the fact Callum was born rich is more likely to annoy her than anything; she's got a real resentment of unearned privilege. But she's also only human, Mum. He can give her the sort of life I could never even aspire to. Plus he's gorgeous and sexy and he's got that little-boy-lost thing going for him. And I'm just... me.'

Sheila looked again at the photo of Callum, her gaze flitting to the curl at the corner of his lip. 'Hmm. Looks full of himself to me. Entitled. I know the sort: thinks anything's his for the taking, women included.'

'I think he seems kind of sad. In his eyes.' Nick took a sip of his watery drink, which was going cold. 'Money might not work with Elodie but that will. She claims to loathe people but she's soft as hell inside. She hates to see anyone hurting.' He fell silent. 'She asked me to be business partners with her tonight.'

'In her Santa agency?'

'That's right. She offered me a choice between a flat instructor fee of £1200 or a twenty-five-per-cent profit share plus £900 fee.'

'That's encouraging then, isn't it? She's not asking Callum Ashley to be business partners.'

'And she's not asking me to be non-business partners.'

'Will you take it?'

'Well, it's a risk. If I take the partnership and we're a flop, I lose out on £300 per course. That's money that could make a big difference to us. But if the idea's a hit, I could make a lot more than the £1200 flat fee.'

His mum examined him. 'And if you go for a partnership, you'll get to see more of the girl.'

'Yes.' He roused himself. 'What do you think I should do, Mum?'

'Is there any point me telling you? You've already made up your mind.'

He smiled. 'I suppose I have. You always know.'

'Well? What are you going to do?'

'I'm going to take the partnership, aren't I?'

***

'...and I've rescheduled your eleven o'clock Pilates session to the afternoon to make way for a meeting with the supplier for the new petite swimwear range.' Sam looked up from her tablet. 'Callum?'

'Mmm. Great.'

She glanced at the pad he was doodling on while she went through his appointments. He was currently adding some curly antennae to a cigar-smoking alien.

'Have you been listening to a word I've said?'

'Of course. Something about swimming.'

Sam put her tablet down. 'All right. What's taking up all your brain space today?'

Callum shrugged. 'Just thinking about a social engagement I had last night.'

She smiled. 'That good, was she?'

'This was strictly business.' He started doodling a little rose on his pad. 'Drinks with a contact. That's all.'

A contact he hadn't been able to stop thinking about all morning. Callum had almost skipped out of bed. He'd vowed on Christmas Day to make Elodie his by the time the next one came around, and he was thrilled at what a strong start he'd been able to make. Not only had they buried the hatchet from a business point of view: they'd actually become friends. He'd shared things with her that he'd never talked about with anyone. Experienced a whole rollercoaster of emotions, after what felt like a lifetime of feeling almost nothing. And she'd shared things with him too. Personal things and things about her business, which meant she now trusted him enough to believe he wouldn't try to stab her in the back.

The problem was, how to get her to see him again? She'd seemed reluctant to repeat the experience, even though she'd enjoyed it. Their worlds were just too different: that's what she'd said. There wasn't much he could do about the social divide between them, short of giving all his money away. Or marrying her, but there'd be another time for that.

Elodie wasn't wrong: their worlds were different. Yet he was still convinced that Elodie was like him. That despite the accidents of birth, they were, in essentials, the same. Callum was born into his world: he didn't choose it, and it had never made him happy. What he needed was a way into Elodie Martin's world, where he could be with her.

'Sam?' he said. His PA was tucking her tablet into her satchel, obviously having decided that her boss was in too much of a dream to be of use to anyone.

'What is it, Cal?'

'I was thinking, I'd like to invest in something – something new. I've got plenty of cash sitting around doing nothing. Would you help me set it up?'

She blinked, surprised at his sudden re-engagement with the world of business. 'OK, sure. I can set up an appointment with your broker next week sometime.'

He shook his head. 'Not shares. A business. This contact I met last night was launching something new and I'd like to back it.'

'What is it?'

'It's an academy.'

'An academy? What, for underprivileged kids or something?'

'No. Santas.'

She looked baffled for a moment. Then she started

laughing. 'Very good. You really ought to wait for 1st April though, Callum. I'll see you later.'

'Honestly, I'm not pulling your leg. This friend of mine is starting an agency and training programme for grotto Santas.'

Sam took a seat again, looking worried.

'Callum, are you OK?'

He waved a hand. 'I haven't flipped, I promise. It sounds mad, but when you think about it it's actually a really sound idea. Someone has to provide all those Santas, don't they?'

'But why invest in something that's going to damage your own business? The more grottoes are out there, the more Ashley's has to fight to get kids into ours. I don't want to cross a line here, but it's... well, it's kind of insane.'

'There'll always be grottoes,' Callum said, echoing Elodie's words of the night before. 'If you can't beat them...'

Sam gave a wry smile. 'Buy them?'

'Exactly. It's the Ashley's way,' Callum said. 'If I get in touch with my contact, can you put together the necessary paperwork?'

'If you're determined to do this, all right.' Sam stood to go, then paused. 'Who is the contact?'

'Hmm?' Callum was doodling again. 'Oh. Elodie Martin.'

Sam frowned. 'Of Martin's Toy Kingdom? You want to back your biggest grotto rival financially so she can create even more grotto rivals?'

'That's right.'

'But... why?'

Callum smiled without looking up. 'Let's just say I think it'll work in my favour. In the long run.'

26

It was two weeks after their impromptu park bench drinking session when Elodie took the lift up to Callum's office.

'Thanks for coming, El,' he said when she walked in, smiling at her. 'Sit down and I'll get Sam to bring us in some drinks. We'll sort the paperwork out in here, then when the others arrive we can go into the big meeting room.' Nick, Pops and Kenny were joining them in half an hour.

Elodie sat down, feeling a little dazed, while Callum rang for some coffees. It had been the day after their night out that Callum's PA had called with an offer from Mr Ashley to invest in her new venture. The woman had been very friendly and businesslike, in a way that left Elodie in no doubt that it was all legit, but a fortnight later she was still struggling to get her head around the fact that Callum wanted to join her and Nick as a partner in the Santa School.

'So you're definitely happy you've made the right decision?' Callum asked when they both had a hot drink. 'It's not too late to tell me to get lost, if you'd rather go it alone. I only want to do it if you're certain, Elodie.'

'Well I am, but… look, Callum, are you absolutely sure you want to do this?'

'I'm sure if you are. I told you, I think it's a great idea. That wasn't the sparkling wine talking.'

'And you're not just…' She trailed off.

'Just what?'

'Well, you said a lot of stuff that night. Stuff about trying to impress me and do the right thing and…'

Callum raised an eyebrow. 'You think I'm doing this to impress you?'

'Yes. I mean no. But it did occur to me that this might be no different to those offers you made to buy the shop and give me a job.'

He frowned. 'You still think the worst of me? I told you, Elodie, I'm not trying to steal your business. When I offered to buy the shop I really just wanted—' He stopped.

'Wanted what?'

'To make sure… you didn't lose anything else,' he said quietly. 'That was what was behind it, although I'm not sure I properly understood that at the time. As a kid I felt so helpless when your parents died, knowing I couldn't buy them back into existence for you, and I think offering to buy the shop was my subconscious's way of trying to remedy that. I know that sounds stupid, but it's how my brain works.'

'I don't think the worst of you,' Elodie said. 'Not any more. I believe you when you say you offered to buy the shop because you wanted to help. But if offering to invest in the Santa School is the same thing, Callum, then I wish you wouldn't. I don't want charity. If you genuinely believe in it as an idea then welcome on board, but if you don't then I'd rather try my luck with the bank.'

'If I believe in Santa,' Callum murmured. 'The irony.'

'Well? Do you?'

'I told you I did and I meant it,' he said firmly. 'I'm impressed by the idea and by your drive to make a success of it, and I know that if Elodie Martin sets her mind to something then it can't fail. Believe me, I came to you with the investment offer purely as a businessman. Is that good enough?'

She smiled. 'Well, all right. Shake on it then.'

Callum held out his hand solemnly and Elodie gave it a shake.

'Last time I offered you a handshake, you recoiled like you thought it was something venomous,' she said.

He laughed. 'I thought you were about to slap me. Not unreasonable given your attitude to me until that point. What changed, El?'

'The bet helped. When you were so gracious about losing, it made me think you couldn't be all bad.'

'Oh, I'm sure I could if I really tried,' he said with a quite uncharacteristic grin. He pushed a contract to her. 'So we just need to sign this – Nick too, when he gets here – and presto. We're officially partners.'

After the paperwork had been signed, making the business relationship between Elodie, Callum and Nick official, there was a brief meeting between partners and instructors about the course and how to promote it. The course content was being developed by their team of Santas, with Nick, Kenny and Pops all working together to produce an impressive itinerary of classes, and Elodie's aim was to start running their first course in six weeks' time. That wasn't long to bring in a decent number of students, she knew, but eighteen weeks was a good chunk of the year and it wouldn't be long after the course before the Christmas season was looming again. They needed enough time to help their first cohort of Santas find grotto jobs this year – the new school's reputation would depend on it.

After the meeting, Kenny stayed behind to have a chat with Callum while Nick, Pops and Elodie took the lift downstairs.

'As one-third of this partnership, I'm voting for future meetings to not be here,' Nick announced as they walked to the car park. 'I hate this place.'

'I guess Callum wants to feel like he's helping, given he's new to the operation,' Elodie said. 'Better than sitting in our dark storeroom.'

'We could've gone to a caf or something.'

'I suppose. It's nice that Callum wants to contribute though.' Elodie nudged him. 'Come on, grumpy chops, cheer up. It's not like you to sulk.'

'I'm not.' He sighed. 'Sorry. I'm tired, that's all.'

'You work too hard, lad,' Pops said.

Elodie unlocked her car. 'Need a lift home, Nick?'

'No thanks, I'll get the bus. My mum asked me to pick up a few bits while I'm in town.' He gave Elodie a kiss on the cheek and clapped Pops on the shoulder. 'See you, guys. Keep me posted on how enrolment's going.'

Pops watched him go.

'Well, are you getting in the car?' Elodie asked him.

'Hm?' Pops turned to look at her. 'Sorry. Just… thinking about my book.'

'The memoirs?' Elodie said as they climbed into her car. 'How far have you got?'

'I've just met your nana and… well frankly, I'm not impressed. I think she might win me round though.'

Elodie started the engine, laughing. 'Spoilers.'

'So you and young Callum looked friendly,' Pops observed when they were driving home.

'I guess. That's what you wanted, isn't it?'

'Perhaps.'

She glanced at him. 'What's that supposed to mean?'

'You and him… you're more alike than you realise, Ellie.'

'That's what he says. That's good, isn't it? If we're going to be friends.'

'Sometimes. Other times…' Pops fell silent, staring at his reflection in the rear-view mirror. 'Well, never mind. What changed your mind about him?'

Elodie hesitated.

'I suppose… he did,' she said at last. 'We went for that hatchet-burying drink you seemed so keen on, and when he talked about his feelings when his dad died… It was a side to him I hadn't seen before. I've known him a lifetime, but I never really understood him.' She paused, smiling. 'It's funny really, because once we got talking I found out he understood me pretty well. Better than I did, anyway.'

'I'm glad of it. It always upset me to see you two fight.'

But Pops looked worried. Elodie parked the car outside his house and turned to look at him.

'You're worried about something,' she said gently. 'What is it? Are you not feeling so good?'

'I feel fine, Ellie. There's just… something I can't help thinking about.'

'Not about me?'

He smiled. 'What else have I got left to worry about except you?'

'I'm OK. I'm great. Better than I have been for ages.'

'Are you sure?'

'I'm sure,' Elodie said firmly. 'I've got people in my life finally – people I like, people who get me – I've got an exciting new project to put my energy into, and I might even be able to drag Martin's out of its slump. For once it feels like life's moving in the right direction.'

'Would you say… maybe in a romantic sort of direction?'

She frowned. 'You can't mean with Callum?'

'I noticed him looking at you.'

'That doesn't mean romance. It probably means I had something on my face,' Elodie said. 'Callum's… well, let's just say I'd have a *lot* of competition if my thoughts ever tended that way – which, by the way, they absolutely don't.'

'You're sure?' Pops said, raising an eyebrow. 'I saw you… looking at him too.'

Elodie laughed. 'You and your looking. Looking's just looking, Pops.'

'Just keep an open mind, kiddo, OK?'

'What, about Callum?'

'About love. It isn't always what you think it is. Or… where you think it is. You can trust me, I'm old.'

She laughed. 'All right, wise elder, I'll keep my mind open. Come on, let's go in and I'll cook you a decent tea for once.'

27

Nick arrived at Martin's half an hour before his first session as a Santa instructor, dressed in his red suit. He was going to be putting the new recruits through their paces alongside Jim in the training grotto Elodie had created in the upstairs storeroom.

It was now late March, two months since Nick had agreed to go into business with his friend, and he still couldn't decide if it had been a genius idea or a huge mistake.

Of course, it gave him the perfect excuse to spend time with Elodie. They'd been seeing a lot of each other: creating and perfecting the course content; working together on the advertising; creating the branding for what they'd decided to name Martin's Santa Superstore.

The problem was, they were so rarely alone. If Nick had realised he was going to be getting another business partner alongside Elodie – and that partner was going to be none other than Callum Ashley – he'd certainly have thought twice about agreeing. Nothing had prepared him for the pain of seeing the person he loved growing closer to someone else right in front of him, while being absolutely powerless to prevent it.

And they were getting closer – anyone with eyes could

see that. Not that Elodie seemed to have romantic feelings for Callum exactly – not yet – but every time Nick saw her with her one-time rival, he noticed her letting her defences down a little more. Just as she had once done with him.

And there was something else too. There was a solicitous care in Elodie's eyes when she looked at Callum that suggested she'd come to feel quite tender towards him. Nick knew he'd been right when he'd observed to his mum that Callum's air of vulnerability was likely to succeed with Elodie where all his money would fail. Yes, her attitude at the moment suggested more friendly concern than romantic attraction, but that would certainly change if Callum had his way.

Nick had no illusions about Callum's feelings. He'd suspected it the very first time he'd seen the department store millionaire bickering with Elodie, and when he learnt that Callum had decided to invest in Elodie's new business just one day after their non-date… he knew. Besides, Nick recognised a look on Callum's face that he was, sadly, all too familiar with from his own. And if Callum Ashley – Chessory's most lusted-after bachelor – had set his sights on Elodie, then what hope was there for someone like Nick Winter?

Months ago when Nick had gone over to Elodie's flat to discuss her new business idea, his plan had been to start preparing the ground in the hope his friend might come to see him as not an entirely unappealing romantic prospect. That plan had gone out of the window as soon as he'd seen Callum and Elodie together once they'd acknowledged themselves no longer enemies, that day at the department store. The interaction between them had confirmed his deepest fear: Callum was in love with Elodie, which left Nick so out in the cold he might as well be in the bloody North Pole.

The other thing Nick had started feeling on a regular basis was guilt. Guilt over wishing things were different. At first he'd tried to convince himself that his love rival's feelings were as selfish as might be expected of someone who lived the life Callum did; that he only wanted Elodie because she'd always been something he couldn't have. But the more he'd observed the pair of them, the more he'd been forced to acknowledge that Callum's feelings were, in fact, genuine. There was a softness in his attitude that spoke of more than a selfish desire to possess and to own. So Nick felt guilty, because Callum genuinely loved Elodie, Callum was good-looking and wealthy, and Callum had everything he needed to make her happy. Nick loved Elodie too, but what did he have to offer her? A life spent eating out-of-date tins of chicken soup, top-and-tailing every night in his dismal single bed as they listened to his mum snore through the thin walls?

Callum was the handsome prince in the storybook of Elodie's life, and he, Nick, was very much the Buttons: the loyal but fundamentally unsexy friend with nothing to offer. If Nick was genuinely a good man as his mum liked to believe, he'd step nobly aside so his friend could get the happily-ever-after she deserved. Still, there it was. He felt how he felt.

Nick was starting to have other suspicions about Callum too. Suspicions about how well things seemed to have worked in his favour, in a way that was almost too convenient. At the start of the last Christmas season, Elodie had been more hostile towards her business rival than ever. Then suddenly, practically overnight, the decades of animosity were all but forgotten. Elodie, the one person who'd always been oblivious to Callum's charms, seemed to be falling more under his spell every time they saw each other.

Nick had spent a lot of time trying to figure out what had changed, and eventually he realised that the turning point had been Elodie winning the bet. Callum's gracious acceptance of his defeat and Elodie's winner's guilt had been the main reasons she'd been willing to go out with Callum that night, and ever since then the department store prince had had it all his own way. It was so convenient, in fact, that Nick couldn't help thinking… had Callum planned this all along? Exactly when had he set his sights on Elodie, and what lengths would he go to, to win her? The Ashleys always won, didn't they? Even when they lost, they won.

Nick jumped as someone put a hand on his shoulder. Jim had appeared, similarly kitted out in his red suit.

'All set, son?'

'I think so.' Nick turned to face him. 'Hardly seems worth turning up for five recruits, does it? But Elodie seems convinced we'll be able to build the thing up. Where is she?'

'In the grotto, making sure everything's shipshape.'

Callum walked in, soaking wet from the driving rain. For once he wasn't wearing some sort of suit – in fact he looked rather scruffy, in faded jeans and a raincoat. He was holding a lead with a small brown puppy of indeterminate breed attached to it. The little dog wagged its tail when it saw the other humans, straining at the lead to greet them.

Jim laughed as he bent to stroke the tiny thing. 'Who's this little chap, Cal?'

'She's called Polly,' Callum said, looking a little bashful. 'She's from the shelter my PA Sam volunteers at.'

'You adopted a puppy?' Nick asked, raising an eyebrow.

'That's right.' He smiled down at the dog. 'She's even got me out in the rain, look. I don't mind though. Polly's already the best thing I've done in my life.'

Oh, brilliant. So now the sexy, swoonsome, brooding-yet-vulnerable millionaire had an adorable little puppy.

'And a great way to impress women, right?' Nick said, only narrowly changing 'Elodie' to 'women' in time. He tried to keep a lid on his resentment of Callum, who was always perfectly pleasant to him – almost too pleasant, as if he felt that befriending Nick would be a good career move when it came to getting into Elodie's good books – but it would spill out occasionally.

Callum shrugged. 'Probably depends on the woman. My mum was pretty horrified when I told her. She had visions of suspicious-looking puddles all over my exotic hardwood flooring.'

'Why did you bring your puppy to the shop?'

'She was due her walk so we thought we'd pop in to wish you guys luck tonight.' Callum slapped Nick chummily on the back. 'Hope it goes well, Nick. I know you've really worked hard on this.'

He smiled warmly, and Nick fought against an urge to grimace in return.

'Thanks,' he said curtly.

'Where's El? I want to introduce her to Polly.'

'Up here,' Elodie called from upstairs. 'Hang on, I'll be there in a sec.'

She came down, sniffing the air.

'I thought I could smell wet dog,' she said as Polly jumped up to greet her. Elodie couldn't restrain a simper as she tickled the dog's ears. 'Aww, what a darling. Whose is she, Callum?'

'Mine,' Callum said, flushing. 'I adopted her from a shelter.'

'You got a dog? I wouldn't have thought you'd be up for a puppy getting hair on your designer suits.'

'I thought the company might do me some good. Actually, I'm not sure why I didn't do it years ago. I'd rather have Polly to hang out with than any number of pristine suits.'

Elodie shook her head, smiling. 'I'd never have had you down as a dog person.'

Callum shrugged. 'For years now I've been a lonely, bitter man who works too hard. I thought Polly might bring something into my life it was missing.'

'Like what?'

'Something to care for.' He picked up the little dog, who seemed to have terrier in her heritage, and laughed as she licked his face. 'She's a loving little thing.'

'I'm glad you've got someone to go home to, Cal,' Elodie said earnestly, giving his arm a squeeze. 'If you ever need a sitter, let me know. I generally prefer the company of dogs to people.'

Callum put Polly down again. 'Me too.'

They smiled at each other, and Nick crouched to stroke Polly so he had an excuse to look away. The little pup pressed her head against his hand, and he found himself welling up suddenly. He fought it back.

'Our student Santas ought to be here soon,' he said. 'Jim, let's head up to the grotto. Bye, Callum.'

Callum was too absorbed in Elodie to offer more than a vague 'Yeah, bye' in return.

'You should tell her, you know,' Jim murmured as they climbed the stairs.

Nick adjusted the angle of his Santa hat. 'Tell who what?'

'Come on, Nicky. While there are many parts of me... about ready to give up the ghost, my eyes are fortunately still in working order.'

'I don't know what you mean.'

'Yes you do.'

Luckily Nick was saved by the bell, as the jangle of the front door announced the arrival of some of the Santa School recruits.

Nick followed Jim into the grotto – if grotto was the right word. There was certainly a North-Pole-like air to it, with the jolly decorations they'd had over Christmas reinstated: snowflakes, fairy lights, paper chains and masses of tinsel. But the two rows of desks facing a smartboard made it look more like a schoolroom for elves than a Santa's grotto. Next to the board was Santa's throne, with a smaller chair beside it.

'Your seat, I believe, Santa,' Nick said, with a flourishing gesture towards the throne.

Jim smiled. 'Our seat.' He settled into the painted chair with a deep sigh. 'Still... it feels good to be back.'

Nick opened his folder of course notes. They'd decided to start their handful of recruits off easy, with a general improv and Santa banter session.

'Nervous?' Jim asked.

'No.' Nick grimaced. 'Yes. They're paying good money for this, aren't they? I feel like I've got a sudden case of impostor syndrome.'

'You know this, Nick. You did it every day for five weeks... over Christmas.'

'I guess. Still, I'm glad you're here.'

'I'm here to be the face of it, that's all. Ellie seemed to think... that was important.'

They looked towards the door as Elodie came in with the recruits.

They were a mixed bunch. There was only one older gent who Nick would have picked out of a police line-up as a potential Santa. The others... well, there was a lad who certainly had the right physique, but age-wise didn't look much over twenty-five. He was also sporting a buzzcut and a large neck tattoo of the name 'Chesney'. Then there was a middle-aged chap who resembled the vicar in an Edwardian farce: sort of stuffy and parsonic, with too much Adam's apple and a general air of living on the edge of his nerves. And the other two weren't quite the right... didn't have quite the required... were women, in fact.

So much for Elodie's Top Gun of shop Santas. These guys were as motley a crew of potential Father Christmases as Nick had ever seen, and given his own experience, he was pretty open-minded about the right type for the job.

And poor Elodie. She looked genuinely gutted at the unlikely bunch who were to be her first class of Santas. For her sake, Nick forced himself to smile brightly.

'Welcome to Martin's Santa Superstore, class of 2022,' he said. 'Let's get to know each other, shall we? Take a seat.'

The group of five all claimed a desk, most leaving a gap between them as they regarded their fellow Santas warily. All except the elderly chap, the one Nick felt had the most Santa potential, and the older of the two women. From the way they sat so comfortably in each other's personal space, Nick wondered if they might be a couple. The other female Santa hopeful looked like she might be with them as well, taking a seat in front of the older woman. Elodie stationed herself at one side of the room to observe.

'I'm Nick Winter, Martin's current Santa-in-residence, and I'm sure I don't need to introduce my legendary colleague here,' Nick said, gesturing to Jim.

'Ho ho ho,' Jim greeted them affably. The younger woman, who was of an age to have visited Jim as a kid, giggled.

'You're the actor, are you?' the man of the Chesney tattoo demanded.

'That's right,' Nick said. 'Three years of drama school, and you can find a list of my acting credits on my agent's website.'

'How come you're here teaching people how to be Santas, if you're an actor?'

'To earn money to buy food. Sadly the days of the barter economy, when I could offer to perform a sonnet in lieu of payment, are long gone.'

'And because he's one of the best in the business,' Elodie chimed in. 'Our instructors are recruited from the finest Santas in the area.'

Nick's gaze roved to the man and woman he suspected were a couple. 'Shall we do introductions? Perhaps you two would like to tell us a bit about yourselves.'

'It's… Robert, isn't it?' Jim said, squinting at the man. 'Robert Adaway, from the allotments?'

Robert smiled. 'Evening, Jim. I thought you might remember my strawberries.'

'What made you want to join us?'

'It all started at church.' Robert nodded to the woman at his side. 'Margery and I met through the church bereavement group after we lost our other halves. We're getting married this year.'

'Congratulations,' Nick said.

'Thanks. Anyway, St Michael's is after a new Santa for their Christmas fair, and I said to Margery, well, why the heck not? I reckon I could make a good job of it.'

'We'd been looking for a new hobby when we saw your advertisement,' Margery said, beaming at her future husband. 'We thought if Rob was going to be Santa for the fair, why not learn to do it properly? It sounded rather fun.'

'Right,' Nick said. 'And you're here for... moral support?'

'Oh no, I'm here to learn.' She patted the shoulder of the shy-looking woman in front of her. 'As is young Siobhan here – my daughter. We thought we could make a family affair of it.'

Nick blinked. 'You all want to train to be Father Christmas?'

Robert laughed. 'No, just me. Margie fancies being Mrs Claus, and Siobhan said she wouldn't mind having a go as an elf. We can have a whole team for the church's grotto.'

Nick shot a helpless look at Elodie. 'Do we do elves and Mrs Clauses?'

Elodie shrugged. 'We do now.'

'Right.' Nick turned to the vicary-looking man with the watery eyes. 'And are you here for Santa training, or did you fancy something else? The Easter Bunny maybe, or the Tooth Fairy?'

'I'm here for Santa training. Malcolm Sommerville.'

The man licked his lips, fiddling with a tissue in his skinny fingers as his protruding Adam's apple bobbed frantically. 'Um, I've been rather volunteered against my will. My wife, you see, she teaches at a nursery school, you see, and she told them I'd play Father Christmas for the tots this year. I honestly don't know what possessed her.' He leaned towards Nick, looking desperate. 'I'm a quantity surveyor, Mr Winter. I don't do public speaking. I don't do people! And as for gangs of toddlers, the very idea of them staring up at me with their chocolate-covered little faces brings me out in a cold sweat.'

'Why did your wife volunteer you, if that's how you feel?' Elodie asked.

'She said it would help me to conquer my fears.' The man gave a high-pitched laugh. 'Conquer my fears! I'll be a nervous wreck by December. Tell me, do you really believe you can make a Santa out of me?'

Nick hesitated, but Elodie jumped in before he could think of a diplomatic answer.

'Absolutely,' she said firmly. 'We can make a Santa out of anyone. Satisfaction guaranteed, or your money back.'

Nick raised an eyebrow. They'd never discussed any money-back guarantee. She grimaced and mouthed the word 'sorry'.

'And what do they call you?' Nick asked, turning to the man with the tattoo. He looked like his natural place was on the door of a nightclub, not enthroned in a grotto.

'Albert,' the man muttered, staring down at the desk as if aware his name didn't suit him.

'What made you want to train as a Santa, Albert?'

Albert shrugged. 'In it for the money, me. I could use some extra dosh around Christmastime.'

Nick's gaze drifted to the tattoo on his neck. 'For your… son?'

'That's right, my boy Chesney.' Albert puffed up with pride. 'He's five this year, as bright a little lad as you've ever met. Nothing like his old man, see? His mum and me aren't together but she lets me see him regular. I want to make sure I can give him a good Christmas. He deserves it.'

'So you're looking for a grotto job from this?'

'Aye, well, it's not so easy to get work when you've got a record. I said to myself "Al, you've got the belly for it, so why not try something new?"' He caught Nick's expression. 'Oh, don't worry, it weren't nothing bad. A bit of shoplifting when I were too young to know better. Still, it puts people off.'

Nick wondered what sort of grotto Albert was expecting to find employment in: one that wouldn't mind their Santa's inked neck and record of petty theft, apparently. But since thanks to Elodie they were now offering a money-back guarantee, he hoped they could find one.

28

Elodie watched as Nick clapped his hands to get the attention of his class.

'Right, I want these gaps closed up,' he said to the students with his usual luvvie-esque exuberance. 'There are no strangers at the North Pole, guys and gals. Just friends we've yet to make.'

Grudgingly the students shuffled up so they were sitting next to each other. Albert shot an interested look at Siobhan in the seat next to him.

'We're going to start with a simple improv game,' Nick said. 'We call this Line at a Time, where we each contribute one sentence to a story. I'll start us off. "It was Christmas Eve at the North Pole, and Sidney the elf was…"'

He nodded to Malcolm the quantity surveyor, who looked panicked at being picked on first.

'He was, umm… umm… wrapping presents,' he supplied, Adam's apple going like the blazes. 'He was careful to use two strips of Sellotape per seam and fold the edges very neatly, because he knew it was important to get it right or—'

'Or Father Christmas would send him to work in the stables shovelling reindeer poo,' Siobhan chimed in. 'That's when he…'

Nick nodded to Albert, who was watching Siobhan with fascination.

'Oh right, is it me now?' He hesitated, looking lost. 'That's when he... when he... um, he decided he was bored of all this North Pole bollocks, so he got out his Honda RCV bike with the V5 engine and whizzed off to...'

'Narnia,' Robert supplied promptly. 'There he discovered it was always winter but never Christmas, which is rather depressing when you're a Christmas elf. The only thing he could do was...'

Margery looked flustered. 'Oh gosh, do I have to do it too? Well, I suppose the only thing he could do was defeat the, um... the evil wardrobe or whatever it was and... zoom away on his motorbike for a lovely holiday in the Canaries. They'd be cheap that time of year, with it being out of season.' The old lady looked rather pleased with herself for this bit of invention.

'And as in all good fairy tales... he lived happily ever after,' Jim finished.

Nick nodded approvingly. 'Well done, everyone. You're a creative bunch, aren't you?'

'I don't see how this is teaching us to be Santa,' Albert grumbled. 'Making up daft stories about elves on motorbikes.'

'It's what's called a warm-up, Albert, to get your dramatic juices flowing.'

'Plus if there's one skill you need to work a grotto, young man... it's the ability to think on your feet,' Jim said. 'Believe me, kids will not pull their punches if you don't have a prompt answer ready... to even the most unexpected question.'

Albert seemed to accept this from the senior Santa present, acknowledging it with a grudging nod. Malcolm, on the other hand, looked about ready to assume the foetal position.

'I'll leave you to it,' Elodie said. 'You're all doing fantastically.'

She gave them a thumbs-up before heading downstairs, where Callum was waiting for an update.

'How's it looking?' he asked.

She grimaced. 'Honestly?'

'That bad, eh?' He nodded to Polly. 'Do you want to join us for our walk? I'm going to take her around the woods for half an hour, now the rain's stopped.'

The little dog put its paws against Elodie's calf, as if personally requesting her company, and she smiled. 'How could I resist those big brown eyes?'

'Thanks,' Callum said. 'I've been complimented on them before.'

Elodie laughed. 'Do you crack jokes now?'

'Only with you. You're the only one who laughs at them. Come on.'

Ten minutes later, they were watching Polly frolic happily in the little patch of woodland near the shop.

'So what's the problem?' Callum asked. 'Is Nick struggling?'

'No, he's doing great. I knew he would; he's a natural at this stuff.' She sighed. 'But as far as recruits go, this bunch are… not exactly what I had in mind.'

'In what way?'

'Have you seen *Police Academy*?'

'No.'

'Oh. Really? Well, there's about half as many as I hoped for. I was banking on the Martin's name bringing in at least ten for our first course,' Elodie said. 'And there's only one that's got "potential Santa" stamped on him. The others are a tattooed biker, a nervous wreck and two women.'

Callum blinked. 'Women?'

'Yeah,' Elodie said gloomily. 'Apparently we're now training elves and Mrs Clauses too. I couldn't say no, could I? Otherwise we'd be down to three.'

He gave her arm a pat. 'It'll build up.'

'Will it? I'm starting to worry I've made a terrible mistake, Cal. It seemed like such a good idea when I thought of it, but…' She looked at him. 'I guess you want to back out now you know what a hopeless bunch we've got, do you?'

Callum picked up a stick and threw it for Polly, who ran delightedly after it. 'I do not. It's a good idea, Elodie, regardless of teething troubles. I believed that when I backed it and I still believe it.'

'Surely you must have better things than my daft schemes to invest in.'

'Maybe I do, but this is more interesting. Besides, you thought of it, and I know that when Elodie Martin decides something's worth doing, she flogs that horse until it's dead.' He paused. 'I'm not sure that was the analogy I wanted it to be.'

'You mega-double-promise you didn't get into this as a way of doing me a favour?'

'I mega-double-promise,' Callum said, smiling at the playground slang from schooldays. 'I got into it, Elodie, because I know a winner when I see one. I'm an Ashley, aren't I?'

She smiled. 'Not as much as I used to think.'

'I'll take that as a compliment.'

'You should because it is.'

'Thanks.' He paused. 'I suppose, in the interests of full disclosure… it wasn't why I did it, but I may have felt a little guilty too.'

Elodie frowned. 'Guilty?'

'About all the years of competing over the grotto. You were right: it was your thing and I tried to take it from you. My father drummed it into me that I had to win at everything and I couldn't let go of that. It wasn't fair on you or your grandad.'

Elodie stopped walking to look at him. 'What's happened to you lately, Callum? You seem… different.'

'In what way?'

Elodie watched as his dog came running up and he crouched down to make a fuss of the little thing. Polly put her filthy paws on his thighs and Callum laughed, unconcerned about the dirty marks.

'More… laid-back, I suppose,' she said. 'I can't imagine the Callum of this time last year with a dog, or muddy pawprints on his expensive clothes. I definitely can't imagine being in business with him.'

'I couldn't imagine it either.' He stood up again. 'It just felt like things had to change. It eats you up, that lifestyle. Everything so shiny on the surface, but empty and hollow underneath. I felt like that was me too: shiny on top with nothing under the surface. Like the world I occupied was sapping whatever was real about me. Can you understand what I mean?'

'Better than you think,' Elodie said quietly.

'Really?'

She nodded. 'I'd started to feel like that too. That whatever was left of the *me* of me was getting eaten up by bitterness at the world. I felt like I resented everything and everyone.'

Callum laughed. 'And look at you now.'

'I know, what a transformation. These days I probably only resent about... eighty-four per cent of everything and everyone.'

'I stand by my opinion that you're secretly as soft as a marshmallow that's been left on the radiator. So what changed?'

She smiled. 'Nick. There's something about that man. He's got a stash of sunshine that infects people like a plague.'

'You think a lot of him.'

Elodie nodded. 'I did all I could to push him away and he wouldn't give up on me. I don't like to think who I'd have turned into otherwise. Nick's the best friend I've got.' She threw another stick for Polly. 'What about you?'

'I think... it was you, probably. When you accused me of exploiting your grandad's illness so my grotto could win...' Callum paused. 'I never rejoiced in him being ill. But there was a truth in what you said, all the same. I realised I wasn't much of a man – never had been.'

'Oh, I wouldn't say that.'

He smiled at her. 'I never thought I'd hear that from you.'

'No. You were right though: we are alike.' She smiled too. 'Maybe that's why we always found it so hard to get along.'

'Heh. You might be right.' He put Polly back on her lead. 'We'd better go. The class ought to be finishing soon.'

***

In the grotto, the recruits were working on improvising some Santa chat. Nick occupied the kiddy chair while Albert sat in Santa's throne.

'Ho ho ho,' Albert said in a bored, mechanical tone.

Jim shook his head. 'I think... you could manage to sound a bit merrier than that, Albert.'

In the mind of Albert, 'merry' obviously equated with 'as loud as possible'.

'HO HO HO!' he roared, practically blowing Nick's hat off.

'Er, yes. It needs practice, but... better,' Jim said weakly. 'Nick?'

'Right.' Nick assumed the persona of a shy child of eight, making his eyes wide. 'Hello, Santa,' he whispered.

'All right?' Albert said jovially. 'Who're you then?'

'Nick,' whispered Nick.

'And what're you after?'

'I said in my letter.'

'Oh yeah, the letters.' Albert looked him up and down. 'Something... girly, was it?'

'OK, stop,' Jim said, raising a hand. 'That won't do – sorry, Albert. No present judgements; that's an unwritten rule.'

Albert folded his arms.

'Was only doing it like you said,' he muttered. 'Act like I know it already and that.'

'That's... not how you do it. And we're going to have to work on your general manner too.'

Nick broke character to join in. 'You're supposed to be

warm and fatherly, Albert. You'll terrify the poor mites, yelling like that.'

'I am fatherly,' Albert said. 'I'm a dad, aren't I?'

'Then draw on that,' Jim said. 'Imagine you're reading your lad Chesney... a bedtime story. What does he like you to read to him?'

'Well usually I read from the *Leeds United Annual*. That or his book on dirt bikes.'

'And what sort of tone would you use?'

'Well, sort of...' Albert pondered. 'Quiet, like. I want him to sleep, see, don't I?'

'Exactly,' Jim said, nodding. 'Calming and quiet... like a lullaby. That's how Father Christmas speaks... when he needs to put a shy child at their ease. You work on that and we'll come back to it next session.'

'And your homework is to read the Biography of Father Christmas sheet ready for a session on Christmas lore next week,' Nick said as they started to file out. 'Good job, everyone.'

He followed them out and peered over the edge of the mezzanine to check Elodie was there to unlock the door.

Yes, she was there – and so was Callum Ashley with the little dog. They looked like they were just back from taking a walk together. As Nick watched, Callum reached out to squeeze Elodie's elbow.

A hand appeared on his shoulder.

'So?' Jim asked gently. 'Are you going to tell her?'

'We'll never make Santas of this lot, Jim. Albert and Malcolm are complete no-hopers.'

'Don't... change the subject.' Jim guided him back into the grotto. 'Well?'

'I really don't know what you mean.'

Jim nodded to the Santa throne. 'Sit. In the big chair, the one you earned last Christmas. Then put your hand on your heart… and swear to me as a fellow Santa that you don't know what I mean.'

Nick sat on the throne and took his hat off, sighing. 'I can't, can I?'

'I thought so.' Jim sat beside him on the smaller chair. 'How long?'

'Christmas. Maybe before.'

'And she doesn't know.'

'Course she doesn't.' Nick rubbed his face. 'She doesn't see me like that. You know she doesn't.'

'Perhaps not – not yet. But she doesn't see Callum… like that either.'

'She will though. He's set his cap at her, and Callum Ashley is a man who always gets what he wants.' Nick looked at him. 'Don't tell me you wouldn't approve? That you'd rather see her with me than your old friend's grandson, who, by the way, just happens to be the richest man in Chessory?'

'I'd rather see her… with the person who'll make her happy. That's all I ever wanted for her.'

'And you think that's me?'

Jim shrugged. 'I don't know yet. But I care about your happiness too, Nick, and I know you'll regret it… if you lose her to Callum without ever showing your hand.'

'You think I haven't thought about this? I've been thinking about it since Christmas Day.' Nick ran a palm over his forehead. 'Option one. I tell her, she chooses Callum, and the ensuing awkwardness means she's out of my life for good.

Option two. I don't tell her, she still chooses Callum, and eventually the fragments of my broken heart heal enough that I can at least stand to be friends with her. Neither are great, but the second still has an Elodie in it.'

'What about option three, where you tell her and she chooses you?'

'That was so far in the realms of fantasy it didn't seem worth including.'

'Let me tell you a story, kiddo.' Jim gazed into the distance; whether queueing up the words he needed or looking into the past, Nick couldn't tell. 'When I was a young man… I used to knock about with this girl – Sandra. Then one day, a mate of mine set his sights on her too. Well, Sandra and me… weren't exactly what you'd call an item so I couldn't complain when she started spending time with him as well. Things were pretty free and easy in the Sixties. But it galled me, because I did have feelings for her and I'd never told her. I could've kept my mouth shut and let him have her, but I knew I'd always be wondering then… what might've been. If it was him she really wanted.'

Nick sat up in his chair. 'What, and that was Elodie's nana?'

'No, that was Callum's nana. She did end up marrying my friend – Terry Ashley, if you hadn't guessed. But I'm still glad… I told her.'

Nick shook his head. 'Jim, if this was a pep talk then it's really not doing the job.'

'What I'm saying is, it all worked out. Two years later… I fell in love with my Mandy. Terry and Sandra remained friends of ours… and I never had to live with the regret of knowing I hadn't spoken up. Do you see what I mean?'

'Not really, no.'

'All right, let me tell you another story.' Jim went to stand behind Nick's chair and rested a hand on his shoulder. 'When Elodie was eight years old… she lost both her parents, suddenly and in the most painful way imaginable. Between then and last autumn, I could count the number of times I've heard her laugh on my fingers. Then over Christmas… her whole outlook seemed to change. For the first time in her life, there was someone in her world she could be herself with. Someone who… put a smile on her face.'

'Callum.'

Jim flicked his ear. 'You, you young pillock.'

'But… we're friends, Jim. That's all she sees me as. All she ever will be able to see me as.'

'You don't know that.'

'And you don't know differently.'

'No. But I know it's better to take a chance… than to risk losing what the two of you might be able to have if you just grew a pair of Santa balls and spoke up.' Jim slapped him on the shoulder. 'Think about it, eh?'

29

Nick did think about it. He thought about it while he was teaching in the Martin's grotto-classroom. He thought about it when he watched Elodie bonding with Callum, and when he lay in his too-small single bed with his feet dangling off the end, wondering what his future held. And finally, he made his mind up. Jim was right. If he didn't tell Elodie what his feelings were and she chose Callum, he'd spend the rest of his life wondering what could've been. OK, so his out-of-the-blue love declaration was almost certainly going to freak her the hell out, but he was never going to be able to move on, stuck in limbo like this.

They were now three weeks into the Santa School course, and their little class had grown a bit. Siobhan had brought along a female friend who also hankered to be an elf, and Albert had recruited a beefy fellow biker also hoping to make some extra cash this coming Christmas. It wasn't much but it was something, and Elodie had been thrilled at the increase in their numbers.

'And that's just the beginning,' she'd gleefully observed to Nick and Callum after one evening class – Callum had taken to coming over on Santa School evenings to entice Elodie out on his walk with Polly. 'I knew word of mouth was going to be our best friend. Next time we run the course I bet we get twice as many.'

'It's great that numbers are building, Ellie, but try not to get too excited,' Nick had said. 'Slow and steady wins the race.'

But Callum had been less cautious.

'You're right, El: things do seem to be taking off. We just need to keep the momentum going. This time next year, we'll be millionaires – I mean, those of us who aren't already.'

Elodie had laughed at this cross between a joke, a humblebrag and a palpably obvious attempt to curry favour by agreeing with her, and Nick had barely concealed a dirty look. Whether or not Callum had intended to emphasise the vast chasm between his wealth and lifestyle and Nick's... lack of wealth and lifestyle, that's what it sounded like. Nick had really started to miss the old days, when he and Elodie could happily agree on what a smug preening wanker the guy was before snuggling up at her place for a film night. Now whenever Nick tried to get her alone, there was Callum. There was always Callum, these days.

Anyway, tonight was the night. Nick wasn't going to stand back and let Callum Ashley flirt with Elodie while he ate his heart out upstairs in the grotto school. He was going to tell her, and then... then what happened would happen.

He wasn't actually due to teach tonight. Kenny Ross was running a solo session called 'Mind-reading Like Santa', so Nick and Jim had the night off. But Nick was a partner in the business, so it didn't look too odd that he'd requested to come along and observe.

When Nick arrived, there was no Elodie around – she was probably out with Callum, helping him walk his puppy – so he headed up to the grotto, where Kenny had started the session.

'Lesson one: use your elves,' Kenny was saying to his class. 'The children are here to see Santa. Elves and other helpers are invisible to them once they get sight of him. Train them to observe clothes, toys or phone apps that might give some clues as to the child's interests. And always, always make sure the elf gets the child's name before you meet them.'

Malcolm was scribbling frantically on a notepad, desperate not to miss a word.

'Lesson two: parents are your allies,' Kenny went on. 'Keep it vague at first and look at them for hints that'll help you fine-tune your patter. It's in their interest to help you out.'

Scratch-scratch-scratch went Malcolm's pen. Nick felt sorry for the poor chap. After three weeks on the course, he'd written down every word his instructors had said and he seemed more terrified about playing Santa now than he had the day they'd started.

Kenny went through some more tips, all eagerly noted down by Malcolm. They were essentially the sort of cold-reading skills a phoney medium might employ, but used for good. Clothing styles, Kenny told them, could give a clue as to the personality of a child. Broad statements can provide an opening, then honed with the assistance of elves and parents to give an appearance of true magic. And finally, a kid is at the centre of their world in a way adults aren't. If you get a talkative child, let them chatter about themselves and they'll give you plenty of clues that'll help you read their minds when it's your turn to speak again.

Once he'd delivered his lecture, Kenny gave them a

practical demonstration using Robert as the child and Siobhan as his elf. It was incredible how effective it could be, just keeping your eyes and ears open and using a few verbal tricks.

'All right, nice job, everyone,' Kenny said when he dismissed them at the end of the session. 'Keep up the good work, and don't forget to fill in your Santa journals before Jim's class on dealing with doubters next week.'

'Thanks for that,' Nick said when the students had gone. 'You're like a North Pole Derren Brown, Ken. I even learnt a few tricks of the trade myself. Hope you don't think that's cheeky, stealing professional secrets off a rival Santa.'

'Ach, no worries,' Kenny said genially as he packed away his notes. 'Glad to be earning my keep. I've been enjoying myself.'

'What do you think of our recruits?'

'Oh, we'll soon have them whipped into shape,' Kenny said, displaying an unquenchable optimism with the capacity to rival even Nick's. 'I'll see you later, young man. I'm due at a pub in the near future. Rob'll have got me a drink in.'

Nick frowned. 'Rob from the course?'

'That's right. I know him and Jim a bit from the allotments – and Jim from his tenure in your grotto, of course, although that was more of a hero worship from afar situation. We've got into the habit of going for a drink on Thursday nights.'

Nick tried to picture this. Robert, the most enthusiastic and impressive of their wannabe Santas, had thrown himself into the part with gusto and already had a full white beard to complement his tummy. What the local landlords must think when three full-bearded Father Christmases walked into their pub, bellies shaking like bowls full of jelly, could only be imagined. There was a punchline in that somewhere.

'Well, enjoy your sherries, Santas,' Nick said.

Kenny laughed. 'When Santa's a Scotsman, he drinks whisky – good whisky. I'll have none of that Sassenach Ribena. See you later, lad.'

When Kenny had gone Nick sat on the throne, head resting on his palms. He wished he was wearing his Santa hat so he could hyperventilate into it.

This was it. It was now or never. Nick was about to make an utter fool of himself, potentially ruin the best friendship he'd ever had and give himself 3am cringe material for a lifetime of sleepless nights. That was what they called romance, apparently. But at least he'd have taken a step towards a future with the person he loved instead of letting himself stagnate in his mum's spare room. And perhaps… just perhaps… there was a chance. God, if there was only that then it would all have been worth it.

She might agree to a date, at least. Just one night together to explore what they might be able to have.

Nick girded his loins – whatever the hell that meant – and headed downstairs. He hoped Elodie was alone and not giggling and pawing with Callum bloody Ashley.

He swore under his breath. Elodie wasn't there. There was only Callum and the puppy.

OK, so plan B. Nick would wait till she got back, hang around till Callum sodded off and hope he could drag her to a quiet corner of the pub where he could bare his soul with the aid of a tongue-lubricating pint of lager.

'Hey, Nick,' Callum said, smiling warmly.

'Hiya.' Nick bent to stroke Polly, giving him an excuse to avoid eye contact. 'Where's El?'

'Locking up at the back. How was class?'

Nick shrugged. 'They seem to be enjoying themselves. Whether we can make Santas of them is another matter.'

'Well, at least numbers are up. We ought to get more for the next course, now word's getting around.'

'Yeah, I was thinking about that. I was going to suggest we contact the *Chessory Herald* and see if they'd be interested in running a feature on us. I think they might give us a couple of column inches.'

'That's a great idea. Yes, I think they would.'

'What're you still doing here then?' Nick asked, in a tone that came out more hostile than he'd intended.

'Waiting to talk to you, funnily enough.'

'Me?'

'Look. Nick.' Callum met his eyes with such an earnest expression that Nick couldn't doubt he meant whatever he was about to say. 'I can't help feeling that after the bet and everything, me and you have got off on the wrong foot.'

'Why do you think that?'

'I'm just sensing that you feel a bit… I don't know, intimidated by me.'

Nick frowned. 'Intimidated?'

'Sorry, that came out wrong,' Callum said, wincing. 'I'm not good at this stuff – I always pick the wrong words. I mean, it's not just you, it's everyone. People can't see past the money.'

'You think I care about your money?'

'God, no! I just…' Callum took a deep breath. 'Let me

start again. The thing is, I know you're important to El. You're the best friend she's got.'

'Did she tell you that?'

'That's right. And since I'm her friend too, and since we're all in this thing together, I'd like you to… well, to like me, I suppose. So if, um, I can buy you a beer or something…' He grimaced again. 'Sorry. Like I said, I'm not good at this.'

'You want me to go out for a drink with you? For what, male bonding?'

'I doubt I'd be much good at male bonding. I was actually thinking all three of us – you, me and El. Tonight, or whenever you like. My PA's offered to dog-sit. I dropped Poll's overnight bag off with her earlier, just in case.'

Nick wasn't sure what to make of this. Callum looked like he meant it, and it wasn't the first time he'd made overtures of friendship. Nick had always suspected this was just another way of trying to impress Elodie, but Callum could be a hard man to read. He was like Elodie in some ways – isolated from anyone genuine, with few real friends. Elodie had chosen her isolation, but Callum had been born into his. If it wasn't for the very obvious feelings Callum had for the person Nick loved, he could pity the guy.

The thing was, he very much needed to get Elodie to the pub alone. It had taken him a long time to get up the nerve to tell her how he felt and he wanted to ride the adrenaline wave before it wore off.

'Well, the problem is—' he began, then broke off when Elodie appeared from the kitchen.

'All locked up.' She glanced at Nick. 'So, boys, are we pubbing?'

Elodie was in on the plan too, was she? She and Callum

must've decided to invite him during their cosy dog walk earlier.

'I think Nick was about to make an excuse,' Callum said, flashing her a conspiratorial smile that dug straight into Nick's heart.

God, couldn't he just cry? Look at them there: sharing each other's space, their bodies subtly brushing against each other like they were a couple already.

That's it – that's what this was. A happy couple, taking pity on their lonely, single friend who had no one to go out with. Nick was at an age where most of his friends had coupled up, so this wasn't the first time he'd been invited out just to be the pub's resident gooseberry. The big difference was that he wasn't usually in love with one half of the couple, and the other half tended not to be a super-hot millionaire.

'I know you're not working,' Elodie said. 'Come on, come for a pint. It's ages since we went to the pub.'

'I… can't tonight,' Nick said. 'I've, um, got a date.'

'Oh. OK.' Elodie did look disappointed. She didn't ask for details though, so jealousy obviously wasn't an issue. It had been worth a try.

Callum had his hand on Elodie's shoulder, for all the world like an adoring boyfriend. And she looked happy; happy with his touch, his proximity, his… him. So, so happy. Nick couldn't have imagined that look of benign contentment on the face of the sarky little thundercloud he'd met all those months ago.

'You two go,' he said in a flat voice. 'I'll drop Polly off with your friend, Callum. You can WhatsApp me the address.'

Callum frowned. 'Are you sure?'

'No worries. You guys go have fun.'

Elodie gave his elbow a depressingly platonic squeeze. 'Thanks, Nicky. We'll all go out another time, OK?'

'Sure thing.'

Nick followed them outside, now holding Polly's lead limply in one hand. He watched as Elodie walked away with Callum at her side. Polly let out a whine to see her dad heading in the opposite direction, and Callum cast a guilty look back.

'I know how you feel,' Nick murmured to the little dog. 'It hurts to watch them walk away from you, doesn't it?'

Polly whimpered in agreement and Nick picked her up for a cuddle, reflecting that this must be what it felt like to be noble. Funny how it felt a lot like dying a little inside.

30

Callum glanced back at Nick, who was walking in the other direction with Polly.

'I hope she'll be all right,' he said. 'I've never left her before. I'd bring her to the pub but she's not fully housetrained yet.'

'I'm sure Sam will know how to take care of her, if she volunteers at a shelter.' Elodie glanced back too. 'Do you think Nick's OK?'

Callum was on his phone, texting Nick Sam's address. 'He seems fine to me.'

'Yeah, but you don't know him like I do. He's been chipper enough in classes, but outside of the Santa School he's been distinctly glum.'

'Has he?'

'Well, glum for him, which is like you and me on a good day. I'm worried about him.'

'What do you think's wrong with him?' Callum asked.

'Work stuff maybe. I know he gets down about the struggle for acting jobs, stuck behind a checkout.'

'I'm surprised he struggles. I've watched him in a couple of classes; he's really pretty good.'

'I know. He says it'd be different if he was in London or Manchester, but with caring for his mum that's not possible,'

Elodie said. 'I had hoped a stint as a drama instructor might boost his self-esteem, but he does seem to be dwelling on something. Wish I knew what it was.'

'Maybe his date'll cheer him up.' Callum glanced at the thumbs-up emoji Nick had sent in response to Sam's address. 'If he's really got one.'

'How do you mean?'

They were at the nearest pub now, the door of the White Hart glowing invitingly.

'Just a thought.'

'I hope we don't attract attention,' Elodie murmured as they headed inside. 'I was thinking it'd be the three of us. Now it's just me and you… I don't fancy being the talk of the town if they think we're more than just mates.'

'Don't worry about that. We're old friends, aren't we?'

'I'm not sure that's quite how I'd describe us.' She nodded to a pair of semi-enclosed monks' seats. 'We'll sit there.'

Elodie glanced around the pub. She probably didn't need to worry. There was hardly anyone in: just a couple of oblivious lads watching football on the big TV. Still, there was no harm in being cautious. Callum seemed pretty blasé about these things, but then he was used to it, wasn't he? Not that Callum was a celebrity, exactly – not in the sense of attracting screaming fans whenever he went out like Harry Styles or someone – but he was well known locally as a playboy and the women he was seen with did tend to attract attention.

'This is nice and cosy,' Callum said when they reached the monks' seats.

'It was the privacy that appealed to me,' Elodie said. 'You hide there while I go to the bar. Try not to look too rich.'

Callum sat down, looking bemused. 'Right. How do I do that?'

'Just… I don't know, slum it like a regular Joe. Kick back, slob about, scratch yourself. What do you want to drink?'

'I don't know. A Blue WKD?'

Elodie raised an eyebrow. 'Seriously? What is this, 2006?'

'I was trying to slum it like a regular Joe. That's what kids used to drink back in the day, isn't it?'

Elodie shook her head, smiling. 'I'll get you a pint.'

'You want some money?'

'No, it's my round. Don't think I'm going to let you buy just because you're loaded.'

She started to turn away, then stopped. 'Cal?'

'Yes?'

'Why did you say "if he's got one"? About Nick's date, I mean.'

'Oh.' Callum looked like he regretted making the remark. 'I just had an idea… that he might be trying to make you jealous.'

Elodie raised her eyebrows. 'Me? Why?'

'Elodie, haven't you ever considered that Nick might think about you like that? It must've crossed your mind.'

'Well yeah, it's crossed it, but… we're friends, that's all. He'd have given me some kind of hint by now.'

'Has he not?'

'No. Just friend stuff. The sort of thing even someone as socially inept as me can't misinterpret.'

'Seems to me he might have and you missed it,' Callum said as he started rearranging the beer mats. 'He compliments you on your hair and your clothes. He notices small changes in your appearance. When I do that kind of thing with women… well, you can fill in the blank.'

'But he's not you. He's Nick. Trust me, he does that to everyone. The first time I ever met him, he was fluttering his eyelashes at a pensioner and complimenting her on her hairstyle.'

'Maybe with you he means it.'

'If he does he's keeping it to himself.' Elodie shook her head. 'No, Cal, that's just what he's like. He's a luvvie. They do that stuff.'

'But why drop a fake date into the conversation?'

'You don't know it's fake.' She smiled. 'Maybe it's you he's trying to make jealous. You're the one with the penny-bouncing bum.'

'Sorry?'

'Oh, nothing. I'll go get our drinks.'

'El?' Callum called as she started to walk away.

'What now?'

'How would you feel about it? If Nick did mean it when he flirted with you?'

She turned back. 'What's the point thinking about that? He doesn't, I promise you.'

'But if he did. If this best friend of yours told you tomorrow that he had feelings for you. Would you be pleased or mortified?'

'Mortified, probably, but since it's not going to happen then there's not much point me imagining it. Why do you care?'

'I do, that's all,' Callum said quietly, looking down at his beer mat arrangement.

Elodie stared at him for a moment before leaving to go to the bar.

Of course she'd thought about it – quite often in the early days, before the misunderstanding about his sexuality. Nick might not have Callum's gym-bothering physique but he was a very attractive person, in every sense of the word. Human beings flocked to him like ants to jam, whether it was Janine and the other old dears in the supermarket who alternately flirted with him and mothered him, the kids who genuinely believed he was Santa Claus, or the mums and dads who'd gigglingly dubbed him Father Dimples when he'd pulled in the crowds at Christmastime. His personality, everything about him, had a magnetic quality.

It took a lot to make a friend of Elodie Martin – at least, of the person she'd been before Nick had worked his Christmas magic on her. She had wondered at one time if what she'd started to feel for him was reciprocated, even daring to hope that it might be. It was hard to tell given her hugely limited experience, but there'd seemed to be... something. Chemistry, did they call it? Elodie had failed chemistry at school, which showed how much she knew about it, but there had seemed to be a certain frisson.

What had changed? Their Kurt Russell conversation, of course, when she'd believed Nick was trying to tell her it was only men he was interested in. She'd concealed her disappointment well, she thought – been glad to have at least made a friend, and counted herself lucky he'd dropped her a hint before she'd let her feelings grow any deeper.

Then when Elodie had discovered romance could have been on the cards after all, their friendship seemed to be so firmly established as platonic that she'd become convinced

Nick had no interest in her. She was certain he didn't. All right, she was by no means an expert on flirting, but when she'd occasionally tested the water with a hopefully sexy compliment, Nick had laughed in the same way as when he was doing his checkout-boy banter with Janine at the supermarket. And when she'd tried subtle touches on the arm or leg to give him a hint – a flirting technique she'd learnt from a copy of *Bliss*, circa 2003 – he'd totally failed to respond. Surely someone as touchy-feely as Nick, skilled actor and master in the art of body language, would know when someone was trying to indicate they liked him?

No, Elodie was sure. They'd known each other for six months, and in all that time Nick had never given a hint he saw her as anything but a friend. Perhaps he thought they were just too different to be compatible in a romantic relationship – temperament-wise they were certainly chalk and cheese. Perhaps she'd put herself too firmly in the friend zone for him to think of her like that. Perhaps he just didn't fancy her. The list of men she'd met who didn't fancy her was long and distinguished, and Elodie was resigned to adding another member to its ranks. Nick was a good mate: the best – and until quite recently the only – one she had. She should be grateful for that and not expect more from him.

The barman, who'd been outside having a fag, had reappeared behind the bar.

'What can I get you, love?'

Elodie pulled herself out of her thoughts. 'Evening, Joe. Pint of your pissiest lager and a medium pinot please.'

He raised an eyebrow. 'Pissiest?'

'Yeah, whatever's cheapest. My friend's trying to learn how to slum it.'

Joe shrugged and started pouring a pint from one of the taps.

She glanced at Callum while she waited for the drinks. He was still amusing himself with the beer mats, making sure they were all evenly spaced and at the exact same angle.

Her other new friend, until recently her bitterest enemy, was another mystery. Men were all mysteries, Elodie decided. As were women. In fact, people generally puzzled the hell out of her.

Callum was different to most people though. After spending a lifetime misunderstanding him, within a couple of months Elodie felt like she'd got to know him almost as well as she knew herself. Funny how quickly her feelings had changed, once she'd made up her mind to stop hating the world and open herself up to it a little.

Callum had been right: they were alike. Nature had intended them both to be good, happy people, Elodie was sure, and then life had come along with a big old 'mwahahahaha!' and turned them into the miserable people-shunning misanthropes they'd become. When they'd first connected at the wine-tasting they'd both been people desperate to fix themselves, with neither of them quite sure how. It felt good to have someone in your life who understood what made you you, even if they couldn't help fix the parts of you that were broken because the same parts were broken inside them.

She knew how Nick felt about her, but how did Callum feel? Thanks to Nick declining the drinks invitation, she and Callum were out on another not-quite-date tonight – in her territory this time. And Elodie was sure… OK, she was bad at this stuff. She had limited experience of the world of romance, and she'd clearly got it wrong with Nick in the early days when she'd thought – hoped – he might be interested. But Callum was like her, and that made him easier for her to read. Elodie had hardly dared to believe it, knowing the type of woman he was generally attracted to and how very many options there were for him, but she was sure – like, sixty-eight per cent sure at least – that Callum liked her as more than just a friend. Weird to think of, but all the signs were there. And when he'd said what he'd said about Nick, the worry in his face when he'd asked if she might be open to a romantic connection with her friend…

But if he was interested, what then? Callum's world wasn't her world. Callum's world was fast cars and designer suits and penthouses. It wasn't cheap lager and the pub and slobbing with a takeaway in your pyjamas.

'Elodie? Hello?'

'What?' Elodie forced her attention back to Joe the barman, who was waving a hand in front of her face. 'Ugh, sorry. How much?'

'£8.45 please, love.'

She paid and headed back to her table with the drinks.

'You looked lost in thought over there,' Callum said as she sat down next to him.

'Yeah. Just… pondering.'

'About what?'

'The mystery of men. I don't suppose you can shed any light?'

He smiled. 'That's the sort of thing us lot are supposed to say about you, isn't it?'

'Exactly. High time we turned the tables.'

He took a sip of his beer and pulled a face. 'What is this?'

'Lager. Cheapest they've got.' She grinned. 'Welcome to my world, rich boy.'

He took another sip. 'I suppose you develop a taste for it after a while.'

'Growing on you, is it?'

'God, no, it's rank.' He turned to her. 'So what were you musing on about us that's so mysterious?'

'I don't know. Just your general mysterious manniness.'

'Like, why can't we put the toilet seat down, that type of thing?'

She smiled. 'A little more weighty than that.'

'Was it me you were thinking about?'

'Partly.' Elodie hesitated, wondering if this was flirty banter and whether she should hint at what she'd actually been thinking, when a man approached them with a pint glass full of biros.

'Here for the quiz?' he asked, shaking his pens at them. 'Quid each.'

Elodie grimaced. 'Ugh, sorry, we hadn't realised it was quiz night. We just wanted a quiet drink really.'

The quizmaster glanced around the pub. 'Well if you fancied having a go, tonight could be your lucky night. I think there are only two other teams – Easter break, you see, so everyone's on their hols. Never seen it so dead.'

'That means we only stand to win about eight quid,' Elodie pointed out.

'Yeah, but it's the kudos, right? Plus we've got a special prize donated by Ashley's Department Store as well as the cash.' He nodded to a huge cuddly panda sitting on one end of the bar.

Elodie raised an eyebrow at Callum.

'What do I – I mean, what do they get in return for that?' he asked.

'We put an ad for them in the bogs and their logo on the question sheets. Pretty sweet deal, if you ask me.'

Callum glanced around the nearly empty pub. 'You think so, do you?'

'So are you in then?' the man asked.

'I've never done a pub quiz.' Callum nudged Elodie. 'What do you think?'

She stared at him. 'You've never done a pub quiz? Seriously?'

'Not yet.'

'And you've never seen *Police Academy*? Cal, you're wasting your life,' Elodie said, echoing the words Nick had said to her when he'd discovered her lack of Christmas film exposure.

'So what do you say?' Callum asked. 'Fancy popping my quiz cherry?'

She dug out a couple of pound coins for the quizmaster. 'Sounds like an offer I can't refuse.'

'I'm going to call him Quentin,' Callum announced as he walked Elodie home, holding the giant panda in his arms.

'Admit it, you rigged that. You donated a panda deliberately to win him back.'

'I swear I had no idea I was sponsoring the pub quiz at your local. Probably something Sam ran past me when I was thinking about something else. She always knows when she can smuggle things like that through.' He held out the panda. 'You want him? Just know that if I give him to you, his name's Quentin and it has to stay that way.'

She smiled. 'No, you keep him. You got more questions right than me.'

'I'd rather you took him. Polly'll only try to eat him.'

'All right, go on.' She took the panda, and Callum smiled watching her carry it. It was as big as a toddler and twice as chunky, and Elodie had to peer round it to see where she was going.

'How was your first pub quiz experience?' she asked him.

'Well we won, so I'm calling that a positive.'

'The spirit of all those Ashleys past can rest easy in their graves, eh?'

Callum was silent, and Elodie grimaced. 'Cal, sorry. I never thought... that wasn't a reference to your dad. I just meant... you know, because of your family motto about winning or whatever.'

'Hmm?' Callum glanced at her. 'Oh. No, sorry, that wasn't what I was thinking.'

'What were you thinking?'

What was he thinking? He was thinking things that weren't quite decent, all of a sudden. He was thinking of Elodie Martin, in his four-poster bed at home without a stitch on. He was thinking of his hands on her skin and his lips on her neck. He was thinking... that cheap fizzy lager really went to your head.

'Um, nothing,' he said. 'Nothing important.'

'Well, was slumming all you hoped it would be?'

'I don't know what I hoped it would be but I had a good time.' The lager making him brave, Callum reached for her hand and gave it a squeeze. 'I always do with you.'

Elodie looked a little bashful suddenly. She hid her face behind her panda.

'Cal?'

'What?'

'You know the last time we went out for a drink?'

'You mean when you dragged me off to a park bench and plied me with fizzy Blue Nun?'

'And I said it had better not be a date, and you swore to me it wasn't.'

'I did say that.'

She peeped out from behind her panda, then quickly hid again. 'How about tonight?'

'You mean, was tonight a date?'

'I suppose that's what I mean, yeah.'

He smiled. 'You tell me. You were the one who asked me to the pub.'

'Because I thought it'd be all three of us. Nick too.'

'But you didn't call it off when he couldn't come. Which makes me think you want it to be a date.'

They were taking the scenic route home, a little country lane that meandered through a patch of woodland. An owl hooted a mating call into the night air, waiting for an answer. The only illumination was the moonlight and a faint glow over the town centre – the perfect atmosphere for what he was about to do. Callum grasped Elodie's elbow and guided her into the trees out of sight.

'Well? Do you?' he asked quietly.

'Mmmf.'

'Stop sucking on that panda. They retail at £34.99.' He took it from her and put it on the ground, then claimed her hands.

'Do you?' he asked again.

'If I do... what happens?' Elodie murmured.

'No get-out clause. Answer first, then you'll find out.'

'I... I do. I think I do. Probably. If you do.'

'OK,' Callum said evenly. 'Well, then I guess this happens.'

Callum took her in his arms, his heart thumping, his brain hazy from the beer but determined he wasn't going to mess up this, his one shot. He lowered his lips to Elodie's and kissed her – gently with soft, exploring lips, not in the passionate, no-time-to-waste way he usually kissed his dates. It wasn't easy to hold back but he did it, waiting for her response before deepening the kiss, letting her arms wrap around him before he pressed her closer.

'Well?' he asked breathlessly when he drew back.

Elodie looked pink in the moonlight, and faintly puzzled.

'I don't know what just happened,' she said after a moment.

'It's called a kiss, Elodie.'

'I don't know what just happened... to me. It's all... new.'

He drew her close again, inhaling the sweet, uncomplicated scent of her hair. 'Do you want to come home with me and we'll work it out together?'

'If I did... if I do... what will we be tomorrow? Me and you?'

He leaned round to kiss her ear.

'Happy,' he whispered.

31

Elodie didn't have time to wonder where she was when she woke up next morning in a large, pristine room in a large, less-than-pristine four-poster bed – or at least, less pristine than it had been when she'd arrived. It was looking distinctly dishevelled this morning. Callum was already awake, lying naked beside her twirling a strand of her hair around his finger.

She tapped his nose. 'Stop looking so pleased with yourself.'

'I'm entitled, aren't I?'

'If you have to ask, then no.'

'I don't have to ask, you were pretty clear. I was just making polite post-coital chit-chat.' He leaned over to kiss her. 'I've been waiting ages for you to wake up. I'll get up and make us breakfast.'

'Don't you have people to do that for you?'

'It's the butler's day off.' He smiled when she stared at him. 'Joke, Elodie.'

'Sorry. I'm still coming to terms with the fact you make jokes now.'

'They don't really suit me, do they? But I'll get the hang of them.'

Elodie pushed herself up to look around Callum's bedroom. She hadn't been paying much attention when he'd led her in here last night. Her tummy had been too full of can-can-dancing butterflies, excitement and anticipation managing even to drown out the voice in her head desperate to remind her that she hadn't had sex in five years and had no idea if she could remember how to do it. Luckily Callum had known what he was doing, so that had made one of them.

The room was large and kind of bare, other than a few modern-art canvases on the walls. It reminded Elodie of an art gallery: clean and untouched. There was storage space here somewhere, she presumed, but wherever it was, it was cleverly disguised. Only the four-poster marked it out as someone's living space.

'Jesus, Callum,' she muttered. 'You know the floorspace of my entire house is smaller than this room?'

'Sorry.'

'You don't need to apologise for it. It's kind of overwhelming, that's all. I knew your life was different, but…' She looked down at him, lying beside her trailing the backs of his fingers over her thigh. 'Do you feel guilty? Is that why you're apologising?'

'I don't know.' He thought about it. 'Maybe on some level, but I mostly just feel embarrassed.'

'Embarrassed?'

'Or ashamed. When people say things like that about my money or the size of my house, it just hammers home that I'm the outsider. That I'm not like them.'

'Sorry. I didn't think about that.'

Callum smiled. 'I didn't mean you. You can say whatever

you want.' He shuffled into a sitting position too. 'I'll go make breakfast.'

'What do you have for breakfast?'

'Just a black coffee and an avocado smoothie. But I was going to make you French toast with strawberries and whipped cream.'

She laughed. 'You don't need to try so hard, Cal. You already got me into bed.'

He kissed her before pushing the duvet off his body. 'Exactly. Now it's my job to keep you there.'

Callum got out of bed and pressed a button on the wall that caused a door to swing open. It led to a walk-in wardrobe that was roughly the size of Elodie's bedroom at home – her guess had been correct, the storage space was indeed cleverly concealed. That had to be a rich people thing. It was probably terribly vulgar, letting your lovers see where you kept your pants.

Elodie tilted her head to appreciate Callum's backside as he fished for a pair of briefs. Nick was right, you probably could bounce pennies off it. There was a home gym in this place somewhere, she'd bet her life.

Nick. Why did thinking that name make Elodie feel unsettled? Half of her was desperate to ring her best friend as soon as Callum was out of the room and fill him in on this exciting development in her previously non-existent love-slash-sex life, to talk it all through with him and see what he thought of it, but the other half... the other half kind of didn't want him to know. Why?

He'd never approved of Callum – she could sense that. It all went back to Christmas, and that bet over the grotto when Cal had sneered at Nick's attempt to be Father

Christmas. But if that was all water under the bridge for her, after her history with Callum and his family, surely Nick could get over it too – especially since he'd won. Maybe it was a man thing.

'What's up?' Callum asked. 'You look preoccupied.'

He was partly dressed now, in jeans but bare-chested. It was still a novelty for Elodie to see him in anything other than a suit. He went to perch on the bed by her.

'I was just thinking about Nick,' she told him.

Callum shook his head. 'Thinking about another man in my bed? I'm going to withdraw my offer of French toast if you can't save your lustful thoughts for me.'

She smiled. 'I was thinking it's a shame you two don't get on better. He means a lot to me, Cal. It'd be nice if you could be better friends now we're...'

She trailed off, suddenly bashful.

'Now we're what?'

'Now we're... whatever we are.' She looked up at him. 'What are we?'

Callum cradled her cheek with his palm.

'You're a puzzle, you know,' he said softly.

'Am I?'

'For years I thought I knew you. I thought you were just like me – hard and jaded from the things that had happened to you, pushing people away but always wishing you could find a way back from the void.'

'Back from the void,' she murmured to herself. 'Yes.'

'But there's... something else. Something different. You really care about people, don't you?'

She laughed. 'How very dare you.'

'Yes you do. You care in a way I have to remind myself

I should. It comes naturally to you in a way it doesn't to me.' He stroked her cheek with his thumb. 'That's why you're good for me. Why I needed to have you in my life. I get it now.'

She blinked. 'You needed me in your life? When did you know this?'

'Primary school, probably. When you cried so much over that bird you couldn't save.' He smiled at her puzzled look. 'Elodie Martin. You've really got no idea.'

'About what?'

'About how I feel – how I've felt. About life. About anything. You pretend to be tough and cynical, then you look at me with those big blue eyes like you've been locked in a tower all your life and this is the first time you've ever slept with someone.'

'Come back to bed.' She pulled the duvet back for him. 'French toast can wait.'

'For some things it can wait,' he said as he wrapped her in his arms.

She tapped his nose. 'Not that. I want to talk to you.'

He frowned. 'It's not, is it?'

'Not what?'

'The first time you've slept with someone. Because if it was, I'd have appreciated a heads-up beforehand.'

She smiled. 'It's not my first time. But… well, let's just say opportunities have been more limited for me than they have been for you.'

'None of it meant anything.'

'Then why do it?'

'I guess it took away the numbness. I could be really alive – for a short while anyway.' He paused. 'It wasn't real though. I think… I really think the only time I've felt anything real in my life…'

'What?' Elodie said softly.

'It's been with you, Elodie. The most genuine emotions I've had have been because of you.'

'Me? All we ever used to do was argue.'

'Right. Whether I was rowing with you about your grotto or getting jealous because I thought you and Nick had something going on or railing against fate because I couldn't bring your parents back or fighting the urge to pull you into my arms and kiss you, the extremes you could make me feel… not to sound clichéd, but they were genuinely better than sex. Better than the sex I used to have.' He kissed her. 'That's why I need you. Without you, who knows if I'll ever get to feel anything again?'

Elodie wasn't sure what to make of this. She could sympathise with the feeling of numbness Callum described – she'd experienced it herself. When feelings became overwhelming, it was easier to shut them down than try to deal with them, until eventually you started to wonder if you'd forgotten how to feel anything at all. But to be told that the reason he needed her to be part of his life was because she was the only person with the power to stir Callum's dormant emotions… that was scary stuff. As much as she wanted this – wanted him – Elodie could wish that being with Callum didn't come with such a weight of responsibility attached.

But this was all new still. Things, feelings, would settle as they became more used to each other as lovers – assuming that was what they now were.

She ran a thumb over the stubble on Callum's jaw. 'So are we boyfriend and girlfriend then?'

'Is that what you want?'

She took a deep breath. 'I think so. I mean, yes. If you think Melissa and all those women with the diamond necklaces and horizontal boobs can bear the loss.'

'I'm sure they'll get over it in time.'

He drew her to him, and Elodie let herself get lost in a deep kiss. She was just unzipping Callum's jeans to restore his previous state of nakedness when the doorbell sounded.

'I bet that's Sam with Polly,' he murmured. 'Terrible timing. Hang on.'

He grabbed his phone.

'Aren't you going to get it?' Elodie asked.

'Just checking who it is. This is the app for my Ring camera.' He raised his eyebrows at the image on the screen. 'Heh. Speak of the devil.'

'Who is it?'

'Your friend Nick, with Polly.'

She blinked. 'Nick?'

'That's right. You want to go answer it?'

'I'm naked, Callum.'

'All right, then I'll answer it.'

He stood up to leave the room.

'Put a shirt on first!' Elodie called. 'And for God's sake, don't tell him I'm here.'

He turned to look at her. 'Why not?'

'I just… I don't want him to know yet, OK?'

'He'll have to know eventually, El.'

'Yes, but not now. I'll tell him when the time's right.'

Callum shrugged and grabbed a polo shirt from the cupboard. 'OK, if that's what you want. Don't go anywhere.'

***

'Sorry for the delay,' Callum said when he answered the door, tucking in the polo shirt. 'I was, er… entertaining.'

'So I see.'

Nick nodded to Callum's open fly, and Callum grimaced as he zipped it up. 'Sorry. You know how it is.'

'I have a vague memory, yes.' He raised an eyebrow. 'Anyone I know?'

'No. Someone I know through work.' Callum bent to fuss Polly, who was going mad at the reunion with her dad. 'And how's my best girl? Were you good for Aunty Sam?'

Nick looked awkward. 'Actually, I took her home with me. Your PA was in bed with the start of a cold so I said I'd look after Polly.'

Callum glanced up at him. 'Thanks, that was good of you. Did she behave?'

Nick smiled at the little dog. 'She was a darling. I nearly had to wrestle her off my mum to get her back to you.'

'I'm sorry you had to cancel your date, Nick. You should've given me a ring.'

'Oh right, that. Don't worry about it. He was happy to reschedule.'

'Long-term thing, is it?'

'No. Not yet. We'll see.'

Nick might be a good actor but he'd never make a poker player. Not with that nervous twitch at the corner of his eye. Callum was now more convinced than ever that this date of his didn't, and had never, existed.

'Anyway, any time you need a dog-sitter let me know.

Polly and me are great friends.' Nick handed over Polly's overnight bag before giving the pup's ears a goodbye tickle.

'Thanks. I might just take you up on that.'

Nick started to go, then stopped as if he'd just thought of something. 'Sorry, I forgot to ask if you had fun at the pub.'

'Yeah, it was quiz night. We won a panda.'

'And still found time for a date afterwards. That's impressive even by your standards.'

'It wasn't really a date. More of an ongoing arrangement. I'm sure you know how it works.' Callum remembered what Elodie had been saying, about wishing he and Nick could be better friends. 'So will you join us next time? At the pub?'

'I'll... play it by ear. See you, Callum.'

Callum watched him go.

He liked Nick, genuinely. He didn't quite get him, but he liked him. What he couldn't make up his mind on was what Nick felt for Elodie. Sometimes Callum thought he could see the same smitten, moonstruck expression on the man's face as he was constantly trying to suppress on his own. Other times, Nick was exactly the brotherly best friend Elodie seemed to believe he was. Callum thought he'd had the measure of Nick's feelings for Elodie way back before Christmas, but he could be a hard one to read.

But if Nick was a love rival, he only had himself to blame now he found himself with the losing hand. He'd had a head start on Callum of several months, and as much as Callum couldn't help liking the guy, when it came to Elodie Martin he wasn't going to step aside for anyone.

But he didn't need to step aside, did he? He'd got her. He was the one she wanted – the one she'd chosen. Not for his money, which he knew she hated, but for himself. It hit Callum afresh like a thunderbolt: the memory of Elodie, in his bed, asking if she was now his girlfriend. He was still determined to make her more than that by the time he'd seen this thing through. He'd make her love him by the end of the year, just as he'd sworn he would on Christmas Day, and then… then he'd make her his wife. That was the plan, and no one – not Nick Winter, not anyone else – was going to stand in the way. Elodie was the best thing he had in his life, the only thing he knew could really make him happy, and he was determined to keep her now he'd got her.

'I guess the best man won in the end,' he murmured as he watched Nick get into his car.

Polly blinked puzzled brown eyes at him, and he smiled as he picked her up. 'Come on, girl. You can have cuddles with Dad's new friend while he makes us something to eat. One big happy family, eh? I never thought I'd be part of one of those.' He carried her into the house, whistling to himself.

32

When Nick arrived at Martin's for his next session, he found Elodie humming a tune as she wiped down the counter.

He'd rethought his plan over the course of that evening a week ago when he'd looked after Callum's puppy, and he knew now what it was he'd done wrong. He'd dived in at the deep end, working himself up to a love declaration to a woman who had absolutely no clue his feelings tended that way.

Of course it was too late to resurrect Plan A, where he subtly prepared the ground with Elodie by dropping hints about deeper feelings – not now Callum was sniffing around, waiting for his chance to pounce. And Plan B, he could see now, had been too much, too soon. That was where Plan C came in.

A date. A proper date, just them, that was clearly designated as such – not just mates hanging out. He'd come in today with the definite intention of asking Elodie if she'd like to go out with him.

It was a plan with no downside – well, no downside except a broken heart if she said she could never see him that way, but he'd resigned himself to that no matter what happened. If she'd given her heart to Callum, she could say no without it being too weird. If she was still undecided, she could say yes without feeling she was committing herself to something too deep. And if it was Nick she wanted after all… then they could both live happily ever after.

He'd come early tonight especially so he could get her alone. Elodie rarely went home after the shop closed on Santa School nights, bringing her tea with her to heat up in the little kitchen, and it was half an hour until they could expect any of the students. Best of all, Callum wouldn't be lurking about with Polly, putting Nick off his game.

'You sound happy,' he said to Elodie, with reference to her humming.

Elodie looked up to smile at him. 'I suppose I am, for me.'

'Why?'

'It's been a funny old week. I'll tell you all about it sometime. How come you're early?'

Nick had an explanation for this all ready. He'd been practising playing it cool so he could make the date request sound like not too big a deal when he casually dropped it in.

'I wanted to show you the press release I've been working on for the *Chessory Herald*.' He fished out a printout. 'Do you mind casting your eye over it?'

'Of course.'

She read it through then gave him an impressed nod.

'That's good stuff, Nick. They'll want to cover us, won't they? I mean, we're unique.'

'And unique sells papers.'

'Well, I'm happy to give my approval as senior partner. You should probably let Callum take a look when he gets here, then we can get it sent out.'

'He's coming over again, is he?'

'I guess so. He usually does.'

Nick hesitated. 'El?'

'What?'

She'd taken out her phone and was smiling at a message she'd received.

'El, I wanted to ask… um, can you look at me a minute?'

She glanced up from her phone, surprised. 'Sure.'

'I wanted to ask… if you fancied going out to the pub next week. With me.'

'Sounds good to me. We can arrange it with Cal and find a day that works.'

'That's not what I—' he began. Then that cursed bell over the door jangled and Callum Ashley walked in. When it came to upsetting all of Nick's carefully laid plans, the man had perfect timing.

There was something different today though. No Polly, and Callum wasn't alone. There was a woman with him: around his age and very pretty.

That cheered Nick up a little. He'd been suspicious about the friend with benefits Callum had mentioned the morning he'd gone round to drop off Polly. For a moment Nick's heart had sunk, until it occurred to him that if Callum had spent the night with Elodie, he'd almost certainly want to rub Nick's face in that fact. But if he was bringing dates to the shop, maybe he did have a few casual girlfriends on the go. While Nick was still convinced it was Elodie Callum wanted, the fact that sex with other women was still one of his favourite hobbies was unlikely to endear him to her. Score one to Mr Winter.

Elodie certainly didn't look impressed.

'Hiya,' she said, a hint of coolness in her tone. 'Who's your friend, Callum?'

'This is Tiffany Berens,' Callum said. 'Tiff, this is Elodie Martin, who owns the shop, and Nick Winter, one of the Santa School instructors.'

The woman smiled. 'It's lovely to meet you both.'

'I don't mean to be rude, Callum, but why are you bringing dates to the Santa School?' Nick asked.

'It's nothing like that. Tiff is the features editor for the *Daily News* Sunday supplement – we go way back. I asked if she'd be interested in running a feature on the Santa Academy and she said she would.'

Tiffany nodded. 'It's the sort of quirky, feel-good story our readers enjoy, and at just the right time too. The *Coronation Street* actor I was supposed to be interviewing today blobbed on me so I need something to fill a page in a hurry.'

'That was my idea,' Nick said to Callum.

'I know, and it was a good one. I just thought we could aim higher than the *Chessory Herald*. After all, why should we limit ourselves to some local rag? We're interesting enough for the nationals. I had a contact at the *Daily News* so I went for it.'

'We do want as much exposure as possible,' Elodie said with an apologetic grimace for Nick. 'We can still use your press release as a news item on the Martin's website.'

'I didn't realise you'd written it already,' Callum said. 'Sorry, Nick, you should've said.'

'No worries,' Nick said automatically, trying to contain his glower. For the first time in his life, he felt like he was on the edge of a full-on sulk. Why did his plans never seem to work out when everything went so right for Callum – always? Had the man sold his soul to Lucifer in exchange for every blessing life had to offer? It just wasn't fair.

Elodie beamed at Callum. 'Thanks for this, Cal. It was good of you to arrange it.'

Callum simpered back at her, and Nick only just resisted the urge to gag.

The front door opened again and Malcolm came in, followed by the SEN expert they'd invited as a guest speaker.

'People are starting to arrive,' Nick said. 'I'll go up to the grotto; you guys deal with the press.'

When Nick had disappeared with the student Santas, Tiffany excused herself to fetch some item of journalistic importance she'd left in the car. Callum stole the opportunity to give Elodie a kiss.

'I'm leaving you to handle this, as the brains of the operation,' he said. 'I'd better go walk Polly. I'll come back later to see how it went, OK, sweetheart?'

'OK. See you then.'

Elodie smiled as she watched him leave.

The 'sweetheart' was new. It sounded odd, but she supposed it was sort of nice. Elodie wasn't sure she'd ever been sweethearted by a boyfriend before. Endearments had never really been her thing. They always sounded so… gushy. She didn't mind them from Callum though. They showed how hard he was trying to get the whole relationship thing right. It was new ground for both of them, really.

It had been a hell of a week: her first seven days in this strange but exciting new romance. Callum couldn't get enough of her. Actually it felt like he wanted too much of her, sometimes – Elodie was enjoying the honeymoon period, and the joy of being with someone she could be completely her own self with, but she would have appreciated a little time alone. But when she'd suggested to Callum that they take a night off from each other, he'd sounded so hurt that she'd ended up agreeing to go over.

She was getting more used, now, to this weird alternate reality he lived in. It wasn't becoming familiar, exactly – she still found it odd that Callum could and would make expensive purchases on a whim, almost without thinking. The only row they'd had so far had been about an expensive gift he'd bought for her: an antique cabinet he thought she'd like that was worth about five times her monthly salary. He'd seen her point in the end, and the cabinet had gone back to the shop. But in general Elodie was becoming accustomed to how Callum lived his life, and finding it easier to fit into his world.

His world was an empty place though. They'd gone to the pub that first night, but Callum wasn't generally a fan of going out. Elodie could see why. People did stare when they recognised him, and she wasn't keen on being conspicuous either. Still, she'd rather spend time with him in the warm, cosy pub than his bare mansion. There was something bleak about that place, for all its luxury.

The sex side of things… that was rather good. Elodie had always thought of herself as one of those people who doesn't really get much out of sex but goes along with it because it's part of a relationship; a way of being close. It had made her feel awkward and self-conscious on the handful of occasions she'd done it, and she'd become wary of entering relationships where she suspected the other person was going to expect a lot of it. Callum had quickly shown her that she could, in fact, be a passionate person if she was with someone she trusted enough to relax with. Elodie loved being with Callum, being held by him, and the tender way he touched her. Sex wasn't always earth-moving, but it was always nice: just him and her, together like that.

She could wish there was a bit less of it though. Callum's appetite for it easily outpaced hers. Still, it was early days. Once the novelty had worn off a bit then it was sure to settle down.

Tiffany came back in with her Dictaphone or whatever it was she'd gone to fetch. Elodie fixed on a smile, wondering how Callum knew her. Was Tiffany someone else who'd once been in his bed? She was typical of the sort of woman Callum used to date, before he'd incomprehensibly decided that what he really wanted in his life was a scruffy toyshop owner with unbrushed hair and no skincare routine.

'So, where do you want to start?' Elodie asked.

'I thought we could go upstairs and observe the class, then you can give me an overview of the course,' Tiffany said. 'I'd appreciate getting some photos too, if the students and instructors would be willing to sign consent forms.'

'I'm sure they will. Shall we go up? The instructors will have got the ball rolling by now.'

Tiffany nodded and followed Elodie to the second floor.

'What is today's session?' she asked, notepad at the ready.

'It's called Neurodivergent-friendly Santaing – awareness training on how to make the grotto a comfortable space for children with additional needs such as autism,' Elodie said.

'Most of our classes have just one or two tutors, drawn from our pool of instructors, but today we have all three present in addition to an SEN specialist. All are working Santas with experience of this issue.'

'When you say working Santas…'

'The best in the business,' Elodie said proudly. 'Jim Martin, my grandad, was the resident Santa here for forty years. He's a bit of a legend in these parts. Kenny Ross is a professional Santa who mans the grotto at Callum's place, and Nick Winter's the bright young thing who saved our backsides last Christmas when my grandad had to step down due to ill health. Father Dimples, the local mums call him. There are advantages to being a young Santa.'

Elodie felt nervous as she showed Tiffany into the grotto classroom, but she didn't need to worry. For once, their motley gang of potential Santas seemed to be on best behaviour. Malcolm seemed less anxious, listening with intense interest to the guest speaker but not scribbling everything down like his life depended on it, and even Albert's sullenness had disappeared.

The specialist talked to them about how the grotto could be adapted to ensure it was a safe space for those with sensory issues; how Santa and his helpers could assist children and parents to feel more at ease; behaviours they needed to be aware of and how to respond; helping families to avoid overwhelming experiences such as crowds, flashing lights, lack of personal space and long queues; accommodations such as special Quiet Grotto days, and appropriate gifts such as fidget toys. Then Jim, Nick and Kenny discussed some of their experiences with neurodivergent grotto visitors, with the specialist giving advice so the students could see how it would work in a practical sense.

'And of course, while being aware of all these things, don't forget the magic,' the expert said when the session was coming to an end. 'The children coming to see you are making memories to last a lifetime, regardless of their personal needs. There's nothing more rewarding than that. I think it's wonderful that everyone in this room has committed to giving children who might struggle to see Santa under ordinary circumstances that opportunity.'

Elodie wasn't sure why, but something in what the woman had said made her feel a bit tearful. It was lucky the lighting was low.

When the specialist had said her goodbyes, Tiffany asked the class if it was OK for her to get some photos. After those had been taken and consent forms signed, she started asking questions.

'How did you find that session?' she asked Albert, biro at the ready.

'Yeah, dead interesting.' Albert looked more enthused than Elodie had seen him yet. 'My little lad's autistic. He had a meltdown in the queue to see Santa one year and me and his mum never dared take him again. It's a shame the shops don't all send their Santas on courses like this, that's what I reckon. Why should our Chez have to miss out just because his brain don't work the same as the other kids'? He's entitled to a magical Christmas same as they are.'

Tiffany nodded, noting that down.

'How about you?' she asked, turning to Malcolm. 'Are you finding the course useful?'

'Useful? It's a lifesaver,' Malcolm said, surprising Elodie

with the vehemence of his answer. 'If I'd not had this, there's not a chance I'd have dared to dress up as Father Christmas and step out in front of thirty nursery children. And now… do you know, I'm almost looking forward to it.'

When Tiffany had asked everything she wanted, the students headed home. Kenny, Robert and Jim took off to the White Hart for their regular Thursday pub session, and Elodie left Nick to tidy the grotto while she discussed the course with Tiffany downstairs.

'Cup of tea?' Elodie asked Tiffany.

'A coffee, thanks.'

Elodie led her to the kitchen, where she made them both drinks.

'Well I must say I'm impressed,' Tiffany said, sipping her black coffee. 'Your students seem to be giving you rave reviews, your instructors clearly know their stuff, and your guest speaker was excellent. I have to admit, when Callum told me about this Santa School I thought it was going to be not much more than a PR stunt to promote your toyshop. But he's an old friend, and I was hopeful I could make a fluff piece of it. Now I've seen what you're offering, I can see I shouldn't have jumped to conclusions.'

Elodie flushed. 'Thank you. Um, how do you know Callum?'

'Oh, we used to knock about together when we were at university.' She turned to a fresh page in her notepad. 'What other classes are you offering in addition to tonight's session?'

'It's an eighteen-week course and there are two one-hour sessions a week, using a combination of our instructors. We try to tailor it to their specialisms. Nick's a professional actor, and he works with the students on general acting techniques, improvisation, body language and that sort of thing, as well as Santa lore and history – he's our resident Christmas expert. Kenny's excellent at mind-reading tricks to convince the kids he's the real thing, whereas my grandad tends to run the sessions on what we call Santa banter: how to chat naturally with the children. That's divided up by age group, so one to fours, five to eights and eight plus. I can send you the course brochure if you leave me your email address.'

'That'll be very helpful, thank you.' Tiffany looked up from her notes. 'You've worked hard on this, haven't you?'

'We have.'

'Aren't you creating competition for your own grotto though?'

'Yes, but that's inevitable anyway. I think the important thing is that wherever they go, children get the proper magical experience of a Santa they can believe in.'

'You don't seem to have many students yet.'

'It's been a slow start,' Elodie admitted. 'I had been hoping for at least ten, with the idea that we'd eventually run courses with classes of fifteen. Still, it's early days.'

'Well, best of luck with it.' Tiffany closed her notepad and shook Elodie's hand. 'I've never heard of anything quite like it, and it's clear your students love being part of it.'

Elodie smiled. 'Thank you.'

Tiffany handed her a business card. 'This is my email for the brochure. The feature will appear in next Sunday's supplement – or it will if I go home and actually write it. Thanks for your time, Elodie.'

'You too.'

Tiffany left, leaving Elodie feeling slightly dazed. She

was still in the kitchen nursing a quickly cooling cup of tea when Callum appeared.

'Well, how did it go?' he asked.

'Yeah, great.' She forced herself out of her reverie to beam at him. 'It went great, Cal.'

'Tiff got some good material for her feature?'

'I think so. She seemed really enthused by it. I got the impression she'd turned up mainly as a favour to you, but she was quite carried away by the idea by the time she left.'

He smiled. 'I know. She texted me.'

'Did she?'

'Yes, she was very impressed with you. Complimented me on my bright, articulate new girlfriend.'

'You told her about us?'

'Didn't need to. She guessed.'

Elodie narrowed one eye at him, smiling. 'Why was she so keen to do you a favour?'

He took her in his arms. 'Not jealous, are you?'

'Might be. A little bit. Is she an ex?'

'Sort of. We had a thing as kids, the first year of university. But that was a long time ago.' He drew her closer. 'Whatever I might've done in my misspent youth, El, there's only one woman for me now. You do know that, don't you?'

Elodie smiled. 'Convince me.'

'Now that I can do.'

He pulled her to him for a long kiss, and Elodie wrapped her arms around his neck. Her eyes fell closed, and she was only vaguely aware of a shadow being cast over them as something blocked the light from the doorway – until Callum broke away and she opened her eyes.

It was Nick.

33

Elodie blinked. 'Nick. Um... I'd forgotten you were here.'

'I could tell.'

She seemed flustered, her face flushed from the kiss Nick had just walked in on. Callum looked awkward too. As for Nick, he just felt... numb.

'I should probably go,' Callum said. 'El, I'll, er, see you tonight.'

He looked like he was going to kiss her goodbye, then he took a look at Nick and thought better of it. He shot out of the back door, evidently relieved to be making his escape.

Elodie busied herself with the kettle while she regained her composure, not looking at him. Nick was glad of that. It gave him the chance to fix his mask in place, ready for when she turned back. This was where he found out how good an actor he really was.

The numbness was subsiding, to be replaced by a hollow, empty feeling in the pit of his stomach. Nick wasn't sure why. He'd known this was coming. It had only been a matter of time until Callum's attentions to Elodie, his good looks, his success, his general charm, paid off. Nick knew he'd never stood a chance with her; not really. And yet seeing her there in Callum's arms, her eyes closed and her expression blissful as he'd kissed her with tender passion, had been so much worse than anything Nick had conjured in his nightmares.

And now he had to pretend nothing was wrong. To be the interested, supportive friend, ready to hear all about it. Oh God, he couldn't stand it.

But he had to stand it. His chance was gone, it was too late, and their friendship was all that was left to salvage. He couldn't let Elodie see what he was feeling – he had to hold it in, at least until he got out of this place.

'So how long has this been going on, El?' he asked, in as bright a tone as he could summon. Elodie was still fiddling with the kettle.

'Since last Thursday. The night we went to the pub.'

So Callum had lied to him. It had been Elodie who'd been in his bed that morning, when he'd answered the door with his clothes half off and his cheeks pink from whatever they'd just been doing. And Nick had actually been dogsitting for the man while he spent the night making love to Elodie, so now he felt pathetic as well as heartbroken.

'Do you want tea?' Elodie asked.

'Not really, no.' He flinched. 'I mean, OK. If you're having one.'

Elodie made them drinks. She seemed quite composed by the time she handed Nick a steaming mug, if rather serious.

'You're OK with it, aren't you?' she asked, and oh God, she looked like she really cared what his answer was going to be. 'I know you're not the world's biggest Callum fan.'

'Does it matter if I'm OK with it? I'm not dating him.'

'It matters to me. I want you to like him, Nick. You know you're one of the most important people in my life.'

She looked so eager for his approval, her eyes filled with earnest appeal. It made Nick want to cry.

'Does he make you happy?' he asked quietly.

'He does. Very much.'

'Then I'm OK with it. I'm thrilled for you, El, honestly I am.'

She smiled and took his hand to give it a squeeze. 'I knew you would be.'

'Just make sure he knows he's got me to answer to if he hurts you, OK?' Nick said, forcing himself to return the smile.

'My hero.' She leaned against the edge of the worktop, sipping her tea. 'God, I've been dying to tell you. This week's been… kind of a rollercoaster. In the best sort of way.'

'Why didn't you tell me?'

She flushed. 'I suppose I was worried you wouldn't approve.'

'I'd have been surprised, but I'd rather have known than not. I mean, I approve of you being happy, whatever opinions I might've held about Callum.'

Yes, he'd certainly rather have known. It would've saved him devising Plan C and potentially making an even bigger fool of himself, and he could've avoided the pain of unexpectedly seeing Elodie in Callum's arms.

'I was desperate to tell you all about it, but I didn't know how you might react,' Elodie was saying. 'He really is a nice guy, Nick. I know I didn't always think that, but I understand him now. He's just damaged, same as me. Same as we all are in one way or another.'

Nick was silent, staring into his tea.

'Nick?'

'I am glad you're happy,' he murmured, talking as if to himself. 'Genuinely, in spite of... anything else. But be wary of people who expect you to fix them, El. That's what therapy's for. It's not a relationship.'

'It's part of a relationship, isn't it? You help each other with the things that are tough for you.'

'It's when you start seeing it in terms of a person being broken and in need of repair. I wouldn't like to think of my partner that way.'

'It isn't like that. I mean, I guess Cal can be a bit needy – that's not surprising, when he's found someone who understands him finally after a lifetime of isolation. But he doesn't treat me like a therapist.'

'Just be careful, that's all. I'd hate to see you get hurt.'

She smiled. 'You're a love, you know that? Here, give me a hug.'

A hug was the last thing Nick felt like giving. How could he hold her now, still with that image of her in Callum's arms, with Callum's lips on hers? But he couldn't refuse or he'd give the whole game away.

'Sure.' He wrapped his arms around her, only barely holding back a sob as she burrowed her head under his chin and he inhaled the scent of that shampoo she always used. Orange and passionfruit or something. He'd never be able to experience that scent without thinking of Elodie.

'Thanks for looking out for me, Nicky,' she whispered. 'You're a good friend.'

'That's me. Everyone's favourite cuddly pal.'

'I'm so glad I can tell you about it now. I've been desperate to talk to someone. It's really opened my eyes to some things. Like with boyfriends before, the sex side of it was always kind of… I guess, formulaic. With Callum it's been a revelation. I've never had anything really passionate before.'

Oh God, he couldn't do this. Nick released her from the hug.

'Look, Ellie, I have to go,' he said, trying to keep the tremor out of his voice. 'I've got a shift in half an hour. We'll chat about it another day, OK?'

'OK,' she said, looking surprised at his abrupt manner. 'How about we have a film night soon and a nice, cosy chat? It's been ages since we hung out, just us.'

A night alone, just them. It was exactly what he'd been planning to ask her for when he'd come to work this evening. And now… now it was all too late. Now the idea of spending time alone with her, listening to her sing Callum's praises as a boyfriend and a lover, was too painful to even contemplate.

'That sounds nice,' Nick lied. 'I mean I'm kind of busy. I've got a lot on with the Santa classes and work and my mum and stuff. But we'll work something out.'

He nodded goodbye and hurried to the door, desperate to escape before she started sharing more details of Callum's amazing sexual prowess. He managed to make it to his car before he gave in and burst into tears.

'I take it you're off to work?' Nick's mum asked him one Monday evening, when he trudged into the living room in his Santa outfit.

'What gave it away?'

'All right, sarky bum. No need for that tone.'

He sighed. 'Sorry, Mum.'

'You're still mooning over that girl, aren't you? Months this has been going on. You're a right misery guts nowadays.'

'I know. Life just seems kind of bleak at the moment.'

'She's still seeing the department store chap?'

'Mmm. They're seriously loved up, and she insists on trying to tell me about it whenever we're alone. I'm such a brilliant actor in the role of sympathetic but disinterested friend that she's got no idea it's tearing me up inside.' He shuddered. 'The sex stuff is particularly gruesome. She's stopped talking about it now, thank God. I must've been doing a face.'

His mum turned off the TV. 'You're going to have to do something, Nicky. Tell her, why don't you?'

'We're well past the time for that. If I was going to do it I should've done it after Christmas, before Callum played his hand. I can't do it now, when she's so happy. It wouldn't be fair.'

'You're a good boy,' his mum said softly. 'So what will you do? Smiling while she tells you all about it then coming home and crying your eyes out in your room is not going to help you move on. Yes, I know that's what you've been doing. I'm not deaf.'

Nick perched on the edge of the sofa and took his hat off. He ran his fingers over the soft red velvet.

'I'm going to resign,' he said quietly.

She raised an eyebrow. 'Resign from the Santa School?'

'Yeah. I love it but I can't stay, Mum. It's too painful. If I go now, before Elodie's realised there's anything wrong, maybe I can do some healing and we can manage to at least save our friendship. I can't do that when every time I go to the shop, I have to see her with Callum or listen to her talk about what a fantastic lover and all-round great guy he is. I'll speak to Callum today about buying out my shares and they can recruit another Santa to take my place.'

'I understand,' his mum said gently. 'We'll miss the money though. You'd have to leave your Christmas grotto job too, I'm assuming.'

'I know, it's a shame. I hope I can find something else. I've given up on acting work, but running other drama classes is a possibility.' He glanced at her. She'd had a late shift at the cleaning job she'd started recently, and there were dark circles under her eyes. 'How's your work going? You look exhausted.'

Sheila rubbed her hip. 'I can't deny it's harder than it used to be. But work's work, Nick. It pays the bills.'

'I wish I could earn enough for us to live on my income. I know it kills you scrubbing on your knees for hours.'

'I do wake up a little stiff, I must admit. But what can I do? It's all I know.'

'I wish life didn't have to be such a struggle for people like us. It feels like there are some people who get everything, like Callum Ashley, then too many who get nothing. It isn't fair.'

'Life tends not to be.'

'Well it should be. I've a good mind to write to Father Christmas about it.' Nick put his hat back on. 'I'd better get to work.'

When Nick arrived at Martin's, he discovered things were all in a kerfuffle. Elodie was on the phone, Callum beside her leafing frantically through the book they used to record course booking information. Jim was there too. He was sitting in a chair looking rather weary.

'I'm afraid we're booked up until next May but I can add your name to the January waiting list in case of a cancellation,' Elodie was saying to whoever was on the phone. 'Yes, it's very popular. I can book you provisionally now and send you the course brochure with details of how to pay.'

She hung up and turned to Callum. 'Another one to add provisionally to May's course, but he wants to go on the January waiting list in case someone cancels. Tally him up, can you,? He's going to email his details to confirm the booking.'

Callum made a note in the relevant parts of the book.

'What's going on, you guys?' Nick asked.

'We're a hit,' Jim told him. 'That piece… went in the paper yesterday. Callum's friend gave us a double-page spread. Now suddenly we've got people… wanting to sign up from all over the place.'

Elodie nodded. 'I've expanded the class sizes to twenty per course and we're still booked up. The next course is full and May's is nearly sold out too, with a waiting list of people who want to get in earlier if anyone cancels.'

Nick blinked. 'Wow.'

'It's great, isn't it?' Callum beamed at Elodie. 'I knew you could do it, El.'

She smiled back. 'It was all you really.'

'It was your idea, wasn't it? Don't do yourself down.'

'Yes, but it was you who got us the press.'

Nick bit his tongue before he felt compelled to point

out whose bloody idea contacting the papers had been in the first place. Of course Callum had been able to go one better than anything Nick could do, with his national press contacts.

Jim got slowly to his feet. 'Come on, Nicky. Let's leave… the mutual admiration society to congratulate each other and get the grotto ready.'

Nick walked with Jim up the stairs. The old man nodded down at Callum and Elodie, still gazing into each other's eyes.

'That could've been you, you know,' he said in a low voice.

'But I fluffed my shot and now I'm destined to be miserable forever watching her in the arms of someone else. I know, Jim, you don't have to remind me.' Nick sighed as he followed him into the grotto. 'I'll have to go.'

'What, leave the school?'

'Yeah.' He closed his eyes for a moment. 'Every time I come in she's there with him. I can't stand much more. It… hurts too much.'

'But we're just taking off,' Jim said. 'You heard Elodie: as of today… we're a sell-out hit. This could be the solution to your money worries, couldn't it?'

Nick hesitated, thinking about his mum. That cleaning job was making her worse, and it ate him up that he wasn't able to support them both on what he earned. Thanks to the fact he was a partner as well as an instructor, the improvement in the Santa School's fortunes could make a big difference to his finances.

But at what cost? Having to see Elodie necking with Callum Ashley every time he came to work, all the time keeping up the mask of happy, jolly, cuddly Nick who took everything in his stride? It was tearing him apart.

His mum though. She couldn't stay in that job; it was weakening her every day. If he could just stand it a little while longer...

Jim seemed to read his thoughts in his face.

'Actually, I'm thinking I ought to take a step back myself.' He rubbed his eyes. 'It's been fun... but I'm not as young as I used to be. My body seems keen to remind me of that these days.'

'You do look a bit tired,' Nick said.

'Aye, it's too much for me really. Three classes a week... is more than I can cope with.' He glanced at Nick. 'I was hoping I could hand over to someone younger and fitter. Someone who knows... his Santaing and can take over the bulk of the course.'

'Me?'

'Of course you. You don't need me, Nicky. It'll mean more hours and a higher fee. Maybe you could even... afford to leave the supermarket and focus on your acting.'

'That's worth thinking about, I suppose,' Nick said. 'Thanks, Jim. What would you do with the free time?'

'Tidy up my memoirs. I've finished the first draft now.'

'Really, you've finished them? Well done.'

Jim took a memory stick from his pocket. 'I was going to ask if you'd do me a favour and... be my first reader, if you've got time. I'd like your feedback.'

Nick blinked. 'Me?'

'As one Santa to another,' Jim said, smiling. 'There's no one else I'd trust to do it but the heir to my throne.' He nodded to the gilt chair with its red cushion.

Nick took the memory stick, feeling touched. 'I'd be honoured. Thanks, Jim.'

'And for what it's worth… I still think you should tell her.'

Nick shook his head. 'She's with Callum now. I've left it too late.'

'I don't know. Call it Santa intuition, but Callum or no Callum, I think she'd want to know.'

34

When the students arrived, Callum started putting the paperwork littering the counter into some sort of order while Elodie ushered them upstairs. Today's surprise surge in demand had caused an unprecedented amount of extra admin work. But it had been worth it for the thrilled expression on Elodie's face.

When Elodie joined him again, Callum left off tidying and pulled her into his arms.

'Alone at last,' he whispered, kissing her ear.

She smiled and wriggled away. 'Give over, you randy sod. We have to get this lot tidied away.'

'You're coming over later though, aren't you?'

'No, I won't tonight. I'm pretty tired.'

'Sure?' He kissed her hair. 'I'm happy just to cuddle. We can have a different sort of early night.'

'Not tonight, Cal. I'm craving a night in my own bed. Just me, I mean.'

'Oh. OK.'

It always worried him when she said things like that. When it felt like she wasn't as keen for his company as he was for hers. As far as Callum was concerned, a day spent without seeing Elodie was a day wasted. There was nothing that gave meaning to his life the way she did; nothing that made him happy. He'd actually started to feel quite anxious on those nights she left him to sleep alone – when he reached for her in the dark only to discover no comforting Elodie-scented body beside him.

She looked up to smile at him. 'I'll come over tomorrow, shall I? You'll enjoy me more for having time to miss me.'

Enjoy her… that was another thing. Callum was sure Elodie enjoyed sex with him – she certainly wasn't the faking-it type. He tried his best to make it enjoyable, using all the skills his years as an oversexed playboy had allowed him to acquire. But she rarely initiated it, and Callum wasn't always able to bring her to climax no matter how hard he tried. Sometimes he could swear she was thinking about something else entirely. He thought of it as her 'have I left the gas on?' expression, where he was completely in the moment only to meet her eyes and discover that distracted look that signalled her thoughts were elsewhere.

He'd achieved his goal – Elodie was his girlfriend, Nick was out of the picture romantically, and Callum was happier than he'd ever been. But the plan he'd made last Christmas Day seemed to have stalled in spite of all that. His goal hadn't just been a relationship; it had been to make Elodie love him. Instead, he spent his time constantly wondering what she was feeling. Callum had often said that Elodie was like him, and in this case that was definitely not an advantage. He'd spent a lot of years learning to mask his emotions. Now he was confronted by someone who was even more of a master at it than he was, it was driving him mad with frustration.

Anyway, he'd thought it over last night and he knew

what he needed to do. He needed to make a gesture – to drop the mask and show Elodie just how he really felt. If he wanted to move their relationship to the next level, it was time to go big or go home.

'Hey, I've been thinking about Christmas,' Elodie was saying. 'I know it's months off, but I wondered about doing something a bit bigger this year.' She flushed. 'I mean, now there's us.'

Callum blinked. 'Christmas?'

'Yeah. Usually it's just me and Pops for Christmas dinner, but I thought if you didn't have plans then you could join us too, and Nick – he came last year so I was already planning on asking him. What do you think?'

'I don't celebrate Christmas,' he said automatically.

'Well yeah, neither did I after my parents died – not properly anyway. But now I've got kind of a little family, with you and Nick in my life, I think I'm ready to open myself up to the season again. There is a sort of magic to Christmas, when you let yourself give in to it.'

'I don't know, El. I'm really not a Christmas person. It depresses me, if I'm being honest. Too many years seeing it through the eyes of a department store owner.'

'Oh.' Elodie looked deflated. 'Well, OK, if it's going to make you uncomfortable. It was just an idea.'

'I'm sorry. I didn't mean to ruin your plans. We'll do something for New Year, how about that? A big party for everyone we know. I can hire a venue and a DJ.'

'I'm not big on parties. Besides, I always see my aunty and her kids for New Year, in lieu of joining her and her husband's family for their big Christmas celebration.'

'Well, it's a long time away. We've got months yet to iron

out the details.' He tilted her chin to look into her eyes. 'Forgive me?'

She smiled up at him. 'Nothing to forgive.'

'I'm glad.' He kissed her hair. 'Love you, OK?'

He tried to drop it in casually, and not scan her face too intently for her response. She mainly looked surprised, and a bit unsure of what to say back.

'OK,' she said. 'Um, thanks.'

'You're welcome.' He let her go again as the students started filing down the stairs. 'Looks like class is over. I just want a quick word with Nick before he goes.'

'Nick? What for?'

'In the interests of he and I being better friends from now on. I met an acquaintance from the theatre world recently for coffee and… well, I could have a career opportunity for him.'

Nick had followed his students down. He nodded to Callum and Elodie.

'I need to rush off, I've got a shift,' he said. 'See you later, guys. I'm glad things are picking up for us.'

He was about to leave when Callum called him back.

'Can I have a word in the kitchen, Nick?'

Nick frowned. 'With me? What about?'

'Something I think might be of interest to you. It won't take long.'

One of Callum's dad's favourite life mottos – and he'd had them for every occasion – had been 'never rest on your laurels'. Callum had taken this to heart at a young age. Yes, he'd come out on top in the battle for Elodie's feelings – it was his bed she slept in, not Nick's. It was his arms she laid in at night, naked and happy. But that didn't mean he should allow himself to get complacent. There was still another man in Elodie's life. One she was close to – too close for comfort.

He worried Callum, this best friend of Elodie's. Callum wasn't sure his girlfriend realised just how often she talked about Nick Winter, but it was a lot, and it was making him increasingly uncomfortable.

And then there were Nick's feelings for her. Callum hadn't been quite sure of them before, but he knew now. Ever since Nick had discovered Callum and Elodie were a couple, it had been painfully obvious to Callum that he was in love with Elodie – quite deeply in love. Perhaps it wasn't something most people would notice, but as he'd once told Elodie, Callum was good at noticing what others didn't. Nick did his best to keep up the mask, but it wasn't enough to stop his pain showing through.

Callum did genuinely feel bad for the guy. He liked to win, yes, but it wasn't in his nature to be cruel in victory, and he well remembered that hopeless feeling of loving when it felt like there was no chance of ever being loved in return. But he worried too. Worried that Elodie might have some romantic feelings for this friend of hers – feelings that perhaps she didn't fully recognise herself. Worried that their closeness would allow those feelings to grow and there'd be nothing he could do to prevent it.

He couldn't afford to take any chances; not while his 'I love yous' were still going unanswered. Nick was in pain, and Callum was insecure. If he could fix that situation by doing the guy the biggest favour anyone had ever done him in his life… well, it'd be helping them both out.

'What is it, Callum?' Nick asked when they were alone.

'I just wondered if you were still looking for acting work.'

'I'm looking for it but it's not looking for me. Why?'

'Well, I was having coffee with a friend of my dad's the other day. He's a theatre producer. He's just organising the auditions for a Christmas production of *Calendar Girls* at The Lowry in Manchester.'

Nick raised his eyebrows. 'The Lowry? You've got connections everywhere, haven't you?'

'I suppose I have. Anyway, I was singing your praises to Barry and on the strength of that he's invited you to audition.'

'For *Calendar Girls*?' Nick glanced down his body. 'I'm not the right shape, Callum.'

Callum smiled. 'He wants you to audition for Lawrence, the photographer – that's the biggest male part. It's got your name written all over it, and the theatre's not so far away you couldn't commute. Or Barry can help you and your mum find affordable accommodation if you wanted to stay nearby for the show's run. It's a bloody good salary.'

Nick stared at him. 'I'm struggling to get my head around this. You've used your contacts to get me an audition at The Lowry? I mean, that's proper stuff. That's the big time. If I get it… well, it could change everything for me.'

'And so it should. You're a great actor, Nick: I've seen you in action. You could really make something of yourself if the right doors are opened for you.'

'But… why would you do that for me?'

'Because you're good at what you do. Because you're Elodie's friend, and your career and wellbeing are important to her. And Elodie's important to me, so it follows I'm going to take an interest in you as well.'

'I'd have to leave the Santa School though.'

'I know.' Callum lowered his voice. 'But I did think, under the circumstances... that might be for the best.'

Nick frowned. 'What does that mean?'

'You know.'

Nick stared at him for what felt like a very long time.

'I don't believe this,' he said in a quiet voice. 'You're trying to buy me off? Seriously?'

'No, I'm trying to help you – to help us both. I know it hurts you.'

'The hell you're trying to help me.' Nick pushed his fingers into his hair, laughing. 'The scary thing is that you actually think it's normal, this sort of thing. I always wondered how everything seemed to go so right for you when it never did for me. Now I know. It's because you make it go right, don't you, Callum?'

'What?'

'When someone's in your way, you buy them out of it. When you can't get a woman to spend time with you, you throw some money into her business as a sweetener. When the person you've fallen for hates your guts, you fake-lose a bet to win her over. Money and machination – that's the Ashley family way, isn't it? Christ!'

Callum took a step back, feeling cornered suddenly. How could Nick have found out about the bet? No one knew about that – not even Sam. If Nick told Elodie that Callum had lied about it... he'd acted with the best motives, but it wouldn't look good for him.

'I don't—' he began, but Nick interrupted.

'I'm right, aren't I?' he demanded. 'I didn't win that bet; Kenny won. Ashley's won. You lied about it so Elodie would let you get closer to her, then you followed up your advantage by buying your way into the Santa School. I've had my suspicions about it for months. And now... now you're trying to buy me out of the way because what, you can't bear the idea of sharing her? That's some serious insecurity you've got going on there.'

Callum drew himself up, trying to keep his expression blank. 'You're being ridiculous.'

'Am I, Callum? Am I really?' Nick shook his head. 'You planned this whole thing from the start. Planned it to get to Elodie, months before you ever got involved with her. The bet, the partnership, even the puppy. You planned all of it.'

There was a long pause, the two men locked in a stalemate, glaring at each other.

'All right, so I wanted her, the same way you did,' Callum admitted at last. 'There's nothing shameful in that.'

'So you did lie! I knew it.'

'Yes, I lied about losing the bet, but only because I knew she couldn't afford the debt. Anyway, haven't you been machinating too, as you call it? You'd have done anything to be with her. So would I.'

'I wouldn't have done anything to be with her. I'd only have done what was fair and right – what was going to make her happy,' Nick snapped. 'It's not about me, it's about her.'

'You think I don't believe it's about her?'

'No, I'm sure you do. The problem is your perception's been warped – warped by wealth and skewed family values and too much time alone. The line between what you want and the right thing to do gets conveniently smudged to suit your agenda.' Nick pushed his hair out of his eyes impatiently. 'And so now you're trying to machinate me out of the way, are you?'

'I just thought you'd be happier – that we'd all be happier. You'd get the shot you've been waiting for, plus you could take care of your mum. Like I said, it's good money.'

'Don't you dare bring my mum into this,' Nick growled. 'I presume you guaranteed I'd get the part with this producer friend. What sort of bribe are we looking at here?'

Callum rested a hand on his shoulder. 'Don't be like that. I can see it causes you pain, that's all. Being around El now she and I are together.'

'Yeah, well that's my cross to bear. You don't just get to make me disappear, Callum, and you can't buy me out of the way with any number of dream acting roles. So shove your audition right up your pert little backside, OK?' With a last glare, Nick shrugged off Callum's hand and marched out.

35

Nick was still fuming as he lay in bed that night. It was past 1am, and he hadn't been able to sleep a wink. Every time he closed his eyes he saw the smug, self-assured face of Callum Ashley, with the curl of the lip that suggested he thought he was better than everyone around him, trying to buy Nick out of the way like he bought everything he wanted in life.

He'd won – wasn't that enough for him? Elodie was his girlfriend, and falling harder for him by the day. He had all the blessings that life had seen fit to confer on him and not Nick: wealth, good looks and the person Nick loved. He could at least refrain from rubbing Nick's face in it.

And yet… there was a little voice in Nick's head pleading Callum's case. The man had said a lot of things today that had made Nick's blood boil but there was an essential truth buried among them. It would be easier and less painful for all three of them if Nick was out of the way. He could stop torturing himself with the sight of Elodie and Callum together, Callum could be free to enjoy what was probably his first genuine relationship, and Elodie could be as happy as she deserved to be. Nick's career would get the kick-start he'd long dreamed of, and his mum wouldn't have to make herself ill in a job she wasn't physically capable of doing.

But not like this. Nick had some self-respect, even if he was currently lying in his childhood bed with his feet – socks on to keep out the chill, since heating was a luxury they could ill afford – dangling off one end. Callum thought he could buy Nick out of the way with a job he'd got for him by unfair means, and Nick refused to give him the satisfaction of winning again even if a part of him was tempted.

Nick jerked as his phone started buzzing. He fumbled for it and looked at the screen.

Elodie? Why would she be ringing him at this time?

'El, what's up?'

'Nick, I… I need you. Can you come to me? Please, just… come to me.'

Nick pushed himself up. Her voice was choked with tears. He could barely make out what she was saying.

'Of course, if I'm needed. What's wrong, my love? Where are you?'

'At the hospital.' She struggled to control her sobs. 'It's Pops. He's had another stroke.'

Nick raced to the hospital as fast as his mum's old car could get him there. He found Elodie ashen and swollen-eyed in the waiting room on the acute stroke ward. She stood up when he entered. Wordlessly he gathered her into his arms.

'How bad?' he whispered.

'They won't say. They're waiting until my Aunty Helen gets here – she's his next of kin.' Elodie sniffed. 'But… I don't think it's good, Nick. The doctors… they all look so serious.'

'Who was with him?'

'No one. One of the neighbours heard him cry out and called the ambulance.'

She gave in to sobs, and Nick pressed his lips to her hair.

'Is your aunty on her way?' he asked.

Elodie nodded. 'She was in Leeds at a work party. She's in a taxi now with her husband.'

'What do you need from me? Can I bring you anything?'

'Just… don't leave me alone. It's better when I can feel you.'

'Whatever you need, sweetie. Let's sit down, eh? You look like you'll fall down if you don't.'

Nick guided her gently into a chair and let her cry for a while, her face buried in his shoulder. It was clearly something she needed. Through the glass that separated the waiting room from the hospital corridor, he could see doctors rushing in and out of the ward. Elodie was right: their fixed, determined expressions didn't suggest anything good. Jim wasn't the only patient though, and he was a tough old chap. Perhaps… perhaps it would be all right.

'I knew he'd want you here,' Elodie said after a while in a trembling voice, mopping her eyes. 'He always did think the sun shone out of your backside.'

Nick smiled wanly. 'Yeah. I never could work out why.'

'He lost a son far too young. That leaves a big hole. You're alike in some ways, you and Pops.'

'Certainly in dress sense. But no one carries off that big red suit like your grandad.'

Elodie laughed wetly, but it quickly turned into a sob.

Nick put his arm around her and guided her head to his shoulder again.

'Will he be all right?' she whispered.

Nick sighed. 'I know you want me to say yes, Elodie. I wish I could. But I'm sorry, I just don't know.'

'Christmas…'

'Christmas?'

'Yeah. The last empty chair.' She let out a heart-rending sound, half sob and half gasp. 'Oh God, Nick, I can't bear it. I can't do this alone. I can't do life alone.'

'You're not alone, Elodie,' he said softly, pressing his lips to her hair.

'No.' She lifted her head to kiss his cheek. 'Thanks for coming, Nicky. I've never needed you more than I do tonight.'

'You don't have to thank me. Like you told me last Christmas, I'm part of the family.'

She smiled. 'Like the brother I never had, right?'

'No. Not like that.' He glanced down at her. 'Is Callum on his way?'

'Callum?'

'You rang him, didn't you?'

She pressed her temples. 'Oh God, I didn't even think. You're right, I'd better contact him. His grandad and mine were old friends; he'd want to know what was happening.'

'I meant for you, Elodie. He's your boyfriend. I think you could use his support right now.'

'It's late. I think… I think I'd rather wait until I know. One way or the other.' She looked up. 'But you'll stay though?'

'I'll stay until we've seen it through, and for as long as you need afterwards. I won't leave you until you ask me to. I promise.'

She smiled. 'You're too good for me.'

'I'm really not.'

They were interrupted by a woman and man rushing in. Nick presumed this must be Jim's daughter Helen and her husband.

'What's happening? Is there any news?' Helen asked.

Elodie stood up. 'I don't know – they won't tell me. They say they have to talk to you.'

A doctor with that same serious expression came in. 'Mrs Rowan?'

Helen nodded. 'Can you tell me what's happening please? We're all family.'

The doctor bowed his head. 'I'm sorry. We tried, but… there was nothing we could do.'

It was a drizzly August day when they laid Jim Martin, Chessory's legendary Father Christmas, to rest alongside his wife Mandy. The weather seemed to match Nick's mood as he gave his mum his arm to support her from the church to the graveside.

A large crowd of people were in attendance. All of Martin's student Santas were there, with Robert, Kenny, Albert and Malcolm acting as pallbearers. On top of that it felt like half the town had come to see Jim off. A lot of people had grown up here when it had been a tradition to make the trip out to Martin's to see the 'real' Santa. At the graveside, a small mountain of tributes had been laid: flower arrangements in iconic red and white, toys, knitted tributes and handwritten notes from generations of grotto visitors.

'It's all rather lovely,' Sheila murmured, leaning heavily

on Nick. 'All those parents who brought their children to see him, who then grew up to bring their children. And here they all are to pay their respects. The memory of visiting Father Christmas stayed with them, all this time.'

'Yes. It's sort of beautiful, really.'

Sheila stopped walking for a moment. Nick turned a look of concern on her.

'Are you OK?'

'Just a twinge in my hip. I've been doing too much bending for my old joints lately.'

Nick squeezed her arm. 'You have to quit that cleaning job, Mum. Do me a favour and give them your notice tomorrow.'

'You know we can't afford for me to do that.'

'Yes we can. All right, so I'll have to go on the scrounge at the supermarket, but I'd rather eat out-of-date creamed corn every day for months than see you make yourself more ill.'

'We'll talk about it later.' She nodded to the crowd gathering around the vicar at the graveside. 'Come on. They're waiting for us.'

Nick tried to focus on the service but his gaze would keep drifting to Elodie and Callum, standing with Helen, her husband and children in the section reserved for family.

Elodie didn't look happy, of course. She looked like she'd cried herself to sleep every night for a fortnight, which was no doubt the case. But with Callum's arm around her, gently brushing her hip, and the looks of tender solicitude he turned on her whenever he heard her sob, she looked… like she was where she was meant to be. Content.

Nick let out a sob of his own, and wondered which

Martin he was crying for. He couldn't help feeling he was saying goodbye to them both. He had felt like part of the family, but now, with Jim gone and Callum so deeply in love with Elodie… now everything was different. Things were changing for Elodie, moving forward, and Nick couldn't move forward with her.

It was obvious that Callum did love Elodie deeply – perhaps almost as deeply as Nick did himself. The difference, of course, was that Elodie loved Callum back. It cut Nick up, but he was glad too. Glad she was cared for and cherished. It was just hard not to selfishly imagine what it would feel like if it was him. If he was the one there comforting her, lapping up those little looks of trust and gratitude she gave to Callum.

He'd had a taste of it, that night at the hospital. For a brief moment, it had felt… sort of like they belonged to each other.

He wasn't sure why her instinct had been to call him and not Callum – force of habit, perhaps. Callum was still a relatively new boyfriend, whereas Nick had been in her life for over nine months. As awful as that night had been, when Elodie had rested her head on Nick's shoulder and looked at him with complete trust, it had felt so… right.

Then Callum had turned up. She'd texted him as soon as they knew what the outcome of Jim's second stroke was, and although he hadn't been asked, he'd driven straight to the hospital to be with her. He'd stepped into the space Nick had been occupying, taking over as Elodie's comforter, and Nick had found himself suddenly surplus to requirements. He'd left Elodie with Callum and gone home to cry himself to sleep.

He looked again at Callum and Elodie, holding on to each other in their grief, and closed his eyes.

He had to go, didn't he? His best friend was in the first truly happy relationship of her life with a man who could give her everything, a man who loved her as she deserved to be loved, and Nick was making everything complicated. No wonder Callum resented his presence in her life. It should have been Callum Elodie thought to call when she needed a shoulder to cry on, not Nick. He was muddying the waters, feeding Callum's insecurity, and making himself bloody miserable into the bargain.

'I need to leave here,' he murmured.

His mum looked at him. 'Leave? It's not finished yet.'

'Not here, I mean… never mind. We'll talk later.'

After the service, Nick went to add his own little tribute to the offerings at Jim's graveside. He placed the Mars Bar he'd brought among the toys and flowers.

'From one Santa to another, eh?' he said softly. 'See you, Jim.'

Once he'd shed his quiet tear at the graveside, Nick took his mum's arm and they went to offer condolences to Elodie. He kissed her gently on the cheek.

'I'm so sorry, El,' he whispered. 'There was no one like him. I loved him.'

She smiled weakly. 'He loved you. Like a son by the end.'

'I hope I made him proud.'

'I know you did.' She glanced at Sheila. 'You're coming to the wake at the White Hart, I hope? We can remember him properly there.'

Sheila nodded. 'Of course.'

Nick turned to Callum, who was standing quietly with

his arm around Elodie's waist. 'Callum, could I talk to you in private for a moment?'

Callum looked surprised. 'If you want.'

Nick followed him a little way from the graveside.

'I'm glad you asked to talk,' Callum said. 'I wanted to apologise for how we left things at the shop, when I offered you that audition. I can see why you were offended and I don't blame you. I really did have good intentions, hard as that may be to believe – they always do seem to backfire.'

'You weren't exactly subtle but you got a few things right.' Nick glanced back at Elodie. 'Thanks for looking after her. She shouldn't be alone.'

'That's my job. Looking after her.'

'Yes.' Nick fell silent. 'Yes it is.'

'Thank you for not telling her about the bet, by the way.'

'I couldn't. Not when she's seemed so happy. I thought she might not understand why you did it.'

'But you do?'

'No.' Nick closed his eyes. 'But I know you love her. I decided that earns you the benefit of the doubt.'

'Nick, I really am sorry how things worked out,' Callum said quietly. 'One of us had to win, but it doesn't follow that was necessarily the best man. You deserve to have good things happen to you.'

'Thanks, Callum.'

Callum stretched out a hand, and somehow Nick found himself shaking it.

'I never did bribe that producer, you know,' Callum said. 'I genuinely impressed him with how good you were. It'd be a level playing field if you did decide to audition – yours on merit, nothing else. You've got an excellent chance though.

He was telling me the sort of actor they wanted and it could've been you he was describing.'

'That was what I wanted to talk to you about.'

'Oh?'

A lump formed in Nick's throat. 'Take care of El, OK?' he said in a choked voice. 'For both of us.'

Callum nodded. 'That goes without saying. So you're going for the part?'

'I think… I have to. If not that then something else far away. You were right: I need to be away from her.'

'I understand.' Callum clapped him on the shoulder. 'She's going to miss you a lot. I'm sorry it had to end like this, Nick.'

'So am I.' Nick sighed. 'So am I.'

36

It was a gloomy late afternoon in October when Elodie went to answer the knock she'd been dreading.

Nick was on her doorstep, in a beanie and scarf to keep out the autumn chill. Elodie could see Sheila waiting in the car, the back seat loaded with cases.

'So this is it,' Elodie said quietly.

He nodded. 'This is it.'

'Do you and your mum want to come in? Callum's here.'

'We don't have time. I've got cast drinks at seven, sort of a getting to know each other thing before we start rehearsals.'

Elodie smiled. 'Cast drinks, eh? Get you.'

He smiled too. 'Never thought I'd make it, right?'

'I knew you would,' she said earnestly. 'How was your last day at the supermarket? Did Janine cry?'

Nick laughed. 'I came home laden with gifts – flowers, chocs, woolly things people had knitted to keep me warm in the frozen wilds of Manchester. I never realised how attached some of the customers were to me.'

She took his hand. 'I'm so happy for you, Nick. I know this is everything you ever wanted.'

'Yes. Everything.' Nick looked at his hand in hers. 'Nearly everything.'

'I'll miss you like hell, you know.'

'You won't. Maybe for a few days, but you'll soon bounce back.'

'Shows what you know.' She squeezed his hand and let it drop. 'I don't want to make it all sad when you're off to live your dream life, but I honestly don't know how I'll get by without you. You won't forget me, will you?'

He smiled. 'I'm going to Manchester, El, not the North Pole. I'll stay in touch.'

'You'd better.'

'Speaking of the North Pole, did you find a replacement for me?'

She nodded. 'Kenny's got contacts in the Santa world. He's managed to recruit us a couple of new instructors.'

'What about the grotto? I hope you've got someone worthy to take the throne.'

'Yes, Kenny. Callum's decided not to run his grotto this year. It seems silly to be in competition with each other now we're... what we are.'

'So, no more grotto wars between Martin's and Ashley's. It really is the end of an era.' Nick reached into his pocket and passed her a USB stick. 'Here. I wanted to give you this before I left.'

'What's on it?'

'Your grandad's memoirs. He gave them to me, the last time I saw him before he died. He wanted me to give him my feedback, but it felt more appropriate that it should be you who reads them first.'

'Oh. Thanks.' She put the stick away and smiled wanly. 'So... time for goodbye?'

'I'm afraid so.'

She put her arms around him. Nick squeezed her tightly back, pressing his lips to her hair.

'God, El, I'll miss you so much,' he whispered. 'You've got no idea how you've changed my life.'

'Right back at you. Break a leg, Nicky.'

He held her back to look into her face. Elodie tilted it upwards, expecting him to kiss her cheek as he usually did when he said goodbye. But instead he planted a single, soft kiss on her lips.

'I always wanted to do that,' he whispered, his eyes damp. 'Be happy, OK? I love you.'

'I love you too,' Elodie said, the words spilling out before she'd really thought about them. Nick smiled warmly, then he was gone.

Elodie was half in a dream when she went back inside. She could still feel Nick's last kiss, vibrating on her lips.

It had been… strange. There was nothing about it that wasn't friendly, although he'd never kissed her on the lips before. Soft and brief: exactly the sort of kiss one friend might give another as he prepared to move away. Yet…

And he'd said he loved her. That wasn't a novelty; Nick often said things like that. He was that sort of person. But when he'd said it today, his eyes brimming with tears, and the answer had dropped from Elodie's lips almost without any input from her brain, it had felt… different.

In the living room, Callum was standing by the bookshelf, examining her snow globe.

'This is out a bit early, isn't it?'

'I always keep it out.'

'Really?' He shook it, watching the flurry engulf the little family inside. 'Where's it from?'

'It was a Christmas present. Nick gave it to me.'

He frowned. 'Nick gave you a snow globe of a family Christmas dinner as a gift? That seems in rather poor taste.'

'It isn't like that. It doesn't mean what you think.'

She sat down on the sofa next to a snoozing Polly. Callum put the snow globe back and went to sit beside her.

'I take it that was Nick at the door?' he said gently.

'Yeah.' She snuggled against him. 'I'll miss him so much, Cal. Does that make me a selfish friend, when I know he's going to better things?'

'It makes you a little darling, like I always knew you were.' He kissed her hair. 'I know you'll miss him; that's only natural. But it is a great opportunity. This is going to open a lot of doors for him.'

'I know, and I shouldn't wish him back again. My world just seems so bleak without Pops and Nick.' She sighed. 'I'm dreading this Christmas Day.'

'You've got me.'

She smiled. 'Yeah.'

'I had an idea actually. About Christmas.'

Elodie looked up into his face. Always handsome, always well-groomed. Callum wasn't exactly vain, but he was obsessive about making sure he never had a hair out of place.

'I thought you didn't do Christmas,' she said.

'That's where my idea comes in.' He put one finger on her lips. 'Now no interrupting until I've told you what it is, OK?'

'OK.'

'I know you hate me spending money on you—'

'I hate you spending money on anything, when it's big money. It just feels like a barrier between us, that you're rich and I'm not. I can't stand being reminded of it.'

He raised an eyebrow. 'Did I mention something about not interrupting until I was finished?'

She smiled. 'Sorry. Go on.'

'I thought that since it's going to be a hard Christmas for you, and Chessory's full of painful memories, you might agree just this once to let me take you away from it all. A holiday somewhere hot.'

'Somewhere hot? For Christmas?'

He nodded. 'A complete change, with sun, sea and good times. That way you're not being reminded of your grandfather everywhere you look.'

'I couldn't let you spend that kind of money on me.'

'Please, El.' He took her hands and gave them an earnest squeeze. 'I've always admired that fierce independence, but I wish you'd let me look after you, just this once. You've lost someone close to you. It's OK to be taken care of for a while.'

'Callum… it's very sweet of you. But… I kind of want to be reminded of Pops.'

He frowned. 'You want to?'

'Yeah. I mean, a different sort of Christmas, in another country… that feels like I'd be sticking a plaster on my grief instead of facing up to it.' She put her arms around his neck. 'I'd far rather have it here, with you. A quiet, traditional Christmas making new memories together. I probably won't be very jolly, but… well, it feels like something I need.'

'I hadn't thought of it like that,' he said quietly. 'OK. I'm not one for traditional Christmases, but for you...'

'Thank you.' She kissed him.

'El?'

'Hmm?'

'That night... when you lost your grandfather. Nick was already at the hospital when I got there.'

'Yes. I asked him to come.'

'How come you contacted him before me?'

Elodie frowned. She wasn't really sure why. She hadn't been thinking all too clearly, and it had felt like the thing to do at the time.

'I don't know,' she said. 'I suppose... I was used to Nick being there when I needed someone. Besides, he'd grown very close to Pops. My brain was all over the place that night, to be honest.'

'OK,' Callum said quietly.

She summoned a smile. 'Hey, do you fancy a drink at the pub tonight? I could use some cheering up.'

'Do we have to?'

'Well, no, we don't have to. I just thought it might be nice.'

'We don't need the pub. I've got everything I need to cheer you up right here.' He nuzzled into her neck, and Elodie tried not to recoil. She wasn't really in the mood to have her neck nuzzled, but Callum was a big fan of it.

He drew back, sensing her reluctance. 'You really want to go? We can, if it means that much to you. I just thought we were all nice and cosy here.'

'No, it's OK. Maybe we could go tomorrow after work instead.'

'Not tomorrow. I'm seeing my accountant to discuss something important.'

Elodie frowned. 'Everything's OK, isn't it? At Ashley's?'

'This isn't about Ashley's, it's about me – me and you. There's something I want to do.'

'What can me and you have to do with your accountant?'

He kissed her. 'Don't ask me yet. You'll know all about it in a couple of months.'

'You're not trying to buy me something expensive again, are you? Because I told you, Callum—'

'I'm not trying to buy you anything. Trust me, OK, El? It's nothing bad, I swear to you.'

'Well, OK, if you're determined to be mysterious about it,' she said. 'Listen, thanks for agreeing about Christmas. I know you don't celebrate normally. It means a lot you'd do that for me.'

'Well. I love you, don't I?'

'I know.' Elodie paused for a long moment. 'I love you too, Callum.'

In Manchester, Nick had dropped his mum off at their new accommodation and gone to meet his fellow cast members at a nearby hotel. The flat they were renting wasn't exactly luxurious but it was a palace compared to their old place. Nick had spent a good ten minutes stretching out on the double bed in his new room, relishing the fact his long legs now had room to spare. When he'd left, his mum had been happily running herself a bubble bath.

He couldn't help thinking about his last goodbye with Elodie though. Nick wasn't sure what had made him kiss her like that. Suddenly all the months of lying about his feelings, all those missed opportunities, had hit him in a wave. He'd had to do it just once, before he left her forever. Just so he knew how it would feel.

And it had felt... perfect. It had lasted microseconds, their lips lightly brushing as he held her, but that had been enough. And her eyes had closed, and for a moment he'd almost given in and deepened it into a proper, unambiguously lover-like kiss, until his conscience had prodded him to remember that Elodie was spoken for and happy with someone else.

He couldn't help that 'I love you' slipping out though. She'd have interpreted it as the sort of friendly thing he often said, but he'd put his whole heart into it this time. She'd looked surprised as she'd said it back, almost like it had dropped from her lips in spite of herself.

When Nick arrived, the party was in full swing. The cast was mostly women, of course, with a few male actors who played husbands and other peripheral roles.

'Here he is! The young man who's going places,' Barry, the producer, boomed as he put an arm around Nick's shoulders. 'This is our Lawrence, guys and gals – Nick Winter. Remember his face, as I predict you're going to be seeing a lot of it on stage and screen in future.'

Nick flushed as Barry brought him forward to join the party, giving a little wave. 'Hiya.'

The cast were a friendly bunch. It felt good to be part of a theatre crowd again – to feel he was back where he belonged. Already his years working on the checkout seemed a distant memory. Barry continued to flatter him, the women were keen to mother him, and his champagne glass seemed to magically refill every time it emptied. It was another world, a Callum Ashley sort of a world, and now it was happening to Nick. Yet still his mind would keep flickering to Elodie, and that last goodbye.

After a while, he sneaked off to the bar for a timeout. It was too early to leave, but he felt like he needed a break from people.

'Penny for them?'

Nick glanced up at the man who'd claimed the bar stool next to his. He was good-looking in a cute sort of way, around Nick's age with red hair and freckles. He'd introduced himself earlier as the actor who'd be playing one of the hospital doctors – Marty.

'Sorry,' Nick said. 'I didn't mean to be rude, sneaking off to hide. It's a bit overwhelming, that's all. I've never been to something like this before.'

'We all had to live through the baked bean years before we finally made it to champagne parties.' Marty glanced at a barman who'd approached. 'Can I buy you a drink, Nick?'

Nick looked at the warm champagne in his glass and pushed it away. 'You know what? I'd bloody love a cold beer.'

'Birra Moretti?'

'Perfect.'

Marty held up two fingers for the barman, who oiled away to pour their pints. Not a word was exchanged during the transaction. It was very slick and exotic.

'You seem a bit down,' Marty said. 'Are you nervous about the run?'

'I'm just thinking about… someone I said goodbye to at home.'

'Sorry, I didn't mean to stir up painful memories. Boyfriend? Girlfriend?'

'Just a friend.' Nick took a sip of the beer that had appeared in front of him. 'I once hoped she might be more, but… well, it didn't work out. Anyway, she's happy with her rich hot boyfriend, I'm about to start my dream job… everyone's living happily ever after.'

'You don't look very happily ever after.'

'My face is still adjusting.'

Marty lifted an eyebrow. 'Is it only girls for you then? Shame for me if so.'

'It was only that one – or that's how it felt when I was with her. Like there was no one else in the world.' Nick looked at him. 'I mean, no, it's not only girls.'

'That's good news. Because I came over with the specific intention of telling you that if you fancied getting out of here, my flat's not far away. We could have a nightcap, run through some lines. What do you think?'

Nick sighed. 'That sounds great. It's been a long time since I… ran through lines with anyone.'

Marty laughed. 'Well?'

'I'd love to, Marty, really, but…' Nick hesitated. 'Maybe another time.'

37

December came. Once again Martin's Toy Kingdom was a winter paradise, colourful and twinkling, thronged with parents and kids queueing to see Santa. Summer, who'd been playing the elf to Kenny's Father Christmas, came downstairs to join Elodie.

'He's with the last ones now,' Summer told her.

'It's been a busy season, hasn't it?'

'It has but not as much as I thought. I expected when Ashley's closed their grotto, everyone would come to us.'

Elodie was scrolling through her phone. 'That'll be our Santas,' she said vaguely. 'The Santa School graduates, I mean. We've managed to get a job for every single one of them – even Albert.'

Summer raised an eyebrow. 'The tattooed guy?'

'A red polo neck under his suit worked to hide the neck art. We signed him up for a stint at a garden centre two towns over. I was worried we'd have problems finding him anything because of his criminal record, but they were open-minded about overlooking a couple of juvenile offences. They're running a Quiet Grotto for kids with additional needs. Albert had the training, and he's the parent of an autistic child too. He's doing really well.'

Elodie's gaze was still fixed on her phone. Summer nudged her.

'Are you OK?' she asked. 'You sound like you're thinking about something else.'

Elodie shook herself. 'Sorry, I was just skimming the new reviews for Nick's play. Several reviewers mention him by name as being one to watch.'

'It's great he's doing so well, isn't it?'

'I know, I'm thrilled for him.'

'And the Santa School's booked up for the next two years, the grotto's doing well, you and Callum are all loved up. Everything's worked out great.'

'I guess it has.'

Summer narrowed one eye. 'Then why do you look like that?'

'Like what?'

'Sort of… sad. Something's on your mind, isn't it?'

Elodie sighed. 'It's Nick. I miss him, Sum. I thought it'd get easier, but… he's left a big hole. The closer we get to Christmas, the more I find myself thinking about him and about this time last year, when he was teaching me to fall in love with the season again.'

'You haven't heard from him?'

Elodie shook her head. 'I've not had a word since we said goodbye. I've sent a couple of WhatsApps but no reply. He's busy, I guess.'

'How come you didn't want to come see him with me and Mum on Christmas Eve?' Summer asked. 'We could've made it a proper girls' night. She was surprised when I said you didn't want her to book you a ticket.'

'I don't know. I just felt like… I needed Nick to invite me.'

Summer frowned. 'Why?'

'Things were a bit strange when we said goodbye. When he didn't reply to my texts, I felt weird about just turning up.' She looked at the stairs, where the last grotto visitors were descending. 'Can you get everything shut up? I need to give Callum a ring.'

'Sure.'

Elodie pulled up Callum's work number and went into the kitchen to call him.

'Cal, can you come over tonight?' she asked.

'I'd love to.' Callum sounded pleased. 'What's brought this on?'

'I've got something to do when I get home that's going to be a bit emotional. Something I've been putting off.'

'Your grandad's memoirs?'

'Yeah.'

'Why tonight, sweetheart?'

'They've been on my mind lately, with it being grotto season,' Elodie said. 'I think I'm ready. I could use a hug afterwards though.'

'I can always manage that.'

'Thanks, Cal.' She took a deep breath. 'I love you.'

'I love you too. Bye, El.'

Callum hung up the phone in his office, feeling pleased and a little puzzled.

That had been two firsts. It was the first time Elodie had invited him over rather than him suggesting they got together, and it was the first time in their nearly eight-month relationship that she'd told him she loved him unprompted.

He said it often, and she usually said it back, but she'd never offered an 'I love you' first until today.

Callum had been worried lately. He'd been convinced that once Nick Winter was out of sight, he'd quickly be out of mind for Elodie too, but he'd been wrong. She'd been down about him leaving for far longer than Callum would have felt a friend, however close, really merited. Yes, she was still grieving, which partly accounted for her low mood – especially now they were in the run-up to Christmas, with all the painful memories of her parents' accident that went with the season. But he knew she regularly checked Nick's Facebook page to see what he was up to, or looked up photos and reviews of the show he was in.

It tore Callum up to think he was still sharing her, although Nick had been out of their lives for more than two months. The fact she seemed to have lost interest in sex concerned him too. He'd explained it at first as a natural response to the loss of her grandfather – grief could do that to people. But he'd been starting to worry it might have more to do with Nick Winter than he liked to imagine.

That was where the next stage of Callum's plan came in. He took a small box from his drawer and flipped it open.

There was a knock at the door and Sam walked in.

'Cal, I—' She stopped when she spotted the box in his hand. 'Bloody hell, what's that?'

'An engagement ring,' he said, handing her the box. 'I'm going to propose to Elodie tonight. Do you like it?'

'No offence, Callum, but it's… I mean, the box says Argos on it.'

He smiled. 'I know.'

'Is it a joke? I'd be pretty insulted if a man proposed to me with an Argos ring even if he wasn't a millionaire.'

'It's symbolic,' Callum said, taking the ring back. 'The whole time Elodie and I have been together, my money's created this barrier between us. She told me once I could never be part of her world, living the way I do, and I know she still feels that way deep down. I need to show her I want to be with her, properly – in her world, not mine.'

Sam shook her head. 'Sorry, Cal, but I don't get it.'

'If she says yes... I'm giving it all up. I'll sell the store, and give everything I don't need to people who do. I'd rather have Elodie Martin than any of it. All it's ever done is make me miserable.'

'Jesus Christ! That's a bit extreme, isn't it?'

'It's a gesture, Sam. A gesture to love. If it isn't extreme, I might as well not bother.'

Sam rested a hand on his arm. 'Callum, I wish you'd think about this.'

'I have thought about it. I've been thinking about it for months. I talked it through with my accountant back in October.'

Sam looked dazed.

'You've always lived for this place,' she said at last.

'I know, and what has it brought me? Nothing but loneliness.'

'But... what will you do? Without Ashley's, what will you do?'

He shrugged. 'Anything I want. Charity work seems appealing – something with animals maybe. Start a family, do up a campervan, learn how to garden. Just be a regular guy.'

Sam raised an eyebrow. 'You're going to take up gardening? You?'

'Why shouldn't I take up gardening? I might be good at it.'

She paused before taking a seat. 'Callum, can I say something to you? Not as your PA. As a friend.'

Callum smiled. 'If you can't, I don't know who can.'

'It's just… well, ever since you and Elodie started seeing each other it's like that's all you can focus on. Like she's taken the place of work in your life. And as annoying as that is for me when I'm trying to get you to focus on this place, I am pleased you've got love in your life. You deserve it. Only…'

'Only?'

'I've never seen you like this over a woman before. I've seen you with plenty, but this is… new. Proposing after eight months – giving everything up for her. That isn't at all like the Callum Ashley I know.'

'I'd tend to see that as a good thing, wouldn't you?'

'To an extent. I still can't help thinking…' She met his eyes. 'Can I speak frankly, Cal? Human to human?'

'I wish you would.'

'I've known you a long time now. You've always got what you wanted, and I know you've enjoyed it most when you've had to work for it. Do you ever think you might be obsessing over Elodie Martin because… well, because she's something you can't get easily?'

Callum didn't even hesitate before answering.

'Yes,' he said. 'That's exactly what I was doing. Back when I started this.'

'Started seeing Elodie?'

'Started *this*. This plan I had, to get El to marry me.' He stared at the cheap ring in its Argos box. 'But now... Sam, I'm not doing it for me any more. I'm doing it for her. It's not about winning. It's about Elodie – her future. Her happiness.'

Sam looked puzzled. 'You really think it'll make her happy if you give up all your money?'

'I think that's what it'll take for her to be happy with me, yes. But...' He sighed. 'It might not be enough.'

'How do you mean?'

'I don't know yet. I'll know when she gives me an answer. That's what this is all about – finding out the answer to something.'

'So you think she might say no?'

Callum smiled a little sadly at the ring. 'I'm not sure. But one way or another, it'll be an ending.'

Elodie slotted the USB stick into her laptop, then took a deep breath as she opened the document on it.

The title page appeared. *Miracle on Whitsun Avenue: Memories of a Toyshop Santa*. She remembered now. The day he'd started writing, Pops had said he hadn't worked out yet what his miracle was going to be. Had he found out before he reached the end? She started reading.

Elodie had expected reading Pops's memories to be an emotional experience, and it was, but she was laughing along with her tears. He'd included all the best anecdotes from his days in the grotto: the woman who'd brought her puppy to see Father Christmas and he'd left a little present of his own on the grotto floor; the sulky child who, when asked what he wanted for Christmas, had announced loudly 'a new dad because mine's rubbish!'; and the one he'd enjoyed telling more than any other, when he'd visited Elodie's class at school and she'd told the other children proudly that 'he's not always Santa – sometimes he's my grandad!'

It wasn't all anecdotes though. Pops had dug deep, aware, perhaps, that he was living on borrowed time. He talked about how he met his wife Mandy, Elodie's nana, and how she'd healed the heart broken when his first love Sandra had married someone else. Elodie hadn't realised Pops had been in love before. Then there was an emotional account of the loss of his son and daughter-in-law, and how he'd found himself a parent to their little daughter at an age when he'd believed his child-raising days were over. How he worried he was getting it all wrong as he and his wife tried to help the grieving girl who just wanted to close the doors on the world, and feared she was becoming too isolated to ever find happiness.

That wrung out a few tears. Still, Elodie felt like she was holding it together pretty well until she got to Pops's final sentence.

So I'm dedicating this story to you, Elodie – yes, I know you'll be reading this. You were my miracle. Never stop believing in people, kiddo, and never shut out those who love you. Throw open the doors, and be happy. Pops x

When Callum let himself in a little later with a bottle of wine and a bouquet of red roses, he found Elodie in a huddle on the sofa, laughing and sobbing her eyes out.

'Hey.' He put down the gifts and put his arms around her. 'What's all this? Were they that upsetting?'

'They weren't upsetting.' Elodie wiped her eyes on her sleeve. 'It's just he... there was a dedication at the end. To me. He said I was his miracle.'

Callum stroked her hair. 'That's beautiful, El.'

'I know. That wasn't what first set me off though. It was when he was talking about falling in love with my nan.'

He guided her head to his shoulder. 'Tell me.'

'Did you know my grandad was in love with your grandma, back in the Sixties?'

'I'd heard they went out with each other. I didn't know he'd had strong feelings for her.'

Elodie nodded. 'They sounded a lot alike, although she was never as keen on him as he was on her. It broke his heart when she picked your grandad over him.'

'And then he met your nan.'

She smiled. 'Yeah, not exactly a match made in heaven at first. She was a real free spirit, whereas my grandad was always one to play by the rules. For their first date, she invited him for a picnic by the lake. He was scandalised when she stripped off and jumped in to cool down.'

'Skinny-dipping in the lake? They sound a bit racy, these memoirs.'

'I know, shocking.'

'So how did he end up falling for her?'

'I think… they were kind of what each other needed. Perhaps my grandad and Sandra were more alike, but Pops became less rigid and more adventurous through being with my nan, and… he was happier for it, in the end.' Elodie gave a wet laugh, wiping her eyes. 'Sorry. Here I go again.'

'You let it out.' Callum waited until she'd got her emotions under control, then brushed a tear from her cheek. 'Elodie…'

'What?'

'I've never known anyone like you.'

She smiled. 'Thanks. Would you say it's the streaky mascara or the sexy Batman hoodie that's doing it for you?'

'Both,' he said, smiling too, but he looked nervous. 'El, I need to ask you a question. It's important. How you answer is important.'

Elodie blinked. 'Is it?'

'Very. Whether you say yes or no, your answer will tell me all I need to know.'

'OK, what is this important question?'

He untangled himself from her so he could drop to one knee. 'It's this one.'

Elodie stared at him. 'What, you mean... you don't mean...'

'I'm afraid so.' He produced a box and held it out to her.

Elodie blinked at it. 'Argos?'

He nodded. '£74.99, this set me back.'

'But... what does it mean, Cal?'

'The ring's a symbol,' he said softly, taking her hand. 'I know my money comes between us. I know you hate that I'm rich, and that our lifestyles are so different. It means that if you'll agree to spend the rest of your life with me, I'll give it all up. The house, the cars, the suits, the money. Even the store. You mean more to me than any of that, El. I want to be with you, in your world, where I can feel like a real human being. Where I can feel.'

'I can't...' She stared at the ring, then looked up at Callum. 'You'd really do that for me?'

'I'd do anything for you, Elodie, because I love you. I knew that a long time ago. Last Christmas I swore I'd make you fall as deeply in love with me as I was with you, and that one day you'd be my wife. Well, if it takes giving up all my money for that to happen then so be it.' He took her hand and kissed it. 'What do you say?'

'I wasn't expecting this.' She pressed two fingers to her temple. 'I… I need time to think.'

'I thought you would.' He squeezed her hand. 'Take all the time you need. I'll be waiting for your answer.'

Elodie lay in bed in the dark, but she could still see the engagement ring in its open box, glinting in a stray beam from a streetlight outside her window. Callum had insisted she hang on to it until she'd come to a decision. It had been two days now since his proposal, and she still hadn't made up her mind. The stone – cubic zirconia or whatever – sent dancing lights skittering over her bedside table.

She was still struggling to process what had happened. Callum Ashley, born with every advantage life could bestow, offering to give it all up for her. Callum, who was so sweet, so thoughtful, so like her in so many ways, and ought to be her perfect man.

But there were those treacherous words: *ought to be*. Callum ought to be her perfect man. He was considerate, affectionate, desirable. Yet when he said he loved her, something in her hung back.

Elodie had always found it hard to let people in, and she'd assumed she would find it easier as time passed to show Callum the same amount of affection as he showed her. But if anything, it was getting harder. Her tongue felt thick whenever she tried to respond to his 'I love you' with one of her own, as if rebelling against the words. And it had been months since she'd been able to enjoy sex with him. Perhaps that was grief, but it didn't seem to be getting any easier. She still liked Callum – very, very much. She knew he was an attractive, sexy man, who could and had made her happy in the bedroom on many occasions. But when she thought about physical intimacy with him… it just didn't feel right.

The strangest thing, though, was the feeling that as alike as they were, Callum didn't really *get* her. It was almost as if their very similarity made it harder for him to anticipate what she needed. It reminded her of her grandad's memoirs, and the story of his doomed romance with Sandra Ashley.

She had to do something. She couldn't expect Callum to wait forever. The fact it had taken her this long to think it over was surely a sign in itself that she wasn't ready for marriage.

She reached for her phone.

'Cal?'

'Elodie, it's 2am,' he mumbled.

'I know. I couldn't sleep.'

Callum sounded more awake now. 'You're ringing with an answer?'

'Yes.' She took a deep breath. 'Cal, I… you're great, really. Like, you're seriously Mr Wonderful, and I'm so, so lucky to be with you. When you offered to give up everything to be with me, that's the sweetest, most amazing thing anyone's ever done for me.'

'But?' Callum's voice sounded flat.

Elodie pressed her eyes closed. 'I'll probably regret this, but I… I can't marry you. It feels wrong, somehow – wrong in my gut. Maybe that'll change in time, but it's how I feel right now. I'm sorry.'

He sighed. 'I know.'

'You know?' Elodie said, blinking.

'Just… give me a minute. Don't hang up.'

'Um, OK.'

The phone went silent, but Elodie could hear Callum in the background, sounding as if he was pacing around the room. There was a muttered exclamation, and the noise of something breaking.

'Sorry,' he said when he came back on the line. 'I just… needed to get that out.'

'Get what out? Are you angry with me?'

'I'm not angry. At least, not with you.' He fell silent, and when he spoke again his voice was choked. 'Do you know why you can't marry me, Elodie? Because I do.'

'I guess… because I'm not ready yet. It's only been eight months, Cal.'

'That's not it. I wish it was. If it was only a matter of waiting for you, I could wait forever.' He choked back a sob. 'For months I've been trying to lie to myself about it. You were grieving for your grandad, and I told myself that was why you jumped whenever I touched you and made excuses when I wanted to be with you. Why you sounded like it hurt you to say you loved me.'

'Trying to lie to yourself… about what?'

'Elodie, I told you when I proposed that whether you said yes or no, it'd tell me everything I needed to know.' He was silent for a moment. 'I've known for a long time that Nick Winter was in love with you – he told me so himself. When you said no tonight, I finally knew for certain that you were in love with him too. You always have been.'

***

Elodie lay staring at the cheap engagement ring, her head whirling.

In love with Nick! Yes, she missed him. He was her closest friend; that was natural. But that's all they were, surely: just close friends.

Slowly, various puzzle pieces in Elodie's brain started to shift and rearrange themselves.

Nick, who'd made a friend of her when all she'd wanted was to shut out the world and everyone in it. Nick, who'd been there for her the night Pops had died and a hundred times before that. Nick, who'd kissed her so tenderly the night he'd said goodbye, and told her he loved her in a way that felt… different to the way those words had ever sounded before. And she hadn't held back, as she so often found herself doing with Callum, but had sunk into the kiss as if it was the most natural thing in the world. The 'I love you' that had dropped from her that night seemed to have bypassed her brain and come straight from her heart.

She loved Callum. She loved him because he was like her: isolated from the world and damaged by the things his life had done to him. But it was Nick who'd shown her you could have happiness and love in your life if you only had the courage to open yourself up to people. Nick who'd pulled her out of the dark. She loved Callum… but not like she loved Nick.

That was why the words 'I love you' stuck in her throat. That was why sex with Callum had felt wrong since the day Nick had kissed her goodbye on the doorstep – almost like a betrayal. It was Nick she loved – she always had. And Callum said Nick loved her too… that Nick had told him so, in his own words, with his own mouth…

But he'd been gone for two months now. Had Elodie realised too late what she felt for him? He was ignoring her texts, which suggested all he wanted to do was put her out of his mind and move on. Perhaps he already had.

She grabbed her phone and googled the ticket website for the Lowry Theatre.

'Shit!' she muttered as she looked at bookings for tomorrow – Christmas Eve, the last night of the run. They were all sold out. She needed to see him! To find out if there was still a chance…

Christmas Eve… that was when Summer and her mum were due to go see the show, wasn't it? That meant she had one last hope. Elodie closed the website and pulled up a number.

'Aunty Helen? I need a huge, huge favour.'

38

'I really owe your mum one for this,' Elodie whispered as she and Summer settled into their seats at The Lowry.

Summer shook her head. 'I still don't get it. Why are you suddenly so desperate to come and see Nick's play?'

'Because I… I have to see him. It's complicated.'

Summer glanced at her cousin's costume. 'And is there a reason for the Santa hat and Christmas jumper, or is that complicated too?'

Elodie smoothed down her psychedelic snowman jumper – the same one she'd worn the night she'd talked Nick into withdrawing his resignation. 'Just getting into the spirit of the season.'

'Did you honestly break up with Callum?'

'Yeah. Well, technically he broke up with me, but it was by mutual agreement.'

'Why? I thought you really liked him.'

'I do. I like him a lot. But not the same way he likes me, I think.' Elodie sighed. 'I feel dreadful about how it ended. But I'm not the right fit for him, and I can't ever give him what he needs. We're bad for each other, Cal and me.'

'And you think you and Nick—'

Elodie put a finger to her lips as the lights went down. 'Hush now. It's starting.'

'Great show tonight, gang,' Nick said to the rest of the cast after the curtain had gone down for the last time. 'A standing ovation too. I think we've earned our after-party.'

Marty slapped him on the back. 'Are you going down to the lobby to do autographs with the other principals?'

'I'll have to,' Nick said, pulling a face. 'I don't know why Barry insists on me doing it. It's the girls who get the queues; I only ever have a couple. But I'd better do as I'm told. I'm auditioning for *Blood Brothers* in the new year so I need to keep him sweet.'

'I'll wait with you.'

'You don't need to do that. You go ahead to the party.'

'I'd rather hang here till you're ready, then we can go together.'

'All right.'

'I'll grab us a couple of drinks from the bar and join you at your table,' Marty said. 'Maybe someone'll even want my autograph. Doctor Number Two is actually the lynchpin of the whole story, I reckon.'

Nick laughed, then went to his dressing room to change out of his costume.

Once he was scrubbed clean of makeup and back in his civilian clothes, he headed to the lobby to join the other cast principals. Tables had been set out for them to sign autographs. Their names and characters were printed on cards, and there were already long queues for the infamous stripping WI members. Nick's queue was smaller – audiences seemed not to notice you as much when you kept your clothes on – but there were still a gratifying number of people waiting for him. He slid into his chair, noting the large crowd around the bar. If Marty was queueing among that lot, Nick might be waiting a while for his pint. Shame: the heat from the stage lights had really helped him work up a thirst.

He was still waiting for a beer when he got down to the last few autograph hunters. The crowds had started to dwindle as people left the theatre for their nice warm beds. It was Christmas Eve, of course. They needed to be under the covers before Father Christmas came to fill up their stockings.

Nick smiled sadly at the thought. On this day last year, he'd finished his final stint in the grotto and gone to the pub with Elodie, Jim and Summer to celebrate winning the bet. The bet he'd never really won at all, not knowing Callum had lied about it for purposes of his own. Those happy early days at Martin's felt like another world, now.

'What name is it?' he asked as a programme was slid across the table for him to sign.

'Summer Rowan.' Summer smiled as he looked up at her. 'Greetings, fellow season.'

'Oh my God!' He laughed, coming out from behind the table to embrace her. 'Summer! What the hell are you doing here?'

'I came to see you, didn't I, your megastarliness? And…' Summer moved aside. 'I brought someone else.'

He stared. 'Elodie.'

'Hi, Nicky.' She waved awkwardly.

'What… why're you…'

'Summer's mum was supposed to come but she gave me her ticket. I didn't want to miss your big break.' She gestured to the Christmas jumper she was wearing. 'Er, ta-da.'

He smiled. 'I'm glad you haven't forgotten how to Christmas properly while I've been gone.'

'I knew you'd never forgive me if I did.' She met his eyes. 'You were fantastic tonight, Nick. I was ever so proud of you.'

Summer nodded. 'I practically had to gag her before we got thrown out. She was determined to tell everyone sitting near us how she knows you *in real life*.'

Nick smiled. 'That's sweet, Elodie.'

'So you're a star.' Elodie's smile looked a little sad. Or wistful, anyway. 'I knew you would be one day. I guess life is pretty different now, with your new theatre crowd.'

'Yeah. It is different.'

'I hope you haven't forgotten us lot at Martin's,' Summer said.

'I could never do that.'

'How's your mum doing?' Elodie asked.

'Blooming and healthy,' Nick said, smiling. 'She's even got a new man in her life. City living seems to suits her.'

'I'm glad.'

Nick rubbed his neck. 'Um… so how's Callum, El?'

'He's fine.'

'And the Santa School?'

'Still going strong. We've taken on Robert as a trainee instructor for next year, now he's graduated. He's been a big success in his first grotto.' Elodie smiled. 'We miss you though. My grandad's first student.'

'I miss you too. And the shop and the grotto and… everything.'

'I texted you.'

'Sorry. I've been busy.'

Nick was just casting around for something else to say, feeling hot under the glaring lights of the theatre foyer, when Marty appeared finally with a couple of drinks.

'Sorry it took so long, love.' He put the drink down and kissed Nick's cheek. 'Mad queues. Shall we have them in your dressing room? Then we can book an Uber to get us to the party.' He caught sight of Elodie and Summer. 'Oh, sorry. You're still signing.'

'Um, no. These are some friends from back home. El, Summer, this is Marty. He's one of the cast.'

Marty nodded to them. 'Pleased to meet you.'

'And you.' Elodie sounded subdued. She tapped her cousin's elbow. 'We'd better go, Sum. Nick's obviously got plans.'

'Honestly, you'd be more than welcome to join us,' Nick said. 'We don't have to go to my dressing room. We can all go sit in the bar.'

'No, we don't want to intrude. We just wanted to say hi and tell you how good you were.' She flashed him a weak smile. 'Well done, Nick. I'm glad it all worked out. You're really living the dream.'

'Thanks, Elodie.'

'Pops would be so proud of you.'

'I hope so.'

Marty looked at Nick. 'This is Elodie? The Elodie you told me about?'

'Er, yeah.'

'Well, bye, Nick. It was nice to see you again. And great to meet you too, Marty.' Elodie paused before offering Nick a sedate hug: very cool and aloof compared to the one she'd given him the day he'd said goodbye. 'Come on, Summer. We'll grab a taxi back to the hotel.'

'So that was Elodie,' Marty said when they'd gone. '*The* Elodie.'

'Yeah. That was the Elodie,' Nick said, gazing at the door.

Marty shook his head. 'And you're seriously going to let her walk out of your life *again*?'

'How do you mean? She's got her own life back at home. With Callum.'

'My God, Nicky, how do you even function with that brain?' Marty took Nick by the shoulders and turned him around. 'She was waiting for you to make a move, you utter dingbat. She came tonight because she wanted you to say something.'

'No. What?'

Marty shook his head again. 'And they say actors are good at reading people. Go after her, you wally. Do it or I'll never speak to you again.'

'You really think that's what she wanted?'

'I'd bet my life. Go on, run, before she gets in a taxi.'

Nick stood stock-still for a moment. The next minute, he was pelting as fast as he could towards the door.

Outside people stood about in gangs, waiting for taxis and Ubers. Light snow had just started falling, the flakes showing up red and green and gold under the colourful Christmas lights. Nick looked about wildly for Elodie, but there was no sign of her. Then he caught sight of a red Santa hat, bobbing above a cab. He fought his way through the crowds of theatre-goers to reach her.

'El,' he panted. 'Please don't get in that taxi.'

She stood on tiptoes to peer at him over the car. 'Nick? I thought you had a date.'

'No date,' he said, struggling to catch his breath.

'But that was your boyfriend, right?'

'No, Marty's just a friend.'

'Oh. You just… seemed close. With the kissing and the endearments and all that.'

Nick laughed breathlessly. 'Darling, this is the theatre.'

Elodie finally smiled at him. She turned to Summer.

'You go on,' she said. 'I can make my own way to the hotel.'

'Right.' Summer grinned at Nick before climbing in. 'Good luck.'

'Come on. You're getting soaked.' Nick took Elodie's arm and guided her across the road to a place called the Footlights Bar, where they could escape the snow now falling in a flurry. Nick got them both a drink and they sat down in a private corner.

'Like old times,' Elodie said softly.

'Yes.' He rubbed his neck. 'Elodie, I… that is, my friend Marty said I should go after you.'

'Why?'

'Because he's spent the last two months listening to me talk about you until he was heartily sick of the subject. He said I'd be a fool to let you walk out of my life again.'

'Well, technically it was you who walked out of mine. Not that I blame you.'

'Look, I know this is probably hopeless, but I might as well do it now I've got nothing to lose,' Nick said, his voice tinged with death-or-glory desperation as he finally laid all his cards on the table. 'There's something I've tried to tell you so many times, but I'm a coward, El. I couldn't see how I could ever stand a chance against Callum, and you seemed to see me as such a friendy-type friend, I thought it was a lost cause. But I have to say it so you know I mean it, even if this is the only time. I love you. I've loved you for nearly as long as I've known you. Not as a friend – I'm talking about the proper, soul-tingling, once-in-a-lifetime stuff. So... there it is.'

Elodie held his hands in hers. 'Nick, I—'

'You don't have to say anything. You're with Callum, I know that. Callum makes you happy. I'm glad about that, honestly; he's a good man. I just needed to tell you this one time.'

'Can you stop talking and listen?' She pressed his hands softly. 'I'm not with Callum. Not any more. We broke up yesterday.'

'You broke up! Why?'

'Because he asked me to marry him. And as soon as I started asking myself if that was what I wanted, everything seemed to click into place. I knew, then, that it was never Callum for me. It was always you. The man who changed my life, and taught me to throw open the doors again. My best friend.'

Nick stared. 'What?'

'I love you, Nick. I didn't realise it until... probably until that day you said goodbye and kissed me the way you did, although I was such a mess after losing Pops that it took me a while to really understand what it meant. But it was always you.' Elodie pressed one of his hands to her lips. 'Pops said in his memoirs that I was his Christmas miracle, and... I guess you were mine.'

Nick continued to stare at her. He couldn't take it in. Was this really Elodie Martin, telling him she'd left the hot millionaire who wanted to marry her because what she really wanted, what she'd realised… was that she wanted to be with him? She loved him. Really, actually loved him.

'I don't know how to… what to do,' he whispered. 'It's all so… dreamlike.'

'Well, you could put your arms around me. That's a thing people do.'

'Yes. It is, isn't it?' He wrapped his arms around her and pulled her body against his, feeling like he was finally starting to get to grips with this strange but wonderful new reality. 'Any tips on where to go from here?'

She stroked his cheek. 'That was a good kiss you gave me the day you said goodbye. It was a bit on the short side though. Have you got anything longer?'

'I can provide kisses in a range of lengths. What's your preference?'

'I think if we start with around two minutes, we can decide where to go from there.'

He tilted her chin so he could look into her eyes.

'Do you know how many times I've tried to do this?' he murmured.

'Do it now.'

He lowered his lips to hers, his eyes closing. It felt like their bodies melted into each other while they kissed – like they just seemed to fit with each other somehow. The pain of the last two months, when Nick had missed her every day while he tried to leave her to what he thought was her happy ending, were washed away as he felt Elodie Martin kiss him back with passionate tenderness.

'God, Elodie,' he whispered when they finally had to break apart.

'I know.' She glanced out of the window at the twinkling Christmas lights and the now thickly falling snow. 'It had to happen on Christmas Eve.'

'Miracles only can happen at Christmas. I think I've shown you enough films to demonstrate that.'

'A kiss while the snow falls. I think I just won your Christmas bingo.'

Nick smiled. 'That's my girl. So what happens now, El?'

'I've got a hotel room. You can come see me there after your party.'

He laughed. 'Sod the party. I'll flag down a cab, before this snow gets any worse.'

'So is this it?' she whispered. 'Happily ever after?'

'No, Elodie. This is just the beginning.'

Epilogue

Two years later…

'Say baubles!'

'Baubles!' yelled the crowd who'd gathered in front of Martin's Toy Kingdom, most clad in Santa suits with a small scattering of elves. The photographer from the *Chessory Herald* snapped a few pictures before giving them a thumbs-up.

Elodie was front and centre with Nick, both in Santa costumes. Nick had one of his arms around her and the other hand rested gently on her huge baby bump. They were flanked by Callum on one side and Kenny Ross on the other. Nick's mum Sheila was there too, leaning on the arm of her new husband Terry. The rest of the ranks were filled by current and former Santa School students, who'd gathered today to celebrate their one hundredth graduate.

'That was great, folks!' Elodie said, turning to beam at them all. 'We've hired the function room at the White Hart for the party. Mince pies and sherry for all our Santas, and carrots for any reindeers you'd like to bring along. Feel free to make your way there.'

Sheila approached with Terry.

'I'm going to skip the party and get off home,' she said. 'I'd better have a lie-down before we see you both this evening. I can't party the day away like I once could.'

'Yes, go and have a rest.' Nick gave her a kiss on the cheek. 'We'll see you later, Mum. Terry, you look after her.'

'That's my job,' Terry said, shooting his wife a fond glance. 'See you tonight, kids.'

They disappeared into the crowd of Father Christmases, which was starting to disperse.

'Can I get changed before we go to the pub?' Callum asked Elodie, gesturing to his Santa suit.

'Don't you dare, Cal. No getting changed until after your mince pie.'

'He looks better in that than me.' Nick turned to Elodie. 'That's not right, is it? That he looks better than me? I'm the pro.'

Callum laughed. 'Better watch your throne, Nick. I quite like the idea of my own grotto.'

Elodie pulled out her stretchy red trousers. 'Tell you what, these make great maternity wear. I might stay in them till the baby comes.'

'When's it due again?' Callum asked.

Nick shook his head. 'Your own godchild and you don't know?'

'Second of January,' Elodie said. 'But I've got a horrible feeling it's going to turn up early. I'd put money on it being a Christmas baby.'

Callum smiled. 'With Nick's genes? It'll be a Christmas baby whenever it turns up.'

Sam approached them, holding Polly's lead.

'Are you coming to the pub, Cal?' she asked.

'I just want a quick word with Elodie.' He gave Sam a kiss. 'I'll see you there, OK, sweetheart?'

'All right.' She waved to Nick and Elodie. 'See you in a bit for some reindeer games.'

'Are you still set to pop the question on Christmas Day?' Nick asked Callum when Sam was out of earshot.

'Yep. I've got something arranged with a fairy-lit pagoda and a violinist.'

'That sounds a bit more romantic than when you proposed to me,' Elodie said.

Callum shrugged. 'I know my prospective wives. You'd have been horrified if I'd sprung a violinist on you.'

'True.'

'And I did think offering to give up all my money was pretty romantic, as gestures go.'

'Well, yes, I have to give you that.'

He smiled after Sam. 'Funny, isn't it? How sometimes it takes you so long to see what's right in front of you?'

Elodie gave Nick a fond look. 'Tell me about it.'

'She's good for you, that woman,' Nick said to Callum.

Callum nodded. 'We fit together, I think, the same way you guys do. Plus she's finally got me doing something good with my money, sponsoring the animal shelter Polly came from.'

'You made the right choice, selling the store,' Elodie said. 'You've been a new man since you left Ashley's.'

'Best thing I ever did. I've actually got something like a life now.' He glanced at her. 'El, can I have a word?'

'OK. We can go in the shop.' She gave Nick a kiss. 'Don't go anywhere, sexy.'

'I'll be right here.'

She went inside with Callum.

'What's up?' she asked when they were alone.

'I wanted to thank you for something,' Callum said. 'I should've done it before now.'

'What is it?'

'Sam.'

She blinked. 'You want to thank me for Sam?'

'Yeah. Nick's right, she is good for me. And you were right when you said me and you were so alike we were bad for each other. I was devastated when you turned me down, but it worked out, didn't it?'

'It did. Just like it did for our grandparents.'

'Plus if I hadn't needed a shoulder to cry on, I'd never have turned to Sam.'

Elodie smiled. 'And the rest is history.'

He rested a hand on her arm. 'I thought it was you I needed to fix me, El, but being with you made me realise that what I really needed was to work on fixing myself. I'm a better man because of you.'

'You always were a good man, Cal. You just needed to break free of those warped values of your dad's.'

'God, I was so close to turning into him for a while. When I swore to myself in a drunken rage three Christmases ago that I'd make you love me, I never even thought about whether that was right for you; it was all about me getting what I wanted. It was seriously messed up – I was messed up.'

Elodie patted the hand on her arm. 'But you stepped aside when you realised it was Nick I loved. The real, decent you won out in the end. I always knew he would.'

'You helped me break free of my dad's obsession with winning. That's the reason I was able to find happiness with Sam.' He kissed her cheek. 'Thanks, Elodie.'

'Here. Give us a hug, if you can fit your arms around this gigantic godchild of yours.'

He smiled and hugged her as best he could.

'I want you to know that I don't regret a second of the time we spent together, Cal,' she said quietly while she embraced him. 'As a couple we weren't meant to be, but I loved being with you.'

He laughed. 'Nearly as much as you loved scrapping with me for all those years beforehand.'

'Well, that was fun too. But I think I prefer being your friend.'

'Me too.' He nodded to the window. 'You'd better get back to your handsome husband. He's looking anxious at going so long without you. I'll see you at the pub.'

Callum pecked her cheek before he left her. Elodie went back to Nick outside.

'What did he want?' Nick asked.

She smiled, putting her arms around him. 'You're not still jealous?'

'Well you're eight months' pregnant with my baby so I'd say at this stage I'm feeling pretty secure,' he said, kissing her ear. 'No, just nosy.'

'Just… laying some ghosts to rest before we move into the next stages of our lives.' She watched the last of their Santas disappearing. 'I never thought we'd make it, did you?'

'I know. The Santa School going from strength to strength, Callum happy and settled, my mum all loved up with Terry, us with a baby on the way like proper grown-ups…'

'And you a top-of-the-bill star, of course. Let's not forget that.'

Nick smiled. 'Thanks to Callum being so desperate to

get me out of your way before you realised you couldn't resist me.'

'That worked well, didn't it?'

He patted her tummy. 'Evidently.'

She looked up at him. 'Thanks, Nick.'

'For what?'

'For taking a chance on me. I'm still not quite sure how you ended up falling for that grumpy, spiky, Christmas-hating, people-shunning cow you met the day you turned up here.'

He drew a finger down her cheek. 'You could never hide from me, Elodie Martin,' he said softly. 'I see you. I always did.'

'I love you, you know.'

'I should hope you do. I've got a strict policy about the people I agree to impregnate.'

'Are you going to kiss me or what? I always seem to be waiting for you to make the first move.'

'Sexism. Why don't you make the first move? Ideally after you've taken me home and torn my clothes off.'

She smiled and drew him to her for a lingering kiss.

'We could go home, couldn't we?' she whispered. 'They'd never miss us at the pub.'

'We're just two Santas among a hundred.' He gave her hat a playful flick.

She sighed. 'I don't suppose there'll be time for all this after the baby comes. I mean I can't wait to meet him, obviously, but I'll be sad to see the end of the fun-and-games stage of our relationship.'

'I don't believe there are any such things as endings – not in life. Just lots of beginnings.' He kissed her again. 'Like I told you once before, Elodie, this is just the beginning. One of many, many more.'

Acknowledgements

A big thank you to my agent, Laura Longrigg at MBA Literary Agents, to whom this book is dedicated, and to my wonderful editor at Aria, Martina Arzu, for all her hard work. Not to mention the rest of the team at Aria, who have again done such an amazing job.

Thanks too to all of my friends and family for their continued support, as well as to the Romantic Novelists' Association for being such a fantastic and supportive organisation.

I'd also like to thank the author Mark Forsyth, whose fabulous little book of Christmas miscellany, *A Christmas Cornucopia*, provided my Christmas-loving hero Nick with much of his festive trivia.

About the Author

Mary jayne baker grew up in rural West Yorkshire, right in the heart of Brontë country… and she's still there.

After graduating from Durham University with a degree in English Literature, she dallied with living in cities including London, Nottingham and Cambridge, but eventually came back with her own romantic hero in tow to her beloved Dales, where she first started telling stories about heroines with flaws and the men who love them.

Mary Jayne's novel *A Question of Us* was the winner of the Romantic Novelists' Association's Romantic Comedy Novel of the Year Award 2020. She also writes uplifting women's fiction as Lisa Swift, and World War II sagas as Gracie Taylor.